THE
TRISTAN
BETRAYAL

THE
TRISTAN
BETRAYAL

ROBERT LUDLUM

ORION

First published in Great Britain in 2003 by Orion
an imprint of The Orion Publishing Group
Orion House, 5 Upper St Martin's Lane,
London WC2H 9EA

A CIP catalogue record for this book
is available from the British Library

ISBN 0 75285 747 9 (hardback)
ISBN 0 75285 748 7 (trade paperback)

Printed and bound in Great Britain by
Clays Ltd, St Ives plc

THE
TRISTAN
BETRAYAL

Moscow, August 1991

The sleek black limousine, with its polycarbonate-laminate bullet-resistant windows and its run-flat tires, its high-tech ceramic armor and dual-hardness carbon-steel armor plate, was jarringly out of place as it pulled into the Bittsevsky forest in the southwest area of the city. This was ancient terrain, forest primeval, densely overgrown with birch and aspen groves interspersed with pine trees, elms, and maples; it spoke of nomadic Stone Age tribes that roamed the glacier-scarred terrain, hunting mammoths with hand-carved javelins, amid nature red in tooth and claw. Whereas the armored Lincoln Continental spoke of another kind of civilization entirely with another sort of violence, an era of snipers and terrorists wielding submachine guns and fragmentation grenades.

Moscow was a city under siege. It was the capital of a superpower on the brink of collapse. A cabal of Communist hard-liners was preparing to take back Russia from the forces of reform. Tens of thousands of troops filled the city, ready to fire at its citizens. Columns of tanks and armored personnel carriers rumbled down Kutuzovsky Prospekt and the Minskoye Chausse. Tanks surrounded Moscow City Hall, TV broadcasting facilities, newspaper offices, the parliament building. The radio was broadcasting nothing but the decrees of the cabal, which called itself the State Committee for the State of Emergency. After years of progress toward democracy, the Soviet Union was on the verge of being returned to the dark forces of totalitarianism.

Inside the limousine sat an elderly man, silver-haired, with handsome, aristocratic features. He was Ambassador Stephen Metcalfe, an icon of the American Establishment, an adviser to five Presidents since Franklin D. Roosevelt, an extremely wealthy man who had devoted his life to serving his government. Ambassador Metcalfe, though now retired, the title purely honorific, had been urgently summoned to Moscow by an old friend who was highly placed in the inner circles of Soviet power. He and his old friend had not met face-to-face for decades: their relationship was a deeply buried secret, known to no one in Moscow or Washington. That his Russian friend—code-named "Kurwenal"— insisted on a rendezvous in this deserted location was worrying, but these were worrying times.

Lost in thought, visibly nervous, the old man got out of his limousine only once he glimpsed the figure of his friend, the three-star general, limping heavily on a prosthetic leg. The American's seasoned eyes scanned the forest as he began to walk, and then his blood ran cold.

He detected a watcher in the trees. A second, a *third! Surveillance.* He and the Russian code-named Kurwenal had just been spotted!

This would be a disaster for them both!

Metcalfe wanted to call out to his old friend, to warn him, but then he noticed the glint of a scoped rifle in the late-afternoon sun. *It was an ambush!*

Terrified, the elderly ambassador spun around and loped as quickly as his arthritic limbs would take him back toward his armored limousine. He had no bodyguard; he never traveled with one. He had only his driver, an unarmed American marine supplied by the embassy.

Suddenly men were running toward him from all around. Black-uniformed men in black paramilitary berets, bearing machine guns. They surrounded him and he began to struggle, but he was no longer a young man, as he had to keep reminding himself. *Was this a kidnapping? Was he being taken hostage?* He shouted hoarsely to his driver.

The black-clad men escorted Metcalfe to another armored limousine, a Russian ZIL. Frightened, he climbed into the passenger compartment. There, already seated, was the three-star general.

"What the hell *is* this?" Metcalfe croaked, his panic subsiding.

"My deepest apologies," replied the Russian. "These are hazardous, unstable times, and I could not take the chance of anything happening to you, even here in the woods. These are my men, under my command, and they're trained in counterterrorist measures. You are far too important an individual to expose to any dangers."

Metcalfe shook the Russian's hand. The general was eighty years old, his hair white, though his profile remained hawklike. He nodded at the driver, and the car began to move.

"I thank you for coming to Moscow–I realize my urgent summons must have struck you as cryptic."

"I knew it had to be about the coup," Metcalfe said.

"Matters are developing more rapidly than anticipated," the Russian said in a low voice. "They have secured the blessing of the man known as the *Dirizhor*–the Conductor. It may already be too late to stop the seizure of power."

"My friends in the White House are watching with great concern. But they feel paralyzed–the consensus in the National Security Council seems to be that to intervene might be to risk nuclear war."

"An apt fear. These men are desperate to overthrow the Gorbachev regime. They will resort to anything. You've seen the tanks on the streets of Moscow–now all that remains is for the conspirators to order their forces to strike. To attack civilians. It will be a *bloodbath*. Thousands will be killed! But the orders to strike will not be issued unless the *Dirizhor* gives his approval. Everything hangs on him–he is the linchpin."

"But he's not one of the plotters?"

"No. As you know, he's the ultimate insider, a man who controls the levers of power in absolute secrecy. He will never appear at a news conference; he acts in stealth. But he is in sympathy with the coup plotters. Without his support, the coup must fail. *With* his support, the coup will surely succeed. And Russia will once again become a Stalinist dictatorship–and the world will be at the brink of nuclear war."

"Why did you call me here?" asked Metcalfe. "Why me?"

The general turned to face Metcalfe, and in his eyes Metcalfe could see fear. "Because you're the only one I trust. And you're the only one who has a chance of reaching *him*. The *Dirizhor*."

"And why will the *Dirizhor* listen to me?"

"I think you know," said the Russian quietly. "You can change history, my friend. After all, we both know you did it before."

PART ONE

CHAPTER ONE

Paris, November 1940

The City of Light had gone dark.

Ever since the Nazis had invaded, then seized control of France six months earlier, the world's greatest city had become forlorn and desolate. The *quais* along the Seine were deserted. The Arc de Triomphe, the place de l'Etoile—those magnificent gleaming landmarks that once lit up the night sky—were now gloomy, abandoned. Above the Eiffel Tower, where once the French tricolor rippled, a Nazi swastika flag waved.

Paris was quiet. There were hardly any cars on the street anymore, or taxis. Most of the grand hotels had been taken over by the Nazis. Gone was the revelry, the laughter of evening strollers, carousers. Gone, too, were the birds, victims of the smoke from the burning gasoline during the first days of the German incursion.

Most people stayed in at night, intimidated by their occupiers, the curfews, the new laws that had been imposed on them, the green-uniformed *Wehrmacht* soldiers who patrolled the streets with their swinging bayonets, their revolvers. A once-proud city had sunk into despair, famine, fear.

Even the aristocratic avenue Foch, the widest, grandest thoroughfare in Paris, lined with handsome white stone facades, seemed windswept and bleak.

With a single exception.

One *hôtel particulier,* a private mansion, glittered with light. Faint music could be heard from within: a swing orchestra. The tinkle of china and crystal, excited voices, carefree laughter. This was an island of glittering privilege, all the more radiant for its gloomy background.

The Hôtel de Châtelet was the magnificent residence of the Comte Maurice Léon Philippe du Châtelet and his wife, the legendary and gracious hostess Marie-Hélène. The Comte du Châtelet was an industrialist of enormous wealth as well as a minister in the collaborationist Vichy government. Most of all, though, he was known for his parties, which helped sustain *tout Paris* through the dark days of the occupation.

An invitation to a party at the Hôtel de Châtelet was an object of social envy—sought after, anticipated for weeks. Especially these days, with all the rationing and food shortages, when it was just about impossible to get real coffee or butter or cheese, when only the very well connected could get meat or fresh vegetables. An invitation to cocktails at the du Châtelets' meant an opportunity to eat one's fill. Here, inside this gracious home, there was not a hint that one lived in a city of brutal deprivation.

The party was already in full swing by the time one of the guests, a very late arrival, was admitted by a manservant.

The guest was a remarkably handsome young man, in his late twenties, with a full head of black hair, large brown eyes that seemed to twinkle with mischief, an aquiline nose. He was tall and broad, with a trim athletic build. As he handed his topcoat to the maître d'hôtel, the butler, he nodded, smiled, and said, *"Bonsoir, merci beaucoup."*

He was called Daniel Eigen. He had been living in Paris off and on for the last year or so, and he was a regular on the party circuit, where everyone knew him as a wealthy Argentine and an extremely eligible bachelor.

"Ah, Daniel, my love," crooned Marie-Hélène du Châtelet, the hostess, as Eigen entered the crowded ballroom. The orchestra was playing a new song, which he recognized as "How High the Moon." Madame du Châtelet had spotted him from halfway across the room and had made her way over to him with the sort of exuberance she normally reserved for the very rich or the very powerful—the Duke and Duchess of Windsor, say, or the German Military Governor of Paris. The hostess, a handsome woman in her early fifties, wearing a black Balenciaga gown that revealed the cleft of her ample bosom, was clearly besotted with her young guest.

Daniel Eigen kissed both her cheeks, and she drew him near for a moment, speaking in French in a low, confiding voice. "I'm *so* glad you could make it, my dear. I was afraid you might not show up."

"And miss a party at Hôtel de Châtelet?" Eigen said. "Do you think I've taken leave of my senses?" From behind his back he produced a small box, wrapped in gilt paper. "For you, Madame. The last ounce in all of France."

The hostess beamed as she took the box, greedily tore off the paper, and pulled out the square crystal flask of Guerlain perfume. She gasped. "But . . . but Vol de Nuit can't be bought *anywhere!*"

"You're quite right," Eigen said with a smile. "It *can't* be bought."

"Daniel! You're too sweet, too thoughtful. How did you know it's my favorite?"

He shrugged modestly. "I have my own intelligence network."

Madame du Châtelet frowned, wagged a reproving finger. "And after all you did to procure the Dom Pérignon for us. Really, you're too generous. Anyway, I'm delighted you're here— handsome young men like you are as rare as hens' teeth these days, my love. You'll have to pardon some of my female guests if they swoon. Those you haven't already conquered, that is." She lowered her voice again. "Yvonne Printemps is here with Pierre Fresnay, but she seems to be on the prowl again, so watch out." She was referring to the famous musical-comedy star. "And Coco Chanel is with her new lover, that German fellow she lives with at the Ritz. She's on a tirade against the Jews again—really, it's getting tedious."

Eigen accepted a flute of champagne from the silver tray borne by a servant. He glanced around the immense ballroom, with its floor of ancient parquet from a grand *château,* the walls of white-

and-gold paneling covered at regular intervals with Gobelin tapestries, the dramatic ceiling that had been painted by the same
artist who later undertook the ceilings at Versailles.

But it was not the decor he was interested in so much as the
guests. As he scanned the crowd he recognized quite a few people. There were the usual celebrities: the singer Edith Piaf, who
made twenty thousand francs for each evening's performance;
Maurice Chevalier; and all sorts of famous cinema stars who
were now working for the German-owned film company Continental, run by Goebbels, making movies the Nazis approved
of. The usual assortment of writers, painters, and musicians,
who never missed one of these rare opportunities to eat and
drink their fill. And the usual French and German bankers, and
industrialists who did business with the Nazis and their puppet
Vichy regime.

Finally, there were the Nazi officers, so prominent on the social
circuit these days. All were in their dress uniforms; many affected
monocles and had little mustaches like the Führer himself. The
German Military Governor, General Otto von Stülpnagel. The
German ambassador to France, Otto Abetz, and the young
Frenchwoman he'd married. The *Kommandant von Gross-Paris*,
the elderly General Ernst von Schaumburg, who, with his close-
cropped hair and Prussian manner, was known as the Bronze
Rock.

Eigen knew them all. He saw them regularly, at salons such as
this, but more to the point, he'd done favors for most of them.
The Nazi masters of France didn't just tolerate the so-called black
market; they *needed* it like everyone else. How else could they
get cold cream or face powder for their wives or lovers? Where
else could they find a decent bottle of Armagnac? Even the new
German rulers of France suffered from the wartime privations.

So a black-market dealer like Daniel Eigen was always in
demand.

He felt a hand on his sleeve. Right away he recognized the
diamond-encrusted fingers of a former lover, Agnès Vieillard. Al-

though he felt a spasm of dread, he turned around, his face lit up in a smile. He had not seen the woman in months.

Agnès was a petite, attractive woman with blazing red hair whose husband, Didier, was a major businessman, a munitions dealer and racehorse owner. Daniel had met the lovely, if over-sexed, Agnès at the races, at Longchamp, where she had a private box. Her husband was in Vichy at the time, advising the puppet government. She'd introduced herself to the handsome, wealthy Argentine as a "war widow." Their affair, passionate if brief, lasted until her husband returned to Paris.

"Agnès, *ma cherie!* Where have you been?"

"Where have *I* been? I haven't seen you since that evening at Maxim's." She swayed, ever so slightly, in time to the orchestra's jazzy rendition of "Imagination."

"Ah, I remember it well," said Daniel, who barely remembered. "I've been terribly busy—my apologies."

"Busy? You don't have a job, Daniel," she scolded.

"Well, my father always said I should find a useful occupation. Now that the whole of France is occupied, I say that gets me off the hook."

She shook her head, scowled in an attempt to conceal her involuntary smile. She leaned close. "Didier's in Vichy again. And this party is altogether too full of *Boches*. Why don't we escape, head over to the Jockey Club? Maxim's is too full of Fritzes these days." She whispered: according to posters on the Métro, anyone who called the Germans *"Boches"* would be shot. The Germans were hypersensitive to French ridicule.

"Oh, I don't mind the Germans," Daniel said in an attempt to change the subject. "They're excellent customers."

"The soldiers—what do you call them, the *haricots verts?* They're such brutes! So ill-mannered. They're always coming up to women on the street and just *grabbing* them."

"You have to pity them a bit," said Eigen. "The poor German soldier feels he's conquered the world, but he can't catch the eye of a French girl. It's so unfair."

"But how to get *rid* of them—?"

"Just tell them you're Jewish, *mon chou.* That'll send them away. Or stare at their big feet—that always embarrasses them."

Now she couldn't help smiling. "But the way they goose-step down the Champs-Élysées!"

"You think goose-stepping is easy?" said Daniel. "Try it yourself someday—you'll end up on your derriere." He glanced around the room furtively, looking for an escape.

"Why, just the other day I saw Göring getting out of his car on the rue de la Paix. Carrying that silly field marshal's baton—I swear, he must sleep with it! He went into Cartier's, and the manager told me later he bought an eight-million-franc necklace for his wife." She poked Daniel's starched white shirt with her index finger. "Notice he buys French fashion for his wife, not German. The *Boches* are always railing against our decadence, but they *adore* it here."

"Well, nothing but the best for Herr Meier."

"Herr *Meier?* What do you mean? Göring's not a Jew."

"You know what he said: 'If ever a bomb falls on Berlin, my name won't be Hermann Göring; you can call me Meier.' "

Agnès laughed. "Keep your voice down, Daniel," she stage-whispered.

Eigen touched her waist. "There's a gentleman here I have to see, *doucette,* so if you'll excuse me . . . "

"You mean there's another lady who's caught your eye," Agnès said reprovingly, smiling in an exaggerated moue.

"No, no," chuckled Eigen. "I'm afraid it really is business."

"Well, Daniel, my love, the least you can do is get me some real coffee. I can't stand all that *ersatz* stuff—chicory, roasted acorns! *Would* you, sweetheart?"

"Of course," he said. "As soon as I possibly can. I'm expecting a shipment in a couple of days."

But as soon as he turned away from Agnès, he was accosted by a stern male voice. "Herr Eigen!"

Right behind him stood a small cluster of German officers, at the center of which was a tall, regal-looking SS *Standartenführer,* a colonel, his hair brushed back in a pompadour, wearing tortoiseshell glasses and a small mustache in slavish imitation of his Führer. Standartenführer Jürgen Wegman had been most useful in getting Eigen a *service public* license, allowing him to operate one of the very few private vehicles allowed on the streets of Paris. Transportation was a huge problem these days. Since only doctors, firemen, and for some reason leading actors and actresses were allowed to drive their own cars, the Métro was ridiculously overcrowded, and half the stations were closed anyway. There was no petrol to be had, and no taxicabs.

"Herr Eigen, those Upmanns—they were stale."

"I'm sorry to hear that, Herr Standartenführer Wegman. Have you been keeping them in a humidor, as I told you?"

"I have no humidor—"

"Then I'll have to get you one," Eigen said.

One of his colleagues, a portly, round-faced SS *Gruppenführer,* a brigadier general named Johannes Koller, sniggered softly. He had been showing his comrades an assortment of sepia-toned French postcards. He quickly put them away in the breast pocket of his tunic, but not before Eigen saw them: they were old-fashioned lewd photographs of a statuesque woman wearing only stockings and garter belt and striking a variety of lascivious poses.

"Please. They were stale when you gave them to me. I don't think they were even from Cuba."

"They were from Cuba, *Herr Kommandant.* Rolled on the thigh of a young Cuban virgin. Here, have one of these, with my compliments." The young man reached into his breast pocket and pulled out a velvet pouch containing several cellophane-wrapped cigars. "*Romeo y Julietas.* I hear they're Churchill's favorites." He handed one to the German with a wink.

A waiter approached with a silver tray of canapés. "Pâté de foie gras, gentlemen?"

Koller snatched two in one swift movement. Daniel took one.

"Not for me," Wegman announced sanctimoniously to the waiter and the men around him. "I no longer eat meat."

"Not easy to come by these days, eh?" said Eigen.

"That's not it at all," said Wegman. "As a man ages, he must become a grass-eating creature, you know."

"Yes, your Führer is a vegetarian, isn't he?" Eigen said.

"Quite right," Wegman said proudly.

"Though sometimes he swallows up whole countries," Eigen added in a level tone.

The SS man glowered. "You seem to be able to turn up everything and anything, Herr Eigen. Perhaps you can do something about the paper shortage here in Paris."

"Yes, it must drive you bureaucrats mad. What is there to push anymore?"

"Everything is of inferior quality these days," said Gruppenführer Koller. "This afternoon, I had to go through an entire sheet of postage stamps before I found one that would stick to the envelope."

"Are you fellows still using the stamp with Hitler's head on it?"

"Yes, of course," Koller said impatiently.

"Perhaps you're licking the wrong side, *hein?*" Eigen said with a wink.

The SS *Gruppenführer* flushed with embarrassment and cleared his throat awkwardly, but before he could think of a reply, Eigen went on: "You're entirely right, of course. The French simply aren't up to the standards of German production."

"Spoken as a true German," said Wegman approvingly. "Even if your mother was Spanish."

"Daniel," came a contralto voice. He turned, relieved at the chance to break free from the Nazi officers.

It was a large woman in her fifties wearing a gaudy, flouncy floral dress that made her look a little like a dancing circus elephant. Madame Fontenoy wore her unnaturally black hair, run through with a white skunk stripe, up in a bouffant. She had enormous gold earrings that Daniel recognized as louis d'or, the antique gold coin, twenty-two karats each. They pulled at her earlobes. She was the wife of a Vichy diplomat, herself a prominent hostess. "Pardon me," she said to the Germans. "I must steal young Daniel away."

Madame Fontenoy's arm was around a slender young girl of around twenty in an off-the-shoulder black evening gown, a raven-haired beauty with luminous gray-green eyes.

"Daniel," said Madame Fontenoy, "I want you to meet Geneviève du Châtelet, our hostess's lovely daughter. I was astonished to hear she hadn't met you—she must be the only single woman in Paris you don't know. Geneviève, this is Daniel Eigen."

The girl extended her delicate long-fingered hand, a brief warning look flashing in her eyes. It was a look meant only for Daniel.

Daniel took her hand. "A pleasure to make your acquaintance," he said with a bow of his head. As he clasped the young beauty's hand, his forefinger gently scratched her palm, tacitly acknowledging her signal.

"Mr. Eigen is from Buenos Aires," the dowager explained to the young woman, "but he has a flat on the Left Bank."

"Oh, have you been in Paris long?" asked Geneviève du Châtelet without interest, her gaze steady.

"Long enough," said Eigen.

"Long enough to know his way around," said Madame Fontenoy, her eyebrows arched.

"I see," Geneviève du Châtelet said dubiously. Suddenly her eyes seemed to spy someone across the room. "Ah, there's *ma grande-tante*, Benoîte. If you'll excuse me, Madame Fontenoy."

As the girl took her leave, her eyes alighted on his, then swept meaningfully in the direction of an adjacent room. He nodded, almost imperceptibly, understanding the semaphore at once.

After an interminable two minutes of empty chat with the dowager Fontenoy, Daniel excused himself as well. Two minutes:

enough time had gone by. He elbowed his way through the thick crowd, smiling and nodding at those who called his name, wordlessly indicating that he couldn't stop because of pressing personal business.

A short distance down the grand hallway was the equally grand library. Its walls and inset bookcases were lacquered Chinese red; the rows of volumes leather-bound, ancient, never read. The room was empty, the cacophony from the ballroom a dull, distant murmur. At the far end, sitting on a divan among Aubusson cushions, was Geneviève, ravishing in her black dress, the skin of her naked shoulders pale and magnificent.

"Oh, thank God," she whispered urgently. She got to her feet, rushed to Daniel, threw her arms around him. He kissed her long and passionately. After a minute she pulled back. "I was so relieved you came tonight. I was dreadfully afraid you'd have other plans."

"How can you say that?" Daniel protested. "Why would I pass up a chance to see you? You're speaking nonsense."

"It's just that you're so . . . so discreet, so careful not to let my parents know about us. Anyway, you're here. Thank God. These people are so boring, I thought I'd die. All they talk about is food, food, food."

Eigen was stroking his lover's creamy shoulders, running his fingertips down to the swell of her breasts. He could smell the aroma of Shalimar, a gift from him. "God, I've missed you so much," he murmured.

"It's been almost a week," said Geneviève. "Have you been a bad little boy? No, wait—don't answer that. I know your ways, Daniel Eigen."

"You can always see through me," Eigen said softly.

"I don't know about that," Geneviève said archly, her lips pursed. "You're a man of many layers, I think."

"Perhaps you could peel a few of them off of me," Daniel said.

Geneviève looked shocked, but it was pure affectation, both of them knew. "Not here, where anyone could walk in on us."

"No, you're right. Let's go somewhere where we won't be interrupted."

"Yes. The second-floor drawing room. No one ever goes in there."

"Except your mother," Daniel Eigen said, shaking his head. An idea had just occurred to him. "Your father's study. We can lock the door."

"But Father will kill us if he sees us there!"

Daniel nodded sadly. "Ah, *ma cherie,* you're right. We really should rejoin the others, I think."

Geneviève looked stricken. "No, no, no!" she said. "I—I know where he keeps the key. Come, let's hurry!"

He followed her out of the library, through the doorway that gave onto a narrow servants' stairway to the second floor, then a long way down a dark hall, until she stopped at a small alcove, at a white marble bust of Marshal Pétain. Daniel's heart was thudding. He was about to attempt something dangerous, and danger always excited him. He liked living on the edge.

Geneviève reached behind the statue and nimbly retrieved a skeleton key, then unlocked the double doors of her father's study.

The lovely young Geneviève had no idea, of course, that Daniel had been in her father's study before. Several times, in fact, during their secret rendezvous here at the Hôtel de Châtelet, in the middle of the night when she was asleep, her parents were traveling, the servants excused for the day.

The Comte Maurice Léon Philippe du Châtelet's private study was a very masculine chamber that smelled of pipe tobacco and leather. There was a collection of old walking sticks, an array of Louis XV armchairs upholstered in dark brown leather, a massive, ornately carved desk covered with neat piles of documents. On the fireplace mantel was a bronze bust of a family member.

While Geneviève locked the double doors, Daniel circled the

desk, quickly scanning the piles of papers, picking out from among the personal and financial correspondence the most interesting ones. At a glance he could see the dispatches from Vichy concerned top-secret military matters.

But before he could do any more than identify the piles of interest, Geneviève had finished locking the doors from the inside and rushed up to him.

"Over there," she said. "The leather divan."

Eigen, however, did not want to move from the desk. He gently pressed her up against the edge of her father's desk as he ran his hands down her body, along her tiny waist, and around to her small, tight buttocks, where they paused, gently kneading her flesh. Meanwhile he was kissing her throat, her neck, the tops of her breasts.

"Oh, my God," she moaned. "Daniel." Her eyes were closed.

Then Eigen ran his fingertips along the silk-covered cleft of her buttocks, softly teasing the private regions, which so distracted her she didn't notice that his right hand had left her posterior and was reaching behind, to one particular stack of documents, nimbly lifting the top layer of papers.

He hadn't expected this opportunity. He'd have to improvise.

Noiselessly he slipped the papers into the vent at the side of his dinner jacket. As the documents disappeared into the silk lining of his tuxedo, he slid his left hand up to the zipper at the back of her neck and tugged at it, pulling the fabric down, freeing her breasts, exposing the brown disks of her nipples to the butterfly-like tremor of his tongue.

The papers, stiff inside the lining of his dinner jacket, made a slight crinkling sound as he moved.

Suddenly he froze, cocked his head.

"What?" whispered Geneviève, her eyes wide.

"Did you hear that?"

"*What?*"

"Footsteps. *Near.*" Daniel's ears were unusually sharp, but he was particularly on the alert now that he was in a compromising situation in more ways than one.

"No!" She pulled away, fumbling with her dress, pulling it up to cover her breasts. "Zip me up, Daniel, please! We have to get out of here! If *anyone* finds out we're in here—!"

"*Shh,*" he said. Two sets of footsteps, he realized, not just one. From the sound of the shoes on the marble-tiled floor of the hallway just outside, he knew it was two males. The sound echoed, growing louder, coming closer.

As Geneviève crept across the room to the locked door, he could make out their voices now. Two men speaking in French, but one had a German accent. One voice, that of the native French speaker, was low and rumbling; he identified it as belonging to the *Comte,* Geneviève's father. The other—was it General von Stülpnagel, the German Military Governor? He wasn't sure.

Geneviève stupidly reached for the key—to do what, to unlock the doors, just as her father and his German colleague arrived? Daniel touched her hand, stopped her before she turned the key. Instead, he pulled it from the lock.

"That way," he whispered. He pointed toward the door at the far end of the study. The last time he'd entered the room it had been through that door. Perhaps Geneviève would think he'd just noticed it, though in her panic she probably wouldn't be thinking clearly at all.

She nodded, ran toward the other door. When she'd reached it, he switched off the lights in the room, plunging them into darkness. But Daniel moved easily in darkness, and he had a mental picture of the layout of the room, the obstacles in his way.

She gasped when she got to the door, realizing as she turned the knob that it was locked. But Daniel produced the key. Had he not done so, the wasted few seconds would have meant they'd be caught. Swiftly he unlocked the door. It stuck a bit as it came open; the door was seldom used. Shoving her into the narrow, dark corridor, he closed the door behind them, deciding not to lock it. The cylinder was somewhat rusty and noisy, and the sound would be heard by the two men.

He could hear the main door to the study open, the men enter, conversing with each other.

Geneviève clutched at Daniel's arm, her fingernails sharp, claw-like against the silk of his sleeve. If she heard the rustle of the stiff papers inside the lining of his jacket, she seemed not to notice it. "What now?" she whispered.

"You take the stairs down to the kitchen and return to the party."

"But the servants—"

"They won't know where you came from or why, and in any case, they'll be discreet."

"But if you follow, even a few minutes later—!"

"I can't, of course. They'd figure it out, and then you'd be done for."

"But where will you go?" She was whispering, but a bit too loudly.

"Don't worry about me," he said. "I'll catch up with you soon. If your mother asks where I disappeared to, you have no idea, of course." Daniel felt it necessary to spell this out for Geneviève, who wasn't the brightest woman he'd ever met.

"But where—?" she began.

He put his finger to her lips. "Go, *ma cherie.*"

She turned to leave, but he touched her shoulder. She turned back, and he gave her a quick kiss on the lips. Then he straightened the neckline of her dress and rapidly made his way up the servants' stairs. The soles of his shoes were rubber, which was even harder to get these days than leather, and almost noiseless.

His mind raced, going over what had just happened and where he'd go now. He had known he'd see Geneviève tonight, but he hadn't planned on the opportunity to enter her father's study— an opportunity he surely couldn't have passed up. But now, with a thick sheaf of documents stuffed into his dinner jacket, it wasn't a good idea to return to the crowded party, where anyone might bump into him, hear them rattle, detect what he was hiding.

Still, there were ways around that. He could look for the cloak-room, for his topcoat, pretending if anyone happened to ask that he was searching for his cigarette lighter. There he could transfer the papers to his coat. But there was a risk that he might be seen doing so; the cloakroom was probably not unattended.

And that risk was as nothing compared to the far more serious possibility that by returning to the party it would become known that he had been with Geneviève in her father's study. The service stairs led directly into the kitchen, where the servants would see him enter, a few minutes after Geneviève had passed through. They would put two and two together. The servants weren't dis-creet at all, despite what he'd assured Geneviève, and surely she knew the truth as well: they lived for gossip of this kind.

Eigen didn't care a bit about whispers and gossip and rumors. Who cared if Marie-Hélène du Châtelet learned that he'd been furtively canoodling with her daughter? No, it was the chain of revelations that concerned him, for he could see all the way down the chain. The time would come when the *Comte* realized that certain papers vital to national security had gone missing from his study, and he would immediately ask his wife, his servants. Accusations would fly. One of the cooks, perhaps, in order to defend the household staff, was likely to reveal that she'd seen the young man coming down the stairs directly from the study.

And then, even if the master of the house couldn't be sure that Daniel had stolen the papers, Eigen would be the most likely culprit. And his cover—his greatest asset of all—would be blown. That he most certainly could not jeopardize.

True, there were other ways out of the house. He could take the service stairs to the third floor or the fourth, and he could cross one of the no-doubt dark upper floors to another of the stairways. There he could climb down to the back courtyard, now a garden but once used to park carriages. The courtyard was walled in by a high wooden fence, which was locked. He could vault the fence, but he was certain to be seen doing so from the windows of the ballroom, several of which gave onto the courtyard. A man in a tuxedo running through the back courtyard and jumping the fence—no, he'd be spotted at once.

There was only one safe way out of the Hôtel de Châtelet.

In a minute he had reached the top floor, which was the servants' quarters. The ceiling was low and sharply pitched, and the floor here wasn't marble or stone but creaky old pine. There was no one up here: all the servants were downstairs at the party. The young man had done his advance reconnaissance—not that he expected trouble, far from it, but because he considered it crucial always to have an emergency exit. That was his modus operandi, and it had saved his life more than once.

He knew that there was a way to get out through the roof and that since this mansion was built right up against the neighboring town houses in a block-long row there should be any number of possible escape routes.

The Hôtel de Châtelet had a mansard roof, into which were set mullioned windows in arched dormers. He saw at a glance that all the windows that led to the roof were located in the front of the building, in the servants' rooms. It was unlikely that any of the servants would lock their rooms; still, he was relieved when he tried the first one he came to and the door came right open.

The room was tiny, with little furniture in it besides a single bed and a dresser. It was illuminated by the pale moonlight that filtered in through the dusty window. He ran to the window, ducking his head as he squeezed through the narrow dormer, and grabbed the lever handle. These windows obviously weren't opened often, if at all. With great force, though, he was able to yank one side of the window open, then the other.

As the frigid night air flooded in, he looked out and confirmed what he'd noticed when he'd studied the building a few days earlier. The window opened directly onto a steeply sloping tar-covered roof, which dropped precipitously down ten feet or so to a parapet. The parapet, a tall ornamented stone railing, would conceal his movements from passersby on the street below. At least, as long as he was maneuvering along the roof of this building. The neighboring buildings, built in other variants of the Second Empire style, didn't have parapets. Well, he'd take whatever cover he could get.

The tar on the roof had rippled and bubbled from years, decades, of summer heat. Now it was dusted with snow, slick with ice. It would be treacherous.

He'd have to climb out feet first, which wouldn't be easy, since his evening attire constricted his movements. Also, his rubber-soled shoes, though excellent for moving furtively through a house, weren't meant for climbing. This was not going to be easy.

Grabbing the top of the window frame, he swung his legs up, then straight out the window. As soon as his shoes hit the tar roof, they slid on the ice. Instead of releasing his grip on the inside of the window, he hung there, his body half-outside, dangling. Meanwhile he scraped the soles of his shoes back and forth on the tar until he'd abraded away enough of the ice so that the surface was rough enough to allow him some traction.

But he couldn't trust the surface of the roof, not enough to let go of the window. To the left of the window, a few feet away, was a tall brick chimney. He released his right hand, then swung his body around, using his left foot as a pivot point so that he was able to grab hold of the chimney while still holding on to the window sash.

The brick was cold and rough in his hand. The roughness was good, though. The mortar between the bricks was old and crumbling, enough for him to sink his fingertips into the cracks and grab on tightly. His body went rigid, his weight balanced, his grip on the chimney bricks secure enough to allow him to release his left hand from the window, fling it around, and grab the chimney, now with both hands.

Carefully shuffling his feet along the icy roof, one at a time, he scraped with his shoes until he had another reliable spot to stand on. Now he was close enough to the chimney that he was able to hug it, in an approximation of a rock climber's grip. Daniel's upper-body strength was considerable, and he needed all of it to pull himself up the chimney, scrambling his feet against the tar until he found another foothold.

He knew that in the last century thieves often traveled this way from town house to town house. He'd done it a few times himself and knew it was much harder than it looked. But he doubted any thief was insane, or suicidal, enough to clamber around this way in the ice and snow of a Paris winter.

Daniel scaled the chimney a few feet until he reached a low brick wall that separated this roof from the adjoining one. The next roof, he was relieved to see, was not tar but terra-cotta barrel tiles. They might be slick with ice, but their undulating surface would provide some traction. He found he was able to lumber up the tiles fairly easily. The ridge of this roof was not pointed, he saw, but flat, a curb about two feet wide. As he climbed up onto the curb, he tested his footing and found it secure. Now he was able to make his way across the roof, carefully balancing his weight, swaying slightly as if walking on a tightrope.

Far down below was the avenue Foch, dark and deserted, its streetlights extinguished in this time of electrical shortages. He knew that if he could see the street, anyone on the street could see him, since there was no parapet to obstruct the view.

And there were other ways he could be spotted. Anyone looking out the window of a flat on one of the higher floors of a nearby building would see him. People were abnormally vigilant these days, with talk of saboteurs and spies. Nobody who saw a man climbing across the roof of a building would hesitate to call *La Maison*, the *Préfecture de Police*. It was a time of the anonymous letter of denunciation, when the great threat bandied about by Frenchmen was to tell the *Kommandantur*. The risks of Daniel's being spotted were real.

He moved more quickly, as fast as he dared, until he reached the low brick wall that separated this building from the next. The

roof on the next was a mansard, like that of the Hôtel de Châtelet, but it was tiled in slate. It also had a flat curb at the ridge-
line, though this one was narrower than the last, no more than
a foot or so.

He advanced across it carefully, sliding one foot after another.
He looked down at the avenue, and for an instant he was overcome with fear, but he focused his mind on the importance of
his mission, and in a moment the scare passed.

In thirty seconds or so he'd reached the next dividing wall.
This was a thick stone wall into which was set a row of clay vent
pipes and chimney pots. Smoke plumed from a few of the vents,
indicating that the occupants of the house below were among
the privileged few in Paris who had coal to burn for heat. He
reached up to grab a vent, which was cold to the touch, then the
one next to it, and as he hoisted himself up, he noticed something interesting.

The stone wall projected a good ways out from the roof into
the backyard of the town house. About ten feet from the roof
eaves a line of iron rungs were set into the wall, going all the
way from the top of the wall down to the dark courtyard below.
The rungs were used as ladders by chimney sweeps to gain access
to the flues.

For a moment, Daniel was stumped. The rungs were too far
off. He couldn't stand on the stone wall and try to maneuver
among the vents: the wall wasn't quite wide enough at the top.
He had no choice but to reach back up to the clay pipes, grab
hold of one and then the next and the next, his legs swinging,
advancing laterally, bit by bit, across the face of the wall like an
ape. The vent pipes were cylindrical and of a narrow enough
diameter that he was able to hold on to each one securely.

He sidled this way for a few minutes until he reached the
column of iron rungs. He grabbed the top one at the same time
as he swung his feet over to a lower rung. Now he was able to
climb down the rungs, slowly at first and then more quickly, until
he'd descended to the ground.

For a moment he stood there in the deserted courtyard. The windows of the town house that overlooked the yard were dark. Judging from the smoke rising from the vent pipes, the house was occupied, though its inhabitants were probably asleep. He walked slowly, quietly, across the cobblestones. Set into the tall wooden fence was a gate, which was locked. Compared to what he'd just been through, this was barely a challenge. He climbed up the fence, vaulted over it, and entered an alley behind the avenue Foch.

Daniel knew this part of the city well. He sauntered down the alley, resisting the impulse to run, until he reached the narrow side street. He patted his jacket, felt the papers still in place.

This street was dark, eerily deserted.

He passed the darkened windows of a bookshop that had once been owned by a Jew and had been taken over by the Germans. A large white billboard covered its sign, the word FRONTBUCH-HANDLUNG in black Gothic lettering nestled among swastikas. Once it had been an elegant foreign bookstore; now it was foreign in another way: it sold nothing but German books.

Traces of the Germans were all over the place, but strangely, they hadn't demolished any of the famous landmarks, any of the beloved buildings. The Nazis hadn't tried to eliminate Paris as it had always been known. Instead, they wanted simply to annex it—to make Europe's crown jewel theirs. But there was something peculiarly slapdash and *temporary* about the way the Nazis had put down their imprint. Like the white FRONTBUCHHAND-LUNG poster that had been hastily pasted over the bookstore's engraved sign. All that big white cloth could be removed in an instant. It was as if they didn't want to scratch their new jewel. When they'd first tried to put up the swastika flag over the Eiffel Tower, it had ripped in the wind and they'd had to put up another. Even Hitler had visited for only a few hours, like an abashed sightseer. He hadn't even spent the night. Paris didn't want them, and they knew it.

So they put up their posters all over the place. He saw them on the walls of the buildings he passed, pasted up so high they could barely be seen, but there was a reason for that: when the Germans put them at eye level, their stupid placards were inevitably torn down or defaced. Some angry Parisian would scribble on them: "Death to the *Boche!*" or "God bless England!"

He glimpsed a poster of a portly Winston Churchill smoking a cigar and grinning, while next to him stood a woman with a scrawny, screaming baby in her arms. "See what the blockade is doing to your children?" the slogan said. They meant the British blockade, but everyone knew that was nonsense. Even on this one, posted up so high, someone had scrawled: "How about our potatoes?" Everyone was angry: all the potatoes grown by French farmers were sent to Germany; that was the truth.

Another poster, this one just words: *Etes-vous en règle?* Are your papers in order? Or, Are *you* in order? You always had to have your papers with you, your *carte d'identité*, in case you were stopped by a French *gendarme* or some *fonctionnaire*—they were worse than the German soldiers.

The young man always had his papers with him. Several sets, in fact. In different names, different nationalities. They enabled him to make the quick changes he so often was forced to do.

Finally he arrived at his destination: an ancient, crumbling brick building in an anonymous block. A decrepit wooden sign hung from a forged iron bracket: LE CAVEAU. The cellar. It was a bar, located below street level, down a small flight of decaying brick steps. Blackout shades had been drawn in its single, small window, but light peeked out on either side.

He glanced at his watch. It was after midnight, just past the curfew that *Ces Messieurs*—the Nazis—had imposed on Paris.

This bar, however, hadn't closed. The *gendarmes* and the Nazis looked the other way, allowed it to operate late into the night. Bribes had been paid, the right palms greased, free drinks dispensed.

He climbed down the steps and pulled at the old-fashioned crank doorbell, three times. Inside he could hear the buzzer sound, over the cacophony of voices and jazz music.

In a few seconds, a dot of light appeared in the peephole in the center of the massive black-paned wooden door. The light flickered, as someone checked him out, and then the door swung open to admit him.

The place was truly a *caveau*—uneven, cracked stone floor, sticky with spilled drink; buckled brick walls; a low ceiling. The place was thick with smoke, and it stank of sweat, stale tobacco— cheap tobacco, at that—bad wine. Tinny music played from a radio. Along the scarred wooden bar sat six or seven rough-looking workingmen and one woman, who looked like a prostitute. They looked up at him, vaguely curious and at the same time hostile.

The bartender, who had let him in, greeted him. "Long time, Daniel," said Pasquale, a scrawny old man as weathered as his bar. "But I'm always happy to see you." He smiled, exposing an uneven row of brown tobacco-stained teeth and two gold ones. He leaned his leathery face close. "Still can't get Gitanes?"

"I think I've got a shipment coming in tomorrow, the day after."

"Excellent. They're not still a hundred francs, are they?"

"More." He lowered his voice. "For others. For you, the special bartender's discount."

His eyes narrowed suspiciously. "How much?"

"Free."

Pasquale laughed heartily, a rattling, smoker's laugh. Eigen couldn't imagine what kind of *merde* the bartender normally smoked. "Your terms are reasonable," he said, returning to his place behind the bar. "Can I get you a cocktail?"

Eigen shook his head.

"*Le scotch whisky?* Cognac? You need to use the phone?" He gestured to the phone booth at the far end of the bar, whose glass had been broken—by Pasquale, as a warning to his patrons to guard their tongues. Even here, where strangers weren't admitted, you couldn't be sure who was listening.

"No, thanks. Just the WC."

Pasquale's eyebrows shot up for a second; then he nodded, understanding. He was a coarse, cantankerous fellow, but he was the soul of discretion. He knew who really paid his rent, and he hated the Germans as much as anyone else. Two of his beloved nephews had died in the battle of the Ardennes. But he never, ever talked politics. He did his job, served his drinks, and that was that.

As Eigen walked the length of the bar, he heard someone snarl, *"Espèce de sans-carte!"* Cardless person—the standard imprecation uttered against black marketers. Obviously he'd overheard what Eigen and Pasquale had been discussing. Well, that couldn't be helped.

At the end of the long, narrow room, where it was so dim Eigen could hardly see a thing, was a doorway that opened onto a set of wooden stairs in poor repair. They groaned and squeaked as he made his way down. The odor of urine and feces was strong, even though the door to the doubtless even more foul-smelling WC had been left closed by a thoughtful patron.

Instead of entering the toilet, however, Eigen opened the door to a broom closet. He entered, stepping over and through buckets, mops, and jugs of cleaning solution. A short-handled broom was mounted on the rear wall. He grabbed the handle—it was actually mounted quite firmly on the wall—and pulled it down, counterclockwise. As he did so, he pushed, and the wall, which was in fact a door, swung open.

Now he stepped into another dark area, maybe six feet square, mildew-smelling and dusty. The foot traffic from the bar above was audible. Directly in front of him was a steel door that had recently been painted black.

There was a doorbell here, far more contemporary than the one outside the bar. He pressed it twice, then once more.

A gruff voice came from within. *"Oui?"*

"It's Marcel," the man known as Eigen said.

In French, the voice continued: "What do you want?"

"I have some goods that might interest you."

"Like what?"

"I can get you some butter."

"From where?"

"A shed near the Porte des Lilas."

"How much?"

"Fifty-two francs a kilo."

"That's twenty more than the official rate."

"Yes, but the difference is, I can actually get it for you."

"I see."

A pause, and then the door opened with a mechanical click, then a pneumatic sigh.

A small, neat young man with ruddy cheeks, black hair worn in high bangs à la Julius Caesar, and round black glasses gave a crooked smile.

"Well, well, well. Stephen Metcalfe, in the flesh," the man said in a Yorkshire accent. "Done up like a dog's dinner. What've you got for us, mate?"

CHAPTER TWO

Stephen Metcalfe—aka Daniel Eigen, aka Nicolas Mendoza, aka Eduardo Moretti, aka Robert Whelan—pulled the door closed behind him, making sure it sealed. The steel door was set into a rubber gasket, a soundproofing measure.

The entire room he was entering was, of course, soundproofed, using the most advanced technology available. It was actually a room-within-a-room, double-walled, resting on and surrounded by steel plates, six-inch rubber walls; even the air ducts were insulated with rubber and fiberglass. It was low-ceilinged, the inner walls constructed of new cinder block painted U.S. Army gray.

Not much of the shiny new gray paint was visible, though, for the entire perimeter of the room was lined with complicated-looking consoles. Even Metcalfe, who came by at least weekly, didn't know what half of it was. Some of the equipment he recognized—Mark XV and Paraset shortwave radio transceivers, teletypewriters, scrambler telephones, an M-209 cipher machine, wire recorders.

The consoles were manned by two young fellows wearing headphones and taking notes on pads, their faces bathed in the eerie green glow emanating from the round cathode-tube screens. They were wearing gloves, carefully turning knobs, calibrating frequencies. The staticky Morse signals they monitored were bolstered by aerial cables that ran throughout the building—which was owned by a sympathetic Frenchman—to the roof.

Every time Metcalfe paid a visit to the Cave, as this clandestine outstation was called—no one remembered whether the nickname came from the bar upstairs, Le Caveau, or from the fact that the base resembled an electronic cave—he was impressed with the array of equipment. All of it had been smuggled into France in parts via ship or parachuted in, and all of it was strictly outlawed, of course, by the Nazi occupiers. Simple possession of a shortwave radio transmitter could send you to the firing squad.

Stephen Metcalfe was one of a handful of agents who operated out of Paris for an Allied network of spies whose existence was unknown but to a handful of powerful men in Washington and London. Metcalfe had met few of the other agents. That was the way the network operated. Each part of the network was kept separate from the others; everything was compartmented. One node never knew what the other node was up to. Security dictated the procedures.

Here in the Cave, three young radiotelegraph operators and cipher clerks monitored and initiated covert radio links with London, with Washington, and with a far-reaching web of deep-cover agents in the field, in Paris, in the other cities of the occupied zone of France, and across Europe. The men—two Brits and one American—were the very best, trained by the Royal Corps of Signals at Thame Park near Oxford and then at Special Training School 52. Qualified radiotelegraph operators were rare these days, and the British were far ahead of the Americans in training personnel.

A radio, tuned to the BBC, was playing low: the wireless was closely monitored for encoded signals delivered in the form of curious "personal messages" before the evening news broadcast. At a small folding table in the center of the room, a chess game had been abandoned. Evening was the busiest time, when the radio frequencies were least crowded and they could transmit and receive most easily.

The walls were lined with maps of Europe, of the borders and coastlines of France, of each arrondissement of Paris. There were navigation charts, topographical maps, charts of ship and cargo movements in Marseille, detailed maps of naval bases. Yet the room was not entirely devoid of human touches: amid the maps and charts was a *Life* magazine cover photo of Rita Hayworth, and another magazine clipping, of Betty Grable sunbathing.

Derek Compton-Jones, the ruddy-cheeked man who'd opened the door for him, clasped Metcalfe's hand, shook it hard. "Glad you're back safe and sound, mate," he said solemnly.

"You say that every time," Metcalfe teased. "Like you're disappointed."

"Bloody hell!" Compton-Jones spluttered. He looked at once embarrassed and indignant. "Anyone tell you we're in the middle of a war?"

"That right?" Metcalfe replied. "Come to think of it, there did seem to be an awful lot of military uniforms out there."

One of the men wearing headphones and sitting at a console across the room turned to look at Compton-Jones and remarked wearily, "Maybe if he kept his willy in his trousers, he might notice what's happening outside of the bedrooms he spends so much time in." The adenoidal voice and upper-class British accent belonged to Cyril Langhorne, an ace cryptographer and cipher clerk.

The other one, Johnny Betts, from Pittsburgh, a topflight radiotelegraph operator, turned and said, "Roger that."

"Ha," said Langhorne. "Stephen here would roger anything in a skirt."

Compton-Jones laughed, blushing. Metcalfe joined the laughter good-naturedly, then said, "I think maybe you boffins need to get out a little more. I ought to take you all over to One Two Two." They all knew he was talking about the famous bordello at 122 rue de Provence.

"I'm all set there," boasted Compton-Jones. "I've got a regular girl now." He winked at the others and added, "I'll be seeing her later on after I pick up the latest shipment of spare parts."

"That your idea of a deep penetration of France?" asked Langhorne.

Compton-Jones's face turned an even deeper crimson, while Metcalfe roared with laughter. He liked the men who worked here, particularly Compton-Jones. He often referred to Langhorne and Betts as the Bobbsey Twins, though they looked nothing alike. Their Morse and cipher work was the crux of the operation. It was grueling and tense, and Metcalfe knew that their japery was one of the few ways they had of relieving the grinding tension. They also considered Metcalfe their own personal Errol Flynn and regarded him with a combination of jealousy and awe.

He cocked his head, listening to the music playing low from the radio. " 'In the Mood,' " he said. "Good old American music— that's Glenn Miller, broadcasting from the Café Rouge in New York City."

"No, sorry," corrected Compton-Jones, "I'm afraid that's the Joe Loss Orchestra, mate. From London. That's their signature tune."

"Well, I'm glad you guys have all that leisure time to listen to the radio," Metcalfe said. "Because somebody's got to do some work."

He reached inside his dinner jacket and pulled out from its lining the wad of papers, somewhat the worse for wear. He held them aloft, smiling proudly. "Complete plans of the German sub base at Saint-Nazaire, including details on the U-boat pens, even the water-locks system."

"Good show!" marveled Compton-Jones.

Langhorne looked impressed despite himself. "Get that from your little Gestapo crumpet?"

"No, actually, from the private study of the Comte Maurice Léon Philippe du Châtelet."

"The Vichy arsehole?" Langhorne said.

"The very one."

"You're codding me! How'd you get into his private study?"

Metcalfe inclined his head. "A gentleman doesn't kiss and tell, Cyril," he mock-scolded.

"His *wife!* Good Lord, Stephen, have you no pride? The *madame*'s an old mare!"

"And the *mademoiselle*'s quite a little filly. Now we've got to smuggle this out to a courier as soon as possible and fly it over to Corky in New York. I also need you to key in a digest of this and put it over the airwaves for further analysis."

He meant, of course, Alfred "Corky" Corcoran. His boss. The brilliant spymaster who ran the private network of agents that included Metcalfe.

Private network: they answered only to Corcoran, not to some government agency, not to a committee. But there was nothing illegal about this, nothing extragovernmental. For it was the inspiration of President Franklin Delano Roosevelt himself.

It was a strange time in America. Europe was at war, but America was not. America watched, waited. The voices of isolationism were loud and strong. As were the voices that argued passionately that the United States must get involved, must attack Hitler and defend her European friends—or all of Europe would be under the sway of Nazi Germany and it would be too late. Then Hitler would be an overwhelming foe.

Yet there was no centralized intelligence agency. Roosevelt desperately needed reliable, unbiased information on what the Nazis were really up to, on how strong the resistance to Hitler was. Would Britain survive the war? Roosevelt didn't trust Military Intelligence, which was amateurish at best, and he despised the State Department, which was both isolationist and prone to leak to every newspaper around.

So, late in 1939, Franklin Roosevelt called in an old friend and fellow Harvard man. Alfred Corcoran had served in G-2 Military Intelligence during the First World War, then attained great prominence within the top-secret world of MI-8—known as the "Black Chamber," the New York–based code-breaking unit that cracked Japan's diplomatic ciphers in the 1920s. After the Black Chamber was shut down, in 1929, Corcoran played a major behind-the-scenes role in resolving a series of diplomatic crises throughout the 1930s, from Manchuria to Munich.

FDR knew that Corky was the best—and most important, FDR knew he could trust him.

With funding buried in the White House budget, and the full backing of the President, Corky set up his shop, deliberately outside of the gossipy corridors of Washington. His top-secret private intelligence ring, which reported directly to the White House, was headquartered in the Flatiron Building in New York, disguised as an international trading firm.

Corcoran had a free hand to hire the best and the brightest, and he drew heavily from the young graduates of the Ivy League colleges, well-bred young men who would be comfortable in the rarefied social circles of Europe. So many of his recruits came from the Social Register, in fact, that wags began to call Corcoran's network the Register, and the nickname stuck. One of his earliest hires was a young Yale graduate named Stephen Metcalfe.

The son of a millionaire industrialist and his Russian wife— Stephen's mother had come from a noble family that had left the country before the Revolution—Stephen had traveled widely with his family and had been schooled in Switzerland. He spoke German, Russian, French, and Spanish fluently, virtually without accent: the Metcalfes had extensive holdings in Argentina and spent part of winter there for years. Too, the Metcalfes did a steady trade with the Russian government.

Stephen's brother, Howard—the reliable one—now ran the family's business empire, since the death of their father four years ago. Stephen would occasionally join Howard, travel with him, assist in whatever ways he could, but he refused to be tied down by the responsibility of running a major business.

He was also fearless, rebellious, and fun-loving to excess— qualities that Corcoran insisted would be useful in his new cover, as an Argentine playboy in Paris.

Derek Compton-Jones cleared his throat nervously. "No need to dispatch a courier, actually," he said.

Langhorne looked up, then quickly looked back at his console.

"Oh really? You have a faster way to get it to Manhattan?" said Metcalfe.

Just then the door at the far end of the room opened.

It was a face he did not expect to see: the grave, drawn face of Alfred Corcoran.

CHAPTER THREE

The old man was dressed fastidiously, as always. His tie was tied in an elegant four-in-hand. His charcoal-gray suit emphasized his rail-thin frame. He smelled of peppermint, as he usually did—he was addicted to Pep-O-Mint Life Savers—and he was smoking a cigarette. He gave a hacking cough.

Compton-Jones immediately returned to his station, and the room fell silent. The high spirits had evaporated at once.

"Christ on a raft, these damned French smokes are godawful! I ran out of Chesterfields on the airboat over here, somewhere over Newfoundland. Stephen, why don't you ingratiate yourself with your boss and get me some American tobacco? Aren't you supposed to be a damned black marketeer?"

Metcalfe stammered a bit as he came forward and shook Corky's hand. In his left hand he clutched the stolen documents. "Of course . . . Corky . . . what are you doing—?" Corcoran was far from a desk jockey: he made frequent trips into the field. But travel into occupied Paris was difficult, complicated, and decidedly risky. He didn't often come to Paris. There must be a good reason why he was here.

"What am *I* doing here?" replied Corcoran. "The real question is, what are *you* doing here?" He turned, headed back toward the room he'd just come from, and gestured for Metcalfe to follow.

Metcalfe closed the door behind him. Obviously the old man wanted to speak in private. There was an urgency about Corky that Metcalfe hadn't seen before.

The adjacent room stored an array of equipment including a German-letter typewriter for issuing passes and ID cards. There

was also a small printing press, used in simple documentary forgery—most of the serious work was done in New York or London—for creating French travel and work permits. One table
held an assortment of rubber stamps, including a good copy of
a German censor stamp. In one corner of the room, near a rack
of uniforms, was an oak desk piled with papers. A green-shaded
library lamp cast a circle of light.

Corcoran sat down at the desk chair and motioned for Metcalfe to sit. The only other place was an army cot against the
wall. Metcalfe sat, anxious. He placed the bundle of stolen papers
on the cot beside him.

For a long while Corcoran regarded him in silence. His eyes
were a pale, watery gray behind his flesh-colored horn-rimmed
glasses.

"I'm sorely disappointed in you, Stephen," Corcoran said
softly. "I established you here at the enormous expense of scarce
resources, and what do you have to show for it?"

"Sir," Metcalfe began.

But Corcoran was not to be deterred. "Civilization as we know
it is being engulfed by Hitler's devouring maw. The Nazis have
conquered Norway, Denmark, Holland, Belgium, Luxembourg,
and now France. They forced the British to turn tail at Dunkirk.
They're bombing London to pieces. The man has the whole sandbox to himself. Good God, young man, this may be the end of
the free world. And you—you're unlacing *bustiers*, for God's
sake!" He pulled out a roll of Pep-O-Mint Life Savers and popped
one in his mouth.

Metcalfe, meanwhile, snatched the papers from the cot, bran-
dished them at his boss and mentor. "Sir, I've just laid my hands
on the top-secret plans for the German strategic naval base on
the Atlantic coast, at Saint-Nazaire—"

"Yes, yes," Corcoran interrupted impatiently, crunching on a
Life Saver. "The German improvements to the water locks that
control entry to the submarine pens. I've already seen them."

"*What?*"

"You're not my only agent, young man."

Metcalfe flushed, unable to suppress a surge of indignation. "Who got this for you? I'd like to know. If you've got multiple agents covering the same turf, we risk stepping all over each other and blowing the whole thing."

Corcoran shook his head slowly, tsk-tsked. "You know better than to ask me that, Stephen. One of my agents never knows what the other's up to—that's an inviolable law."

"That's also crazy . . . sir."

"Crazy? No. It's prudent. The almighty principle of compartmentation. Each one of you must know only what's strictly necessary about your assignment, about your colleagues. Otherwise, all it takes is for one of you to be captured and tortured and the entire network is compromised."

"That's why we're all given cyanide pills," Metcalfe objected.

"Yes. Which works only if you have sufficient notice. But what if you're taken suddenly? Let me tell you something: one of my agents—whom I'd managed to place in an important position in the Compagnie Française des Petroles—was picked up by the Gestapo a week ago. Haven't heard from him since. This is a fellow who knows of the existence of this place right here." Corky waved his hands around, indicating the Cave. "What if he talks? What if he's turned? These are the sorts of questions that disturb my sleep."

A moment of silence passed. "Why are you here, sir?"

Corky bit his lower lip. "Your code name, Stephen. It's Romeo, is that right?"

Metcalfe rolled his eyes, shook his head in embarrassment.

"I often find myself despairing at your lack of restraint when it comes to the fairer sex." Corky chuckled dryly and munched at a candy. "But once in a while your trail of broken hearts actually benefits our cause."

"How so?"

"I'm referring to a woman with whom you had a dalliance a while ago."

Metcalfe blinked. That could describe any number of women, and he didn't particularly feel like guessing.

"This woman—this old flame of yours—has taken up with a very important Nazi official."

"I don't know who you're talking about."

"No, there's no reason you should. It was six years ago. In Moscow."

"*Lana!*" Metcalfe whispered.

He felt a jolt, like an electric shock. Just hearing her name, a name he'd never thought he'd hear again, summoned her, still vivid in his memory.

Lana—Svetlana Baranova—was an extraordinary woman, impossibly beautiful, magnetic, passionate. She had been the first great love of his young life.

Moscow in 1934 was a gloomy, frightened, and mysterious place when Stephen Metcalfe, fresh from Yale, first visited the city. The Metcalfe family did a small amount of business in Russia—back in the twenties, the elder Metcalfe had helped set up a half-dozen joint ventures with the Soviet government, ranging from pencil factories in Novgorod to oil exploration in Georgia. When a hitch had arisen, as invariably happened with the Soviet bureaucracy, Metcalfe senior had sent his two sons over to negotiate the dispute. While his stolid brother, Howard, sat through endless, inconclusive meetings with Soviet functionaries, Stephen explored the city with wide-eyed fascination. He was drawn especially to the great Bolshoi Theater, its sweeping colonnade topped with a copper sculpture of a chariot-drawn Apollo.

It was there, at that vast nineteenth-century edifice, that he found himself transfixed by a beautiful young ballerina. Onstage, she floated, hovered, flew, her ethereal aura heightened by her porcelain skin, dark eyes, and silky black hair. Night after night, he'd watched her effortless, astonishing movements in *The Red Poppy* and *Swan Lake*. But never was she more memorable than in her starring role in Igor Moiseyev's version of *Tristan and Isolde.*

When Metcalfe finally arranged for them to meet, the young Russian girl seemed overwhelmed by the attentions of the rich American. But she had no idea how overwhelmed the rich American—though he pretended to be sophisticated and worldly—was by her. After a few months, the Metcalfe sons left Moscow, the family business concluded. Stephen found parting with Svetlana Baranova to be as painful a breakup as he'd ever been through. On the overnight train from Moscow to Leningrad, Stephen had sat up the entire night, grim-faced. His brother, Howard, had slept comfortably, and when he was awakened by the dour old lady serving tea, an hour outside of Leningrad, he joked with his younger brother, poked fun at him. Howard was as sensible and insensitive as only an older brother can be. "Come on, forget her," he urged Stephen. "She's a *ballerina,* for God's sake. The world is full of beautiful women—you'll see."

Stephen just stared dismally out the window at the forest speeding by.

"Anyway, you can't have been serious about her. I don't want to think about what Father would say if he ever found out you've been seeing a ballerina. That's almost as bad as an *actress!*"

Metcalfe grunted, staring out the window.

"Though I will admit," Howard said, "that girl was a real dish."

"Svetlana Baranova is now a prima ballerina at the Bolshoi," said Alfred Corcoran. "In the last few months she's become the mistress of a high-ranking member of the German Foreign Ministry stationed in Moscow."

Metcalfe shook his head, as if to clear away cobwebs. "Lana?" he said again. "With a *Nazi?*"

"Evidently," Corcoran said.

"And . . . and how did you know I'd had a . . . a fling with her?"

"You'll recall that when you joined I had you fill out a long and tedious form, some fifty pages long, in which I required you to list all your contacts in foreign countries—friends, family, relations, everyone. You listed relatives in Buenos Aires, schoolmates in Lucerne, friends in London, in Spain. But you didn't mention anyone in Moscow, though you did list Moscow as one of the places you'd visited. I pushed you on that—how could you spend months in Moscow and *not* meet anyone? And you fessed up that, well, you did have this fling. . . ."

"I'd forgotten."

"My New York staff is quite small, as you know, but they're resourceful. Skilled at cross-referencing names. When a stray intelligence report crossed one of my researchers' desks concerning an attaché of the German embassy in Moscow named Rudolf von Schüssler and rumors that he might not be entirely pro-Nazi, one of my girls was alert enough to connect two dots. The surveillance report on von Schüssler linked him with a ballerina at the Bolshoi named Svetlana Baranova, and the name struck a chord in my researcher's memory."

"Lana is seeing a German diplomat?" Metcalfe mused aloud, mostly to himself.

"Ever since Hitler and Stalin signed their nonaggression pact last year, the German diplomatic community in Moscow has been able to socialize reasonably freely with certain privileged Russians. Of course, the German Foreign Ministry is full of old-money, old-line aristocrats—the Social Register isn't limited to our country, you know—and a number of them are less than discreet about their distaste for Hitler and his rabid Nazis. We've surmised that von Schüssler may count himself among those secretly opposed to Hitler. But is this true? And how opposed is he, really? So opposed that he might help out the white hats a bit? That's what I need you to find out."

Metcalfe nodded, feeling the excitement build. Moscow again! And . . . Lana!

"So here's what I'd like you to do," Corcoran went on. "These days it's fiendishly difficult for a foreigner to get into Russia. It was never easy, but it's harder than ever now. I suppose it's not impossible to infiltrate an agent under some sort of cover, but that's extraordinarily risky. And in any case, it's not necessary. I want you going over there without cover. In the clear—as yourself. You will have a perfectly plausible reason for going to Moscow, after all. Your family needs to finalize some asset transfer concerning some of the old joint ventures."

"I don't know what you're talking about."

"Oh, you'll come up with something. Work out the details with your brother. We'll facilitate that. Take my word for it, if there's a promise of an infusion of hard currency, the Soviets will be most eager to arrange meetings. Even these days, when they denounce us in *Pravda* every day."

"You're talking about bribes."

"I'm talking about whatever it takes. It's really not important. The point is to get the Russians to grant you a visa, so that you have a legitimate reason for being in Moscow. While there, you will 'happen' to run into your old flame, Svetlana, at an American embassy party. You will get together, as is to be expected."

"And?"

"The specifics I'll leave to you. Perhaps you'll rekindle an old romance."

"That's the past, Corky. We ended it."

"On good terms, if I know you. All your old lovers seem to regard you with misty-eyed affection. How you do it I don't understand."

"But *why?*"

"This is an extremely rare opportunity. A chance for you to spend time in an informal, personal setting, outside official circles, with a very important German diplomat who has a direct line to von Ribbentrop himself, and thus to the Führer."

"And do *what?*"

"Assess him. See if you can confirm the reports we've been receiving—that he's secretly disaffected."

"If you're receiving reports, his feelings can't be all that secret."

"Our American diplomats are skilled at reading nuance. They report subtleties, joking asides, that sort of thing. But that's not the same as an all-out, close-up assessment and development by a trained intelligence officer. If von Schüssler is indeed secretly opposed to Adolf Hitler's madness, we may be able to cultivate a most valuable intelligence lead."

"You want me to turn him, is that it?"

"Let's take this one step at a time, shall we? I want you to apply for a visa in your own name at the Soviet consulate here, on the boulevard Lannes. Even given your family's privileged status with the Sovs, the paperwork will certainly take a few days to a week. Meanwhile, you'll tie up your business here in Paris but burn no bridges. Tomorrow you'll meet with a very clever associate of mine who specializes in some of the tricks of the trade you'll need in Moscow."

Metcalfe nodded. The notion of going to Moscow was enormously exciting, but it was nothing compared to the thought of seeing Svetlana Baranova again—and for such an important reason.

Corcoran stood up. "Go, Stephen. We have no time to lose. Every day that goes by, the Nazis gain another victory. Invade another country. Bomb another city. They grow stronger, more rapacious, while we sit on the sidelines and watch. We're short on quite a few things, as you know—sugar and shoes, gasoline and rubber, munitions. But the thing we're shortest on is time."

CHAPTER FOUR

The violinist was playing his favorite piece, Beethoven's *Kreutzer* Sonata, but he was not enjoying himself at all. For one thing, the pianist was terrible. She was the dowdy wife of an SS official, only minimally talented: she played like an adolescent at a school recital. She was no musician. She was hammering the keys with no sense of dynamics at all, completely overpowering him in some of the more urgent, sensitive passages. And she had an annoying habit of breaking her chords by playing the left hand an instant before the right. The first movement, the stormy allegro, had been simply adequate. But the old hag had no feeling for the subtleties of the third movement, the *andante cantabile*, with its virtuosic rhythmic ornamentations.

Then again, the piece was complex, even for an accomplished musician such as himself. When Beethoven had sent the manuscript to the great Parisian violinist Rodolphe Kreutzer, to whom he'd dedicated it, Kreutzer himself proclaimed it impossible to play and never once performed it in public.

Also, the acoustics here were godawful. This was the home of the violinist's immediate boss, Standartenführer H. J. Kieffer, the Paris chief of the counterespionage department of the *Sicherheitsdienst*, the Nazi secret service. The room was carpeted, hung with heavy drapes and tapestries, and the sound just died here. The piano was a very good Bechstein, but it was woefully out of tune.

Kleist did not know why he had ever agreed to play this evening.

It was, after all, a very busy time, and the violin was only his avocation.

A smell suddenly assaulted his nostrils. He recognized the ber-gamot, orange, and rosemary notes on top of a base of neroli and musk and knew it was 4711, the cologne made by the German fragrance firm Muelhens.

Kleist knew without even looking up that Müller had just en-tered the room. Müller, his local control in the *Sicherheitsdienst*, was one of the very few men in the SD who wore aftershave. Most of the SD men considered such a thing an unmanly affec-tation.

Müller had not been at the dinner, nor at the house concert, so he must have had some urgent piece of business on his mind. Kleist decided to skip the repeat and hurry the fourth movement to its conclusion, get the thing over with. There was work to be done.

The applause was enthusiastic, heartfelt, and loud, given that there were no more than twenty-five people in the room, all of them SD men and their wives or consorts. Kleist nodded his appreciation and hurried to the side of the room, where Müller awaited him.

"There's been a break in the case," Müller said quietly.

Kleist, his violin in one hand, his bow in the other, nodded. "The wireless station."

"Correct. There was an RAF parachute drop in Touraine in the middle of the night last night. Several containers of com-munications equipment. Our informant alerted us to the drop." He added smugly, "Our informant has never been wrong. He insists that the drop will lead us to the *réseau*." That was the term for a nest, a clandestine espionage ring.

"The equipment was delivered to Paris?" Kleist said. Someone was lingering nearby, no doubt to compliment him on his per-formance. Kleist turned, didn't recognize the woman, nodded brusquely, and turned back to Müller. The woman went away.

"To a flat on the rue Mazagran, near the Porte Saint-Denis."

"That's the location of the wireless station? On the rue Ma-zagran?"

Müller shook his head. "Just a transfer point. An apartment owned by some old whore."

"Has the equipment been delivered?"

Müller smiled and nodded slowly. "Picked up, actually. By an agent we believe to be a British national living here under cover."

"Well?" Kleist said impatiently.

"Our team lost him."

"*What?*" Kleist sighed in disgust. There was no end to the incompetence of the SD's field teams. "You want me to talk to this whore," he said.

"I would not delay," said Müller. "Your playing was quite nice, by the way. Was that Bach?"

The whore plied her trade at the base of the grand arch, at the end of the rue du Faubourg Saint-Denis, which had been built in the seventeenth century to celebrate Louis XIV's victories in Flanders and the Rhineland. There were five whores gathered there, in fact. They chattered among themselves, turning their faces and bodies toward the pedestrian passersby, harried men rushing home to beat the curfew. She could be any one of them, Kleist realized.

As he strolled past them in his crisp green SD uniform, he noticed that three of them were too young to be the "old whore" that Müller had described, the one whose apartment had been used to transfer equipment dropped in Touraine by the Royal Air Force. According to Müller, the whore was around forty and had an illegitimate son of twenty-four who was active in the Resistance. She often let her son use her apartment as a transfer site. Only two of the prostitutes here looked old enough to have a twenty-four-year-old son.

His nostrils flared. He caught the unmistakable mingling of odors that he associated with French prostitutes—the stench of cheap cigarettes, and the cheap perfume they invariably used to mask their lack of hygiene. Their feminine odors came through strongly, along with the smell of male discharges that had not been washed away. Quite revolting, actually.

They all noticed his uniform, which he had kept on deliberately. Several of them had turned his way, smiling lasciviously, saying good evening to him in bad German. The two who did not were both the older ones, which did not surprise him. The older women probably detested the German occupiers, at least more actively. He stopped, smiled at the women, turned back toward them. He walked more closely past them.

When he was close enough, he could smell the fear. It was a myth that only dogs could smell fear on human beings, Kleist had learned. He was an amateur student of biology. Turbulent emotion, particularly terror, stimulated the apocrine glands in the armpits and the groin. The secretions came out through the hair follicles. The odor was pungent, musky, and sour, instantly recognizable.

He could smell her fear.

The whore didn't just dislike Germans; she was afraid of them. She saw his uniform, recognized the security police, and she was terrified that her role in the Resistance had been discovered.

"You," Kleist said, pointing.

She avoided his glance, turning away. This was further confirmation, as if he needed confirmation.

"The German gentleman prefers you, Jacqueline," teased one of the younger whores.

She reluctantly turned to meet his stare. Her blond hair had been bleached badly, in peroxide, and not recently. "Oh, a handsome soldier such as you can do much better than me," she said, attempting a frivolous tone. Her voice was cigarette-raspy. He could hear her rapid heartbeat in the tremor of her voice.

"I prefer a mature woman," Kleist said. "A woman who has been around. Who knows a thing or two."

The other women tittered and cackled.

With great reluctance, the blonde came up to him. "Where shall we go?" she said.

"I have no place," Kleist said. "I am not posted in the city."

The whore shrugged as the two of them walked. "There is an alley very close to here."

"No. That will not do for what I have in mind."

"But if you have no place . . ."

"We need a bed, and some privacy." Her reluctance to take him to her apartment verged on the comical. He enjoyed toying with her like a cat with a mouse. "You have a flat near here, surely. I will make it worth your while."

Her apartment building on the rue Mazagran was disheveled, in poor repair. They walked the four flights of stairs to her flat in silence. She took a long time to find her keys in her purse, clearly nervous. Finally she let him in. It was surprisingly large, sparsely decorated. She took him to her bedroom, pointing to the bathroom door. "If you need *la salle de bain*," she said.

The bed was large, the mattress lumpy. It was covered in a threadbare scarlet spread. He sat on one side, and she sat next to him. She began unbuttoning his tunic.

"No," he said. "You undress first."

She got up, went into the bathroom, and closed the door. He listened carefully for the scrape of a drawer, the sound of a weapon being retrieved, but there was nothing except the running of water from the tap. She emerged a few minutes later wrapped in a turquoise dressing gown, which she flapped open briefly to give him a glimpse of her naked flesh. She had surprisingly firm breasts for a woman of her age.

"The gown, please," Kleist said.

She hesitated only a few seconds before dropping the gown to the floor, displaying her body with haughty pride. Then she went to him, standing close to him, naked, and began once again to unbutton his tunic.

"You get into the bed, please," said Kleist.

She did so obediently, moving with studied grace. She lay back on the bed, still posing. "You are a modest man," she said. "You prefer not to be naked."

"Yes," Kleist said shyly. "Also, I prefer to talk a little first, hmm?"

She paused. "You want me to talk dirty to you, is that it?"

"You are a woman who could teach me a good deal, I'll bet." He smelled the wet burlap even before he noticed the corner of the burlap sack under the bed. The sack had been used to transport the equipment, Kleist reasoned. That was why it was still damp. Perhaps it had been raining in the countryside. "Ah, the scent of your glorious countryside."

"Pardon me?"

He reached down to the floor and tugged at the burlap, pulling the neatly folded sack all the way out. "Yes, I can smell the fertile soil of the Loire Valley. The flinty clay, the limestone soil. Touraine, yes?"

She looked instantly fearful, but she quickly masked her terror with a shrug. She reached for him, placing one expert hand on his crotch. "You German soldiers have such large packages," she murmured. "It is always very exciting for me."

Kleist's organ did not respond. He placed a hand on her grasping, kneading claw and lifted it away. "Speaking of packages," he said. "The fields of Touraine make convenient drop sites for packages, do they not?"

"I don't know what you are talking about. I have never been to Touraine—"

"Perhaps not, but your son, René, has, has he not?"

The whore looked as if she had been slapped. She flushed. "I have no idea what you're talking about," she said. "What do you want from me?"

"Just a little information. You are a woman who knows a thing or two, as I said. I want a name from you."

She drew herself up, folded her arms around her naked breasts. "Please, go," she said. "You are mistaken. I am a working woman, that is all I know."

"You believe you are protecting your only son," Kleist said

softly. "But you are in reality harming him. Him and his wife and his two-year-old son—your grandson. For if you do not tell me what I need to know, they will be shot before the sun comes up. This I can assure you."

The whore cried out, "What do you *want?*"

"Just a name," he said. "The name of the British man who picked up the equipment. And how he is contacted."

"I don't know *anything!*" she said. "They only use my apartment!"

Kleist smiled. She had cracked quite easily. "You have a very simple choice, Mademoiselle. I have no interest in the business of your son. I am interested only in the British man. You will give me the contact information for the British man, and you will save your son and grandson. Or else they will be dead within the hour. This is your choice."

She told him everything he wanted to know. The information tumbled out of her in a terrified rush.

"Thank you," Kleist said.

"Now get out of here, *Boche!*" the whore spat at him. "Get out of my apartment, you filthy Nazi!"

Kleist was not disturbed by the prostitute's sad attempt at retrieving a scrap of dignity. She had told him everything, after all. That was not what bothered him. No, it was the certainty that she would tell her son about the visit from the SD officer. The word might get to the British man before he could be picked up, and that wouldn't do at all.

He leaned over her, stroking her breasts, her shoulders. "You really mustn't talk that way," he said quietly. "We're not as bad as all that."

She stiffened at his touch, turning her head away. She did not see the flash of the catgut E string as Kleist whipped it from his pocket, gripping it like a garrote. When she felt it tighten against her throat, however, she attempted to scream, but no sound emerged. Mixed with the coniferous aroma of the violin string's rosin, Kleist could smell, within a few seconds, the cloacal discharge. Sometimes his extraordinary olfactory sensitivity was a burden. When she was dead, he removed the gut string and put it back in his pocket.

Then, after washing his hands fastidiously to remove the stench, he left the whore's apartment.

CHAPTER FIVE

There was, as Corcoran had so urgently insisted, no time to lose. There was a Soviet visa to arrange. This he could do in Paris, at the Soviet consulate on the boulevard Lannes. The German occupiers of Paris were partners with the Russians now; Moscow would be cooperative. More important, Metcalfe's family still did a small but consistent business with the Soviet government. So the Metcalfes would be considered VIPs in Moscow. He'd be granted a visa without a problem, he was sure.

But he'd have to contact his brother, Howard, in New York. Since Howard was in charge of the family business operations, it would have to be he who made arrangements with the Soviet government to send his brother over. Howard would no doubt be surprised at his younger brother's request. He knew that Stephen was now working for the government, in some undercover capacity, but for reasons of security he hadn't been told much more than that.

By the time Metcalfe left the Cave, the bar upstairs had quieted down. A few people remained at the bar, the more subdued sort of drunks who sat by themselves and medicated themselves into a stupefied, quiet oblivion. Only the bartender, Pasquale, noticed him coming up. Pasquale was bent over an abacus and a stack of receipts, tallying the evening's business. He looked up when he heard Metcalfe's footsteps, gave him a wink. Pasquale made a quick gesture—finger and thumb together at his lips, pantomiming a smoke—and Metcalfe nodded. The bartender hadn't forgotten about the cigarettes he so desired, and wordlessly Metcalfe had indicated he hadn't forgotten, either. Metcalfe patted the bartender's arm as he passed wordlessly through the bar and out onto the street.

He glanced at his watch: a little after one in the morning.

At this time of night, the streets of Paris were deserted. Metcalfe was weary and could use a good night's sleep, but at the same time the meeting with Corky had energized him, pumped him full of adrenaline. No matter how much he needed his rest, he couldn't possibly sleep now.

It was late, certainly, but was it too late? There was a woman he knew: one of his most important sources, in fact. She was a code clerk . . . a night owl, she liked to stay up late, even though she was required to be at her desk by nine o'clock in the morning.

She'd welcome his presence no matter what time of night; hadn't she often said so? Well, a visit at this time of night would certainly put that to the test.

Flora Spinasse was a rather plain woman indeed, but a dear woman: a bit mousy and reticent at first, yet when she began to open up, she became playful, then passionate. Before the German occupation five months ago, she'd been a code clerk at the *Direction Générale de la Sûreté Nationale,* the French office of national security. When the Nazis moved in, the Gestapo seized control of the *Sûreté,* and the *Sûreté* headquarters, at 11 rue des Saussaies, just around the corner from the Palais de l'Élysée, became Gestapo headquarters. After a purge of those deemed unreliable, *la Gestapo* kept as many of the French-speaking employees as they could, since they were short on French speakers. Most of the secretaries and file clerks remained. The Frenchwomen didn't like their new bosses, but those who stayed were smart enough to keep their mouths shut and keep their jobs.

But they all had their personal lives, their family backgrounds, and Flora Spinasse had her own little tragedy. Her beloved grandmother had died when the Nazis invaded. The nurses at the Paris hospital where her grandmother had been at the time had been in a hurry to escape Paris, and some of their patients had been too ill to move. Those—including Flora's adored *grandmère*—were administered fatal injections. Flora had grieved in silence, but her anger at what the Nazis had done to Paris, and in effect to her grandmother, continued to burn deep inside.

Stephen knew all this about Flora—Corky's network had done its prep work, collating hospital records with lists of employees at sensitive offices throughout Paris—even before he "happened" to meet her at the Parc Monceau. She was flattered and embarrassed by the attentions of this handsome, rich Argentine, and they both found themselves joking about the stupid, freshly painted German signs that had suddenly been put up all over the park: RASEN NICHT TRETEN—keep off the grass. Before the Germans moved in, you could picnic anywhere in the Parc Monceau. But now? It was so . . . so *German!*

The Nazi-imposed curfew was midnight, so anyone with an ounce of brains in their heads was at home or at least inside somewhere and not walking around. Violation of the curfew could mean a night in jail. Curfew violators were sometimes made to polish German soldiers' shoes all night or peel potatoes in the military kitchens.

It was a long walk to Flora's apartment on the rue de la Boétie. He had left his powerful old Hispano-Suiza near his own apartment, on the rue de Rivoli. Just as well: if he'd driven to the party, he'd have had to abandon it near the avenue Foch anyway. He heard the throaty rumble of an automobile. A black Citroën—a Gestapo car, for sure—roared by. But its occupants were too busy to stop and harass the lone pedestrian who should have been at home, not wandering about.

The night had gotten colder, the wind gusty. Metcalfe felt his ears, his fingers, go numb. He half-wished he'd gotten his topcoat before he left the party, then realized that was impossible.

A minute or so later, a Black Maria passed by—a *panier à salade,* the French called it, a salad basket—bearing prisoners. Metcalfe felt a twinge of paranoia, then remembered that most of the vehicles out this late at night were Nazi ones. Spotting a telephone booth, he crossed the street. As he approached the booth, noticing the sign the Germans had posted on the glass, thoughtfully in French—ACCÈS INTERDIT AUX JUIFS, Jews not allowed—he heard a shout, and footsteps coming his way.

"Hey! You! *Arrêt!*"

Metcalfe glanced up casually, saw a *flic*, a French cop, running toward him. He kept going toward the booth.

"Hey! You! Let me see your papers." The policeman was in his early twenties and didn't look like he shaved yet.

Metcalfe shrugged, smiled pleasantly, and handed him a *carte d'identité* in the name of Daniel Eigen, issued by the *Préfecture de Police.* The Frenchman looked it over suspiciously. When he realized he'd stopped a foreigner, he straightened visibly.

"The curfew is midnight," the young man scolded. "You're not allowed to be out; you know that."

Metcalfe pointed backhandedly at his dinner jacket, gave a crooked smile. *I'm a lousy drunk, a reprobate,* he implied by his stance, his rueful grin. He was grateful he hadn't had time to change into street clothes. His tuxedo was a good alibi, a kind of proof that his reason for violating the curfew was fairly innocent.

"No excuse," the *flic* snapped priggishly. "The curfew hours are posted everywhere. You are in violation. I'm going to have to keep this, and you're going to have to come in to the station for questioning."

Oh, great, Metcalfe groaned inwardly. *Just my luck.* He'd been stopped for curfew violations countless times since the rules had gone into effect, but never had he been taken in. This was trouble. He was reasonably certain his forged papers would withstand close scrutiny, and he certainly had plenty of people of influence who'd vouch for him. Hell, he could call any number of powerful friends in Paris who could get him released in an instant. But that was only if he got to that point. If this fellow dug too deep into his records . . . Metcalfe couldn't be sure how thorough the backstopping had been, how many layers of validating records existed to back up the Daniel Eigen identity. He might not withstand an interrogation. . . .

The best weapon against an authority figure was authority, Metcalfe knew. *Rule number one,* Corky had often told him, *when challenged by authority, you must always lay claim to a greater authority. If you learn nothing else from me, learn this.*

He drew closer to the policeman, scowling. "What's your number?" he said in French. "Come on; let's have it. When Didier hears about you, he's going to go apoplectic."

"Didier?" the young cop said suspiciously, his brow furrowed.

"I suppose you don't even know the name of your own boss, Didier Brassin, the chief of the *Préfecture de Police,*" replied Metcalfe, shaking his head in disbelief and taking out the velvet pouch of cigars from his breast pocket. "And when Didier hears that one of his own men—a mere *patrolman*—attempted to prevent the delivery of these *Romeo y Julietas* to his home on the Quai des Orfèvres, cigars needed for an urgent late-night meeting, you will be out of a job. And that's if Didier's in good spirits. Now, your number, please."

The cop stepped back a bit. His expression was transformed: now he was genial, wreathed in smiles. "Please, sir—don't take offense. Go on, sir. My apologies!"

Metcalfe shook his head as he turned and walked away. "Don't let it happen again," he said.

"Of course not, sir. It was entirely a mistake!"

Metcalfe strode on past the phone booth, deciding against stopping to place a call. He would just show up at Flora Spinasse's flat unannounced.

Her apartment house on the rue de la Boétie was shabby and in poor repair. The little foyer, like all the walls in the building, was painted a hideous mustard-yellow, and the paint was peeling. He let himself in—she'd given him a key to the front door—and took the self-service elevator to the fifth floor. He knocked on her door, using their secret code: three quick raps followed by two. A dog yapped somewhere inside. It was a long while before the door opened. Flora gasped when she saw him.

"Daniel!" she said. "Why are you here? What time is it?" She was dressed in her long cotton nightgown, her hair in curlers. Her poodle, Fifi, ran in circles at her feet, growling and yapping.

"May I come in, Flora dear?"

"Why are you *here?* Yes, yes, come in—good heavens! Fifi, *down,* my little *toutou!*"

Flora was not looking her best, but then, few did at this hour of the morning. She was embarrassed; her hands fluttered up to her curlers, then down to her nightgown, not knowing what to conceal first. She shut the door quickly behind him. "Daniel!" she said again, but he kissed her at once, on the mouth, and she kissed him back with growing urgency.

"Is everything all right with you?" she said at last when they had pulled apart.

"I had to see you," Metcalfe said.

"But . . . but Daniel, you should have called me first! You know that! You can't simply show up unannounced at a woman's flat, when she is unprepared!"

"Flora, you don't need preparation. You don't need to paint your face. You look loveliest in your natural state, I've told you that."

She blushed. "You must be in trouble, that's all there is to it."

He looked around her tiny, forlorn apartment. Her windows were draped in black satinette for the *blaqueoute,* the blackout. There was even a blue shade on the standing lamp in the corner of the living room. Flora was a young woman who did everything by the book, observed all the rules. Her greatest transgression was her dalliance with a foreigner—and the information she provided him. It was the single act of naughtiness in a life of orderliness and respectability. And it was no small violation.

But then, it was always the plain women, Metcalfe had learned, who made the best agents. They were paid less attention, assumed to be dutiful and hardworking. While secretly deep in their hearts lurked the spirit of rebellion. In the same way, it was always the plainer girls who were the most ardent, most inexhaustible lovers. The beautiful girls like Geneviève, vain and self-absorbed, tended to be far more nervous and self-aware in bed. Whereas Flora, who was no beauty queen, had a voracious appetite for sex. Metcalfe sometimes found her demands exhausting.

No, Flora was happy to see him anytime. That he was sure of.

"It's ice-cold in here, darling," he said. "How can you sleep?"

"I have just enough coal to heat this one room for a few minutes a day. I save it for the mornings. I'm used to sleeping in the cold."

"I think you need a warm body next to you in the bed."

"Daniel!" she said, shocked but pleased.

He kissed her again, a quick, affectionate peck. Fifi the poodle had settled down on the threadbare rug near the couch and was watching the two with interest.

"I think you should get me some extra coal," Flora said. "You can do that, I know you can. Look at what I have to burn." She motioned toward her fireplace, in which were half-burned balls of paper pulp, made from newspapers and cardboard boxes, even books, soaked in water until they turned back into pulp, then molded into balls. All over Paris the French were burning these paper balls for heat, since hardly anyone had enough coal anymore. Often they burned their own furniture. "My friend Marie is lucky—a Gestapo agent moved into her building. Now the whole building gets enough coal to keep everyone warm."

"You shall get your coal, my pet."

"What time is it? It must be two in the morning. And I have to work tomorrow morning—no, *this* morning!"

"My apologies for disturbing you, Flora, but it's important. If you'd rather I leave—"

"No, no," she said hastily. "So I will be a wreck tomorrow at work, and the gray mice will make fun of me." That was what everyone called the Nazi women auxiliaries of the Gestapo, the

Blitzmädchen, who wore gray uniforms and seemed to be everywhere. "I wish I had some real tea to give you. Can I offer you
some Viandox?" Metcalfe was heartily sick of Viandox, a kind of
beef tea made of some mysterious meat extract, which was served
all over Paris. Some people made a whole meal, these days, of a
cup of Viandox and some crackers.

"No, thanks, I don't need anything."

"I'm sure you can get me some real tea, and you must get me
some at once."

"I'll do my best." Flora never stopped angling for black-market
goods from her Argentine lover. She was so mercenary, so re-
lentless in demanding things from him, that he no longer felt
that he was using her to provide him with intelligence. If anything, she was using *him.*

"Really, Daniel," Flora scolded. "The idea of you just popping
in on me like this! And in the middle of the night! I don't know
what to say." She went into her bathroom and closed the door.
She emerged ten minutes later in a pretty, if threadbare, silk
dressing gown, the curlers gone, her hair done up. She'd put on
lipstick and pancake makeup. Though she was no beauty, she
was now almost pretty.

"Look at you!" Metcalfe said.

"Oh, please," Flora said with a dismissive flip of her hand. But
she blushed; Metcalfe knew she enjoyed his compliments. She
did not receive compliments often, and she luxuriated in them.
"Tomorrow I will get a permanent."

"You don't need one, Flora."

"You men. What do you know? Some women get a permanent
every week. Now, I have hardly anything to serve you. I made a
chocolate cake using a recipe my neighbor gave me—it's made
of pureed noodles with a drop of chocolate, and it's *horrible.*
Would you like some?"

"I'm fine, I told you."

"If only I had some real chocolate . . ."

"Yes, my dear, I can get you some."

"You can? Oh, that would be delightful! When I went to Paquet the grocer after work yesterday, all he'd give me was one bar of soap and a pound of noodles. So there's no butter for breakfast."

"I can get you butter, too, if you'd like."

"Butter! Really? How wonderful. Oh, Daniel, you don't know how terrible it's all gotten. I have nothing to feed my Fifi. There's no poultry, no game." Her voice dropped to a whisper. "Why, I've even heard of people *eating* their own dogs!"

Fifi looked up and growled.

"People are using *cats* in stews, Daniel! And a few days ago I saw a respectable old woman braining a *pigeon* in the park to take home to cook!"

Metcalfe suddenly remembered the little square flask of Guerlain's Vol de Nuit he had in the pocket of his dinner jacket, out of the same cache from which he'd gotten Madame du Châtelet's bottle. He'd meant to give a bottle to Geneviève but had forgotten. Now he pulled it out and put it in Flora's hands. "Until then, this is for you."

Flora's eyes widened, and she gave a little squeal. She threw her arms around Metcalfe. "You are a miracle worker!"

"Flora, listen. I have a friend who's going to Moscow this week—he just told me—and I'd like to do a little business there."

"Business? In Moscow?"

"The Germans there are just as greedy as the Germans here, you know."

"Oh, the Germans—*ils nous prennent tout!* They're swiping everything. This evening, some Fritz soldier gave up his seat for me on the Métro, but I refused to accept it."

"Flora, I need you to get something else for me at the office."

Her eyes narrowed. "The gray mice are always watching me. It's dangerous. I must be careful."

"Of course. You're always careful. Listen, my dear. I need a complete personnel list of all Germans stationed at the embassy in Moscow. Can you get that for me?"

"Well . . . I can try, I suppose. . . ."

"Excellent, my darling. It will be a big help to me."

"But then you must do two things for me."

"Of course."

"Can you get me a pass to the unoccupied zone? I want to visit my mother."

Metcalfe nodded. "I know someone in the *Préfecture.*"

"Wonderful. And one more thing."

"Certainly. What is it?"

"Undress me, Daniel. Right this minute."

CHAPTER SIX

It was very early in the morning when Metcalfe finally returned to his apartment, on the fifth floor of a Belle Epoque building on the rue de Rivoli. It was a large and lavish flat, expensively furnished, as befit the international playboy that was his cover. Several of his neighbors were high-ranking Nazi officials who had seized apartments in the building from Jewish owners. They appreciated the convenience of having this wealthy young Argentine living nearby, who could procure for them the unobtainable luxuries, and so of course they left "Daniel Eigen" alone.

At the front door to his apartment, he inserted the key in the lock and then froze. He felt a tingling sensation, some kind of premonition. Something that told him that all was not quite right.

Quietly he pulled the key out, then reached up to the top of the door, where it jutted out an eighth of an inch. The pin he placed there whenever he left was gone.

Someone had been in his apartment.

No one but he had the key.

Although he was exhausted, having been up the entire night, his every instinct was now fully alert. He backed away from the door, looked both ways down the dark, empty corridor, then placed an ear against the door to listen for a few seconds.

He could not hear any sound, but that didn't necessarily rule out the possibility that someone was inside.

In all his time in Paris, this had not happened before. He had lived his cover, attending dinners and parties, having lunch at Maxim's or the Chez Carrère in the rue Pierre Charron, and conducting his affairs, and all the while collecting sensitive intelligence on the Nazis. Never had he had even an inkling that he might have been suspected. His apartment had never been searched; he had never been taken in for questioning. Perhaps he had grown complacent.

But something had changed. The evidence of that was as minute as the absence of a pin atop his front door. But it meant something. He was sure of it.

He touched the ankle holster under his trousers, assuring himself that the compact .32 caliber Colt pistol was in place, ready to whip out if he needed it.

There was only one entrance to his apartment, Metcalfe reflected. No, not quite. Only one *door* to his apartment.

Silently, swiftly, he ran down the hallway to the end. The casement windows there were rarely opened except on the most sweltering of summer days, but he had tested them, knew they worked. *Always know your exits,* Corky had drummed into him from day one of his training on the farm in Virginia.

The *volets,* the wooden shutters, were always left open to let in the light. He peered out, confirmed his recollection that a fire escape ran along this side of the building, accessible through the windows here. There was no one in the alley that he could see, but he would still have to move fast. The sun had risen; it was a bright, clear morning, and he risked being seen.

Moving quickly, he twisted the lever of the *crémone* in the center where the windows met. The rack and pinion assembly turned with a soft moan. He opened the windows inward, reached up to the sill, and climbed out onto the iron railing of the fire escape.

Stepping gingerly along the icy, slick iron slats, he made his way around until he reached the window that he knew opened into his bedroom. It was, of course, locked, but he always carried with him his trusty Opinel penknife. Having satisfied himself that there was no one in the bedroom, he slid in the blade and pried the lock, then worked the *crémone* open. *Quiet,* he commanded himself. He had oiled the window locks not that long ago, so he was able to work without making much of a sound, but it was not silent. Perhaps the slight scrape of the window opening would be masked by the ambient noise from the street. He stepped down into his bedroom, landing softly on his feet, crouching slightly as he touched down to minimize the sound of the impact. Now he was inside. He stood still for a moment, listening. He heard nothing.

Then something caught his eye: something subtle, imperceptible to anyone else. It was the gleam on the top of his mahogany credenza, the sun reflecting off the burnished surface.

There had been a fine layer of dust there this morning—no, it was yesterday morning already. The Provençal woman who came in to clean twice a week wasn't due in until tomorrow, and in this old apartment dust tended to settle quickly. Metcalfe hadn't polished it, of course. Someone had wiped it down, no doubt in order to eliminate any traces of a search. Someone had been here, he now knew for certain.

But *why?* The Nazis didn't break into apartments in Paris, as a rule. Furtive entry was not their modus operandi. When they conducted their house-to-house searches for criminals, for British servicemen in hiding, it was almost always in the middle of the night, yes, but always in the open. And always with a pretense of legality. Papers were produced, signatures waved about.

Who, then, had been here?

And: Was it possible that the intruder was still here?

Metcalfe had never killed anyone. He was entirely comfortable with the use of a gun, going back to his boyhood days on the *estancia* in *las pampas.* At the training farm in Virginia, he had been trained in the lethal techniques. But he had never had the opportunity to shoot a man to death, and it was an opportunity he was not looking forward to.

Still, if he had to, he would.

But he would have to be extraordinarily careful. Even if there was an interloper in his apartment, he could not fire unless his life was threatened. Far too many questions would arise. If he killed a German, the questions would not stop. His cover would be blown for sure.

His bedroom door was closed, and that was another thing. He always left it open. He lived alone, and when he was not there, there was no reason to close his bedroom door. The little things, the tiny unnoticed habits. They made up a scrim of normalcy, a mosaic of everyday life. And now that mosaic had been disturbed.

Approaching the bedroom door, he stood still and listened for a minute. Listened for the creak of footsteps, the movements of a stranger who did not know which floorboards squeaked. But nothing: not a sound.

Standing to one side of the doorway in a sniper stance, he turned the knob and pulled the door open slowly, let it swing open. His heart hammering, he stared into the living room, waiting for a minute shift in the light, a movement in the shadows, *expecting* it.

Now he shifted his gaze, sweeping the room, pausing at the places where someone might try to hide, assuring himself that no one was there. He reached for his gun, withdrew it from the holster.

Suddenly he stepped into the room, gun extended, and said, "*Arrêt!*"

Whipping his body from one side to the other, he thumbed the safety, cocked the hammer by pulling back the slide, and prepared to fire.

The room was empty.

No one was there. He was fairly certain of it. He did not sense the presence of an intruder. Still, keeping the weapon pointed, he swiveled from side to side, advancing along the wall until he reached the door to the small library.

The door was open, as he had left it. The library—really just another, smaller sitting room furnished with a desk and chair and lined with books—was empty. He could see every inch of the room; there were no hidden corners.

But he would take no chances. He raced to the kitchen, pushed open the double doors, entered with his weapon extended. The kitchen was empty, too.

He searched the potential hiding places that remained—the dining room, the pantry, his large clothes closet, a broom closet—and satisfied himself that they were all empty.

He relaxed his vigilance a bit. No one was here. He felt a little foolish, but he knew he couldn't take chances.

Returning to the living room, he noticed another tiny change. It was his bottle of Delamain Réserve de la Famille Grande Champagne Cognac on the bar. The label normally faced out; now it faced in. The bottle had been moved.

He opened his ebony cigarette box and saw that the double layer of cigarettes had been shifted as well. The gap in the row of cigarettes had been third from the end; now it was fifth from the end. Someone had taken out the cigarettes to search underneath—for what? Documents? Keys? He concealed nothing there, but the intruder didn't know that.

Other traces. The switch on the antique brass lamp was now on the right, not on the left, indicating that someone had lifted it to search its base. A good hiding place, but not one he used. The telephone handset had been hung up differently, so that the cloth-wrapped cord now hung on the opposite side from the way he had left it. Someone had picked up the phone for some reason: To make a call? Or simply to move the phone in order to look inside the chest on which it rested? The heavy ornate marble mantel clock above the fireplace had been shifted a fraction of an inch: the dust outline told the tale. The search had been remarkably thorough: even the ashes in the fireplace had been swept aside and then moved back; someone had looked in the ash box, another clever hiding place he hadn't used.

Now Metcalfe raced to the clothes closet, in the alcove off his bedroom. His suits and shirts still hung in the proper order, though the precise gaps between the hangers were different. Obviously someone had carefully removed his clothes and searched pockets.

But he, or they, had apparently not noticed the compartment that had been skillfully built into the wall by one of Corky's craftsmen. He slid the panel open, revealing the heavy iron safe. Its dial still pointed to the number seven, and the fine patina of dust had not been disturbed here. The safe, which contained cash, encoded telephone numbers, and various identity papers in different names, had not been touched. That was a relief.

Whoever had searched his apartment so thoroughly—and with such neatness—had not discovered his safe, the only evidence that Daniel Eigen was in fact the cover of an American spy. And they hadn't learned his true identity.

They had not found what they were looking for.

But . . . but exactly what *were* they looking for?

Before leaving his apartment, he placed a trunk call to Howard in New York.

His brother was surprised, if pleased, to hear from him. He was even more surprised at Stephen's sudden interest in the family's manganese mining concession in Soviet Georgia, which the Metcalfes still operated in partnership with the Soviet Ministry of Trade. It was a minor operation, and with all the Soviet restrictions and the necessary payoffs it barely eked out a profit. The Russians had long expressed an interest in buying the Metcalfes out. Stephen suggested that maybe this wasn't such a bad idea. Maybe he could go to Moscow, meet with some people, and further the discussion. After a long silence—the hiss of the transatlantic call loud—Howard understood what his brother was asking. He promptly agreed to make arrangements. "I can't tell you how thrilled I am," Howard said dryly, "that my baby brother wants to play a more active role in the family business."

"You shouldn't have to shoulder all the burden."

"I don't suppose a certain ballerina has anything to do with this resurgence of interest in business, right?"

"How dare you impugn my motives," Metcalfe replied, a smile in his voice.

He changed quickly out of his tuxedo, putting on the more casual suit and tie of the international businessman he pretended to be. Fortunately, the fashion in the last few years had been loose, almost baggy trousers: they concealed the revolver, whose holster he strapped to his ankle.

He walked out of his building into the bright, cold morning, unable to suppress a feeling of dread.

About an hour later he was sitting in the dark nave of a gloomy, decrepit church in Pigalle. Barely any light filtered through the grimy stained-glass window in the apse. The only other parishioners here were a few old women, who knelt, prayed briefly, and lit candles. The place smelled, not unpleasantly, of matches and beeswax candles and sweat.

This small church had been neglected for years, but at least it had survived the Nazi invaders. Not that they had demolished any buildings in Paris, nor had they destroyed or even shut any churches. Far from it. The Catholic Church had struck its own, separate accommodation with the Nazi occupiers, hoping to safeguard its rights by accepting the new dictators.

Once again he felt for his gun.

Now, Metcalfe noticed a cassocked priest in a Roman collar, his rail-thin figure mostly concealed beneath the loose black vestments, enter and kneel at the statue of a saint. He lit a candle and then got to his feet. Metcalfe followed him to the ancient door that led to the underground crypt.

The small, dank room was dimly lit by a hanging overhead fixture. Corcoran removed the hood of his cassock and sat at a small round table next to an unfamiliar man. He was a fireplug of a man: short, ruddy-faced, rumpled. His shirt collar was too tight, his necktie too short, his suit jacket cheap and ill-fitting.

Next to the elegant, gaunt Corky, he looked markedly out of place.

"James," Corcoran said pointedly to Metcalfe. "I want you to meet Chip Nolan."

Interesting: Corcoran had called him by a fake name. Of course, Corky was famously paranoid, always making sure one hand never knew what the other hand was doing. He wondered whether "Chip Nolan" was a real name, either.

Metcalfe shook the smaller man's hand. "Nice to meet you," he said.

Nolan's grip was firm; his clear eyes regarded him steadily. "Same here. You work in the field for Corky, that's all I know. But it's enough to impress the hell out of me."

"Chip's on loan from the FBI to our Technical Section. An expert on flaps and seals, and technical equipment."

"You're going to Moscow, huh?" Nolan said, lifting a large, heavy leather suitcase from the floor and placing it on the table. "I don't know beans about your assignment, and that's the way we're gonna keep it. I'm here to outfit you, give you all the toys you might need. The bag of tricks, we like to call it." He ran his hand over the worn hide of the case. "This is yours, by the way. A gen-u-ine Soviet suitcase, made in Krasnogorsk." He popped open the case, revealing a row of neatly folded clothing, including a suit, all of it wrapped carefully in tissue paper. "Real Soviet clothing," Nolan went on. "Manufactured at the October Revolution Textile Factory and bought at GUM, the Soviet department store on Red Square. Artificially aged and distressed, though. The Roos-kies don't exactly get to buy duds often, so they have to wear stuff far longer than we Americans do. Everything's been tailored to your exact measurements." He unwrapped a pair of cheap-looking brown shoes. "These fellas here are the real thing as well. Believe me, you can't buy shoes as lousy as this in the West. And the first thing the Russians look at is your shoes, you'll see. That's how they can spot a foreigner right away."

Metcalfe glanced at Corky, whose expression seemed distant,

as if he weren't quite there. "Actually, I'm not going to be infil-
trated into Russia in the guise of a native," he said. "I'm going
in the open, in the clear—as myself."

Corcoran cleared his throat. "You'll be arriving as yourself,
James, that's true. But you never know all the eventualities. Always know the exits. You may well need to become someone
else."

Metcalfe nodded. The old man was, of course, right.

Nolan next produced a subminiature camera, which Metcalfe
recognized as a Riga Minox. He nodded, no explanation needed.
The FBI man pulled out a pack of playing cards, fanning them
out on the table. "Get a slant at these."

"What are they?" Metcalfe asked.

"Top-secret map of Moscow and its environs. You don't want
to be caught with a map over there, or they'll toss you in the
Lubyanka and throw away the key. Sandwiched in between the
front and back of each playing card is a numbered section of
map. Just peel off the face of the card. You can rub off the excess
rubber adhesive with your thumb."

"Clever," said Metcalfe.

The FBI man produced an assortment of concealed weapons,
all of which Metcalfe had seen before: a wrist pistol, a webbed
belt whose buckle contained a modified .25 caliber Webley pistol,
activated by a length of cable. He then took out a canvas shaving
kit, unzipped it, and pulled out a razor and shaving brush. Nolan
rolled the ivory shaving brush across the table, and Metcalfe
picked it up, examined it. Metcalfe tried to twist the handle, to
pull it apart, but it appeared to be solid. "You can leave that in
your hotel room without worrying about it," Nolan said. He
grabbed it back, then twisted the handle clockwise, revealing a
cavity from which he removed a rolled-up sheet from a onetime
pad, a system of encoding messages that was impossible to crack.
Metcalfe nodded; he had been trained in the use of onetime pads.
"Printed on cellulose nitrate, so it's highly flammable, for rapid
destruction if you gotta screw."

Nolan took out a tube of Ipana toothpaste from which he squeezed out a white ribbon. "The Ivans aren't going to suspect it's mostly hollow." He tugged at the crimped tinfoil end of the tube and withdrew a bladder from which he pulled out a rolled-up silk foulard. A dense grid of numbers had been printed on it. Metcalfe recognized it as a key list, printed on silk for ease of concealment. He nodded.

"More one-time pads in this. You smoke?" Nolan produced a pack of Lucky Strikes.

"Not often."

"You do now. More often. Another key's in here." Nolan showed him a fountain pen. Then Nolan placed another suitcase onto the table. This one was a fine leather Hermés case. "For when you travel as you, an American."

"I've got a case, thanks."

"Concealed in the brass fittings of *this* one, buddy, are the key components of a radio transmitter. Without them, the transmitter won't work."

"What transmitter?"

"This one." Nolan hoisted a third leather suitcase onto the table. This one appeared to be quite heavy. He unbuckled it, revealing a black steel box with a wrinkle finish. "The BP-3," he announced proudly. "The most powerful two-way communicator ever built."

"It's one of the first prototypes," Corky said. "Built by a group of Polish émigré geniuses for MI-6, but I managed to get them first; don't ask me how. This makes everything else obsolete. All those other machines are now museum relics. But please, do guard it with your life. *You* can be replaced, but I'm afraid this device cannot."

"It's true," Chip Nolan said. "It's a pretty nifty toy. And in Moscow, you'll need it. So far as I know, the only other way to communicate with home base is the black channel, right?"

Nolan looked at Corky, who simply nodded.

"But that's to be used only in an emergency. Otherwise, there's this, or encrypted messages passed through trusted intermediaries."

"Are there any?" Metcalfe said. "Intermediaries I can trust, I mean."

"There's one," Corcoran put in at last. "An attaché at our embassy whose name and contact information I'll give you. One of mine. But I want to warn you, James. You're on your own over there. No backup."

"And if something goes wrong?" Metcalfe said. "You're always saying know your exits."

"If anything goes wrong," Corcoran said, drawing himself up within his cassock, "you'll be disavowed. You'll have to fend for yourself."

A few minutes later the FBI man left. Corcoran took out a pack of Gauloises and a box of matches, scowling. Metcalfe, remembering, took a pack of Lucky Strikes out of his pocket and placed it in front of his mentor.

"No Chesterfields on the market these days," Metcalfe said, "but I figured this is better than nothing."

Corky unwrapped the pack without saying a word, though his faint smile revealed his pleasure. Metcalfe told him about the break-in at his apartment.

After a long silence, Corcoran said, "This is concerning."

"You're telling me."

"It may be nothing more than an overly exuberant Gestapo. You are, after all, a well-traveled foreigner—automatic grounds for suspicion. Yet it might be a symptom of something more."

"A leak."

Corcoran inclined his head slightly. "Or a penetration. Despite my insistence upon compartmentalization, I have no doubt that lines are crossed, things are said, security is compromised. All we can do at this point is stress vigilance. I don't imagine this Moscow mission will be easy for you."

"Why do you say that?"

Corcoran pulled a cigarette from the pack and, striking a match deliberately, lit it. "This woman, this ballerina—she was someone important to you once, was she not?"

"At one time, yes. No longer."

"Ah, I see," Corcoran said with a cryptic smile as he inhaled a lungful of smoke. "Now she's just part of your long history of romantic entanglements, is that it?"

"Something like that."

"So seeing her again—in the arms of another man—won't be trying?" He held the smoke in his lungs for a long while.

"You've given me far more difficult assignments."

"But never a more important one." Finally he exhaled. "Stephen, do you understand the gravity of what you're about to do?"

"Put that way," Metcalfe said, "no, I suppose I don't. Even if von Schüssler turns out to be genuinely anti-Hitler *and* willing to betray his own government—which is a lot to hope for—then he'll be just one more source. I'm sure we have others."

Corcoran shook his head slowly. The old man looked even gaunter than when Metcalfe had last seen him, in New York. "If we hit the jackpot and you're able to turn him, Stephen, he will be one of our most important lines into the German High Command. He's close to the German ambassador to Moscow, Count Werner von der Schulenberg. His family is upper-class, terribly well connected—you know what that's like." He chuckled dryly. "They look down their noses at this rabble-rousing Viennese upstart Adolf Hitler. They all have contempt for the Führer. But they're all German patriots at the same time. Quite ornate."

"If von Schüssler's a German patriot, as you suspect, he's hardly going to betray his own country in the midst of a war. Führer or no Führer."

"His allegiances may turn out to be more complex than they appear on the surface. But we don't know until we try. And if we—*you*—succeed, the intelligence he may be able to provide will be astonishing indeed."

"The intelligence on what, exactly? Even a highly placed diplomat in the Foreign Ministry isn't going to be privy to the military strategy of Hitler's inner circle," Metcalfe countered. "He's not going to know the details of the Nazi plans for the invasion of England."

"Correct. But he will be quite well informed about the state of relations between Germany and the Soviet Union. And this is where our only hope lies."

Metcalfe shook his head, uncomprehending. "They're allies. Since last year, Hitler and Stalin are partners in this goddamned war. What more can we possibly learn?"

Corcoran shook his head sadly, as if disappointed. "They've signed a scrap of paper. A treaty. But a treaty is like a mirror, Stephen. One sees in it what one wishes to see."

"You've just gone over my head, Corky."

"Hitler offers Stalin a piece of paper to sign, a paper that says we're friends, our interests coincide, we're partners. But what Stalin sees in that treaty is what he wishes to see: a reflection of his ambitions, his hopes, his aspirations. And what Stalin sees reflected in that treaty is not necessarily what Hitler sees in it. Hitler may see a different vision entirely. And we, the onlookers, the rest of the world, we may choose to see reflected in this mirror a pact between two villains genuinely joining together in larceny, or a game of deception in which one is attempting to outmaneuver the other. Why does a mirror reverse left and right but not up and down?"

"You know I'm not much good at your riddles, Corky."

Corcoran sighed in exasperation. "It doesn't, Stephen. A mirror *doesn't* reverse left and right. It merely shows what it sees. It reflects what's in front of it."

Metcalfe nodded again. "You want to know what the Russians are thinking about the Germans, and what the Germans are thinking about the Russians. *That's* the truth you want to learn, correct?"

Corcoran smiled. "Truth is the shattered mirror. Strewn in myriad bits. Each believes his little bit is the whole truth. If you'll permit me to paraphrase Sir Richard Francis Burton's version of the stanzas from the Kasidah of Haji Abdu."

"I'll permit it," Metcalfe said. Corky was often reciting a few lines from that Persian panegyric.

"The alliance between those two tyrants," Corky said, "is the great mystery of the war. It is of the utmost importance. You remember the Peloponnesian Wars, Stephen?"

"I'm afraid that was a bit before my time, old man. You must have been in knee pants yourself."

Corcoran gave a thin smile. "Athens survived only because of discord between their two most formidable enemies."

"You're saying there's some kind of rift developing between Germany and Russia?"

"I'm saying I'd like to find out if there is. That would be valuable intelligence indeed. And our only hope, really."

Metcalfe's furrowed brow told his mentor that he didn't quite follow. Corcoran went on: "While Hitler was busy fighting Britain and France, the Russians were sending iron and rubber, grain and cattle. The Russians were feeding Hitler's soldiers and supplying his army. Bear in mind, Stalin's *own people* were starving while he was selling Hitler thousands of tons of grain! These two tyrants have divided Europe between themselves, now they plan to divide up the British Empire, and together they plan to rule the world."

"Come on, Corky. They're not going to be dividing up the British Empire. Churchill's resolve seems pretty firm to me."

"He's as firm in his resolve as a leader can be. But there's only so much he can do in the face of an enemy as overwhelming as the Nazis. When he says he has nothing to offer but blood, toil, tears, and sweat—well, I take him at his word. England has little else. Its very survival is in serious doubt."

"But you believe Stalin really *trusts* Hitler?" Metcalfe shot back. "Those two madmen are like scorpions in a bottle!"

"Indeed, but they need each other," Corcoran said, exhaling smoke through his nostrils luxuriantly. "They have much in common. They're both totalitarians. Both untrammeled by any concern for individual freedom. The alliance between the two was a stroke of genius. And it's not the first time. Look at what happened in the last war, Stephen. When Russia realized it was losing to Germany, it signed a separate peace with Germany at Brest Litovsk. And then spent the next decade secretly rearming Germany, in absolute violation of the Treaty of Versailles. It's thanks to Russia that we face such a formidable enemy today."

"You don't think Hitler's just biding his time, waiting to attack Russia when the time is right? I'd always thought Hitler despises the Slavs, the Commies. I mean, look at what he wrote in *Mein Kampf*—"

"We *know* he's not planning an attack. We have intelligence, sporadic but reliable, from Hitler's inner circle, indicating such. Hitler's no fool. For him to launch a war against Russia while at the same time fighting the rest of the world—well, that would be utter madness, a deathblow to the Nazi cause. For us, it would be too good to be true. And I'll tell you something else that's really agitating me just now. I'm getting a lot of pressure on the home front from people in military and intelligence circles who believe that Hitler isn't really the main enemy anyway."

"What are you talking about?"

"They consider the Bolsheviks to be the real threat and regard Adolf Hitler as an important bulwark against them."

"But how—how can anyone believe Hitler's anything other than a bloodthirsty tyrant?" Metcalfe asked.

"Many people prefer the comforting lie," Corcoran said. A sardonic smile played on his lips. "I learned that lesson quite early, when I was a child and my aunt died. They told me she'd 'gone to a better place.' "

"How do you know they were lying?" Metcalfe needled the old spymaster.

"You didn't know my aunt," Corcoran replied.

Metcalfe appreciated the old man's mordant wit, all the more at a time of such tension. "All right," he said. "What are my arrangements?"

"I want you to leave Paris tomorrow," Corcoran said crisply. "Do us a favor and forgo the good-byes to your string of lovers. No one must know where you're going. Feel free to write postcards, which we'll have mailed from the Canary Islands or Ibiza. Let them think the elusive and glamorous Mr. Eigen was called away abruptly on pressing business. No one will raise an eyebrow."

Metcalfe nodded. Corcoran was right, of course. Better to avoid explanations. Tomorrow! That meant there would be no time to return to Flora Spinasse and get her list of personnel at the German embassy in Moscow: a loss, but not insurmountable.

"You'll be traveling on the *Chemin de Fer du Nord* from the Gare du Nord to Berlin, and thence to Warsaw. A first-class berth has been reserved for you under the name of Nicolas Mendoza. There you'll exit the Warszawa Centralna station, return two and a quarter hours later, and board the train for Moscow under the name of Stephen Metcalfe. You've reserved a room at the Metropole."

Metcalfe nodded. "Papers?"

"You have contacts here. We don't have time to get them produced by my people and sent from the States."

"Not a problem."

"You will have your work cut out for you. The stakes are immensely high, so no more of your hotheaded showboating. There's a good deal that can go wrong."

"I ask you again: What if something does?"

Corcoran adjusted his chasuble. "If anything goes wrong, Stephen, I suggest you pray."

CHAPTER SEVEN

The violinist waited in the man's apartment.

The *Sicherheitsdienst* had obtained the man's address from the telephone number provided by the whore. Kleist still did not know the location of the wireless station—the whore, of course, had no idea. And their informant, who had alerted them to the parachute drop in the first place, did not know, either: information was strictly compartmentalized. During the hours he had spent waiting for the British agent to return, he had had ample opportunity to search the man's apartment carefully. He now knew the Brit's true identity, which was a start. He knew that the Brit worked at night and slept during the day.

Kleist would just have to wait.

At a little after seven o'clock in the morning he heard a key turn in the lock. The Brit hummed to himself as he bustled about, put on water for tea, went into his bedroom to change into pajamas. He opened the door to his clothes closet, and as he parted the clothes hangers he barely had time to scream before Kleist leaped forward out of the closet, both of his hands grabbing the Brit's throat, slamming him to the floor.

The Brit gurgled, his face deep red. "What the—!" But Kleist shoved a knee hard into the man's groin, so hard that he could hear the coccyx snap.

Now the Brit moaned. His tears flowed copiously. He was crying like a girl.

"All I want to know is the location of your wireless station," said Kleist. His English had a heavy German accent; he had learned English too late in life. Now he released one hand from the man's throat.

"Fuck you!" the Brit said in a high, gurgling voice.

The Brit must have thought he had removed his hand from the man's throat in order to allow him to speak, but in fact Kleist did so to reach into his pocket for the coiled violin string. He snapped it open and had it against the man's throat in a matter of seconds, just above the cartilage of the laryngeal prominence and below the floating hyoid bone. It was the point of greatest vulnerability. As he compressed both the airway and the carotid artery, he could see the Brit's eyes bulge.

The young man was not exactly meticulous about his personal hygiene, Kleist realized. He had probably not bathed for several days. True, hot water was limited, but that was no excuse.

"I ask you again," Kleist said slowly, deliberately. "I wish to know the location of the wireless station where you work; that is all. If you answer my question, my work is done, and I will leave at once. I will let you live. There is no need to be brave."

The Brit was trying to say something. Kleist let up on the catgut just enough to let the man speak.

"Aw'right!" the Brit gasped. "Aw'right! I'll tell you!"

"A false answer will guarantee not only your death, but the deaths of everyone you work with." Kleist had learned from his years of interrogation and torture that the threat of death was usually ineffective. What worked was guilt, the instinct to protect one's friends and colleagues. And pain: pain worked most quickly to loosen the tongue. That was why he had positioned the catgut where he had. For maximum pain.

"I'll *tell* you!" the Brit shrilled.

And he did.

When he had finished telling Kleist everything he needed to know, Kleist abruptly tightened the violin string against the soft tissue of the Brit's throat. There was an expression of bewilderment, indignation, in the Brit's eyes, even before they bulged out. *I've kept my side of the bargain,* his eyes seemed to be saying. *Why have you not kept yours?*

Kleist never understood why his victims always thought they could make a deal with him. What good was a deal when only one side has the power?

When the Brit was dead, Kleist got up and, with a shudder of disgust, washed the foul odors off of his hands.

CHAPTER EIGHT

There was a forger in Paris whom Metcalfe had known for several years and trusted, as much as he allowed himself to trust anyone in his undercover life. Alain Ducroix was much more than a forger, of course, but the Nazi occupation had transformed him, as it had transformed so many. A veteran of the First World War who had been crippled at the Battle of the Somme, Ducroix was a man of many talents: a poet, the owner of a highly regarded bookstore, and a publisher. Editions Ducroix was a tiny press that specialized in chapbooks, beautifully crafted small editions of poets both legendary and unheralded. And on its printing presses, located in a studio behind the bookshop, Alain Ducroix did meticulous handiwork of another sort entirely: *cartes d'identité,* driver's licenses, SD credentials, German identification cards, whatever was required by the small army of brave Resistance fighters. He was a good man who did valuable work.

As Daniel Eigen, Metcalfe had asked Ducroix to produce documents for him and for friends. Metcalfe had made a point of not revealing his true identity, and not just to protect his own cover. Metcalfe wanted to protect Ducroix. The old forger knew that Eigen was a black marketer who had been useful to him and his colleagues in the Resistance. Eigen was not a political type, Ducroix had long ago concluded, but he was sympathetic, or at least trustworthy.

And Metcalfe needed Ducroix's help now. Since he would be leaving France by rail, under the name of Nicolas Mendoza, he would need departure documents issued by the Vichy government. And Ducroix was the only documents man in all of Paris who had paper of just the right weight and composition and who could reproduce the government seals and typography perfectly.

The Librairie Ducroix was located on the avenue de l'Opéra. Its windows were an elegant stage set, a display of the stunningly beautiful books Alain Ducroix printed and bound by hand. Passersby would stop and marvel at the volumes bound in crimson morocco leather with raised bands on the spine and hand-applied gold leaf. Some were bound in calfskin or vellum, with hand-marbled papers, hand-sewn spines, the front and back boards ornamented with gold, red, and blind tooling, the edges gilded.

The only jarring note in the display windows was a small framed portrait of Marshal Pétain, a sign beneath it that said: VENDU—sold out. This was a pun, a bitter joke: Pétain had sold all of France out. Not a wise thing to put in his window, Metcalfe reflected. He would have to chide Ducroix. Given his important secret work, it was all the more vital that he keep his political beliefs cloaked.

Metcalfe pushed open the door. Bells mounted on the door jingled as he entered. The shop, which was crowded with tables and shelves stacked with volumes of poetry and belles lettres, some of them Ducroix's own publications, was deserted.

Not entirely empty, of course. "Ah, Daniel!" came a rich baritone from the back of the shop. "Where have you been?"

Ducroix, a handsome, stout man in his sixties with a shock of white hair, propelled his wheelchair with great speed from the back of the shop down the narrow center aisle. Although he had been paralyzed since the last war, he was a powerful, even athletic-looking man. His hands were large and callused, his forearms muscular.

Ducroix extended a hand and shook Metcalfe's hand firmly. "You have come to buy my new edition of *Les Fleurs du Mal, hein?* Yes, a good choice. The binding is in full black morocco, with red morocco doublures, the flyleaves hand-marbled. A beautiful volume, even if I say it myself. Not to speak of the typography—"

"This picture of Pétain in the window," Metcalfe interrupted.

"Yes," Ducroix chuckled. "The hero of Verdun, but I spit on him."

"Well, you'd better do your spitting in private. I'd take that little joke out of the window if I were you."

Ducroix shrugged. *"D'accord,"* he said. He lowered his voice. "We shall talk in the back."

Metcalfe followed Ducroix through the shop and through a set of double doors into the cavernous stone-floored room that held the hand-operated letterpress, the monocaster that was used to cast type from molten lead, and the workbenches where Ducroix did his bookbinding.

As Metcalfe explained his needs, Ducroix nodded, his eyes closed in concentration. "Yes, yes," he said at last. "It is possible, yes. I may have a few of the blanks left; I will have to check. They are extremely difficult to obtain. I had to go to the manager of one of the larger Paris printing firms, who is an old friend. He does work for the government, so he had a stock of the blank forms. The official Ministry of Foreign Affairs seal I have cast myself in lead. But the typesetting I shall have to do on the Linotype machine, and it must be done most carefully to avoid detection. I mean, the border guards are a stupid lot, but every so often you come across a sharp one who looks carefully, and we do not want a catastrophe."

"No, that we don't," Metcalfe agreed.

"Perhaps I have been reading too much Baudelaire recently, but I keep thinking of what he says: *'Il n'y a pas de hasard dans l'art, pas plus qu'en mécanique.'* The best art takes much work, yes? Not that I am a great artist, of course, but to do this kind of work right does require some artistry and much concentration. *Alors!*" He spun around, reached over to the bench behind him, and retrieved a slim volume from a stack. He handed it to Metcalfe.

"This, *mon cher,* is a gift for you. Racine's *Phaedra.* Perhaps you will read it now while you wait—take the comfortable chair in the shop. The binding is not quite dry, so you must take care. It is beautiful, is it not? The calf vellum is fiendishly hard to get these days—the Germans are sending all of our cows to Germany."

"It's beautiful," Metcalfe said. "I'll read it with pleasure."

"So, if you will sit for a few minutes, I will see what I can turn up. I shall let you know if this document will take me an hour or twelve. Do you need this very soon?"

"As soon as possible, my dear Alain."

"I shall do my best. You go out front and mind the shop while I look back here. And if the Racine is not to your liking, feel free to browse in my shop. You may find some jewels out there. How does Lamartine put it? *'Même dans le rebut on trouve des joyaux.'* Jewels may be found among the dross."

Metcalfe returned to the bookshop and looked through the shelves with idle curiosity. He was not one to frequent bookstores, and now particularly he had little patience. He was tense, worried about involving his friend.

Forging exit visas was of a different order of magnitude from printing fake ration books and the like. If Metcalfe was caught, Ducroix might be ensnared as well. The thought was chilling. After all, Metcalfe had signed on to do dangerous undercover work. Ducroix was an intellectual, a bookshop owner, a man of letters. Not a spy. He was a brave man, doing his part to help the Resistance; it was vital that he be protected.

A few minutes later his thoughts were interrupted by a jingling at the door. A customer had entered: a man of about forty. Metcalfe felt a spider crawl of unease, the prickly sense that something was not right about the man. He looked too well fed, in this time of deprivation. There was something sleek, privileged, about this gentleman, in his expensively tailored suit. His hair was cut short, in an almost military manner, and he wore rimless glasses. Was he a German? His shoes were costly-looking, highly polished leather with leather soles. The French tended not to dress this well anymore.

Metcalfe pretended to examine an edition of Corneille on a shelf at eye level, while secretly inspecting the other man in the shop. The wooden floor creaked underfoot as the man peered around. He seemed to be looking for something, or someone.

Metcalfe watched in silence. It wasn't until the man turned slightly that Metcalfe noticed the slight bulk at his waist: a holstered weapon.

My God, Metcalfe thought. *I've tracked them in.*

A minute later, he heard a car pull up to the curb in front of the shop. He recognized the type of car from the sound of the powerful engine, even before he saw the black Citroën *Traction Avant*. It was a Gestapo car. The driver wore a Gestapo uniform. A man got out of the backseat: another plainclothesman, also dressed in a good suit.

Metcalfe felt a jolt of adrenaline as the second Gestapo agent entered the store. *I must have been followed*, he realized with terror.

He did a swift mental calculation. He had a weapon of his own, holstered at his ankle, where it did not show. In theory he was outmanned, but this was not yet a matter of drawing his pistol and firing. That was the very last resort: he could not risk killing a Gestapo agent, particularly not on the eve of his departure from Paris. That would complicate everything.

Assuming, of course, that he was able to make an escape. There were two of them, and their orders were surely to make arrests, not to kill.

But whom had they come to arrest?

Ducroix was the most vulnerable. After all, Metcalfe was doing nothing more than browsing in a bookshop. Let the Gestapo take him in for questioning; it would lead to nothing. But if they burst into the back room while Ducroix was doing his illegal work, it was the Frenchman who would be arrested, sentenced to execution.

He had to protect Ducroix. He had to warn him; that was the first thing.

Quietly Metcalfe turned, running his finger along a row of books as if searching for a particular title, then moved to the next aisle of bookshelves. He moved slowly, deliberately, with the patience of a browser immersed in literary pursuit.

The first Gestapo agent looked up, watching Metcalfe's movements warily. Instead of speeding up, Metcalfe slowed down in an attempt to divert the German's suspicion. He stopped, pulled a book off a shelf, opened it, and examined it. Then he shook his head, replaced the book, and continued toward the back of the shop. When he was out of the two Germans' sight lines, concealed behind a long, tall shelf, he accelerated his pace, keeping his tread light, moving with very little sound.

Finally he reached the double doors that led to the workshop.

He pushed at them gently, willing their hinges not to squeak. They did not.

Ducroix was on the telephone, his wheelchair pulled up to a bench. Metcalfe was relieved to see that there was no incriminating evidence spread out before him, no *Wehrmacht* seals, no document blanks, nothing of the sort.

Ducroix turned, smiled at Metcalfe. "I am needed out front, yes? We have paying customers?"

"Gestapo," Metcalfe spoke in a whisper. "Two of them. If you have anything out, put it away. Now!"

Ducroix looked at him with an expression of bewilderment.

Metcalfe continued, "Is there a back way out of here?" *Always know your exit:* Corky's First Commandment. Yet Metcalfe had slipped. He wasn't prepared.

"But I forgot to give you the slipcase!" Ducroix protested. "For the Racine!" He lifted a cloth-covered box from the bench, then spun around to face Metcalfe.

"Damn it, there's no time for that!" Metcalfe rasped. He scanned the workshop, looking for the exit door. "You don't understand: The Gestapo is here! I've got to get out of here, and you, you've got to—"

"I've got to do my duty," Ducroix interrupted, his voice curiously flat. The slipcase dropped to the floor, revealing an enormous Luger aimed at the center of Metcalfe's chest.

Ducroix held the immense weapon in a firm, two-handed grip, his elbows steadied on the arms of his wheelchair. Metcalfe stared at the muzzle of the gun, and as he reached one hand around to his back to retrieve his own gun, Ducroix barked out, "Freeze! Or I will fire!"

From somewhere behind Metcalfe there were footsteps. He turned, saw the two Gestapo agents enter, their guns leveled at him.

"Alain!" Metcalfe blurted out. "What the hell are you doing?"

"I suggest you make no sudden moves," Ducroix said. "If you do, we will not hesitate to kill you. These gentlemen want only to talk to you, and I suggest you cooperate. You see, this pistol is aimed precisely at your seventh thoracic vertebra. You move, I fire, and—*voilà!* A lifetime in the *roulant,* just like me. If you survive, that is. Nothing works below the waist, *mon frère.* It concentrates the mind wonderfully. No more chasing after *les femmes.* And the calluses you build up on your palms . . . Not to worry—what does that English poet say? 'For people will always be kind . . .' You will *pray* for death, believe me."

"Excellent job," came a voice from behind Metcalfe.

"I aim to please," Ducroix said with a shrug, but all the while he gripped the weapon firmly, steadily, as if no time had passed since his military days.

Metcalfe's thoughts whirled as his adrenaline surged. He was *trapped.*

He froze, but slowly he looked behind him. The two plainclothes Gestapo agents had their weapons pointed at him. They were less than ten feet away, and they were moving in closer. Three weapons leveled at him. He was outnumbered. If he made any sudden moves, he would be dead in seconds. That he was sure of.

How and *why* this had happened he didn't fully understand. It was astonishing: Ducroix had betrayed him! Ducroix, who claimed to loathe the Germans with every fiber of his being, had for some reason cooperated with the Gestapo to turn him in. More than astonishing, it was almost inconceivable. What kind of pressure must they have placed on Ducroix? What kind of threats? What sort of bribe might they have offered?

Or was it possible that Ducroix had been in league with the Nazis all along?

While Metcalfe tried to make sense of it all, another part of his brain furiously calculated the odds of his lunging for Ducroix. . . . But it was no use. They had him.

But for *what*? What did they know about him? Had his cover identity been somehow blown? Or was it simply that Ducroix had set him up for attempting to procure forged documents— in which case, wouldn't Ducroix be incriminating himself?

"Meine Herren," Metcalfe said in a tone of wry amusement, "don't you think you are overdoing this?"

"Hands at your side," the other Gestapo agent commanded.

Metcalfe slowly lowered his arms to his sides. He shook his head slowly, an expression of sorrowful puzzlement on his face. "May I at least ask you gentlemen what this is all about?"

"Herr Eigen, we will talk later. We have an interrogation chamber outfitted for that purpose. For now, you will come with us, and do not make any sudden moves or we are ordered to shoot."

Ordered: these were men acting under orders from above, from superior officers. They were drones, low-level street agents, and this was good, Metcalfe considered. They did not act on their own initiative. They responded to authority.

Metcalfe smiled, glanced at Ducroix. But the Frenchman's eyes were steely, opaque, his arms still in the firing position, the Luger steady. He radiated no sympathy, no recognition of their old camaraderie. He seemed a changed person—ruthless, unyielding.

"Gentlemen," said Metcalfe, "aren't you required at least to tell me what you're taking me in for?"

He heard the jingling of bells as the door to the bookshop was opened.

"Turn, please," the first German said. "Walk toward the door. Arms at your sides."

"No, the back way, please!" interrupted Ducroix. "No one must see him come out of my shop!" He pointed with his gun toward one end of the workroom, where Metcalfe now noticed a door. It probably led to the alley.

"Is this about documents," Metcalfe persisted. *"Papers?"* He raised his voice. "About the documents I use in order to get Gerhard Mauntner his cognac, his cigarettes, his caviar? To get Frau Mauntner her silk stockings, her *perfume?* Gentlemen, really . . . you can't be serious." By invoking the name of the number two man at the Paris headquarters of the Gestapo, an occasional client of his, Metcalfe was pulling out his heaviest ammunition. These street agents, obedient to the core, would do nothing to contravene the wishes of a man as highly placed as Mauntner.

"Oh, we are quite serious," the second German replied calmly. There was a note of ominous pleasure in his voice. "After all, Gerhard Mauntner's signature is on the arrest form. We are obeying Gruppenführer Mauntner's express personal orders. Move, please."

They had called his bluff! His ruse had been exposed for the lie it was. There was nothing to do now but go along with the agents. He glanced again at Ducroix, who had not relaxed his firing stance at all, though beads of sweat had appeared on the man's forehead. A tiny smile played about the forger's lips. The lover of poetry appreciated the irony, the delicious spectacle of a fabulist being caught in the web of his own fiction.

"Well," Metcalfe said, "there's obviously some terrible mistake, but we'll straighten this out at the rue des Saussaies."

He began walking toward the back of the room, past the great steel Linotype machine. One of the agents fell in beside him, grabbing him by the elbow. In his other hand the Gestapo man pointed his Walther. The second agent followed close behind.

Ducroix, Metcalfe saw in his peripheral vision, had lowered his gun at last and wheeled himself toward his shop, no doubt to attend to the customer who had entered the shop, the crisis having passed. Now it was just the two Gestapo agents and him, but he was still outnumbered, outgunned.

As he walked, he lowered his head shamefacedly, and he began cowering, quivering with visible fear. "Oh, God," he murmured. "This is terrifying. I've been afraid of this happening for so long—"

Metcalfe's knees buckled, and he slumped to the floor with an anguished wail escaping his lips. He was a trembling wreck, overcome with fright. The agent at his side loosened his grip on Metcalfe's arm momentarily as he was pulled downward by Metcalfe's sagging weight.

Collapsing to the floor, Metcalfe pulled the German down with him; then he spun, lightning-fast, slamming the man's head against the stone floor. The crack of the Gestapo man's head hitting the stone was audible: the skull had fractured. His eyes rolled up into their sockets, the whites of his eyes all that showed.

In a split second Metcalfe bounded to his feet, the unconscious man's Walther in his hand. As he lunged to his right, behind the steel machinery, he fired off a shot at the other German.

"Drop the weapon or you'll *die!*" the German shouted. Fear had taken over his once phlegmatic face. He fired at Metcalfe, but the round pinged off the steel hulk of the Linotype press. Shielded by the iron-and-steel press, Metcalfe pointed the stolen weapon between a gap in the machinery, aimed carefully as another round of bullets clanged against the metal. The Gestapo man rushed toward Metcalfe, firing, the shots ricocheting off the metal.

Suddenly Metcalfe felt a jagged pain in his thigh as a round creased his flesh, slicing through the fabric of his pants. He gritted his teeth, fired again, and this time his shot hit the German in the neck. The man screamed in pain, collapsing. He clutched his wound, which spewed bright red arterial blood. His right hand squeezed at the trigger of his gun, which was pointed upward, at the high cement ceiling, a stray last round. The agent collapsed, bellowing like an animal. Peering around the side of the machine, Metcalfe saw at once that his shot had been fatal. The man was not quite dead yet, but he was incapacitated and rapidly losing consciousness. His scream became a faint cry, liquid and burbling.

Metcalfe turned and ran toward the back door, and his right leg spasmed in pain. He heard a scuffling sound and turned to see where it was coming from. It was the first Gestapo man, the one who'd been knocked unconscious: lying on his side, he flung out his hands in what appeared to be an attempt to locate his weapon, not realizing that the gun was in Metcalfe's hands.

Metcalfe fired off a shot, hitting the man in the stomach. The German collapsed to the floor once more. This time, if he was not dead, he was at least seriously wounded, permanently so.

So I've finally killed a man, he thought grimly, heaving a sigh of relief. Suddenly there came another explosion of gunfire. He flattened himself against the wall, beside a long wooden case of type, which jutted out far enough to act as a barrier.

Silhouetted against the bright light from the bookshop was the figure of Ducroix in his wheelchair. The Frenchman was firing at Metcalfe with steady and deadly accuracy. Bullet after bullet splintered the wood of the shelves just inches from Metcalfe's head. A drawer of lead type shattered and scattered noisily to the floor.

Metcalfe squeezed off a round. One shot clanged against the metal seat of the wheelchair, another pitting one of the metal wheels, and the third struck Ducroix in the forehead.

The sight was horrific. A fragment of Ducroix's forehead flew off amid a ghastly spray of blood, and the forger slumped in his chair.

Metcalfe stood still for a moment, stunned, then forced himself to move. He rushed to the bodies of the Gestapo agents and searched their pockets, removing all papers, badges, and identity cards. Any of them might be useful.

Then he ran toward the back door. Grasping the knob, he yanked it open and leaped into a trash-strewn alley.

CHAPTER NINE

There was only one place to go.

The safe house. The Cave. He had to get in touch with Corky and warn him about what had just happened, about Ducroix's betrayal, about the disaster. Corcoran would be enraged that Metcalfe had been compromised, no question about that, but he had to be informed about the breach. Perhaps he would have an explanation as to why the forger had so unexpectedly turned— *been* turned, more likely.

Metcalfe had to reach Corky immediately, and the only way to do so was through channels, through his contacts at the Cave; that was the system Corcoran had devised, his means of preserving security.

He began to run; then, feeling a throbbing from the wound in his thigh, he slowed to a purposeful stride. It was not just the wound, which was minor; Derek Compton-Jones, the radio clerk at the Cave, was trained in emergency medicine and could treat it properly. No, it was important to look unhurried, an innocent and important man on important business. If anyone stopped him for any reason, he could produce papers from either of the dead Gestapo agents. True, he looked nothing like either photograph, but he'd deal with that if and when he had to.

It was already late afternoon, and Parisians bustled along the streets. He was still shaken from the barely averted arrest, by the carnage. He had never taken a life before, and now he had killed three men. He felt numb, appalled at the bloodshed, even as he realized that if he had not killed these men, he would himself be lying there dead.

By the time he reached the crumbling brick building in which

Le Caveau occupied the ground floor and the base station the level below, the pain in his thigh had abated somewhat and his limp was less pronounced. He descended the steps to the bar, cranked the old doorbell three times, and waited for the peephole to be slid aside as Pasquale, the bartender, checked on his identity.

He waited a full minute, then tugged the bell three times again. Pasquale, normally prompt in letting people in, must be occupied, he figured. Yet it was still afternoon, and there would be few customers at this time, the only ones the hard drinkers, the truly dissolute.

Another minute went by, and no reply.

He tried again. Strange, he thought. Was it possible that the bar was closed? There was another, more complicated, way to access the base station, Metcalfe knew. It involved entering the apartment building next door, taking the elevator to the basement, and unlocking a bolted steel fire door that led to a back way to this building. But that entry was reserved for emergencies, since it was less secure: residents of the adjoining building could see anyone entering and would be suspicious.

Metcalfe tried the doorknob and was startled when it turned and the door to the bar came open. It was supposed to be locked.

There were no lights on inside, which was surprising. No one was there. Yet the door was unlocked—it made no sense! As soon as his eyes because accustomed to the darkness and the shadows and shapes became recognizable as the long wooden bar and bar stools, Metcalfe saw something that caused him to freeze.

Several of the bar stools had been knocked to the floor. Along the top of the bar was broken glass—wineglasses shattered, cocktail glasses upturned and cracked. Something had gone on here, something violent.

He stepped into the dim recesses of the bar, saw that the drawer of Pasquale's ancient cash register jutted open, empty.

A burglary?

Thefts, burglaries, still happened in Paris, even in the Germans' police state. But this chaos indicated something more than a mere theft. It was evidence of a struggle.

And no one was here! Pasquale, his patrons—all gone.

What could have happened?

The base station!

Metcalfe ran the length of the bar, dodging overturned stools and broken glass. He bounded down the steps to the subbasement, feeling his way through the dark to the broom closet, pulled the door open.

He grabbed the broom handle, pulled it counterclockwise. The concealed entrance to the station swung open. The black-painted steel door was directly in front of him. Heart pounding, he pressed the doorbell twice, and then one more time.

Please God, he thought. *Let them be here!*

He waited in terrified silence. He knew what had happened. Somehow the Nazis—whether the Gestapo or the SD—had learned of the top-secret location of the station. Someone had talked. Pasquale the bartender? Could that be?

Or was it one of Corky's agents, the one he'd said had been picked up by the Gestapo? But how had *that* agent been uncovered in the first place? There had to be a leak somewhere within the network!

Oh, God, no. What would he do now? What if the men of the base station had been rounded up in one terrible sweep? Metcalfe would be alone in the field, with no way to reach Corky.

No, there had to be a way! He'd been issued emergency backup directives, encoded and imprinted in miniature on the backs of tags in his clothing. There was always a backup; Corky had made sure of it.

He rang again, the same tattoo of two short rings followed by one long one. No answer now, either.

They were gone, too; he was now sure of it. They had been arrested. The ring had been fatally compromised.

But if they had been arrested . . . wouldn't the Germans have set a trap for any stray agents who tried to contact the base? So far, there was no evidence of any such trap, but he would have to be alert for one.

He drew from his pocket his key ring. The key fob was a leather disk. He compressed it at the side, and it popped open; inside was a small steel key that opened this door.

The key unlocked three separate locks along the perimeter of the door. When he'd sprung the third lock, the door came open with a click and the sibilant hiss of the rubber seal.

He hesitated before speaking, alert in case anyone was lying in wait inside.

He saw the greenish glow from the row of transceivers. The machinery was still there, which was a good sign: if the Nazis had somehow discovered the Cave's location and had made a sweep, they'd surely have seized the valuable equipment at the same time.

But where *was* the staff? Why was the machinery unattended?

Metcalfe saw a figure seated at one of the consoles. Metcalfe recognized, from behind, Johnny Betts, the American radiotelegraph operator. He called out: "Johnny! Didn't you hear—?"

Then Metcalfe saw that Johnny still had his headphones on, which explained why he hadn't heard the buzzer. He approached, tapped him on the shoulder.

Suddenly Johnny slumped to one side. His eyes bulged. His face was crimson, his tongue lolling grotesquely.

Blood rushed to Metcalfe's head. He let out a horrified cry as he stumbled. "My God, no!" Johnny Betts's throat looked at first as if it had been slashed, but then Metcalfe realized that what appeared to be a deep gash was in fact a ligature mark with accompanying bruising.

Betts had been strangled, garroted, with some sort of thin cord or wire.

Johnny Betts had been murdered!

Metcalfe whirled around, looked for the others—for Cyril Langhorne, for Derek Compton-Jones. He saw no one else. Rushing to the adjoining room, he opened the door, looked in, but it was empty. *Where were the others?*

He raced to the antechamber that led to the emergency access into the next building, and there, beside the steel door, which was slightly ajar, he found the crumpled body of Cyril Langhorne, a single bullet hole in his forehead.

The station had been entered through the emergency entrance, Metcalfe knew now. Langhorne had gone to the steel door and had been shot, swiftly and probably with a silenced pistol. Betts, wearing his headphones and engaged in his transmission, had heard nothing. For some reason—to ensure silence?—he hadn't been shot but had instead been garroted. Someone had stolen up behind him—there were several invaders, no doubt—and slipped the cord or wire over his neck, strangling the life out of the American.

Dear Jesus, how had this happened?

And where was Derek? He was the only regular staffer not here. Had he been off, at home, asleep? Perhaps—please, God—Derek's schedule may have saved his life.

A noise. The loud squeal of tires, then brakes, from outside. From the street. Ordinarily traffic noise would not be heard in this soundproofed chamber. But the steel door was ajar, letting in noise from the street above.

It could only be the Nazis who would arrive so noisily. Backup of some sort? A follow-on team?

They were here for him.

Metcalfe leaped over Langhorne's corpse, slipped out through the open fire door, and raced up the basement stairs of the apartment building next door. As he ran he caught a glimpse, out of a basement window, of three or four black Citroëns converging on the street. The Gestapo, there was no doubt about it.

This time he knew his exit.

———

He escaped via the roof of the building, along the rooftops for a short distance, and then climbed down to the narrow alleys behind the avenue.

He was short of breath, but his bloodstream coursed with adrenaline, and he barely stopped to think. He just kept on running. He had to get to Derek Compton-Jones's apartment, to warn him not to go to the base station—but also to find out what might have happened, if Derek had any inkling.

Assuming Derek had escaped, that is.

He hadn't been there; at least, his body hadn't been anywhere to be found. Compton-Jones worked at night and slept during the day; the others had the misfortune to have drawn earlier shifts. Maybe Derek was alive after all.

And did Corky know about this nightmare yet?

He slowed only when he approached Derek's apartment building. Despite Corky's strict rules of compartmentation, Metcalfe knew where Derek lived; the Paris station was small, and they were friends, after all. Now he stood in front of a stationer's across the street, feigning interest in the window display, actually tilting his head to catch the reflection in the glass. After a few minutes he was satisfied that there was no suspicious activity in front of the building: no idling cars, no loitering pedestrians. He crossed the street quickly, entered the building, and took the stairs to Derek's flat.

At the apartment door he listened for a moment, then knocked.

No answer.

He knocked again, said, "Derek?" If Derek was inside, afraid to open the door, he might recognize Metcalfe's voice. But a few minutes went by, and nothing.

He looked to either side, saw no one. From his wallet he removed a long, slender metal pick that curved up at one end. It was a rudimentary lock pick, which he'd been trained to use. Inserting the pick, he jiggled it in and out, up and down, as he turned it to the right. Before long the lock gave way. These old French locks were not complicated, Metcalfe realized with some relief. The door came open, and Metcalfe entered carefully.

He had visited Compton-Jones a few times, shared a bottle of whiskey while Derek had listened with rapt fascination as Metcalfe told tales from the field . . . and even, discreetly, from his bedroom. To the young British code clerk, Metcalfe had embodied all that was exciting about this underground war; through Metcalfe, Derek had been able to live it vicariously.

Metcalfe looked around quickly, calling out in case Derek was still here, asleep. Then he knocked on the closed bedroom door. When there was no answer, Metcalfe opened the door.

What assaulted him first was the acrid, metallic odor of blood, smelling the way a penny tastes on the tongue. His heart sped up as he entered the room. A few seconds later he saw Compton-Jones's body, and he could not suppress a moan.

Derek lay on his back on the floor next to the clothes closet. His face was reddish-purple, the color of an old bruise, and his eyes stared, bulging horribly, just as Johnny Betts's had. His mouth was slightly ajar. Bisecting his throat was a thin, deep red line, a ribbon of hemorrhaged tissue.

He had been garroted, too.

Metcalfe shuddered. Tears came to his eyes. He dropped to the floor, felt Derek's neck for a pulse, but knew there would be none. Derek had been murdered.

"Who did this?" Metcalfe said in a low, keening, ferocious voice. "Who the hell did this to you? God damn it all, who *did* this?"

Perhaps it was foolish to think that some murders were more violent than others—a murder is a murder, after all—but Metcalfe believed that this garroting seemed unnecessarily brutal, personal. Then again, Metcalfe realized, garroting had certain tactical advantages. It was a stealthy way to kill, no doubt the stealthiest, if one could bring oneself to do it. By cutting off the victim's ability to produce sound, and the flow of blood to the brain, you ensured that there was no loud cry. Still, most

men would not use a garrote. This killer was not just skilled; he
was a disturbed man.

And the garroting seemed to be his signature.

Metcalfe somehow managed to get to his feet. Light-headed,
on the verge of passing out, he went to the apartment door just
as it opened.

A German strode in. A middle-aged man in a Gestapo uniform
that bore the insignia of a *Standartenführer*.

The colonel's Walther was drawn. "Freeze!" he barked, aiming
his pistol at the center of Metcalfe's chest.

Metcalfe reached for his ankle-holstered gun.

"Please do not pull out a weapon," the German said. "I will
have no choice but to fire at once."

Metcalfe considered pulling it out anyway, but the *Standartenführer* had the advantage of several seconds. To attempt it would
be suicide; the Gestapo colonel appeared to be entirely serious
and poised to fire. There was no choice in the matter.

Metcalfe stared imperiously at the German, slowly folding his
arms.

"Hands at your side," the German said.

Metcalfe complied but remained silent. He continued to stare
defiantly.

Finally he spoke, in flawless German. "Are you quite finished,
Standartenführer? Have you had enough?" His eyes were glacial,
yet his expression was phlegmatic, superior. Metcalfe's German,
acquired in childhood, was perfect, and if it had the trace of an
accent, it was the *Hochdeutsch* spoken by his aristocratic German
language teacher at his Swiss boarding school. Germans were so
class-conscious, Metcalfe knew, that the Gestapo agent could not
help but be intimidated in a subtle, unspoken manner.

"Excuse me?" the Gestapo colonel said, a change in his tone
abruptly evident. His air of arrogant command had vanished;
now he sounded simply worried.

"*Dummkopf!*" Metcalfe snapped. "Who the hell ordered the
Brit to be killed? Was it *you?*"

"Sir?"

"This is absolutely intolerable. I gave express orders that the Brit was to be taken alive and interrogated. You incompetent fool! Show me some ID, you idiot. I'm going to launch an investigation. This entire thing has been botched."

A series of expressions passed over the Gestapo man's face, from confusion to concern to abject fear. He whipped out his wallet and displayed his Gestapo identity card.

" 'Zimmerman,' " Metcalfe read off the card as if memorizing it. "You, Herr Standartenführer Zimmerman, are to be held directly responsible for this botch! Did you order the death of this British agent?"

"No, sir, I did not," the Gestapo man replied, cowed by Metcalfe's onslaught. "I was told only that the American had showed up here, sir, and I thought, mistakenly, that it was you. It was a reasonable assumption."

"Disgraceful! And what took you so long to get here? I've been waiting here fifteen minutes. This is simply intolerable!"

Metcalfe reached into his jacket pocket and pulled out the pack of cigarettes he'd taken from one of the Gestapo agents at the Librairie. It was a pack of Astras, a common Nazi brand. He pulled one out, pointedly not offering one to the colonel, and lit it from a pack of windproof *Sturmstreichhölzer* matches. The signals were subtle, unspoken: Metcalfe was a fellow German officer.

Expelling the harsh smoke through his nostrils, Metcalfe said, "Now get this body out of here at once." He stooped to pick up his pistol, shaking his head in silent disgust, then continued toward the door.

"Pardon me," the German said suddenly. There was another change in his tone, one that Metcalfe found worrying.

Metcalfe turned around sullenly and saw a perplexed look in the Gestapo man's face. The German was gesturing at Metcalfe's right leg.

Metcalfe looked down and saw what the German was pointing

at. His pant leg was soaked in blood. It was the wound he had sustained earlier: though minor, it had bled profusely.

Metcalfe's momentary confusion emboldened the colonel's suspicion. *Something is not right here,* the Gestapo man seemed to be thinking as his facial expression changed to one of wariness.

"Sir, I have the right to inspect your papers as well," the German said. "I want to make sure you are indeed—"

Metcalfe did not wait. He drew his weapon and fired. The round penetrated the man's chest, and the German sank to the floor. Metcalfe fired a second time, aiming precisely for the same spot, and now he was certain that the Nazi was dead.

Yes, the man was dead, but now everything had changed. The Gestapo was looking for him, whether they knew his true name or not. That meant he couldn't risk showing up at the train station. He couldn't take the train from Paris, couldn't follow Corky's prescribed route, which was now far too hazardous. Plans would have to be altered, and Corky would have to be notified.

Metcalfe knew he was now a marked man. He could no longer walk the streets freely.

He approached the dead German slowly, felt for a pulse at the man's throat. There was none. He saw the two small-bore bullet holes at the center of the man's chest. Though the bullets had penetrated the tunic, the holes were in fact small and concealable.

Moving swiftly, he removed the Gestapo colonel's uniform. He stripped off his own clothes, transferring his wallet, papers, keys, and passport to the Gestapo uniform. Wadding up his discarded clothing, he shoved them into a nearby china cabinet, then he donned the Gestapo uniform. The fit was not too bad, though it felt peculiar: highly starched, stiff, scratchy. He adjusted the black tie so that it covered the bullet holes, keeping it in place with the Nazi Party pin that the agent had used as a tie tack.

He took the colonel's papers and weapon, any of which could come in handy. In Derek's medicine cabinet he found some gauze, adhesive tape, and merthiolate. Then, after quickly binding the wound in his thigh, he rushed out of Derek's apartment in search of the one man who could get him out of Paris quickly.

"Jesus Christ almighty!" Chip Nolan exclaimed. "They're all *dead?*"

"Everyone but . . . the man you know as James," Corky replied, a stricken look on his face. He had just entered the modest flat in the Eighth Arrondissement that the Bureau kept as one of several Paris safe-house locations.

"My *God!*" Nolan cried, his voice breaking. "Who was it? Who were the bastards who did it?"

Corcoran approached the window, staring apprehensively out at the street. "That's what I need your help on. One was shot, but two of them were garroted."

"Garroted?"

"In exactly the same way as the Belgian librarian last week— also a member of my organization. I speculate the responsible party is the *Sicherheitsdienst,* and one assassin in particular. But I need verification—a complete forensic workup, the sort of thing the Bureau does so well."

Nolan nodded. "It's risky, but I'll do it for you. The *bastards.*"

Corcoran turned back from the window, shaking his head slowly. "This is a grievous setback to our efforts."

"Setback? My God, Corky, I don't know how you do it. You treat the world as if it's one big board game. For God's sake, these are *human beings* we're talking about! They had mothers and fathers, maybe brothers and sisters. They had *names.* Doesn't the loss of human *lives* mean anything to you?"

"Absolutely," snapped Corcoran. "The loss of human lives all across Europe and the U.S. I don't have time to get sentimental over the fate of a handful of anonymous men who knew full well what the risks were when they signed up. I'm concerned with the survival of freedom on this planet. The individual must always be subordinate to the greater good."

"You could have taken those words right out of Joe Stalin's mouth," said Nolan. "That's the way dictators talk. Boy, you really piss ice water, don't you? You can really be a heartless bastard."

"Only when my job requires it."

"And when is that?"

"All the time, my good fellow. All the time."

CHAPTER TEN

The Spanish diplomat was enraged.

José Félix Antonio María di Liguori y Ortiz, the Minister of Foreign Affairs in the military junta of Spain's Generalissimo Francisco Franco, had come to Paris for a series of secret meetings with Admiral Jean-François Darlan, leader of the armed forces of Vichy France. His private plane was scheduled to depart from Orly Airport in a quarter of an hour, and yet his limousine was stuck on *Autoroute du Sud* halfway between the Porte d'Orléans and Orly Airport.

And not just stalled on the highway, but in the middle of a tunnel! The gleaming black Citroën Traction Avant 11N limousine just sat there, its engine block ticking, the hood up, while the driver hunched over the engine trying to bring it back to life.

The minister glanced at his watch and nervously touched his extravagantly curled, waxed *mostacho*. "*Madre de Dios!*" he exclaimed. "*Caray!* What the hell is going on?"

"My apologies, Your Excellency!" the driver shouted. "It seems to be the transmission. I am doing all I can!"

"My plane is scheduled to leave in fifteen minutes!" the Spaniard retorted. "Make it quick!"

"Yes, sir, of course," the driver said. In a lower voice he muttered to himself in French, "The goddamned plane's not going to leave without him, for Christ's sake." There were three others in the Spaniard's delegation, and they were stuck in the car immediately behind. So they were all going to be late. Big deal.

The driver, whose name was Henri Corbier, cursed the imperious Spanish fascist, with his ridiculous mustache. Ever since

Ortiz had arrived in Paris, two days earlier, he'd been ordering everyone around. He was truly insufferable.

Today, the driver had been forced to sit for eight hours in the cold in front of some damned government building while Ortiz met with some assholes from the Vichy government and a bunch of Nazi generals. The Spaniard wouldn't even allow him to go to a café. No, he had to sit there in the cold, waiting. And with petrol so scarce, he couldn't even keep the engine running!

So when a friend of his, who shared his contempt for the *Boches* and the way they'd ruined Paris, asked Henri to do a minor favor, he wasn't just willing, he was downright ecstatic. "Nothing illegal," Henri was assured. "Just stall the limousine on the way to the airport. Make the goddamned Spanish fascist nice and late for his scheduled departure. That way our friends at Orly will have the time to do what needs to be done to the fascist's Junkers Ju-52; never you mind what that means. Ignorance is your best protection. No one will ever be able to prove that the car didn't have engine trouble."

Henri would have done his part for free, but when they offered him a nice fat Christmas ham if he did his patriotic duty, he was thrilled. Nothing like getting paid in the most valuable commodity of all—scarce ham—for doing something you want to do anyway.

"What's taking you so long?" the minister shouted.

Henri toyed with the engine, pretending to adjust one of the cylinders. "Soon!" he shouted back. "I think I have it figured out." Under his breath, he added: *"Putain de merde!"*

The old Renault Juvaquatre barreled up to the sentry booth that blocked the access road to Orly Field. Two German military policemen snapped to attention.

Metcalfe, still dressed in the stolen Gestapo uniform, rolled down the window. *"Heil Hitler!"* he called out, his face a mask of bland authority as he flashed the Gestapo badge.

The MP saluted, replied, *"Heil Hitler!"* and waved the vehicle through.

It was as Metcalfe had expected. The badge was not inspected, no questions asked. No MP was going to risk his job, or his neck, harassing a high-ranking Gestapo officer who was obviously there on business.

"Well done," said the car's other passenger, who was also its owner. Roger "Scoop" Martin was a tall, rangy man with curly red hair, prematurely receding—at twenty-eight, he was barely older than Metcalfe—and a sallow complexion, his cheeks pitted with acne scars. Martin was an ace RAF pilot who'd just been assigned to the SOE, Britain's Special Operations Executive, the sabotage and subversion agency formed by Winston Churchill just a few months earlier. Martin lived in Paris; as his cover, he worked as a *médecin-chef* for Le Foyer du Soldat, helping feed and treat prisoners of war, visiting wounded men in hospitals. In this capacity he was one of the few Parisians allowed to operate a private car.

"That was the easy part," Metcalfe said. His eyes roamed the asphalt-paved parking lot. Ever since taking over France, the Nazis had turned Orly Field from a commercial airport into a military base. The only flights into and out of Orly now were military or the occasional government dignitary. *Wehrmacht* soldiers patrolled the area with MG-34 light machine guns, Schmeisser 9mm pistols, or MP-38 submachine guns; the field was crowded with troop transport vehicles, Skoda and Steyr trucks, three-ton Opel Blitz trucks.

"There it is," Roger said, pointing at a gate built into the chain-link fence that protected the runways and aircraft hangars.

Metcalfe nodded as he turned the wheel. "Awfully good of you to do this for me, Scoop," he said.

"Like I had a bloody choice," Martin grumbled. "Corcoran gets on the blower to Sir Frank, and next thing I know I'm to fly to goddamned bloody *Silesia.*"

"Oh, you'd have done it for me anyway," Metcalfe said with a sly smile. Roger had used his SOE channels to convey Metcalfe's urgent message to Alfred Corcoran about the nightmarish carnage at the Cave, as well as to inform him about an alteration in his plans. Corky would have to make arrangements in Moscow for one more visitor.

"Hmph. There's a limit to friendship," the pilot replied morosely.

Metcalfe knew well his friend's bone-dry sense of humor. Roger Martin often played at being the martyr, complained about his lot in life, but it was all attitude. In truth, Roger was about as loyal a friend as there was, and he loved what he did. He played poker the same way, moaning about his lousy hand right up until he played a royal flush.

Roger was born and educated in Cognac, of a French mother and an Irish father, and his ancestors had been cognac makers in France since the eighteenth century. He had dual citizenship, spoke French like a native, but considered himself British. Ever since he'd first seen a biplane soaring above the skies over Nord-Pas-de-Calais, he'd dreamed of flying. Uninterested in the family business, he'd become a pilot for Air France, then served with the French Air Force in Syria, where, after the Nazis moved into France, he joined the Royal Air Force Volunteer Reserve and, after a course of training, became a Special Duties pilot with the RAF's "Moon Squadrons." Based in Tangmere, on the south coast of England, he flew a "Lizzie," a tiny single-engine Westland Lysander, during the evacuation of Dunkirk, dropping supplies to embattled troops defending Calais. Plenty of Lysanders were lost, but not Scoop's. He'd racked up thousands of hours flying perilous nighttime clandestine missions into Europe, dropping and extracting British agents. No one was better than Roger Martin at taking off and landing on rough, muddy French farm fields under the nose of the enemy, illuminated only by torchlight. But Scoop was typically modest about his famous skills. "Any bloody fool can drop Joes over France," he'd once told Metcalfe.

"Though scooping them out of there can be a bit hairy." Roger became known for accomplishing the impossible, for executing pickups on the most difficult terrain. His wing commander had dubbed him Scoop, and the moniker had stuck.

"I don't know how the hell you plan to pull this off," Scoop groaned as they got out of the Renault. Painted on the outside of the car was the insignia of Le Foyer du Soldat and the Red Cross emblem.

"All you have to do is keep your mouth shut," Metcalfe said. "You can do that, *mon vieux.*"

Scoop grunted.

"You're my pilot. I'll handle the rest."

They approached the next checkpoint, an MP who stood at attention beside the gate. He saluted when he saw Metcalfe, nodded as Metcalfe flashed the badge, and pulled the gate open for the men.

"Which hangar are we going to?" Metcalfe muttered under his breath.

"Damned if I know," Scoop replied. "We know the tail number of the craft, the scheduled time of departure, and that's about it." He fell silent as they approached another checkpoint. This time Metcalfe simply gave a brisk salute and the MPs did the same.

Once they had passed and were crossing a grassy field next to the paved runway, Scoop continued: "I suggest we stop at the first hangar we come to and ask. As far as anyone knows, I'm an ill-informed pilot reporting for duty."

His voice dropped as they passed a knot of German officers who were smoking and laughing heartily. They were admiring several risqué French postcards, fanned in the pudgy hands of a round-faced SS *Gruppenführer.* Metcalfe froze when he recognized the SS man. It was one of his many Nazi acquaintances, the portly Brigadier General Johannes Koller.

Quickly Metcalfe turned his face away, pretending to be deep in whispered conversation with Scoop. He realized it was only a matter of time before he saw someone he knew—but not now, not *here!*

Scoop noticed the distress in Metcalfe's face. He looked puzzled but said nothing.

It was likely that the *Gruppenführer,* busy showing off his postcards, had not noticed Metcalfe. Even if he had gotten a look at Metcalfe's face, the Gestapo uniform would have surely confused him; the uncertainty would keep him quiet.

Finally they reached the last security checkpoint, which was more elaborate: an open booth on the edge of the tarmac, manned by two MPs. Once they were past it, Metcalfe and Scoop had only to locate the correct hangar. Metcalfe tensed. If the MPs asked to examine his stolen badge or papers, it was all over. The photographs of the dead Gestapo agent did not resemble him at all.

But the military policeman who was clearly the one in charge simply gave a salute and waved the men through. Metcalfe let out his breath noiselessly just as he noticed a movement out of the corner of his eye. It was Koller, walking quickly toward him, the other officers following close behind.

Metcalfe quickened his own stride. "Go," he whispered to Scoop.

"What?"

"Run ahead. You're a pilot who's late for his assigned flight. I can't run—it'll look suspicious."

"You're mad—"

"Just do as I say. I'll catch up to you."

Scoop shrugged, shook his head in perplexity, and broke into a half-run, half-walk, the hurried movement of a man who was late. Metcalfe, meanwhile, kept up his steady, determined pace.

"Excuse me! Excuse me!"

Metcalfe turned, saw the MP who had just waved him through. Next to him stood Koller, pointing at Metcalfe.

Metcalfe shrugged, looked perplexed, and didn't move. He

bowed his head as he pretended to fish something out of his pocket. *Must keep my face as concealed as possible!* Metcalfe glanced over his shoulder, saw Scoop entering one of the hangars, and again considered running. But there was no point to that; he and Scoop would simply be caught. In any case, it was too late. Koller and the MP were advancing toward him. "I *know* this man!" the *Gruppenführer* said. "He is an impostor!"

"Sir," the MP said. "Come here, please. May I see your papers?"

"This is a joke of some sort?" Metcalfe replied in a loud, strong voice. "Come now. I have important business."

The two men came beside him. "Yes, that is Eigen! Daniel Eigen! I knew it was him!"

"Your *papers,* sir," the MP repeated.

"What in the hell do you think you're doing, Eigen?" Koller said, staring at him. "Your criminal actions are—"

"Silence, you fool!" Metcalfe roared. He lunged forward, reaching into the *Gruppenführer*'s tunic and pulling out the lewd postcards. He tossed them into the air. Then he sniffed loudly, his face next to the German's. "Look at what this degenerate spends his time doing!" he snapped in German, addressing the guard. "And smell his breath—he is drunk."

Koller's face turned crimson. "How *dare* you—"

"Whether this is some sort of intraservice *prank* or simple sabotage, consider the source! A drunken degenerate who tries to delay the Reich's work." He pointed at Koller. "You, whoever you are and whatever your degenerate intentions, have no business interfering with security business of the utmost urgency! As our Führer says, the future belongs to the vigilant." He shook his head in disgust. "*Gott im Himmel!* You disgrace us all."

With that, Metcalfe turned on his heel and strode away, in the direction of the hangar he had just seen Scoop enter. But his ears remained attuned to shouts, running footsteps, any signs that his ruse had failed. He could hear Johannes Koller still arguing with the guard, his voice rising until he sounded apoplectic with rage.

Metcalfe's counterattack had worked, but it had probably done no more than buy him a minute or two.

That was better than nothing. The difference between success and failure might be as slim as a few seconds.

Metcalfe ran full out. The hangar straight ahead of him was a large barrel-shaped structure built of prestressed, reinforced concrete. In the early days it had been used as a hangar for dirigibles. Now it held the Junkers Ju-52/3m on which the Spanish Minister of Foreign Affairs had been scheduled to depart this very moment.

But *El Ministro* was unavoidably detained, his pilot, Metcalfe now saw, lying slumped on the ground against the concrete wall of the hangar, a black-haired man in a leather jacket. What had Scoop done to the man? Had he killed him? Scoop was a pilot, not an operative, but if it was necessary to take a life, he would do so.

As Metcalfe approached, he heard the plane's three powerful engines roar to life. The ugly slab-sided craft jolted ahead, rolling forward. Scoop was in the cockpit, visible through the Plexiglas canopy, waving wildly at him to get in. Scoop was shouting as well, though the engine drone made his words inaudible.

The plane was some sixty feet long, almost twenty feet high. On its corrugated light-alloy metal skin were painted the words IBERIA—LINEAS AEREAS ESPAÑOLAS. This was a German-manufactured craft in the service of the Spanish national airline, probably left over from the Spanish Civil War.

Madness! Scoop expected him to leap into a moving plane. There was no choice; Metcalfe could see several guards running toward him, brandishing their weapons. Dodging the giant propeller blades, he raced past the low, cantilevered wing and grabbed hold of the cabin hatch door, which had been left open. No ramp was in place, nor was one necessary. He pulled himself up, hoisted himself into the cabin as the plane accelerated on the tarmac, pulled the hatch closed behind him, and bolted it.

He could hear the explosion of bullets pitting the plane's duralumin skin. The craft was lightly armored, built to withstand ordinary gunfire, though nothing much heavier. The engines revved, whined. Through the small Plexiglas window he could see the runway fly by. The interior of the cabin was equipped with a dozen or so seats and was, by the standards of most Junkers planes, almost luxurious. Metcalfe ran forward, but a sudden lurch threw him to the cabin floor. Crawling the rest of the way, he finally made it to the cockpit.

"Strap in!" Scoop shouted as Metcalfe leaped into the copilot's seat. Another volley of gunfire strafed the nose nacelle. Fortunately, the cockpit sat high, canted upward, out of the line of fire. Through the Plexiglas, he could see the source of the barrage: three or four MPs firing off their machine guns from a hundred feet away.

Suddenly Metcalfe realized that they were headed directly toward the guards. Scoop seemed to be aiming for them! As the plane hurtled forward, the men scattered, diving to the ground on either side, unwilling to risk their lives in a foolhardy attempt to stop fifteen thousand pounds of runaway plane.

As Metcalfe strapped in, he could hear Scoop speaking into the radio, but he couldn't make out the words. The engine drone grew high-pitched as the plane accelerated, the throttle pushed full open. Scoop pulled back on the controls to set full flaps and achieve a climbing angle. There was another spatter of gunfire against the fuselage, somewhere to the rear, and the plane lifted off.

The engine noise had abated somewhat. "Jesus Christ almighty, Metcalfe," Scoop said. "What the *hell* did you get me into?"

"You did it, Scoop."

"Barely."

"But you did it. Are we cleared for takeoff, by the way?"

Scoop shrugged. "Our flight path is cleared, but I had to make a premature departure. We should be okay for a while."

"A *while?*"

"I don't think *Luftwaffe* air traffic control is going to order us shot down. Too much uncertainty. A Spanish plane cleared to take off, the reports will be conflicting—"

"You don't *think?*"

"Like it or not, Metcalfe, we're in the middle of a war. Fortunately, we've got civilian markings, so my buddies in the RAF won't be shooting us down. It's the damned Nazis I worry about. We're flying a goddamned stolen plane through Nazi-controlled airspace. You know what that could mean."

Metcalfe chose to ignore the warning; after all, what could he do about it at this point? All they could do was hope for the best and count on Scoop's extraordinary skill. "You've flown one of these before?"

"Oh, sure. '*Tante Ju.*' The corrugated coffin. No, actually, I haven't, but close enough."

"Jesus," Metcalfe groaned. "How far can this thing take us?"

Scoop was silent for a minute. They were still climbing. "Eight hundred miles or so, with the auxiliary fuel tanks."

"We're going to just make it to Silesia."

"Barely."

"Even then, assuming we get there safely and we're able to refuel, it's going to be dicey."

"What are you talking about?"

"It's *another* eight hundred miles or so. It's going to be close."

"Eight hundred miles to *where?* I thought Silesia was the final destination."

"No," said Metcalfe. "I have a date. With an old girlfriend."

"Have you gone barmy on me, Metcalfe?"

"No. You're taking us to Moscow."

PART TWO

Moscow, August 1991

Ambassador Stephen Metcalfe hung up the phone, shaken.

It was after midnight, Moscow time. He sat in a secure room on the second floor of Spaso House, the ornate putty-yellow mansion a mile west of the Kremlin that served as the residence of the American ambassador to Moscow. This had been Metcalfe's home for four years in the 1960s; he knew it well. The current ambassador, a friend of Metcalfe's, was pleased to give the illustrious Stephen Metcalfe the use of the sterile telephone line.

The President's national security adviser had just provided him with the latest signals intelligence on the growing crisis in Moscow, and it looked ominous.

Soviet President Mikhail Gorbachev, who had been on vacation with his family at the seaside presidential villa in the Crimea, was being held hostage. The conspirators—including the chairman of the KGB, the Defense Minister, the chief of the Politburo, the Prime Minister, and even Gorbachev's own chief of staff—had declared a state of emergency. They had announced, falsely, that Gorbachev had fallen ill and was unable to govern. They had ordered 250,000 pairs of handcuffs from a factory in Pskov and had had 300,000 arrest forms printed. They had cleared two entire floors of Moscow's Lefortovo Prison to incarcerate their enemies.

The ZIL limousine was waiting for him in front of Spaso House. Metcalfe got in next to his old friend the three-star general. The Russian who had used the code name "Kurwenal" was, Metcalfe saw, dressed in civilian attire. The man nodded at the driver, and the car immediately sped through the tank-choked streets.

The general spoke without preamble, the tension in his voice evident. "Gorbachev has no way to communicate with the outside world. All of his telephone lines have been cut, even the special commander-in-chief line."

"There's worse," said Metcalfe. "I've just learned that the conspirators now have control of the nuclear football."

The general closed his eyes. The briefcase that held the top-secret Soviet nuclear codes would enable the junta to launch Russia's entire arsenal of nuclear weapons if and when they so chose. The thought of such power in the hands of madmen was staggering.

"Is Gorbachev alive?"

"Apparently so," replied Metcalfe.

"The coup plotters want change," the general said. "Well, they will get change. Just not the change they imagine. If..."

Metcalfe waited. Then he asked, "If what?"

"If the *Dirizhor* will intervene. He is the only one who can stop this insanity."

"They'll listen to him?"

"More than that. As the chief of my country's entire military-industrial complex, the *Dirizhor,* as he's called, holds vast power in his hands."

Metcalfe settled back in his seat. "It's strange, you know," he said. "You and I seem to speak to each other only at times of extraordinary crises. When the world is at the precipice of nuclear war. The Berlin Wall crisis, the Cuban Missile crisis—"

"Was I not right that Khrushchev would never fire his missiles?"

"You've never compromised the interests of your own country, and neither have I. I suppose we've both acted as...as..."

"As circuit breakers, I've always thought. We've been there to ensure the house doesn't burn down."

"But we're old, both of us. We are respected because of our reputations, our age, our alleged 'wisdom'—though I always say that wisdom is what comes from making a shitload of mistakes."

"And learning from them," the general added.

"Perhaps. Still, I'm superannuated. I'm just about irrelevant in Washington. If it weren't for my money, I doubt I'd still get invitations to the White House."

"The *Dirizhor* will not consider you irrelevant or superannuated."

"I belong to the past. I'm history."

"In Russia the past never remains the past, and history is never just history."

But before Metcalfe could reply, the limousine screeched to a halt. In front of them was a roadblock: traffic cones, road flares, a line of uniformed soldiers.

"Alpha Group," said the general.

"Order them to stand down," said Metcalfe. "You're their superior officer."

"They're not army. They're KGB. The elite commando group that was used in Afghanistan, in Lithuania." He added regretfully, "And now here in Moscow."

The men surrounded the limousine, submachine guns pointed. "Step out of the car," ordered the squadron leader. "You—driver. You two old men in the back. Now!"

"Dear God," breathed the general. "These are men with orders to kill."

CHAPTER ELEVEN

Moscow, November 1940

Moscow had changed dramatically since the last time Metcalfe had been there, and yet it was very much the same place. It was a city of shabbiness and grandeur, desperation and pride. Everywhere he went, from the lobby of the Metropole Hotel to Kuznetsky Most, there was the stench of *makhorka*, the cheap Russian tobacco, a smell he'd always associated with Russia. Too, there was the foul, rancid smell of wet sheepskin, another Moscow odor he recognized.

So much was the same, yet so much had changed. The old one- and two-story buildings had been demolished, replaced by grandiose skyscrapers built according to Stalin's personal taste, in the wedding-cake style of architecture they were calling Stalinist Gothic. Everywhere was frantic construction, excavation. Moscow was transforming itself into the center of a totalitarian empire.

There were no more horse-drawn carriages. The cobblestone streets had been widened and graded and asphalted over, as Moscow had made itself over for the age of the automobile. Not that there were all that many cars on the streets—a few battered old Renaults, but mostly Emkas, the Russian nickname for the GAZ M-1, their knockoff of the 1933 Ford. The dull brown streetcars still screeched noisily on their tracks, and Muscovites still clung to them, hanging out of the open doors, but the trams were no longer as crowded as they used to be when Metcalfe had last visited. There were other ways to get around Moscow now, including the new Metro that had been built in the last few years.

The air was sootier than ever: smoke now belched from factories and trains and automobiles. The old, steep Tverskaya

Street, that grand thoroughfare, had been renamed Gorky Street, for the writer who had championed the Revolution. Most of the small shops had been replaced by huge government stores—stores that were empty, shelves bare, despite their fancy window dressing. Food was scarce, but propaganda was plentiful. Everywhere Metcalfe walked there seemed to be giant portraits of Stalin, or Stalin and Lenin together. Buildings were festooned with immense red banners that proclaimed: "We will overfulfill the quotas of the Five Year Plan!" and "Communism = Soviet Power + Electrification of the Whole Country!"

Still, beneath the strange Communist trappings the eternal, ancient Moscow remained—the golden onion domes of the old Russian Orthodox churches glinting in the sun, the dazzling colors of St. Basil's Cathedral in Red Square, the workers in their tattered outfits of quilted cotton wadding, peasants in bulky coats and babushkas on their heads, hurrying along the streets, carrying *avoskas,* string bags, or dragging homemade wooden suitcases.

In their faces, though, was something new, a harrowing fear even deeper, more profound, than Metcalfe had seen six years earlier: a paranoia, a thick and enveloping terror that seemed to have settled over the Russians like a blanket of fog. That was the most awful transformation of all. The great terror, the purges of the 1930s that had begun only after Metcalfe had last left Moscow, had etched itself onto every face, from the lowliest peasant to the highest commissar.

Metcalfe had seen it in his meeting today at the People's Commissariat of Foreign Trade—a meeting he thought would never be over, but that was necessary for the charade, the pretext for his being in Moscow at all. Certain members of the delegation should have been familiar to him from the old days, but they had changed almost beyond recognition. The jolly, laughing Litvikov had become a beetle-browed, haunted figure. His aides, who in earlier times would have been expansive and gracious in the presence of this great American capitalist, were now impassive and remote. They regarded him, Metcalfe thought, with both envy and fear. He was royalty, yes, but he was also diseased, contagious: if they got too close to him, they could be tainted in the eyes of their superiors. At any moment they could be charged with espionage, with collaborating with a capitalist agent; they could be arrested, executed. People were shot for far less.

Recalling the meeting now, Metcalfe shook his head. Sitting in that overheated reception room, around a table covered with green felt, he'd had to go through an elaborate dance of hints and promises without committing to anything. He had hinted at his family's political connections, dropping names like Franklin Roosevelt, names of the President's trusted aides, of powerful senators. He had confided that the President, despite his public posture of criticism of Russia, actually wanted to increase trade with the Soviet Union, and he could see their ears prick up. It was all smoke and mirrors, but it seemed to have worked.

Now, as he walked across Teatralnaya Square, he could see the gleaming classical facade of the Bolshoi Theater, with its eight-columned portico and, atop its pediment, the four bronze horses of Apollo's chariot. Metcalfe found his pulse quickening.

He passed a *militsiyoner,* a street policeman, who eyed him warily, ogling Metcalfe's garb: his heavy black cashmere coat, his finely sewn leather gloves. It was the attire, after all, of the scion of Metcalfe Industries.

Hide in plain sight, Corky had often admonished him. *Naked is the best disguise.*

To which his old friend Derek Compton-Jones, overhearing, had once cracked, "Stephen's got the naked part down, all right. He thinks a 'one-time pad' is where you go for a one-night stand."

Remembering, Metcalfe felt a stab of grief. His friends in the Paris station were all dead now. Good, brave men murdered in the line of duty, but how? And why?

Now he thought of an old Russian proverb—there were dozens, hundreds of them that he'd heard in the time he'd spent here—that said: "Dwell on the past, and you'll lose an eye; forget the past, and you'll lose both eyes."

He would not forget the past. No, he couldn't forget the past. Here, in Moscow, he was surrounded by it, he was returning to it; and the past that he was returning to was a dancer named Svetlana.

Outside the theater was a crowd of people waiting to enter. Metcalfe had no ticket to this evening's sold-out performance of *The Red Poppy,* but there were always ways. In Moscow, hard currency—the American dollar, the British pound, the French franc—could buy almost anything. There would always be Muscovites desperate for *valuta,* as they called hard currency, which could be used to buy food in the special stores intended only for foreigners. Desperate enough that they would even peddle their highly sought-after tickets to the Bolshoi. Desperation: he could always count on that here in Moscow.

The crowd was better-dressed, in general, than the people he passed on the street, and no surprise about that. Tickets to the Bolshoi could only be gotten through *blat,* the Soviet Russian word for pull, connections. You had to know someone, be someone important, be a member of the Party—or be a foreigner. There were lots of military uniforms in this crowd, red epaulets on the uniforms of officers. The epaulets were a new thing, Metcalfe reflected. Stalin had introduced them recently as a way to restore morale in the Red Army, which had been traumatized by the purges of 1938, when so many of the military leaders had been executed, charged with being traitors in collusion with Nazi Germany.

But what struck Metcalfe about the officers of the Red Army wasn't just their dress uniforms, the embroidered silver stars on their red epaulets; it was that their hair was now clipped short, in the Prussian style. They even *looked* like their Nazi counterparts now. Their chests jingled with bronze and gold medals; they had pistols in highly polished leather holsters suspended from their Sam Browne belts.

Strange, he reflected: now Moscow was allied with the Nazis. Russia had signed a nonaggression pact with Germany, its great enemy. The two great European military powers were partners now. The fascist state had joined hands with the Communist state. The Russians were even providing war matériel to the Nazis. How could the forces of freedom hope to take on both Nazi Germany and the Soviet Union? It was madness!

There was a familiar scent in the air, Metcalfe noticed. It wafted from a number of the Russian women, in their low-cut evening gowns: the hideous Soviet perfume named Red Poppy—how appropriate, given tonight's performance!—which was so awful that the foreigners called it "Stalin's breath."

An old man caught his eye, approached, whispering, "*Bilyeti? Vyi khotitye bilyeti?*" You want tickets?

The man's clothes were threadbare, but they had once been elegant. His gloves were missing several fingertips, and they'd been repaired with packing twine. This was a man who had once been well off but now was reduced to abjection. His speech, too, was cultivated. He was heartrending.

Metcalfe nodded. "Just one," he said.

"I have two," the old man said. "For you and your wife, sir?"

Metcalfe shook his head. "Just one. But I'll pay for two." He produced a small wad of dollars, far more than the transaction required, and the old man's eyes widened as he handed over a ticket.

"*Thank* you, sir! Thank you!"

As the old Russian smiled, Metcalfe caught a glimpse of the gold fillings that crowded his mouth. This was a man who had once been able to afford such luxuries.

So much was in short supply in Russia these days, Metcalfe thought. Food, fuel, clothing . . . but the greatest shortage of all was *dignity*.

He checked his coat in the *garderob,* as everyone had to do. A white-haired, wrinkled old woman took his overcoat, stroking it admiringly as she hung it among the shabby, shapeless garments.

The warning bell sounded, and Metcalfe joined the crush of people moving into the hall to take their seats. As he entered, he was impressed by the opulence of the theater. He had forgotten how lavish it was, what an island of czarist extravagance in the midst of Moscow's gray drabness. An immense crystal chandelier hung from a high domed ceiling decorated with fine classical paintings. Six tiers of private boxes banked the Czar's box, which was outfitted with red drapes and gilded seats beneath a gilt hammer and sickle. The main curtain was of gold cloth, and woven into it was CCCP, the Russian initials for the Communist Party, and all sorts of numbers, the great historical dates of the Soviet Communist past.

His seat was an excellent one. As he looked around the theater, he noticed the young Russian military officer seated directly behind him. The Russian smiled at Metcalfe.

"It's a beautiful theater, no?" the Russian said.

Metcalfe smiled back. "Spectacular." He felt a jolt. The man had spoken to him in English, not in Russian.

Why? How had he known . . . ?

The clothing, it had to be. That was all. To the discerning eye of a Russian, a foreigner stood out easily.

But how did he know to speak English?

"Tonight's performance will be a very special one," the military man said. He had a shock of flaming red hair, a strong nose, and a full, cruel mouth. "Gliere's *The Red Poppy*—you know the story, yes? It is about a dancing girl who is oppressed by a vicious, villainous capitalist." The hint of a smirk appeared on his face.

Metcalfe nodded, smiled politely. Suddenly he noticed something about the red-haired military man: he was no ordinary Red Army soldier. He recognized the green tunic and gold epaulets— the Russian was a major in the *Glavnoye Razvedyvatelnoye Upravlenie*: the GRU. The Main Intelligence Administration of the Soviet military. Military intelligence: a spy.

"I'm familiar with the story," Metcalfe said. "We capitalists make convenient villains for your Russian propagandists."

The GRU man nodded in tacit acknowledgment. "The lead, the role of Tao-Hoa, is danced by the Bolshoi's prima ballerina. Her name is Svetlana Baranova." His eyebrows shot up, but his expression remained impassive. "She is truly extraordinary."

"Is that right?" Metcalfe replied. "I'll keep an eye out for her."

"Yes," the Russian said. "I always do. I never miss her performances."

Metcalfe smiled again and turned around. He was filled with alarm. The GRU man *knew* who he was. It had to be! His face had revealed it; he'd *meant* to reveal it. There was no question about it.

Which suggested that the GRU agent had been placed here, directly behind Metcalfe, deliberately. Metcalfe's head reeled, his thoughts spinning. How could this have been arranged? For it *had* to have been arranged; there was nothing random about this "coincidence."

But how? Mentally, Metcalfe reviewed the last few minutes. He remembered taking his seat, an empty seat surrounded by people already sitting there on either side, front *and* back. The uniformed GRU agent, Metcalfe now realized, was already there. He remembered seeing the shock of reddish hair, the arrogant, cruel face; it had registered in his consciousness on some level. The GRU man could *not* have moved in only after Metcalfe had taken his place!

How, then, had this been arranged? A creeping sense of paranoia prickled at the back of his neck. What were the chances that a seat he had bought at the last minute from a scalper outside the Bolshoi just *happened* to be directly in front of a GRU agent who knew of his connection to Lana Baranova?

Metcalfe shuddered as he realized. The old man who had sold him his ticket: a desperate-looking, once elegant man. Desperate enough to do whatever he was ordered.

It had been a setup, hadn't it?

They knew he was going to the Bolshoi, *they* being the watchers, the Soviet authorities, in this case the elite GRU, and had wanted to communicate to him the *fact* that they knew, that he couldn't make a move without their knowing. Or was he being paranoid?

No. *It was no coincidence.* He had been followed to the Bolshoi, perhaps, although if he had indeed been followed, it had been expertly done; he hadn't picked up on the signals, hadn't seen evidence of the tail, and that was the alarming thing. Normally he was quite adept at spotting surveillance. It was what he did, after all: what he had been trained to do. And Soviet surveillance tended to be clumsy, obvious—subtlety sacrificed for heavy-handed warning.

But how could this possibly have been arranged at the last minute? He had deliberately not tried to buy a ticket at the In-tourist office, which was the standard procedure for a foreign visitor. He had made a point of procuring his ticket at the last minute, knowing that he could always pick one up from a scalper.

Not until he entered Teatralnaya Square could his followers have known he was headed toward the Bolshoi. That had been a matter of a few minutes, hardly sufficient time to arrange a placement of an agent.

And then it occurred to him: he had arrived in Moscow en-tirely in the open, under his true name, with several days' notice, his arrival cleared by the responsible authorities. They had a dos-sier on him; there was no doubt about that. Presumably they had no idea about why he was here. But they knew of his past con-nection to Lana; of that he had no doubt. It was entirely pre-dictable that he'd want to attend the Bolshoi, see a public performance of his old flame. Yes: they had anticipated his moves, put a watcher in place in case he did what they figured he would do.

He was being closely watched by those who knew who he was. That was the message they were sending.

But why GRU? Why an agent from Soviet *military* intelligence? Surely the NKVD was the agency that would be most interested in keeping a close watch on him.

A final warning bell sounded from out in the lobby, the lights began to dim, and the excited hubbub diminished to an electric silence. The orchestra started playing; the curtain rose.

And then, several minutes later, came Tao-Hoa's entrance, and Metcalfe saw her.

For the first time in six years, Metcalfe saw his Lana, and he was transfixed, lost in her beauty, her litheness. Her radiant face seemed to hold nothing except the purest transport, transparency, joy: she was at one with the music. There was heaven in that face. The audience could have been a million miles away; she was ethereal, a creature not of this earth.

Compared to her, the other dancers looked like marionettes. Her stage presence was electrifying, her movements at once fluid and powerful. She soared as if untethered by gravity, as if propelled by magic. She soared like music incarnate.

And for a moment, Metcalfe allowed his heart to soar with her. He was flooded with memories, of the first time he saw her, dancing in *Tristan and Isolde*—the first and last performance of that production. It was foolish of Igor Moiseyev to have attempted to set a ballet to German music, and the Commissariat of Culture soon showed him the error of his ways. Metcalfe's time with Lana was cut short with what seemed equal finality. The memory of their brief yet fevered time together haunted him. How could he have ever let her go? Yet how could he have stayed? It was a brief attachment, no more, a fling; he was never going to remain in Moscow, and she was never going to leave.

And now, he agonized, what had happened to her? Who had she become in the intervening six years? *What* had she become? Was she the same fragile, impetuous girl?

What was he about to get her into?

Suddenly the audience burst into applause as the curtain fell, and Metcalfe was startled out of his reverie. It was intermission. He had been in a daze all this time, lost in his thoughts, his recollections of Lana. He realized that his eyes were wet with tears.

Then he heard a voice from behind, very close. "It is hard to take your eyes off her, is it not? I never do."

Metcalfe turned slowly, saw the GRU man sitting back, applauding vigorously. The movement of his hands and arms caused his tunic to shift just enough to reveal the glint of metal in a holster.

A gleaming nickel-plated 7.62mm Tokarev.

I never do.

What was he implying?

"She's something," Metcalfe agreed.

"As I say, I never miss her performances," the GRU man said. "I've been watching her for years." His tone was confiding, insinuating, threatening: a voice of true malevolence.

The lights in the house came up, and the spectators arose. Intermission at the Bolshoi, as at most Russian theaters, inevitably meant a buffet set out for the patrons. There would be vodka, champagne, red and white wine; there would be smoked salmon and sturgeon, ham and salami, cold roast chicken. Given how poorly fed Muscovites seemed to be these days, everyone living off ration cards, it was no surprise that there was a crush to leave the hall for the banquet.

The GRU man got up as soon as Metcalfe did and seemed to be intent on following closely behind. But the crowd was thick, and as it undulated up the aisle toward the exit door Metcalfe managed to leave the Russian a good distance behind. What was the Russian intent on doing? Metcalfe wondered. He had made his point: Metcalfe was being watched closely. Obviously the man wasn't trying to be subtle. He wasn't trying to disappear into the background.

The GRU man could see Metcalfe elbowing his way through the crowd, to the protests of those he jostled. *"Molodoi chelovyek! Ne nado lyest' bez ocheredi!"* A prim older woman scowled at him. "Young man, don't try to sneak ahead of me." A classic response: Russians, particularly elderly women, were always lecturing strangers, telling them how to behave. They would yell at you for not wearing a hat when it was cold out. Your business was their business.

"*Prostitye,*" Metcalfe replied suavely. "Forgive me."

Once he reached the lobby, he maneuvered his way through an even denser crowd, and by now he was far enough away from the GRU man that he seemed to have lost the watcher, at least temporarily.

He knew where he was going. He had been to the Bolshoi countless times, had visited Lana here. He knew the layout better even than most regular theatergoers here.

Attired as he was in a dinner jacket, his face set in an expression of gravity, he was able to make his way, unhindered, toward a beige-painted doorway on which a sign announced in Cyrillic letters NO ADMITTANCE TO THE PUBLIC. It was unlocked, as he remembered it always was. Just inside, however, was the *dezhurny*, the security guard, a swarthy, pockmarked man in a blue uniform sitting at a table. He was a typical Soviet petty official, no different from the petty officials of the czarist days: indifferent to his job yet at the same time fiercely hostile to any who dared to challenge his authority.

"A gift for the prima ballerina, Miss Baranova," Metcalfe intoned in British-accented Russian. "From the British ambassador, my good man."

The man looked up suspiciously, put out his hand. "You can't go in here. Give it to me; I'll see that it gets to her."

Metcalfe laughed. "Oh, I'm afraid Sir Stafford Cripps would never countenance that, my friend. Far too valuable a gift, and if anything were to happen to it . . . well, I'd hate to imagine the international incident that might result, the investigation . . ." He paused, withdrew a small stack of rubles, and handed it to the guard. The man's eyes widened. It was more than he made in a month, most likely.

"I'm *so* sorry to trouble you," Metcalfe said, "but I really am required to give it directly to Miss Baranova."

The guard swiftly slipped the bribe into a pocket of his jacket, looking to either side as he did so. "Well, what are you waiting for?" he said with an officious frown, waving Metcalfe by. "Go. Move on. Quickly."

The backstage area was a frantic scene of stagehands moving large props, including an immense painted backdrop of the port in Kuomintang, China, with the prow of a giant Soviet ship set against an orange sky. There was a cluster of male dancers, some clad as Russian sailors, others as Chinese coolies, standing around, smoking. Several ballerinas in Chinese costumes with heavily painted faces scurried by in satin tutus and toe shoes. Metcalfe could smell the perfumed smell of stage makeup.

A ballerina pointed him toward a door marked with a red-and-gold star. With quickening pulse, he knocked on the door.

"*Da?*" came a muffled female voice.

"Lana," he said.

The door was flung open, and there she was. The silky black hair pulled up tightly in a bun, the large clear brown eyes flashing beneath the painted Chinese features, the delicate upturned, chiseled nose, the high cheekbones, the red-lipsticked pout. The breathtaking beauty. She was dazzling, even more luminous in the flesh than she was on the carefully lit stage.

"*Shto vyi khotite?*" the petite dancer demanded brusquely without looking up at her visitor. "What do you want?"

"Lana," Metcalfe repeated, softly.

She stared, and then recognition dawned in her eyes. Something in her expression softened for a split second, then hardened into haughty arrogance. The fleeting moment of vulnerability had passed, in its place an amused composure.

"Why, can it be?" she said, her voice velvety. "Can it really be Stiva, my old, dear friend?"

Stiva: that was her nickname for him. Six years ago she would call him that in a soft, silky, almost purring tone, but now she said it in a lilting way that seemed—could it be?—almost *contemptuous?* She smiled graciously, the prima ballerina receiving a fan with imperious condescension. "What a nice surprise."

Metcalfe could not stop himself from reaching for her, encircling her with his arms, and as he went to kiss her mouth, she turned abruptly to offer him her talcum-covered cheek instead. She pulled back, the strength in her slender arms surprising him, as if to get a better look at this dear old friend, but the movement seemed quite deliberate, intended to break the embrace.

"Lana," Metcalfe said, "forgive this intrusion, *dushka*." *Dushka*, or darling: one of his terms of endearment for her from the old days. "I'm in Moscow on business, and when I heard you were playing the lead tonight—"

"How wonderful to see you. How kind of you to drop by." There was something almost mocking in her tone, something excessively formal.

Metcalfe produced a black velvet box from his dinner jacket and held it out to her.

She did not take it. "For me? How kind. But now, if you don't mind, I must finish applying my makeup. It's really a scandal how short-staffed the Bolshoi is these days." She gestured around to her tiny, cramped dressing room with its three-sided mirror, the small dressing table cluttered with makeup and brushes, lignin makeup remover, and ragged white cotton towels embroidered with a large yellow *B* and *A,* for "Bolshoi Artists." Metcalfe took in every insignificant detail, his senses in a heightened state of sensitivity. "There's no one to help me with my makeup tonight; it's terrible."

Metcalfe opened the box, revealing the diamond necklace that sparkled against the black velvet. She had loved jewelry, like most women, but with an unusual appreciation for the artistry, the design, not just the size and flash of the precious stones. He handed it to her; she glanced at it quickly, without interest.

Suddenly she laughed, high and musical. "Just what I need," she said. "Another chain around my neck."

She tossed the case back at him; he caught it, stunned by her reaction. "Lana—" he began.

"Ah, Stiva, Stiva. Still the typical foreign capitalist, eh? You don't change, do you? You would force us into chains and manacles, and just because they are made of gold and diamond, you imagine that we do not see them for what they are."

"Lana," Metcalfe protested, "it's just a little gift."

"A gift?" she scoffed. "I don't need any more *gifts* from you. You have already given me a gift, my dear Stiva. There are gifts that shrink and confine and enslave, and there are gifts that grow."

"Grow?" Metcalfe said, baffled.

"Yes, my Stiva, *grow*. Like the proud stalks of wheat in a collective farm. Like our great Soviet economy."

Metcalfe stared at her. There was not a trace of irony in her voice. All this talk of collective farms and capitalist enslavement—it was so unlike the irreverent Svetlana Baranova of six years ago, who used to poke fun at the Stalinist slogans, the Communist kitsch, the *poshlost'*, she called it, that untranslatable word that meant "bad taste." What had happened to her in the meantime? Had she become a creature of the system? How could she utter such claptrap? Did she actually believe what she was saying?

"And I suppose your great leader Stalin is your idea of the perfect man?" Metcalfe muttered.

A fleeting look of terror appeared on her face, and in a flash it was gone. He realized the stupidity of his remark, the dangerous position he'd just put her in. People were passing by as he stood in the doorway of her dressing room; a single overheard syllable of subversion, even if it came from the mouth of a foreign visitor, would automatically imperil her.

"Yes," she shot back. "Our Stalin understands the needs of the Russian people. He loves the Russian people, and the Russian people love him. You Americans think you can buy anything with your filthy money, but you cannot buy our Soviet soul!"

He stepped into her dressing room, speaking quietly. "*Dushka,* I realize I don't have the charms of certain other men in your life. Such as your Nazi friend, Herr von—"

"You don't know what you're talking about!" she hissed.

"Gossip gets around, Lana. Even in the foreign embassies. I know plenty—"

"*No!*" she said. Her voice shook, and in it there was something even more potent than fear: there was truth. "You know *nothing!* Now get out of here at once!"

CHAPTER TWELVE

"How magnificent you were this evening," Rudolf von Schüssler said as he stroked Svetlana Baranova's hair. "My very own Red Poppy."

She shuddered as he touched the porcelain skin of her neck, and for the barest instant he wondered whether it was a shudder of rapture or one of revulsion—could it be? But then he saw her lips form themselves into the sweetest smile, and he was reassured.

She wore the negligee he had bought her in Munich, made of the sheerest gossamer pink silk, and the way it concealed and yet revealed the swell of her breasts, her tiny waist, the voluptuous flesh of her lean yet muscular thighs, was enormously exciting to him. She was the most appetizing dish he had ever been fortunate to have, and von Schüssler was a cultivated man who had always enjoyed the finest meals. Some might call him portly, but he thought of himself as well fed, a gastronome, a man who liked to live well.

Yet living well in Moscow was well nigh impossible. The food one could get here, even through the German embassy, was simply substandard. The apartment he had been given, which had formerly belonged to some high Red Army official who had been executed in the purges, was spacious enough. And certainly the dacha in Kuntsevo, outside Moscow, which he used as a weekend house, was adequate. He'd had to pay quite a bit under the table to the Russians to secure a lease on the place, and he'd had to suffer the unspoken derision of his colleagues in the embassy who were less fortunate, who didn't have family money that allowed them to make special deals with the Soviet government, but it was worth it.

He'd had to import all his best pieces of furniture, there was no decent help to hire for his dinner parties, and he had long ago tired of the diplomatic circuit here in this gloomy city. All you ever heard about was the war. And now that the Russians had signed the nonaggression pact with Berlin, *that* was all anyone ever talked about. He'd go out of his mind with the tedium of it all if he hadn't found his Red Poppy.

How well everything seemed to work out for him. It wasn't luck; no, it just went to show the truth of what his father had always said: the bloodline was everything. Ancestry—nothing mattered more. He took justifiable pride in his own ancestry, in the grand manor outside Berlin that had been in the family for more than a century, the service his many illustrious forebears had paid to kaisers and prime ministers. And of course there was the great Prussian general Ludwig von Schüssler, the hero of 1848 who led the military forces that had put down the liberal uprisings while Frederick William IV, the King of Prussia, was dithering and capitulating. Von Schüssler was keenly aware of the distinguished name he had to live up to.

Unfortunately, there were always those who would assume that he had gotten as far as he had by virtue of his name alone. Indeed, von Schüssler often found himself gnashing his teeth over the way his talents went unrecognized. He wrote brilliant and beautifully composed memoranda, garlanded with allusions to Goethe, yet they only seemed to molder.

Still, one did not become Second Secretary in the German embassy in an important posting like Moscow without intelligence, skill, and talent. True, he owed his position to an old family friend, Count Friedrich Werner von der Schulenberg, the German ambassador here, who was the doyen of the Moscow diplomatic corps. But for heaven's sake, the German Foreign Ministry was *full* of aristocrats—look at the Foreign Minister himself, Joachim von Ribbentrop, or von Ribbentrop's second-in-command, Ernst von Weiszacker, or Hans-Bernd von Haeften, or the last Foreign Minister, Freiherr Konstatin von Neurath . . . and the list went on. Who else had as deep an appreciation of the greatness inherent in the German *Volk*—the civilization that had given the world Beethoven and Wagner, Goethe and Schiller? The civilization that had given the world civilization itself?

Adolf Hitler hadn't had the privilege of a bloodline as great, but at least he had vision. There was something to be said for fresh blood. As tiresome and vainglorious as *der Führer* could be, at least he had an appreciation of the greatness of the German people. And after all, for all its rhetoric about the masses, the Third Reich craved the legitimacy that could only be conferred upon it by such aristocrats as the von Schüsslers.

It was for that reason that von Schüssler spent every weekend in Kuntsevo writing his memoirs. His illustrious ancestor Ludwig von Schüssler had taken pains to write his memoirs, thus ensuring his place in history. Rudolph had read it five or six times, and he was sure that *his* memoirs would be far more important than those of his forebear. After all, the times he was living in were far more important, far more interesting.

Well, Moscow was tedious, truth be told, but there was glory in his posting to Moscow, he'd simply have to keep reminding himself. Soon enough, Germany would win the war—this was inevitable: the only country remotely powerful enough to vanquish Germany was Russia, and Stalin was being meek and compliant—and then von Schüssler could retire to his *schloss* with the glory of having served his government and ride his beloved Lippizaners in the beautiful German countryside. . . . He would finish, and polish, his memoirs, and they would be published to great acclaim.

And he would take with him his jewel, his Red Poppy, the one thing that brightened the gloom of Moscow. For that he would ever be grateful to another old friend, Dr. Hermann Behrends. Behrends—he now went by the title *SS Untersturmführer der Reserve (Waffen-SS)*—and he had gone to school together, at the

University of Marburg. Both had received their doctorate of law
degrees there, and both had practiced fencing together. Behrends,
who was a far more avid fencer than von Schüssler, proudly bore
his scars: deep slashes in his cheeks from the fencing swords. The
two had taken different paths after university; while von Schüssler went on in the Foreign Service, Behrends had joined the SS.
But they stayed in touch, and Behrends had taken him into his
confidence just before von Schüssler had left Berlin. He had divulged, as one friend to another, a secret of which he had become
aware. A secret he thought his old school chum might find useful.

Behrends had told him the secret of Mikhail Baranov, the Hero
of the Russian Revolution.

And when von Schüssler had met the old man's daughter,
shortly after arriving in Moscow, at a party at the German embassy . . . Well, as the old German proverb had it, *Den Gerechten
hilft Gott.* Good things happen to good people. Ancestry had
proven decisive once again, and this time it wasn't just von
Schüssler's bloodline that had proven decisive. It was the stun-
ning ballerina's ancestry as well. The secret of her father. "The
fathers have eaten sour grapes and the children's teeth are set on
edge." How true, how true.

He hadn't *blackmailed* her—no, no, that was the wrong way
of looking at it. It was merely a way of establishing a connection,
of ensuring her attention. He remembered how she had grown
pale when, in a quiet corner of the embassy party, he had let on
to her what he knew about her father. . . . But all that was in the
past. What his own father had told him was so true: *Mars öffnet
das Tor der Venus. Der erste Kuss kommt mit Gewalt. Der zweite
mit Leidenschaft.* Mars opens the gate to Venus. You get your first
kiss by force. And the second comes from passion.

"You seem quiet tonight, my darling," he said.

"I'm just tired," the lovely girl replied. "It is a strenuous performance; you know that, Rudi."

"But that's not like you at all," he persisted. He stroked her
breasts, squeezed her nipples. She made an expression that at

first appeared to be a wince but which von Schüssler quickly recognized as a twinge of pleasure. He moved his other hand lower and began to stroke her. She did not seem to respond down there, but that was normal: this was a girl who had to be pursued, a fortress that had to be stormed. She was certainly not the most sexually responsive woman he had been with, but every woman was different. She just took a little longer to warm up.

She gave him a smoldering look of what he knew was passion, although from a certain angle one might almost mistake it for . . . banked rage. But no, it was passion. She was a fiery little filly.

He reached over to the box of German chocolates—Russian chocolate was unspeakable, after all—and placed one against her lips. She shook her head. He shrugged, stuffed it into his mouth. "I think I'd go mad without you," he said. "Mad with *boredom*. There's *nothing* worse than boredom, don't you agree?"

But Lana did not meet his gaze. She still seemed distant. There was a strange smile on her face. He never knew what she was thinking, but that was all right. He liked a woman of depth.

She would be an excellent prize to take back with him to Berlin when all this unpleasantness was over.

Washington

The President always insisted on mixing the drinks for himself and his visitors. This evening it was some sort of blend of grapefruit juice, gin, and rum and it was appalling, but Alfred Corcoran pretended to enjoy it.

They sat in the President's favorite room in all of the White House, the second-floor study, a comfortable, homey place crowded with tall mahogany bookcases, leather sofas, ship models, and nautical paintings. This was the place where he read, sorted his stamp collection, played poker, and saw his most important visitors. Roosevelt sat in his high-backed red leather chair. Corcoran always marveled, whenever he saw his old friend, at how powerfully built Franklin was, the wrestler's arms and shoulders so broad that, if one didn't see the polio-withered legs, one would get the impression that the President was a much larger man than in fact he was.

The President took a sip of his drink and made a face. "Why the hell didn't you tell me how awful this is?"

"I'm really not much of a rum drinker," Corcoran said politely.

"You've always held your cards close to your vest, Corky, old man. Now, what happened in Paris?"

"Some very good agents were burned."

"Killed, you mean. Gestapo?"

"We believe it was the work of the Nazi *Sicherheitsdienst.* Obviously there was a leak."

"The fellow who escaped—does he know *why* you've sent him to Moscow?"

"Of course not. The truth must be decanted in measured quantities. And like a fine claret, it must never be served before its time."

"You think he'd refuse to go if he knew?"

"Not exactly. I think he wouldn't do what needs to be done, certainly not as effectively."

"But you're sure he can pull it off?"

Corcoran hesitated. "Am I sure? No, Mr. President. I'm not sure."

Roosevelt turned to look directly at Corcoran. His eyes were a piercing blue. "Are you saying he's not the best man for the job?"

"He's the *only* man for the job."

"An awful lot rides on this one agent. Far *too* much, I'd say." The President put his mother-of-pearl cigarette holder to his lips and struck a match. "Great Britain is in a perilous state. I don't know how much longer they can survive this Nazi bombing. The House of Commons is all but destroyed; Coventry and Birmingham have been leveled. They've been able to beat back the *Luftwaffe,* but who knows how much longer they can keep it up.

Meanwhile, the Brits are on the verge of bankruptcy—they don't have the money to pay us for all the munitions they've ordered, which they need desperately to stave off the Nazis. Congress will never go along with loaning them the money. And we've got all these rabid America Firsters accusing me of trying to drag us into the conflict." He sucked at the cigarette holder; the end of his cigarette flared like a dying sun.

"We're in no shape to go to war," Corcoran put in.

Roosevelt nodded gravely. "Lord knows that's the truth. We haven't begun to rearm. But the plain fact is, without our help, Great Britain is finished in a matter of months. And if Hitler defeats Britain, we'll all be living at gunpoint. And there's something else." The President lifted a folder from the end table next to him and held it out.

Corcoran got up and took it from him, opening it as he sat back down. He nodded as he scanned it.

"Directive Number Sixteen," the President said. "Signed by Hitler. The Nazis call it Operation Sea Lion—their top-secret plans for the invasion of Britain by two hundred fifty thousand German soldiers. Paratroop assaults, then an amphibious landing, the infantry, the panzers . . . I don't think Britain can survive it. If the Germans go through with it, all of Europe will become the Third Reich. We *cannot* allow this to happen. Do you understand, Corky, that if your young agent doesn't pull this thing off, we're all doomed? I ask you again, does your man have what it takes?"

Corcoran narrowed his eyes as he inhaled a lungful of Chesterfield smoke. "It's a huge risk, I admit," he said, his voice muzzy, "but not as risky as doing nothing. Whenever mortals undertake to shift the course of history, things can go horribly wrong."

"Corky . . . if a *single* word of this plan gets out, it could backfire so badly that it'll be worse than our never having attempted it at all."

Corcoran snubbed out his cigarette butt and gave a hacking

cough. "The time will likely come when the young man no longer serves a purpose. Sometimes when your vessel starts taking on water, you must throw the ballast overboard."

"You always were a bloody-minded soul."

"I take it you mean that in the best sense."

The President gave a chilly smile.

Corcoran shrugged. "In fact, I assume he *won't* survive the expedition. If he does, and he has to be sacrificed, so be it."

"Christ, Corky, is that blood or ice water in those veins of yours?"

"At my age, Mr. President, who can tell the difference?"

CHAPTER THIRTEEN

Metcalfe slept badly, tossing and turning throughout the night. It wasn't merely that the bed was uncomfortable, the sheets stiff and coarse, or the hotel room unfamiliar, though all of that contributed. It was the anxiety that flooded his body, made his thoughts race, his heart beat too fast. The anxiety caused by seeing Lana again, realizing how deeply he had loved the woman, though he had pretended for years that she meant nothing more to him than any of the dozens of other women he had had in the years since then. The anxiety caused by her reaction last night—a certain flirtatiousness, a coyness, the scorn and contempt. Did she hate him now? So it seemed, yet she also seemed to be attracted to him still, as he was to her. How much was he imagining, pretending? Metcalfe prided himself on being clear-eyed, never delusional, but when it came to Svetlana Mikhailovna Baranova, he lost the gift of objectivity. He saw her through a distorted lens.

What he was sure of, however, was that she had changed in ways that at once excited him and alarmed him. She was no longer a vulnerable, flighty young girl; she had developed into a woman, self-assured and poised, a diva who seemed fully aware of the effect she had on others, who understood the power of her beauty and her celebrity. She was more beautiful than ever, and she was in some ways harder. The softness, the vulnerability—he thought of the hollow at the base of her neck, that soft porcelain flesh he loved to kiss—was gone. She had developed a toughness, a hard surface. It protected her, no doubt, but it also made her more remote, more unattainable. Where had this hardness come from? From the nightmare of living in Stalin's Russia? Simply from growing up?

And he wondered: How much of this seeming hardness was an act? For Svetlana was not just an extraordinary dancer but also an accomplished actress. Was that shell something she put on and took off?

Then there was the question of her German lover, this von Schüssler. He was a high-ranking official in the Nazi Foreign Ministry. How could she fall in love with such a person? She and Metcalfe had never talked politics, and the last time they had been together the Nazis had only recently come to power in Germany. So he had no idea how she felt about the Nazis, but her father was a Hero of the Soviet Revolution and the Nazis were avowed enemies of the Communists. Did her father, that great Russian patriot, know of this strange relationship of hers?

The mission that Corky had charged him with—to get to von Schüssler through Lana, assess the German's allegiances, and see if he could be turned—now seemed impossible. She would never cooperate with Metcalfe, especially if she figured out what he was trying to do. She would not allow herself to be used.

Yet he could not give up now. Far too much was riding on it.

A loud knock on the door jolted him fully awake. *"Da?"* he called out. The knock came again—two, two, and one—a tattoo that he recognized as Roger Martin's prearranged signal.

"Dobroye utro," a gruff voice said in a bad Russian accent: Good morning. It was indeed Roger.

As soon as Metcalfe opened the door, Roger pushed his way in. He was dressed oddly, in a tattered navy-blue *telogreika*, which was a padded and quilted peasant jacket, felt boots, a fur cap. Had Metcalfe not known it was Roger Martin he would easily have mistaken him for a Russian peasant or laborer.

"Jesus, Scoop, you smell awful," Metcalfe said.

"How easy d'you think it is to buy new clothes around here? I bought 'em off some guy on the street who seemed more than happy to make a deal."

"Well, you look authentic, I'll say that. Straight off the *kolkhoz*." Metcalfe laughed.

Roger pointed to his felt boots. "These *valenki* are bloody warm. No wonder the Russian army defeated Napoleon. The frogs got nothing on this. Now, why the hell didn't you tell me to bring toilet paper?" He was carrying a heavy briefcase, which he set down. It contained the radio transmitter, Metcalfe knew; Roger had kept it with him since they'd checked into the Metropole. It could not be left in the hotel room, of course, and Metcalfe certainly could not bring it with him to his meetings at the Ministry of Trade, nor to the Bolshoi.

"As long as you're dressing like a Muscovite, you might as well go all the way," Metcalfe said. "Use strips of *Pravda* or *Izvestiya*."

Roger grimaced. "Now I get why the Russians look so downtrodden. Plus, it took ten minutes for my shaving water to drain—you try the sink yet? Totally stopped up."

"Hey, just having your own bathroom here's a rare privilege, Scoop."

"Some privilege. How was last night?"

Metcalfe gave Roger a warning look, circled his index finger toward the ceiling to indicate the likelihood that the room had concealed listening devices. Roger rolled his eyes, walked over to a table lamp, and began speaking into it. "There's this really *amazing* invention the capitalists have come up with called *toilet paper,* and I really hope the Russians don't *steal* the technology from us."

Metcalfe recognized what Roger was doing: all his banter, his joking, served as a form of bluster to conceal his underlying fear. The Briton was one of the bravest men Metcalfe knew and accustomed to working undercover, but here in Moscow everything was different. Foreigners were scarce and were watched carefully, and blending in with the native populace was much more difficult than it was in France. Given his heritage, Roger easily passed as a Frenchman; here he couldn't help but stick out. If being an agent in France was hazardous, doing so in Russia was downright treacherous.

Metcalfe dressed quickly, and the two of them went down to the lobby to talk. It was early in the morning, and the lobby was empty except for a few burly men badly dressed in boxy dark blue Russian suits sitting on couches and chairs pretending to read newspapers. Metcalfe and Roger sat in adjoining chairs at the far end of the lobby, far enough from the NKVD men that they couldn't be overheard.

Roger spoke quickly, in a low voice. "Your transmitter won't work indoors—we need an outdoor area, preferably isolated. Plus, it's got to be concealed as soon as possible. Tell me your itinerary today, and I'll figure out a plan."

"There's a party at the American embassy's dacha in the woods southwest of Moscow," Metcalfe said. "Corky told me about it— his man in Moscow will extend an invitation."

"Excellent. There we go. But how'm I supposed to get around this damned city without a car? There aren't any taxis, and my Russian isn't good enough to use the streetcars. I mean, for Christ's sake, I'm supposed to be your driver, and they won't even give us a car!"

"They'll give us a car," Metcalfe said.

"A car *and* driver. Which is an escort and a minder and a jailer, all in one."

"Have you tried the British embassy yet?"

Roger nodded. "No luck. Those guys don't have cars for themselves."

"I'll try the American embassy."

"Pull whatever strings you can. In the meantime, I managed to buy an ancient Harley-Davidson. My Russian's terrible, but it's amazing how far the British pound goes here. That plus some snowshoes and a compass. Then I've got to figure out how to get some aviation fuel. Awfully scarce these days, with all the rationing."

"Surely a strategic bribe ought to do the trick."

"Only once you figure out who to bribe," Roger said. "That'll require a trip out to the airport. I'll need your map of Moscow— I've got my work cut out for me. And you? Did you make contact last night?"

"Oh, I made contact," Metcalfe said ruefully. Then, quietly, he added: "But I've got my work cut out for me, too."

As soon as Roger had left, Metcalfe went to the hotel restaurant for breakfast, where he was seated at a small table with a rotund balding man with a gin blossom over his nose and cheeks. The man, who was dressed in a tweed suit of a garish plaid pattern, shook Metcalfe's hand. "Ted Bishop," he said in English, obviously recognizing Metcalfe immediately as a Westerner. "Moscow correspondent for the *Manchester Guardian*." Bishop had a cockney accent.

Metcalfe introduced himself by his true name. He noticed that there were plenty of empty tables in the dimly lit restaurant, but this was the way Soviet hotels did things. They always seated their foreign guests together, especially those who spoke the same language. Presumably, herding them together made them easier to monitor.

"You a journo, too?" Bishop asked.

Metcalfe shook his head. "I'm here on business."

Bishop nodded slowly as he stirred a lump of sugar into a glass of hot tea. His expression changed somewhat as something occurred to him. "Metcalfe Industries," he said. "Any relation?"

Metcalfe was impressed. His was no household name. "One and the same."

Bishop's eyebrows shot up.

"But do me a favor," Metcalfe said. "I'd really like to keep my visit quiet, so if you don't mind keeping my name out of your dispatches—"

"Of course." Bishop's eyes lit up with the pleasure of having a secret to keep. Metcalfe realized that though he'd have to be careful around a reporter, the man could be a useful contact here, a good man to cultivate.

"Now, I hope you're not too hungry," Bishop said.

"Starved. Why?"

"Notice the sugar in my tea won't dissolve. I've been waiting here so long my tea's got cold. That's the way it is every morning. The service is so slow you think they're waiting for the eggs to hatch. Then when it comes, it's a couple of slices of black bread, butter, and one greasy egg. And don't try to ask for it the way you like it. They give it to you the way *they* like, which is whatever the hell way Olga back in the kitchen feels like making 'em that day."

"At this point I'd settle for sawdust."

"And you'll get it, too," Bishop said with a chortle. His entire belly shook, and his double chin wobbled. "Don't eat anything mashed, I warn you. They like to put sawdust in it. I'm telling you, what the Bolshies have done to bangers and mash, blimey, you wouldn't give it to a starving termite." He lowered his voice. "And speaking of bugs, you've always got to assume they're listening, everywhere you go. Got little bleedin' microphones anywhere they can stuff 'em. I swear they've stuffed one up the desk clerk's arse. Only thing that would explain the expression on the clerk's face."

Metcalfe laughed appreciatively.

"The Russian diet—it's the best diet in the world, in'nt?" Bishop continued. "I must've lost a hundred pounds since I got here."

"How long have you been here?"

"Four years, seven months, and thirteen days." He looked at his watch. "Oh, and sixteen hours. But who's counting?"

"You must know Moscow pretty well by now."

He looked askance at Metcalfe. "More than I'd like to, I'm afraid. What would you like to know?"

"Oh, nothing," Metcalfe said airily. "Nothing in particular." There would be a time for questions, but not yet. *Go slowly with this fellow,* he thought. *He's a reporter, after all, trained to look for the real story, to dig, to penetrate others' lies.* Still, he felt a genuine warmth toward the hardworking English journalist. He knew the type: salt of the earth, totally unflappable, frightened of nothing except boredom. He'd surely know all the angles.

"You know about changing money, right? Do it at your embassy—you'll get a much better rate than what they give you here at the hotel."

Metcalfe nodded; he had already changed some money here.

"If it's restaurant recommendations you're looking for, I may be able to help you out there, but it's a short and sad list. Looking for real American-style apple pie? Your only hope is the Café National. Aragvi, on Gorky Street across from Central Telegraph, serves decent shashlik. Good Georgian cognac, too. The Praga, on Arbat Square—well, the food's lousy, but they have a nice gypsy band, and there's dancing. Used to have a good Czech jazz ensemble here, but they got kicked out in '37 for allegedly being spies. Real reason, I'm sure, was that they made the Russian jazz boys look so bad. Speaking of spies, Metcalfe, I don't know if you've ever been here before, but you'd better watch yourself."

"How so?" Metcalfe asked blandly, masking the surge of tension he suddenly felt.

"Well, have a look around. You've noticed the YMCA boys, right?" Bishop motioned with his ample chin at the lobby.

"YMCA?"

"What we call the NKVD chaps. Bolshie bulls. Bad actors. They're very interested in wherever you go, so be careful who you meet with, 'cause they'll be watching."

"If so, they're going to be awfully bored. Mostly I've got meetings at the Ministry of Foreign Trade. That should put them fast asleep."

"Oh, I have no doubt you're on the level, but that's not enough these days. Often as not, the Reds are looking to frame you capitalists if negotiations don't go well. Ever hear about that British engineering firm Metro-Vickers?"

Metcalfe had. The Metropolitan-Vickers Electrical Company Ltd. had supplied the Soviet Union with heavy electrical machinery. A year before he came to Moscow for the first time, there had been a major diplomatic incident when two of their employees had been arrested on charges of industrial sabotage. "Those two engineers were tried in a Moscow court and sentenced to two years in prison," Metcalfe recalled, "after a couple of turbines they'd installed had malfunctioned. But weren't they released after the whole thing turned into a major diplomatic kerfuffle?"

"Indeed," said Bishop. "But the reason the Bolshies dared to arrest 'em in the first place was that the fellers had so little contact with the British embassy that the Kremlin figured they were safe targets—determined that the British government were prepared to disown them. You have close ties with the American embassy?"

"Not particularly," Metcalfe replied. He had exactly one contact there, an attaché named Hilliard whom Corky had suggested he be in touch with. But the attaché would be careful, circumspect about his contacts with Metcalfe. If anything happened to Metcalfe—if the Soviets caught him in any compromising position—the embassy would disavow any connection. Corky had pointedly warned Metcalfe about this.

"Well, I suggest you make friends there as soon as you can," the Brit advised. "You see what I told you about the service here?" He took a gulp of his tea. "You may need an ally. You never want to be in Moscow without an ally."

"Or what?"

"They'll sense weakness, and they'll strike. If you have some sort of major institutional affiliation, be it a newspaper or a government, you've at least got some kind of protection. But without it, you're always vulnerable. If they think you're trouble, they won't hesitate to grab you. Just a word to the wise, Metcalfe."

———

It was a bitterly cold day, so cold that Metcalfe's face burned. This was, he had overheard some Muscovites commenting, already the coldest winter in years. He stopped into a Torgsin store on Gorky Street, which sold scarce goods, unavailable to any Russians, for *valuta,* hard currency. There he bought a *shapka,* a Russian fur hat—not for disguise, but for needed warmth. There was a reason that Russians wore these hats: nothing could keep one's head as warm, protect one's ears from the fierce Russian winter. He remembered how bitterly cold it could get in Moscow, so cold that if you left a window in your flat open just a crack, the ink in your inkwell would freeze. When he was last here and there were no refrigerators, even for the most privileged foreign guests, he and his brother would be forced to hang perishables outside the transom windows in string bags; inevitably, the milk, the eggs, would freeze solid.

He was being followed, he saw at once. At least two of the burly NKVD agents he had seen earlier sitting around the lobby of the Metropole were tailing him with a clumsiness, a lack of subtlety, that bespoke either poor training or a deliberate intent to let Metcalfe know he was being followed. Metcalfe thought it was the latter. He was being warned. If he hadn't been so familiar with the ways of the Russian secret police, he might have been more concerned, might have wondered whether they suspected that he was not here simply on business. But Metcalfe knew how the secret police here worked, or at least so he told himself. They kept a close watch on all foreigners. They were like guard dogs, growling at any potential interlopers, warning them not to get too close. These thugs—for they really were little more than thugs, knee breakers—were assigned in teams to follow all foreigners, to intimidate them, to make sure that all foreign visitors to Moscow felt the hot breath of the Soviet police state on their necks.

Yet Metcalfe found the presence of these NKVD goons perversely reassuring. It was evidence that the NKVD was not unduly suspicious of him, strangely enough. It meant that the secret police considered him a run-of-the-mill foreigner and nothing more. Had they suspected that he was up to anything else—had they known the *real* reason he was here—the NKVD would not put a team of mediocrities on his tail. They would have assigned far more skilled agents. No, these thugs were ordinary Russian junkyard dogs, there to make sure he stayed on the straight and narrow. He found them reassuring.

At the same time, however, their existence was a problem for Metcalfe. There were times when he not only didn't mind being followed; he actually welcomed it—his visits to the Ministry of Foreign Trade, for instance. He *wanted* the NKVD to see him going about his cover business. But this morning, he had to lose them without appearing to do so. If he shook an NKVD tail too skillfully, he would raise all kinds of alarms in the Lubyanka, the much-feared headquarters of the NKVD. They would know that he was not only up to something suspicious but was also more than a mere American businessman. They would know that he was an intelligence agent.

This morning he would be a sightseer, nothing more than that. A tourist out to see the sights of the Russian capital city. He would have to act in a way consistent with that, which meant an assortment of behaviors: no obvious evasive tactics, no sudden moves, yet at the same time his movements must not be too smoothly coordinated. He could not appear to be too purposeful, as if he were going somewhere, meeting someone, as if he had an appointment. No, he would have to behave with a certain plausible randomness, stopping to look at things that struck his fancy, just as a tourist might.

And yet at the same time, somehow, he would have to lose the followers.

There was an old lady selling some mysterious soft drink from a cart. A sign identified the drink as *limonad,* which was Russian for any kind of carbonated drink. A long queue of Russians, wearing fur hats with the flaps down so that they stuck out like donkey ears, waited with bovine patience to pay a few kopeks to drink her blend of carbonated water and red syrup from one communal glass. Metcalfe stopped as if curious, his eyes scanning the line, at the same time confirming the positions of his followers. One was a few hundred feet behind him, walking with a leaden pace. The other was across the street, pretending to use a phone booth. They were in place.

They were watching, keeping their distance and therefore letting him *know* they were watching. To be any closer would be less than plausible; to be farther away would be impractical.

Metcalfe continued walking up the broad avenue with the leisurely pace and demeanor of a tourist taking in the vagaries of a strange city. The wind blew sharply, at times howling, carrying with it stray flakes of snow, crystals of ice. His boots—the polished leather boots of a wealthy American, not felt *valenki*—crunched on the snowdrifts. A short time later he was accosted by a one-armed newspaper dealer, an old man selling copies of *Trud* and *Izvestiya* and *Pravda*. In his one hand he held several copies of a small red booklet, which he waved at Metcalfe. "Half a ruble for this songbook," the toothless old man called out desperately. "All of our greatest Soviet songs!" He sang in a high, cracking voice, " 'Stalin, our great father, our sun, our Soviet tractor.' "

Metcalfe smiled at the man, shook his head, and then stopped. An idea occurred to him. A tram was coming, a streetcar in the *Bukashka* line, also known as the "bol'shaya krugosvetka," which ran along the Garden Ring Road. He saw it approach slowly, in his peripheral vision. One follower was across the street, examining the window display of a store marked OBUVI, or Shoes; in reality, of course, he was watching Metcalfe in the reflection in the plate glass. The other was coming up the same side of the street as Metcalfe was on, keeping his careful distance. In a moment, this watcher would reach the stand where the old woman was selling her *limonad,* and if Metcalfe timed it right, the watcher's line of sight would be temporarily obscured. He approached the toothless old newspaper dealer as he pulled out his wallet. The watcher down the street could see that Metcalfe was stopping to buy a songbook, a transaction that would take thirty seconds at least, for the old man would also no doubt try to sell others of his wares. Thus, even during the few seconds when the watcher's view was blocked, the NKVD man could assure himself that he was missing nothing.

Metcalfe handed the old man a ruble.

"Ah, *vot, spasibo, baryn,*" the vendor said, thanking him in the polite, almost groveling language in which peasants of old addressed the gentry. The Russian set down his small pile of booklets on his newsstand so that he could take the ruble, but Metcalfe did not wait to receive the booklet. Instead, he vaulted past the man, toward the curb, leaping onto the moving streetcar. His right foot landed on the steel ledge of the three-car tram as his right hand grabbed a steel ring and he managed to pull himself onto the car. Fortunately, it was not moving so quickly that Metcalfe was hurt. A few shouts came from inside the car: a female voice, likely one of the *strelochnitsi,* the older women who helped turn the wheels that kept the trams on track.

He whipped his head around and confirmed that he had made it onto the tram unseen by the watchers. As the streetcar thundered down the road, Metcalfe saw that one of the watchers, the one who had been peering into the plate-glass shoe store window, had not moved from his place. He had noticed nothing. The other watcher was striding around the long *limonad* line; it was evident from the blank look on the man's face that he, too, did not perceive that anything was out of the ordinary. As far as this NKVD man knew, his American target was still haggling with the one-armed newspaper dealer. Only the newspaper dealer had observed him jumping onto the tram, but by the time either of the watchers asked him what had just happened, Metcalfe would be long gone.

Metcalfe shoved his way onto the crowded streetcar and made his way up to the conductor, depositing a handful of kopeks into the coin receptacle. All of the wooden seats were taken—many of them by men, he noticed, while women of all ages stood.

He had pulled it off—temporarily, to be sure, but he had evaded the watchers. But simply by doing so he had changed the rules. Once they realized that he had evaded them, they would regard him with heightened suspicion. They would step up their surveillance, treat him as hostile. Never again would he evade them quite so easily.

He got off the tram on Petrovka Street, one of the main avenues in the city center. It was lined with mansions where Russia's wealthiest merchants had once lived, palaces that had been converted into hotels, embassies, apartment buildings, and shops. He immediately recognized the four-story limestone building with the classical facade. It was where Lana lived with her aging father, Mikhail Ivanovich Baranov, a retired general now employed in the Commissariat of Defense. During his sojourn in Moscow six years ago, Metcalfe had visited her here several times; he could find her apartment by memory.

But he did not stop in front of the building. Instead, he walked past it, as if heading for the Hotel Aurora, halfway down the block. He passed several shops: a bakery; a store selling meat, although Metcalfe doubted there was much of anything for sale inside; and a women's clothing shop, whose plate-glass display windows allowed him to monitor foot traffic behind him. Some people had gotten off the tram when he did—several middle-aged women, a woman with two small children, an old man—and none of them raised alarms. He stopped, presumably to inspect the meager wares on display in the clothing shop's windows, while in fact examining the patterns of the other pedestrians. Reassured that he had not been followed here, he made an abrupt U-turn, crossed the street, pretended to examine a travel poster advertising the splendors of Sochi. The suddenness of his movement would flush out a follower, causing last-minute adjustments. But he saw none. Now he was certain he had not brought a tail to Lana's apartment building. He walked up a block, crossed back over, then circumnavigated her building.

At the Bolshoi, Lana was protected, as were all the ballerinas, in particular the prima ballerina. Here, however, she would be far easier to approach; that, at least, was Metcalfe's plan. He glanced up at the fourth floor, at the row of windows that he knew belonged to Svetlana's father's apartment, and saw a shadow.

Outlined against the sheer curtains in the window was a silhouette that he knew at once, and his breath caught.

A slender young woman stood by the window, one hand on her hip, the other gesticulating at an unseen interlocutor.

It was Lana; he was sure of it.

Even in outline she was extraordinary, achingly beautiful. Suddenly he could not bear to be out here on the freezing, windswept Moscow sidewalk when inside, a few hundred feet away, stood Lana. Last night she had dismissed him scornfully, cast him out with a combination of contempt and—he was sure of it—fear. She would be no less fearful about seeing him now.

But what did her fear stem from? Was it simply the phobia that all Russians had of foreigners, of being seen to consort with capitalist visitors? Or did her fear derive somehow from her latest entanglement, with von Schüssler? Had she been warned? Whatever the source of her fear, it was something Metcalfe had to acknowledge in speaking with her. He had to let her know he understood. He had to defuse her fear by addressing it head-on.

Standing several entryways down from Lana's, he took out a folded copy of *Izvestiya* and pretended to read it. For a few minutes he stood there, perusing the newspaper, waiting. Finally, when no one was in sight, he went to Lana's entrance. Once inside the building—there were no guards, since no high-ranking members of the government lived here—he raced up the stairs to the fourth floor.

The door to her apartment, like all the doors in this and other similar buildings throughout Moscow, was padded and covered with leather. The padding, Metcalfe knew, did more than keep out the cold; it prevented eavesdropping. Always there was a fear that someone might be listening.

He pushed the buzzer and waited. His heartbeat accelerated, a strange combination of apprehension and anticipation. After a minute or so he could hear a heavy tread approaching from inside. They were not Lana's footsteps; might they be her father's?

The door came open slowly and a face appeared: the ancient, weathered face of an old woman who peered at him suspiciously, her tiny eyes rheumy and all but buried beneath wrinkles. She wore a coarse woolen sweater with a delicate lace collar and over it a heavy linen apron.

"*Da? Shto vyi khotite?*" she demanded: What do you want?

Metcalfe immediately recognized not the face but the type. The old woman belonged to that age-old genus, the Russian *babushka*, a word that meant "grandmother" but in reality was applied to any elderly woman and carried with it a bevy of meanings. The *babushka* was the center of the extended Russian family, the stern but loving, hardworking matriarch in a society in which the men so often died prematurely, from war or alcohol. She was mother and grandmother, cook and housekeeper and gorgon all in one.

But this was not *Lana's* grandmother. More likely she was a cook/housekeeper, a rare privilege accorded certain members of the Soviet elite.

"Good morning, *babushka*." Metcalfe spoke gently in Russian. "I'm here to see Svetlana Mikhailovna."

"And you are ...?" the old lady inquired with a scowl.

"Please tell her it's ... Stiva."

The *babushka*'s permanent scowl deepened even further, and she squinted, her eyes all but disappearing beneath the folds of skin. Abruptly she shut the door. Metcalfe heard the heavy tread moving away into the interior of the apartment, the voice of the housekeeper high and muffled, fading away. Lana and her father had not had a housekeeper previously, Metcalfe reflected. A housekeeper or cook was an increasingly rare perquisite these days, he knew. Was this a privilege accorded Lana since becoming the Bolshoi's prima ballerina?

A minute later, the door opened again. "She's not here," the old woman said, her voice now peevish and abrupt.

"I *know* she's here," Metcalfe said.

"She is *not* here," the *babushka* snapped.

"Then when will she be back?" Metcalfe said, playing along with her.

"She will *never* be back. Not to you. Not ever. *Never* come here again!"

And she slammed the door.

Lana was more than frightened: she was terrified. Once again she had pushed him away, just as she had last night—but *why?* This was not the impetuous reaction of a lover who felt spurned, rejected. No, there was something more complex going on. It had to be something more than the widespread fear of contact with a foreigner. That would not explain why she had sent him away *now,* when her housekeeper could see that he was alone. Simple curiosity would have led Lana to admit him, to ask what he was after, why he was in Moscow, why he was so insistent on seeing her. He *knew* Lana. She had always been a woman of insatiable curiosity, endlessly asking about what life was like back in America or on his travels around the world. She was almost like a child that way, her questions never ceasing. No, given the opportunity to find out why Metcalfe was here, trying to see her, she would not have passed it up. He knew, too, that she was not one to hold a grudge long; anger was always a passing emotion with her, appearing quickly and just as quickly gone. It did not make sense that she continued to banish him, and he wondered why.

The scowling, wrinkled face of the housekeeper came into his mind. Why *was* there a housekeeper when neither Lana nor her father had had need of one in the past? It was a household of two, and Lana had always done the cooking for her widowed father.

Was the *babushka* truly a housekeeper? Or was she in fact some sort of *warden,* a watcher, a keeper assigned to Lana? Had the old woman been placed in Lana's household to oversee her, keep her a prisoner?

But that made little sense; Lana was simply not that important. She was a dancer, nothing more. There had to be a simple, plausible, rational explanation for the presence of this housekeeper: the *babushka* was nothing more than a perk accorded to such a prominent artist of national stature. That had to be it. And as for Lana's refusal to see him? Nineteen-forty was a different time from the early thirties. Soviet society had just emerged from the period of the great purges; fear and paranoia were widespread. Didn't it make sense that Lana's affair with Metcalfe was known to the authorities, that she had been warned not to make contact with him again? Maybe that was all it was.

He *hoped* that was all it was. Because another explanation had begun to suggest itself, an ominous theory Metcalfe didn't want to think about. Was it conceivable that the Soviet authorities *knew* why he was here, knew of his secret mission? If that was the case, it was perfectly logical that Lana had been warned not to see him. And if that was the case . . .

He couldn't think about that. If that were the case, he would have been arrested as soon as he arrived in Moscow. No, that could not be.

He descended the stairs, glancing out a narrow window as he passed, and then he saw something that made him freeze. A man was standing in the courtyard outside Lana's entrance, smoking a cigarette. For some reason he looked familiar. He had a typical Russian face: high cheekbones, chiseled features, a Siberian cast to the eyes; but it was a hard, pitiless face. His hair was a thick blond thatch, his eyes pale.

Where had he seen the man before?

It came to him suddenly: Metcalfe now remembered seeing the man standing in front of the Metropole, chatting with another man, so involved in their conversation that Metcalfe took the barest notice of either of them. As was his habit, Metcalfe had taken quick note of the men's faces and stored them away as he so often did. Neither man had taken any notice of Metcalfe, so he had not given them another thought.

But *it was the same man;* he was certain.

How? Metcalfe was certain he had not been followed here. He had evaded the NKVD thugs from the hotel lobby; that he was sure of. Immediately after getting off of the streetcar, he had taken note of the others who had gotten off with him, watched them go their separate ways. There had been no one lingering in the vicinity—he was absolutely convinced of it!

Yet he was equally sure that the blond man with the pitiless face was the same one he had barely noticed standing in front of the Metropole.

Which meant that the man had *not* followed Metcalfe here. And that was alarming indeed. He remembered the old slogan that Corky liked to repeat: *The only thing worse than being followed is not being followed—because they know where you're going.*

The blond man had come here from the Metropole separately, as if he *knew* that Metcalfe would be coming here. How? Metcalfe hadn't told Roger where he was going, so he could not have been overheard in the lobby.

Obviously the blond man, or his handlers, knew of Metcalfe's connection to Lana. Unlike the low-level goons from the hotel lobby, this agent had to be operating on instructions from a well-briefed control, someone who had access to Metcalfe's dossier. That in itself differentiated the man from the run-of-the-mill operatives; he was of another category, a more *dangerous* category.

Metcalfe stood in the stairwell, watching the blond man at an angle so that he could not be detected. His thoughts whirled. The agent had not seen him enter the building, he was sure; instead, he had been stationed as an observer, one who knew Metcalfe's face, knew how he was dressed: that was the point of the man's loitering in front of the hotel, so that he could catch a furtive glimpse of Metcalfe, establish visual confirmation.

He did not see me enter, Metcalfe realized. *He doesn't know I tried to visit Lana.*

And he *would* not, Metcalfe vowed. He was determined to protect Lana as best he could.

Descending the stairs to the ground floor, he continued on to the basement of the building. The smell of smoke grew stronger: this building was heated not with coal but with wood, as were most buildings in Moscow these days, given the coal shortage and the abundance of wood. A splintered heavy wooden door gave onto a dark dirt-floored cellar. Metcalfe let his eyes become accustomed to the dark, then made his way among the stacks of split wood, between the primitive furnace equipment. The floor became muddy and slimy in one area, where Metcalfe realized a black-market shower had been set up for the building's residents. Hot baths were forbidden by law these days, at least for most residents of Moscow; hot-water systems were often disconnected, making it impossible to bathe unless one heated water on the stove. Thus an illegal industry had emerged in the cellars of certain of the larger apartment buildings, where Muscovites paid exorbitant sums to gyrate beneath a trickle of warm water.

The wood had to be brought in some way, he realized. There had to be a service entrance, a *sluzhebnyi vkhod.* Looking around, he at last found what appeared to be a rudimentary delivery chute, a small set of concrete steps that led up to bulkhead doors. The doors were locked from inside, of course, by means of a hook and eye. He unlocked it quietly, then pushed up slowly on one of the hatches, peering out as he did so at an alley. Metcalfe looked around quickly, establishing that no one was within sight. The blond man was surely still at his observation post, waiting to see whether a foreigner either entered or departed the building. He would not leave his station and risk missing his target.

Metcalfe stepped out of the bulkhead, closed the doors behind him, and raced through the cobblestone-paved alley. This was something more than an alley, though, he realized quickly; it was a *pereulok*, a lane between major thoroughfares, used mostly for deliveries. A number of the shops he had passed while walking down Petrovka had service entrances back here. Usually such entrances would be locked, however, making it difficult to gain access. He ran past the rear entrances to the bread shop, the meat shop, the women's clothing shop, until he reached the back of the Hotel Aurora, where he slowed to a leisurely-seeming stroll.

Glancing quickly around to make sure he was not being followed, he mounted a set of wooden steps, past garbage cans, and pounded on the steel door with his fist. No response. He pounded again, then tried the knob and was surprised when it turned.

Inside, a dimly lit corridor that stank of cigarette smoke led to another, broader hallway. A pair of double doors swung open, revealing an immense institutional kitchen. A squat woman with brassy red hair was stirring something in a great cast-iron pot; a middle-aged man in a blue uniform was frying some mysterious kind of cutlets on a griddle. They looked up at him with curiosity, obviously trying to determine what a well-dressed foreigner was doing here, unsure how to respond.

"Oh, excuse me," Metcalfe said in English. "I seem to be lost."

"Nye ponimayu," the red-haired woman said with a shrug: I don't understand. Metcalfe gave an uncomprehending but polite smile, shrugged in reply, and crossed the kitchen, exiting into a deserted hotel restaurant. Now he continued into a shabby high-ceilinged lobby, paint peeling from its walls, threadbare Oriental rugs strewn across the floor. Stuffed reindeer heads stared from wooden plaques.

Two officious-looking young men stood at the reception desk. They nodded as he passed. Neither recognized him, but neither would say anything: he was a well-dressed foreigner emerging from the hotel's interior. Apparently he belonged. He nodded, brusquely but politely, in return, and strode toward the front doors. Here he could simply disappear into the stream of pass-ersby, having left the blond watcher back at Lana's apartment building.

Leaning against a streetcar shelter in front of the hotel was a familiar figure.

The blond man with the pale eyes. Eyes narrowed, he smoked, his body relaxed as if waiting for someone.

Metcalfe turned his face away, pretending to be looking in the other direction. *My God*, he thought, *the man is good.* Whoever he was, wherever he was from, he was of an entirely different caliber from the run-of-the-mill NKVD goons. He was a first-rate operative.

Why?

What did it mean that someone of his skill had been assigned? It could mean . . . it could mean any number of things. But one thing was becoming abundantly clear: for some reason Soviet intelligence considered Metcalfe someone to watch with partic-ular scrutiny. They would not devote such top-notch talent to someone they considered a mere foreign businessman.

A line of perspiration broke out on his forehead as the adren-aline coursed through his veins. *Has my cover been blown?* he wondered.

Do they know why I'm here?

The only solution was to burn the agent, render him useless. He was far too good, dangerously so. But once the agent had been identified by the target, he would no longer be of use in the field; he would have to be withdrawn.

Plastering a friendly, if clueless, look on his face, Metcalfe traipsed over to the wooden shelter, mentally rehearsing his line of patter: *Awfully sorry, but d'ya mind giving a steer? I seem to have gotten lost. . . .* The face-to-face encounter would ensure the blond agent's replacement.

Circling around the structure, Metcalfe stared in astonishment, his heart pounding. Christ, the watcher was good.

He had vanished.

CHAPTER FOURTEEN

The American embassy in Moscow was on Mokhovaya Street, next to the National Hotel, facing Manege Square and the Kremlin. The offices were bleak and run-down, but the security was tight. It was ironic, Metcalfe thought with a grim smile as he displayed his passport to gain admission: both the Russians and the Americans participated in defending and protecting the American embassy. Posted in front of the chancery were both U.S. Marines and agents of the NKVD. The marines were there to keep out the Russians; the NKVD was there to keep out the Russians as well—to make sure Russians didn't try to force their way in and attempt to defect.

The man he was here to see, Amos Hilliard, occupied a small, austere office devoid of personality. He was a third secretary and consul, a small bespectacled man with a balding head, pale skin, and hands so soft that it seemed a paper cut would be fatal to the man.

But the softness of the man's flesh belied an inner core of steel. Hilliard was plainspoken to the point of being blisteringly frank. Metcalfe understood quickly why it was that Corcoran, a man who trusted so few people, trusted Hilliard, the blunt-talking Iowa farm boy who'd spent his career in the Foreign Service. Amos Hilliard was a Russia expert who didn't believe there was any such thing as a Russia expert. "You know what a Russia expert is?" Hilliard had said with a snort a few minutes after Metcalfe had sat down in his office. "Someone who's lived in Russia twenty years—or two weeks. And I don't fit into either of those categories. Hell, there's no *experts* in these parts. Just varying degrees of ignorance."

Hilliard was more than one of the few State Department officials Corky trusted. He was secretly one of Corky's agents as well. It was highly unusual for Corcoran to permit one of his operatives to meet with another: this was a violation of his vaunted principle of compartmentation. "In this case, I have no choice," Corky had said to Metcalfe in Paris. "I have serious doubts about the trustworthiness of the other embassy staffers in Moscow. Hilliard is one of the very few you can trust. Inasmuch," he icily added, "as anyone can be trusted, which is a proposition very much to be debated."

"Even you?" Metcalfe had replied with an impish grin.

Corcoran, however, didn't treat Metcalfe's glib remark as a joke: "Isn't that invariably where we first go wrong—placing too much trust in ourselves?" In the old man's eyes was an indictment, a familiar reproach that hardly needed to be spoken: *Don't get too full of yourself, Stephen—you just might not be as good as you think you are.*

"Welcome to happy valley," Hilliard said, lighting a Camel. "Our . . . mutual friend must think highly of you."

Metcalfe shrugged.

"Obviously he trusts you implicitly."

"And you. It's certainly rare that two of his nodes are permitted to come in contact."

Hilliard shook his head as if clearing it, and he smiled. "Ask our *friend* how the weather is and before he answers he'll stop to ponder on whether you have a need to know."

"Obviously Moscow is a special exception."

"Correct. Simply by entering this building your name has become known to about a dozen of my fellow employees. Of course, you're a visiting American businessman, nothing more than that, but you're meeting with me, which may raise an eyebrow or two."

"How so?"

"Not in the way you may be thinking. I'm just a diplomat who does his job, keeps his head down, but I don't belong to any of

the several factions, those with their own agendas, so I'm automatically suspect. I should warn you—though I'm sure it's a
warning that's unnecessary to you, but indulge me—not to talk
to anyone else in this building. No one can be trusted. It's a rats'
nest here."

"Dual loyalties?"

"Dual?" Hilliard scoffed. "As in *two?* Start counting, my friend.
The Moscow embassy has come to resemble Ankara or Istanbul
in the nineteen-thirties, crawling with agents all with differing
agendas and loyalties. It looks like what you see when you lift
up a rotting log—dozens upon dozens of creatures you've never
seen before scuttling around frantically. For which I blame our
own government. The Roosevelt White House. Which itself is
run through with fault lines. They keep switching the way they
think about Russia, can't make up their minds, and so they've
been sending out wildly mixed messages to those of us in the
field."

"You're not one of those who consider Mr. Roosevelt some
kind of Red, are you?" Metcalfe said dubiously.

"Not now. But for years, since the day he took office, he looked
at Moscow through rose-colored glasses—there's no question
about it. One of the first items on his agenda was to do what no
other U.S. President had done since the Bolshies threw out the
czar—formally recognize the Soviet government. Which he did
right away. And his main adviser, his trusted counsel, Harry Hopkins, he's always bad-mouthing us so-called 'Russia experts' in
the Foreign Service for being too hard on good old Uncle Joe
Stalin. 'Why can't you fellows see the *good* side of these guys?'
he's always saying. I mean, for Christ's sake, look at the last
ambassador Roosevelt sent over here!"

Metcalfe nodded. The last ambassador was famous for fawning
over Stalin, defending Stalin's bloody purges. "What are you saying, that some of your colleagues here are a little soft on the
Russians, a little pink? Or that there may be out-and-out spies
for the *Kremlin* planted here?"

Hilliard looked uncomfortable. He ran a plump hand nervously over the babylike peach fuzz of his balding pate. "There's a difference between a spy and an agent of influence. I'm referring to men who believe in the double-column ledger. Who believe they can work for us while still doing favors for their friends in Red Square—passing along tips, making calls, even trying to work from within to shape American foreign policy in a manner more, shall we say, amenable to Moscow."

"Call them whatever you want," Metcalfe said, "but I call them traitors."

Hilliard shrugged wearily. "I wish it were that simple. Men like that tend to be guided by the actions of the men at the top. And if Harry Hopkins and FDR are seeking to build a strong Soviet–American relationship as a bulwark against the Nazis—which they *were* until Stalin shook hands with Hitler two months ago— then it makes a kind of weird sense for them to leak to their friends in the NKVD or the Kremlin, doesn't it? After all, they're just helping the cause. Freelancing. The most dangerous traitors are those that act out of love—they always think they're the *true* patriots." Hilliard gave him a piercing gaze.

What the hell is he trying to say? Metcalfe wondered. "You're describing an embassy of the United States government where you can't trust your *own colleagues?* Where you don't know who might be working for *Stalin?*"

"As I said, that's only one of the factions here. Only one of the elements. It's only recently that Roosevelt has started admitting that Uncle Joe Stalin maybe isn't a nice guy. He's starting to learn some hard facts about the Bolshies." He lowered his voice. "Look at the latest knucklehead he's sent over as ambassador. A fat-cat campaign contributor, a slick New York lawyer who doesn't know beans about Russia, hates it here even more than the rest of us do. Despises the Soviets, but without knowing anything about it. Nothing worse than fanaticism based solely on ignorance. And he's got his claque, the hate-Russia crowd, guys so frightened of the virus of Bolshevism that they'll do whatever the hell they can to sabotage our relations with the Kremlin. They're happy to help out Berlin any way they can. They see the Nazis as the only hope for stopping the spread of Communism around the world."

"You're seriously talking about people working for *Hitler?*"

"In the same double-entry way, yes. Or worse. Problem is, you just don't *know!* It's a goddamned vipers' nest here."

"Point taken."

"But that's not why you're here. If I read my coded communications accurately, you're looking for some concrete intelligence from me. You want to find out what we know about the Nazi–Soviet alliance—whether it's *real.* Or some kind of tactic on either side."

"That's part of what I'm after."

"And that's the great unanswerable. It's the riddle of the Sphinx. It's what we all want to know. Why *you* want to know, however, intrigues me."

"And we'll have to leave it there."

"Compartmentation," Hilliard said with a nod. "Segmentation. Well, let me tell you this. For over a year and a half, I've been sending telegrams to Washington warning them that Stalin was going to sign a nonaggression treaty with Hitler, and you know what I kept getting back? Complete and utter disbelief. Denial. 'Nope, it'll never happen,' the idiots kept replying. A Marxist government would never make a deal with their ideological enemy. Washington just didn't seem to understand the simple fact that Stalin's only concern is preserving the Soviet system. Ideology has nothing to do with it. It's self-preservation now."

"You *knew* they were going to sign a deal?"

"I had sources."

"In the Kremlin?"

Hilliard shook his head and smiled cryptically. "Everyone knew Berlin and Moscow were talking, but even the *Russians* didn't know they were actually going to come to an agreement. How do we know that? I'll tell you a story. When the German foreign minister, von Ribbentrop, came to Moscow to sign the deal with Stalin, the Russians didn't even have any Nazi flags to put up at the welcoming ceremony at the airport. Searched everywhere, couldn't find any. They'd spent the last six years attacking the Nazis; of course they wouldn't have any. Finally they turned some up at a *movie studio* in Moscow where they were being used in some anti-Nazi propaganda film—which of course got scrapped."

"But you knew," Metcalfe prodded. "You knew a deal was coming." *That means Amos Hilliard must have a source in the German embassy,* Metcalfe thought.

"The secret of what limited success I've had here in Moscow," the diplomat said, "is that I'm able to think like Stalin. Not a pleasant process, I'll admit. But he's a supremely pragmatic man. I've met him; I've had the opportunity to take the measure of the man. He's ruthless, but ruthlessly *practical.* I know how he thinks. He sees that France has fallen, that the Brits have turned tail and pulled out of the Continent. He sees that London has no allies in Europe—none! And Stalin knows he has no other cards to play. He knows you always make the deal with the strong man, not the weakling. Whatever it takes to keep German panzers from the Soviet borders."

"Even better if the Führer throws in half of Poland, the Baltics, and Bessarabia."

"Exactly. And Hitler gets to avoid a war on two fronts. Which would destroy him. It would be sheer insanity for him to attack Russia at the same time he's fighting the Brits. That would spread his army, his resources, so thin that he'd be guaranteed to lose. And Hitler, whatever you say of him, is not stupid. Which brings us back to the riddle of the Sphinx, the great unanswerable. Is this alliance between Hitler and Stalin for real? Well, let me answer it for you. Hell, yes, it's for real. It's as real as warfare. It's as real as self-interest."

Metcalfe nodded, his thoughts spinning. An idea had just occurred to him, something at the back of his mind, not yet wholly formed. . . . "But if this alliance is for real, we're all cooked," he said. "An armed alliance between the two great empires of the European continent, with immense armies and millions of soldiers? They can just divvy up the spoils, divide Europe and then the rest of the world among themselves, redraw the map, and there's nothing we can do about it!"

"Now I see why our mutual friend trusts you. You're a strategic thinker."

"Stalin conducted the negotiations with von Ribbentrop personally, didn't he?"

Hilliard nodded.

"He wouldn't have done that if he weren't genuinely committed to making it work."

"And when the treaty was concluded, Uncle Joe drank a toast to Hitler. Called him a *molodyetz.*"

"A good guy."

"You know Russian."

"Just a bit," Metcalfe lied. "Enough to get around."

"And now the Soviets are buying millions of marks' worth of turbines, gun borers, lathes, and antiaircraft guns from the Germans. This is a matter of record. You think Germany would sell this kind of stuff to Russia if they didn't consider them partners in the war effort? I don't think so. We're in a tough spot, Metcalfe. You think Washington wants to join this war? You think Roosevelt wants to take on both the Soviet Union *and* Nazi Germany?"

"Our only hope is if there's a falling-out among thieves."

"You're whistling in the dark, Metcalfe. You're dreaming. These dictators know how much more powerful they are as allies— how, together, they can split up the world between themselves. And I'm hearing things from my British friends here—that there are highly placed members of Churchill's government, though not Churchill himself, who are pressing for a separate peace with Germany against the Soviets."

Metcalfe chewed his lower lip a moment and pondered. "How well do you know the German embassy staff here?"

Hilliard looked suddenly guarded. "Fairly well. What do you want to know?"

"There's a second secretary in the German embassy named von Schüssler."

The diplomat nodded. "A mediocrity. Aristocrat, comes from a long line of upper-class Germans, which is the only reason he got a job in the German Foreign Ministry. A nonentity. What do you want to know about him?"

"Do you have any sense of his true politics?"

"Ah," Hilliard said, understanding. "There are indeed members of the German embassy here who, shall we say, hold no brief for the Nazis. Loyal German patriots who love Germany but hate the Nazis, who'll do what they can to undermine Hitler. Members of an underground, anti-Nazi resistance. But von Schüssler? Hardly. He knows what side his bread's buttered on. I don't think the man *has* any ideology. He'll do what he's told. As far as I can judge—and I've met the man quite a few times; it's a small town here—he has some sad, self-deluded notion of himself as the heir to the great Prussian nobility. He wants glory, no doubt about it. But he's not brave. He's a weak, vain man. Von Schüssler does what he's told. Just wants to retire to his castle with his ribbons. And write his memoirs, from what I hear. Christ."

"I see," Metcalfe said. He trusted Hilliard's judgment. *A weak, vain man.* Not a hero, not one who would do something brave or be a secret member of the anti-Nazi underground resistance. Not someone, it appeared, who could be turned. Of course, this was just one man's assessment, but if Hilliard was right, von Schüssler was not a good prospect for Corky's assignment. *He's not brave.* It was not the portrait of a potential double agent. Yet Corcoran had sent him here to size the German up as a potential asset. How could Corky have been so misguided? He had a source on the ground in Moscow, Amos Hilliard, who could have told him not to bother. Metcalfe was baffled.

"Look, I don't know what you're up to, but if you're interested in meeting the fellow face-to-face, I'm told he and his Russian ballerina girlfriend will be up at the dacha tonight."

His Russian ballerina girlfriend, Metcalfe thought. *Lana!*

"It's the center of the social whirl in the diplomatic enclave. Yep, it's just one goddamned continuous round of pleasure here in the happy valley."

"I'll be there," Metcalfe said, getting to his feet as Hilliard did the same. The diplomat came around from behind the desk, and Metcalfe extended his hand to shake. He was surprised when the small man instead gave him an embrace, a bear hug. Then at once he understood why when Amos Hilliard whispered in his ear: *"Watch your back, you hear me? Do yourself—and me—a favor, Metcalfe. Don't ever come here again."*

CHAPTER FIFTEEN

Metcalfe retrieved the key to his hotel room from the elderly woman, the *dezhurnaya,* who sat at a desk on his floor, watching all comings and goings. At the Metropole, as in every Soviet hotel, you picked up and dropped off your room key with the *dezhurnaya,* who was often as not an old woman, like this one, and who sat there at all times of day. At night she would doze, her head on a pillow on the desk. Presumably this archaic system was designed to make hotel guests feel safe, to make sure keys were only given out to the proper people, but the real reason, of course, was to keep a close watch on the guests for security reasons. Everything in Moscow was about security—the security of the state.

His first thought when he unlocked the door was that the maid had still not been by to clean and make up the room. Which was strange, since it was late afternoon.

As his eyes adjusted to the dimness, his second thought—and it was a realization that struck him like a blow to the solar plexus—was that his room had been searched. Theoretically this should have come as no surprise; the Russians usually searched the hotel rooms of their foreign visitors. But it had been done crudely, obviously, *ostentatiously.* He had been meant to see the evidence of the search.

His room had been completely torn apart. His suitcase, which he had locked before leaving this morning, was open, the lock cut, its contents, hastily packed in Paris, strewn around the bed and floor. It was complete chaos, *insanity!*

The few suits he had carefully hung up in the closet had not just been tossed to the floor; they had been slit open, as if to check for concealed pockets. Leather belts were slit open, as were the soles of his shoes. Even the lining of his suitcase had been slashed open, without finesse. No care had been taken to conceal the search, which had been conducted with an aggressiveness that shocked him.

He raced across the room, lifted the leather Hermés case, and examined the brass fittings. Concealed in some of the hardware was an array of parts for a miniaturized radio transmitter, which could be assembled when needed. Most of them still seemed to be in place, as far as he could tell, including the crystal, the most important component of the transmitter, without which it could not operate. Luckily, those parts had not been discovered; they had been too well hidden. Of course, they were only the miniature components of the transmitter; the rest of the device had been concealed by Roger somewhere in the pinewoods of Moscow near the American embassy dacha.

Then he remembered the compact, wearable Webley pistol, which he had carefully wired into the frame of the bed. He got down on his knees, looked under the bed, and saw that the netting, which he had untacked before concealing the pistol and then retacked, had been slashed.

The gun was gone, too.

He sat down on a chair, his heart pounding. Why had they tossed the room, conducted their search so openly, so *violently?* What did it *mean?* They—the Soviet security services, presumably, though he didn't know which ones—seemed to be warning him, letting him know in their unmistakable way that they were suspicious of him. They were drawing a line in the sand, telling him to go no further, to watch his step, to be always aware that they were watching.

But to make such a warning required clearance from the top, or near the top, of the security services. That was what was most unnerving. He was in a special category for some reason. Certain highly placed individuals had at least strong reason to suspect that he was not here merely as a businessman. Did that indicate a *leak?*

He had to contact Corky and let him know. Ordinarily he would not communicate with Corcoran unless and until he had a decision that needed to be made at Corky's level—field security demanded isolation of agent from command central as long as possible. But the nature of this assault—for that's what it was— was evidence of a possible security breach, and of that Corky had to be notified at once. Tonight Metcalfe would be going to the American dacha outside Moscow. As soon as he had an opportunity to leave unobserved, he would traipse out into the woods, following the prearranged markings that Roger had left for him. He would find the transmitter, install the crystal and other components that had been fitted into his suitcase hardware, and attempt to contact Corky.

But he had to get out to the dacha without being followed. That was the challenge. The run-of-the-mill goons from the hotel lobby would be following him, which was not a serious concern. But so would the pale-eyed blond man, whoever he was. No one except Amos Hilliard knew he was planning to attend the party tonight, and he would not tell anyone, except perhaps the ambassador. On the other hand, if it was known to the NKVD that Lana was planning to be there tonight—and surely it was known that he had met with Lana backstage at the Bolshoi—the followers could fairly assume that he might try to get invited. Nevertheless, he'd have to take precautions, at least create a semblance of doubt, thereby reducing the contingent of those tailing him.

He began to devise a plan while he washed his face and shaved. There was a knock at the door. Metcalfe dried his face with the rough hotel towel, went over to the door, and opened it.

Standing there was Ted Bishop, the British journalist, looking seedier than normal. His tie was askew, his shirttails untucked, his face flushed. He was clutching a bottle of Scotch.

"Bloody *dezhurnaya* wouldn't give me your bleedin' room number until I told her I was your brother! Now fancy that! Tall, handsome American like you and dumpy little British troll like me brothers!" His words were slurred; he was obviously tipsy. "She must think we're adopted, we—*blimey!*"

Bishop stared at the wreckage of Metcalfe's room. "You really can't get decent help anymore, can you? I mean, I know the maids at the Metropole are subpar, but good Christ!"

Metcalfe pulled him in, closed the door. "Do they search every foreigner's room these days?" he asked. "Even businessmen who've come to try to do a deal? No wonder there's no more Soviet–American trade."

"*They* did that?" Bishop cried, weaving unsteadily into the room and plopping into the only chair. "Gorblimey! I'll be buggered! They get your passport, too?"

"No," Metcalfe said. "That's locked up at the front desk."

"Where they're like as not studying how to forge it—they don't see all that many American passports anymore. What'd you do, shake off one of the cockroaches they put on your trail?"

Metcalfe nodded.

"They don't like that. Makes 'em as mad as hornets. They like to know where all their foreign guests are going. You have a glass here, a tumbler or two?" He waggled his Scotch bottle, which he gripped by the neck.

"Sure," Metcalfe said, grabbing a dusty glass from the bureau and handing it to the journalist.

"Got another?"

"I'm afraid that's all they've given me."

Bishop glugged out several fingers of Scotch. "You're lucky, then." He raised the glass to his lips and drank deeply. "This isn't even Scotch at all. It's goddamned vodka. They put some bleedin' caramel coloring in it, and they get some nice hard currency from us in return. Put the swill in old Johnnie Walker bottles. No wonder there's no seal on 'em."

"None for me, thanks," Metcalfe said unnecessarily. Bishop wasn't exactly offering some anyway.

"Goddamned brown vodka," Bishop said. "Callin' it Scotch. Is that a heartbreaker or what? It's a metaphor for the whole fecking regime, I'd say, if I went in for poofter things like metaphors. You going out somewhere tonight? You got plans?"

"Meeting some friends."

"*I* see." Bishop peered at him over the rim of his tumbler. "Businessmen friends, I assume."

"Something like that."

"Selling 'em the rope?"

"Excuse me?"

"The rope. Selling the Russians the rope. You never heard that?"

"Afraid not."

Bishop fixed him with a beady bloodshot eye. " 'S'what Lenin himself said. 'The capitalists will sell us the rope with which we'll hang them.' "

Careful, Metcalfe thought suddenly. The British correspondent was a drunk, but beneath the alcoholic haze was a deep and abiding hatred of the Soviet regime. He remembered Hilliard's words: ... *the hate-Russia crowd ... happy to help out Berlin any way they can. They see the Nazis as the only hope for stopping the spread of Communism around the world. ...* Was Ted Bishop one of the "hate-Russia crowd" as well? The journalist had been ensconced in Moscow for years, which meant he had good sources from whom he got information—but did the transaction go the other way? Did he in turn *provide* information to some of his favored contacts? Contacts not necessarily in the Soviet government but, instead, in the community of foreigners based here?

Everyone in Moscow seemed to have his own hidden agenda. It was a maze. What was it that the British prime minister had said last year? "I cannot forecast to you the action of Russia. It is a riddle wrapped in a mystery inside an enigma." Even more confounding, more mystifying, was what Hilliard had called the "rats' nest" of the Russia watchers here. *Watch your back,* Hilliard had warned.

Bishop was gesticulating wildly, embarked upon a rant. "You and your fellow businessmen may say you're just out to make a buck, but aren't you really helping to build the Soviet *war* machine? Shit, you got Douglas Aircraft building planes for the Russkies, and if you don't think those birds are going to be dropping bombs on London, I'm the Archbishop of Canterbury. You got United Engineering and Foundry building the Stupino Aluminum Mill outside of Moscow, the most advanced aluminum plant in the world, fancier than anything you Americans have back home, to *make* those bombers. You got General Electric selling turbines and turnkey power plants to the Commies; you're building steel mills and blast furnaces and bloomin' steel plants bigger than what you Yanks got in Gary, Indiana; you got . . . Ah, I don't even know what I'm talking about, Metcalfe. Listen to me go on."

As Bishop raved, Metcalfe began moving about the room gathering his clothes, plucking out those that hadn't been slashed apart. If he was going to make it to the American embassy party tonight, he'd have to move quickly, which meant getting the soused Brit out of here.

Bishop took another deep swig of his "brown vodka." He lowered his voice to a stage whisper. "I probably shouldn't be telling you this, Metcalfe, but I've got it from an *impeccable* source, a bird who works for a bloke at the 'clearinghouse'—"

"The what?" Metcalfe said, suddenly alert.

"That's what I call it—the 'clearinghouse' . . ." Bishop went on. "Anyway, they're tellin' me that Stalin's man Molotov is going to Berlin in the morning, he is. Leaving out of Byeloruskaya Station tomorrow morning with a huge sodding delegation."

"Is that right," Metcalfe said blandly. If this was true, this was a serious piece of news. If Stalin was sending his foreign minister to Germany, that meant he was trying to cement relations with the Nazis. . . .

"The Brits have been playing *footsie* with the Sovs," Bishop said, swaying from side to side, "and when they find out about this they're going to be mighty *pissed*. London's been saying the Russians may have signed some ruddy piece of *paper* with the Krauts, but they secretly *hate* 'em, right? Bollocks! Does this sound neutral to you, Met—"

"This on the level?"

Bishop raised a finger unsteadily, waving it at Metcalfe. He squinted, swaying from side to side, front to back. "Impeccable source, I told you." Suddenly Bishop lowered his finger, drew back, his mouth agape. "Don't scoop me, now."

"Not to worry, Ted."

"Worry and I were born twins, as whatsit said," Bishop roared sloppily. In a low voice, he added, "You're not a spy, are you? This *businessman* thing, it's your classic cover, you know."

Metcalfe froze. He composed a smile, prepared a witty demurral, but then the Brit let loose a loud, braying laugh, which became a choking, gagging sound, and all at once Bishop rushed to the bathroom, flinging the door shut behind him. Metcalfe could hear retching noises, groaning.

"You all right in there?" Metcalfe called, but Bishop's only reply was a groan, followed by more heaving. Metcalfe shook his head as he began to dress quickly. Whatever Ted Bishop's secret allegiances, he was a drunk, plain and simple, which made him less a danger than an annoyance. A few minutes later came the sound of the toilet flushing, then water running, and then Bishop emerged, grinning sheepishly.

"Uh, Metcalfe," he said, "would you mind terribly leaving me your toothpaste and your shaving cream when you clear out of Moscow? Really damned fecking hard to get that stuff here, y'know."

Roger had still not returned to the Metropole. The challenge was
to get to the embassy dacha undetected, which ruled out hiring
a car and driver through Intourist or certainly arranging for a
taxi, if one could be found. One of the front-desk clerks, the
more amiable-seeming of the two young men, smiled as Metcalfe
approached.

"I need a ride," Metcalfe said. He spoke in Russian, but haltingly and with a deliberately poor accent. If your Russian was
too fluent, he knew, alarms would be raised. Better to sound like
a hapless tourist.

"A . . . ride?"

"A car."

"I can call Intourist," the clerk said, reaching for his phone.

"No," Metcalfe said with a grin. "Nothing official. I—well, this
is just between us guys, okay? It's *personal*, you know?"

The clerk slowly raised his chin, eyes narrowing, the sides of
his mouth curling up slightly in a knowing smile. "Personal," he
repeated.

Metcalfe lowered his voice still further. "A situation involving
a woman, you understand? A beautiful girl. *Ochi chorniye*," he
added. Dark eyes: the old Russian folk song. "She's a tour guide
for Intourist, and I know she's nervous about her bosses finding
out . . . understand?"

The Russian understood. "You do not wish to involve anyone
from Intourist," he said with a nod. "But this is most difficult,
sir. Intourist is our official organization for all foreign tourists."
He shrugged helplessly. "Moscow is not like London or New
York, sir. Intourist is the only official transportation service for
foreigners."

"Absolutely," Metcalfe said. Very subtly he slid a thick pile of
ruble notes across the counter, poorly concealed beneath a piece
of Metropole stationery. "It is a difficult situation, clearly. Anything you can think of—any means of *unofficial* transport that
can take me to my *ochi chorniye*—will be most, er, handsomely
appreciated."

"Ah, yes, sir," said the clerk, suddenly enthusiastic. "Love must always find a way." He disappeared into the back office and returned a minute or so later. He tipped his head to make sure that the other clerk did not overhear from the far end of the desk, where he was busy speaking with a group of Bulgarians. "It is difficult to say for sure, sir, but there may be a possibility." He arched his eyebrows. "It may require some inconvenience on my part."

Metcalfe nodded. He shook the clerk's hand, concealing within the grip another, even thicker, wad of rubles. "Anything you can do."

"Ah, yes, sir. Perhaps I may be able to help. If you will come with me . . . ?"

The young Russian came out from behind his counter and walked quickly to the hotel's front doors, Metcalfe following close behind. A few minutes later, the clerk flagged down a large, dented van on whose sides were painted the word MOLOKO: milk. The clerk rushed over to the van's driver, speaking hurriedly. Then he returned to Metcalfe. "This gentleman tells me that gasoline is quite scarce, you know, and very costly."

Metcalfe nodded again and slipped the clerk another wad of rubles. The Russian scurried over to the driver of the van, handed over the cash, and then came back to Metcalfe. "This way, sir," he said, leading Metcalfe over to the back of the van and opening the doors. Metcalfe climbed in. Apart from several crates of milk bottles and, strangely, a box of foul-smelling onions, the interior of the van was empty. As soon as the van's doors were shut, plunging Metcalfe into near darkness, he heard a gruff voice coming from an opening between the cargo area and the driver's compartment. "Where you going?" the driver demanded.

Metcalfe gave quick directions. He avoided giving any specifics about the embassy dacha, instead describing its location. Glancing through the narrow slit, he saw the driver's tattered peasant jacket, the fur hat. "I don't want you touching my onions," the driver said, throwing the van into gear. The vehicle lurched ahead. "Ten rubles for the kilo, and I was lucky to get them. The wife's going to be pleased, I can tell you this." While the driver prattled on in a tedious singsong, Metcalfe's eyes became accustomed to the dark, and soon he noticed a small, dusty window at the back of the van that enabled him to watch for any followers.

There were none. The driver followed the roundabout route Metcalfe had directed, all the while chattering. From time to time Metcalfe would grunt to indicate that he was listening. When at last the van reached Nemchinovka and maneuvered off the Mozhaisk Chaussee down the narrow, tree-lined path that led to the embassy dacha, Metcalfe was certain that they had not been followed. He had made it here undetected. At last, a victory, even if it was a small one. He allowed himself to enjoy a brief, passing moment of pride, the satisfaction that came with accomplishment, with control.

"Right here's fine," Metcalfe said. With a grinding of gears, the van bucked to a halt. Metcalfe pulled open the doors and leaped out. It was dark; evening came early in Moscow at this time of year. The only light came from the dacha, a few hundred feet away. He could hear faint gramophone music, laughter, animated conversation. He wondered whether Lana and her German lover were already there.

Metcalfe pulled out another wad of rubles and strolled over to the front of the van to hand it to the driver. Suddenly, with a burst of speed and a cloud of dust, the van lurched ahead, its engine roaring. Why was the driver in such a hurry to get out of here that he wouldn't even wait for the promised final payment? Baffled, Metcalfe stared, and then, in the instant before the van barreled away down the dirt road, he caught a glimpse of the driver, for the first time, in the van's rearview mirror. Heart thudding, he saw the face of the man who had been disguised beneath the fur hat and peasant jacket. The man who had driven him from the hotel right to the embassy dacha.

It was the man he had been trying so hard to avoid. The blond man with the pale gray eyes.

CHAPTER SIXTEEN

The damage had been done, his attempt at arriving surreptitiously even more incriminating than any aboveboard arrival might have been. There would have been nothing unusual about a scion of Metcalfe Industries who happened to be visiting Moscow attending a party at the U.S. embassy. That was entirely to be expected. His evasive maneuvers, however, were bound to make it seem as if he was hiding something. This was not good. There would be consequences, no doubt, beyond the damage that had been wreaked upon his possessions back at the hotel. Consequences he would have to face later.

The dacha leased by the American embassy was a modest two-story country house built of logs, set on a ridge overlooking this valley in the woods southwest of Moscow. Here was the hub of social life in the foreign diplomatic community in Moscow, the place where ambassadors, counselors, attachés, and their staff gathered to exchange gossip, pass along information to one another, subtly attempt to pry information out of one another. Here, year-round, the most important envoys from America, Britain, Italy and Greece, Turkey and Serbia collected to socialize. More diplomatic business was transacted here, Metcalfe knew, than at any official function; the sheer intimacy and informality of the place was conducive to the sort of idle chatter that enabled trust to be established and thus substantive information to be exchanged. Here the Americans and the Germans often went riding together, on horses jointly owned by the Brits and the Americans. Sometimes the diplomats went for long walks in the woods. There was something pleasantly illicit about these social gatherings, over drinks on the porch or at dinner, over tennis on the courts out back or skating during the long winter months when the tennis courts were flooded. But beneath the facade of social chitchat, what was really being transacted was politics. That was the true hard currency expended at the American dacha. Everything here was politics.

Metcalfe entered the large main room, which was crowded with a motley assortment of people gathered before a roaring fire. Some of the faces he recognized quickly: the British ambassador, Sir Stafford Cripps; the Greek ambassador, left-leaning yet shrewd; Count von der Schulenberg, a tall, gray-haired, distinguished-looking gentleman who was, by virtue of his long tenure here, the dean of the diplomatic community. There were others who looked familiar. He noticed Amos Hilliard, who glanced at him, seeming to indicate recognition with a subtle widening of the eyes before turning away. "How High the Moon" was playing on a gramophone in the corner, an old windup Victrola with a large decorative horn.

He introduced himself to a woman standing near the entrance—the American ambassador's wife, it turned out.

"Gate crasher?" she said. "You? Don't be silly—you're Charlie Metcalfe's boy, aren't you? You know, your father and I . . ." And the woman began prattling about some social dalliance at the Union League Club in New York decades ago. It often went this way when Metcalfe met old-line Social Register types. The Metcalfe name was not only well known, but it carried a certain cachet even among those with cachet, for Metcalfe's father not only was wealthy but also had been a prominent figure on the social circuit, in a way that never interested his sons. Stephen had often reflected upon whether the vocation he had chosen—a spy for his country, requiring impersonation and acting and the assumption of a cover identity—had been his response to the falseness he'd perceived in his father's social whirl.

Now the Madame Ambassador, having removed his coat and glanced curiously at the torn lining—the result of the NKVD's tossing of his hotel room—clutched both of his hands and began giving him the rundown on the party's guests in a low, confiding burble. "That little man over there is the Italian ambassador, Augusto Rosso, with his American wife, Frances. We're *not* supposed to like him but we do, we *do,* he's really lots of fun, he's always taking us around Moscow in his open-topped roadster, he *loves* to play poker all night, and he has the most *lovely* black spaniel, Pumpkin. Ah, and let's see, over there, thick as thieves, are the ministers from Turkey, Greece, and Serbia; they're always gathering for coffee each morning in Stafford Cripps's sitting room; it's a veritable kaffeeklatsch they've got going. That Romanian fellow over there, I shouldn't tell you this, but he's being treated for the clap, and let me tell you, Moscow is *not* the place for VD treatments; he has to fly out to *Stockholm* every other week. Well, Stephen, I hope you're prepared to talk politics, that's *all* they ever talk about here, it's *boring,* I hope you can stand it—"

Metcalfe accepted a drink—a genuine Scotch—from her and excused himself, telling her he couldn't possibly take up any more of her time. The word of his arrival had spread quickly among the assembled. Even amid the important and celebrated here, Metcalfe was a celebrity, though of a minor stripe: he was at the least a curiosity, a visiting businessman here on some unstated family business, a presentable young single man from a prominent family. He was fresh blood, or perhaps fresh meat hurled into a cage of starving lions; everyone wanted to talk to him, to get the latest gossip from the States, to introduce him to their daughters or sisters.

Alcohol flowed, and the food was abundant: caviar, black bread and butter, smoked sturgeon. The crowd pulsed with a kind of nervous splendor, a hollow luxury. Here, in the midst of Russia's privation, the guests enjoyed the best of everything. Metcalfe was a stranger here, but he knew how to play the role. By the end of his adolescence he had been to enough shindigs that he was an expert at the witty repartee, the raised eyebrow, the indirect allusions to Groton and Exeter, Princeton and Yale, to parties in Grosse Pointe and Watch Hill and Bar Harbor.

All around him, just as the ambassador's wife had warned, was talk of politics. Everything concerned the war and whether the U.S. would enter it. Most of all the talk seemed to center on Germany. The tidbit that Ted Bishop had imparted earlier, about Russian Foreign Minister Molotov going to Berlin, was the hot gossip item of the party. What did it mean? the diplomats wondered. Was Russia about to join the war, with the Germans, against Britain? If so, that was a nightmare.

Metcalfe overheard snatches of conversation.

"But von Ribbentrop signed a ten-year nonaggression pact!" an American attaché was saying to a Brit.

"You seriously think the Germans intend to keep it? Get serious."

"They *have* to keep it. The Germans can't fight a war on two fronts!"

"Any treaty Hitler signs is nothing more than a piece of paper, and never forget it. Plus, the man despises Communism!"

"Hitler's no idiot. He'll never attack Russia. That would be insanity—it would be the end of him! His men have to know how strong Russia is, the Red Army—"

"The Red Army? But that's exactly the *point!* Stalin shot ninety percent of his top Red Army commanders in the last couple of years, and Hitler *knows* it!"

Metcalfe chatted briefly with the American ambassador, who told an anecdote, obviously well honed from countless retellings, about how a toilet at his residence at Spaso House had gone on the fritz and they couldn't get anyone to fix it, and so the ambassador had had his telephone operator call the Deputy Commissar of Foreign Affairs, Andrei Vyshinsky, to say that if the toilet wasn't fixed within one hour, the ambassador was going over to the Commissariat to use Vyshinsky's.

The ambassador introduced Metcalfe to Amos Hilliard. "You should come over to the embassy for lunch sometime," the ambassador said.

"Yeah," Hilliard muttered when the ambassador had moved on. "Canned tomato soup made with condensed milk, and canned pineapple for dessert. All the canned goods you can stand." He lowered his voice. "Now, let me see, most of the German contingent is here. They don't miss a party at the dacha. There's General Köstring, their military attaché, and there's Hans Heinrich Herwarth von Bittenfeld, whom everyone calls Johnny— a most useful source and no supporter of the Nazis, but that's *entre nous.* And there's . . ."

But Metcalfe had ceased paying attention. There, across the room, her arm linked in that of a large, pudgy man with a double chin, was Lana.

She was dressed in a gown of white and gold, and she looked a world apart from the ordinary Russian woman. She was smiling at something her lover was saying, but it seemed a sad, tentative smile. She held a champagne glass but did not seem to be drinking from it. Lana was surrounded by uniformed German officers as well as others, dressed in civilian clothes, who had a certain Germanic look about them—the rimless glasses, the Hitler mustaches, the beefy, well-fed arrogance. She was at the center of a knot of admirers, and she appeared to be bored to desperation.

". . . If you want to be that up-front about it," Hilliard was saying. "There's no reason why you two shouldn't just meet— after all, you're an American businessman, always looking to make a quick buck wherever you can; you don't care *who* you make it off. All right?"

"Excuse me," Metcalfe said, drifting away toward her like a moth attracted by a bright light. As he maneuvered through the crowd, she turned abruptly and caught his eye. His breath caught. In her gaze he saw what seemed to be sparks, a smoldering fury, though from a certain angle it might have been mistaken for interest—passion, even, the sort of look she used to give him six years ago. But he knew better, whatever he wanted to imagine. She was furious at him, her fury unabated.

As he worked his way through the crowd—*how many damned cocktail parties must I suffer through?* he asked himself—his mind ran though his store of ready-made quips. Would she think he was pursuing her? If so, there was nothing wrong with that, for women enjoyed being pursued. Yet she could not be sure; after all, this was just the sort of party at which someone like him would naturally be expected to appear. She would wonder whether this was purely a coincidence.

"Stephen!" It was the ambassador's wife again, intercepting him with a hand pressed flat against his chest. "I don't see you talking to any of the available young women here, and I think that's a frightful waste! They're starved for male company, you know. You really ought to do your patriotic duty."

"I'll give it the old college try," Metcalfe replied. He continued edging toward Lana until he was just about at her side.

"Oh, you needn't go *that* far," the ambassador's wife giggled. "I know all about you at Yale, you know. I hear the most *alarming* stories about you."

"My conscience is clear," Metcalfe said serenely. He was now so close to Lana he could smell her delicate perfume, feel the warmth radiating off her bare arms. His heart was beating so hard he wondered if it were audible.

Abruptly Lana turned around and met his eyes. "A clear conscience," she said levelly, "is usually a sign of a bad memory."

He grinned sheepishly and replied in Russian: "I take it you don't have a performance tonight."

She looked at him and smiled right back. Only someone who knew her well would know the smile was not genuine. "They seem to get along fine without me."

"I rather doubt it. May I meet your . . . friend?" Metcalfe's face was composed in an expression of innocence, but she knew better.

A flash of annoyance flickered in her eyes, but she covered it with a polite dip of her head. "Of course. Rudi, I'd like you to meet an acquaintance of mine."

Rudolf von Schüssler regarded Metcalfe incuriously. He extended a damp, pudgy hand and shook limply. He was a tall, rotund man with beady, nervous eyes and a goatee that sat astride a double chin like an animal pelt.

"It's a pleasure to make your acquaintance," Metcalfe said in English. "I'm particularly honored to meet a man with such impeccable taste in women."

Svetlana blushed suddenly. Von Schüssler looked bewildered, as if unsure how to reply.

"I'm told you're a member of what's known as the finest diplomatic mission in all of Moscow," Metcalfe continued.

"And you are here because . . . ?" von Schüssler inquired. His voice was high and soft, almost feminine.

Did he mean in Moscow or at the party? Metcalfe decided he meant Moscow. "I travel a good deal for my work." He turned slightly, forcing von Schüssler to do the same, which took him out of the circle of Germans with whom he had been conversing. The others resumed talking, enabling Metcalfe, Lana, and von Schüssler to speak privately.

"Which is?"

"My family's firm is Metcalfe Industries. Perhaps you've heard of it."

"I am not well versed in American corporations."

"Really? But surely you know that some of our greatest American corporations have helped build up your regime. Why, the Ford Motor Company built troop transport vehicles for the *Wehrmacht*, of course. The trucks that enabled your soldiers to roll through France and Poland were produced by General Motors—trucks that are the backbone of the German army transportation system." He paused, watching the German's expression closely. But von Schüssler only looked bored. "And of course your Führer gave Henry Ford the highest civilian honor awarded by the Nazis—the Grand Cross of the German Eagle—as you may remember." He shrugged. "I'm told Hitler keeps a large portrait of Mr. Ford next to his desk."

"Well, I believe it was an American president who said, 'The business of America is business,' *ja?*" von Schüssler said, reaching for a sevruga-trimmed canapé. For an instant Metcalfe thought the German was winking at him, but then he realized it was merely a twitch.

"Some of us in American business," Metcalfe said carefully, "believe that international trade blazes the path for politics. It's always nice when we can make money while helping to . . . strengthen those historical forces that we cannot *openly* support, if you understand me."

Metcalfe was dangling the bait, but would the German bite? Surely von Schüssler had to understand what Metcalfe was hinting at—that here was another American industrialist who secretly supported the Nazis. If he took the bait, von Schüssler would be revealing something of his own private inclination. But if he was a secret opponent of the Nazi regime, there would be subtle indications, signs in his manner, his expression, to which Metcalfe must remain alert.

"I'm sure that money, like love, will always find a way," von Schüssler said blandly.

"Not all of my colleagues think as I do," Metcalfe said carefully. "There are some businessmen who do not wish the Nazis well. They consider you barbarians."

Von Schüssler seemed to bristle. "You should tell your fellow industrialists that *we* are not the barbarians. The German people—the *real* German people—have always loved beauty and strength, both. We are interested only in restoring civilization and order. A Europe unified under the Führer will be a place of peace, law, and order. And order is good business, no?"

Metcalfe scrutinized the man's expression closely. Was there a flicker of skepticism, a moment of doubt, a hint of irony—of any distance between the words spoken and the man speaking them?

There was not. Von Schüssler's face was composed, impassive; the sentiments he expressed were, to him, nothing more than commonplaces. He might have been a schoolteacher explaining the difference between reptiles and mammals to a particularly slow student. A small man with mousy brown hair and thick-rimmed glasses pulled von Schüssler aside and began speaking to him in rapid-fire German.

At last Metcalfe and Lana were alone, and finally she hissed at him, "Don't you *ever* visit me at home again, do you hear me? *Never!*"

"God, Lana, I'm sorry," Metcalfe said, stricken. "I didn't re-alize—"

"No, you did not realize." She seemed to relent a bit, her outburst subsiding. "There are a great many things you don't realize."

"I'm beginning to see that." *Many things,* he thought. For one, he hadn't realized how much he still loved her. "We've got un-finished business, you and I."

"Business, yes," she said with a sad shake of the head. "Every-thing to you is business. I hear the way you talk to Rudi, the deals you want to make with *those people.* Anything for the al-mighty dollar."

"Perhaps there are some things *you* don't realize," he coun-tered softly.

"You are a businessman. A man of business. You may try to rebel against what you have been given, what you have inherited, but it is no use. The stain is always with you."

"Stain?"

"Of capitalism. Of making money from the blood of the workers."

"*I* see," Metcalfe said. She did not sound like the carefree, apolitical Lana of old; she sounded now like some Komsomol instructor, as if she had somehow absorbed all the Communist Party propaganda that she used to mock. "If enterprise is a stain, then it's a stain Russia has . . . *purged* . . . clean in recent years."

"It is as our great leader says," she intoned solemnly. "You cannot make an omelet without burning down the chicken farm. As the slogan goes, Communism equals Soviet power plus electrocution of the whole country."

What was she trying to say? Was she deliberately misspeaking? There was not a trace of irony on her face.

"I don't think that's quite how Stalin put it. I thought he defended his bloody purges by saying you can't make an omelet without breaking eggs."

She flushed. "Stalin knew long before the Russian people knew that there would always be enemies of what we are trying to create."

"Oh? And what are 'you' trying to create?"

"We are building a new socialist state, Stephen. Everything will be collectivized. And not just collective farms. Everything. Factories are being collectivized. Families are being collectivized. Soon poetry will be collectivized, too! Can you imagine a society that has succeeded in doing that?"

She was talking nonsense, parroting empty slogans. But it was too much, too ridiculous, as if she was almost mocking the propaganda that was all around. Was that possible? Yet if she was truly ridiculing the sinister language of Communist propaganda, she was doing it in such an understated way, with a wit so dry he barely recognized it—or her. What had happened to the sweet, simple Lana, the ballerina with nary a serious thought in her head?

"Lana," he said quietly, "we need to talk."

"We are talking now, Stiva."

"Alone."

She paused as if weighing something in her mind. "Have you ever seen the grounds here? The land is really quite lovely. Shall we go for a little stroll?" She suggested it in an offhand, playful way, but he knew what she was doing. She was, for the first time, acquiescing, *agreeing* to speak with him.

"That would be nice," he said.

It was bitterly cold outside, hardly a night for taking a stroll around the rolling lawn behind the dacha. Lana wore a long fur coat that appeared to be mink, and a matching hat, an ensemble that was an extravagance all but unobtainable in Moscow these days, Metcalfe knew. He wondered whether it was a gift from her new German lover. *"Those people,"* she had disdainfully called the Nazis. What did that mean? Did she hate von Schüssler and what he stood for? If so, why was she with him? The Lana Metcalfe knew was no vapid materialist; she would never strike up an affair with a lover simply for the things he could buy her.

But she had become a complete puzzle to him. What was she all about now? Why *was* she with the German? What did she *really* think of the Stalinist system? Who *was* she anymore?

"Are you really here on business, Stephen?" she asked as they strolled aimlessly, their boots crunching in the icy snow. She kept a certain polite distance from him, he noticed, as if to make it clear—to him and to anyone who might be watching—that they were nothing more than friends, or *acquaintances,* as she'd pointedly told von Schüssler. Far off in the distance Metcalfe could see an outbuilding, presumably the stable.

"Of course. That's what I do. You know that."

"I don't know *what* it is you do, Stephen. How long are you in Moscow?"

"Just a few days. Lana—"

"Did you come here to this party because you knew I'd be here?"

"Yes," he admitted.

"What's past is past, Stephen. We have both grown up and moved on. We had a brief love affair a long time ago, and it is over with."

"Are you in love with the German?"

"He is amusing to me. He is, how do you say, *charmant*." She affected a light tone, but it was not persuasive.

"*Charmant* is not the first word that comes to mind when one thinks of von Schüssler. *Lugubrious*, perhaps."

"Stephen," she said warningly. "It is not your place to delve into the mysteries of the heart."

"No. If we're really talking about the heart. And not something else."

"Meaning what, exactly?" she snapped.

"Well, mink cannot be easy to find in Moscow."

"I make a very good salary now. Six thousand rubles a month."

"All the rubles in the state treasury won't buy you something that cannot be bought."

One side of her mouth turned up in a sly smile. "It is a gift. Though it is nothing compared to the gift you gave me."

"You've said that before—something about a gift I gave you. What *gift*, Lana?"

"Rudi is good to me," she said, ignoring his question. "He is a generous man. He gives me gifts, yes—what of it?"

"It's not like you."

"What is not like me?"

"To take up with a man because he can buy you minks and jewelry."

But she would not be goaded. "It is how he expresses his love."

"Love?"

"His infatuation, then."

"Yes, but somehow I don't think you are . . . *infatuated* with him, are you?"

"Stephen," she said, exasperated. "You have no claim on me anymore."

"I know that. I understand. But we need to meet; we need to talk. It's important."

"Talk?" she scoffed. "I know how you *talk*."

"I need your help. We have to arrange to meet. Can you meet me tomorrow afternoon—will you be back in Moscow by then?"

"I'll be back in Moscow," she said, "but I see no reason to meet."

"Sokolniki Park. Our usual spot, the place where we—"

"Stiva," she interrupted. "Quiet." Suddenly she nodded at a man who had appeared on the veranda not far from where they were walking. He turned to look, and Metcalfe recognized the face. It was the GRU man who had been sitting in the row behind him at the Bolshoi, the one who had struck up a conversation about her.

"I've seen him before," Metcalfe said in a low voice.

"Lieutenant Kundrov of the GRU," she said in a voice just above a whisper. "He's my minder."

"Your . . . *minder?*"

"I must be a plum assignment—he's unusually senior for the job. For the past year and a half, he's become my shadow. At first it was ridiculous. Everywhere I went, he would follow. I would meet friends at a restaurant, and there he was, at the next table. I would be shopping, and he would be in the line behind me. Every performance at the Bolshoi, he would be there, always in the same seat. Finally I invited him in for tea. I did so in front of others, prominent dignitaries at one of the private parties at the Bolshoi, so he couldn't decline."

"Why?"

"I figured I might as well get to know my jailer. Perhaps one day he will be ordered to collect me for my execution. Perhaps one day he will be my executioner. I prefer to know the one who has accepted my destiny as his personal assignment."

"But *why?* Why have they assigned you a minder?"

She shrugged. "I supposed it goes along with my status, with my being the prima ballerina." She added with a tone of amusement: "I have become an important personage, and therefore I am to be watched closely. One of the dancers who got too friendly with a foreigner—a capitalist stage-door Johnny—was sent to live in Siberia. We are caged birds."

"So you've reached an accommodation," Metcalfe said in English.

" 'Accommodation,' " she repeated. "I like this word. How do you spell?"

Reaching an accommodation with one's jailer, Metcalfe mused: it seemed to be a Russian specialty. As he began to spell out the word, he noticed that the GRU man, Lieutenant Kundrov, was coming across the lawn toward them.

"Svetlana Mikhailovna," the Russian said in a strong, resonant baritone. "Good evening. It is very cold to be outside. You will get sick."

"Good evening, Ivan Sergeyevich," Lana said with elaborate politeness. "Allow me to introduce a visiting businessman—"

"Stephen Metcalfe," said Kundrov. "Yes, I believe we met at the Bolshoi."

They shook hands. "You're a ballet fan, I take it," said Metcalfe.

"I'm an admirer of Svetlana Mikhailovna."

"As am I, but I'm afraid we are only two among many."

"Too true," the Russian replied. "Svetlana Mikhailovna, you are spending the evening here, yes? As guests of the ambassador?"

Was it a flash of irritation that appeared briefly on her face? "You know everything about me," Lana said gaily. "Yes, a little skiing and riding. And you?"

"No, I haven't been invited to spend the night, I'm afraid."

"A shame," Lana said.

Kundrov turned to Metcalfe. "You were able to make it out here without too much trouble? It is impossible to get a taxi these days. I assume Intourist provided you with a car and driver."

Clearly he knew about Metcalfe's attempt to elude surveillance. Metcalfe decided to seize the opportunity to do some repair work. "Truth is, I didn't want anybody to know I was coming out here. You wouldn't believe the precautions I took."

"But why? This is Soviet paradise," the GRU man said smoothly. "There are no secrets here. Not from us."

Metcalfe pretended to look sheepish. "That's exactly the problem."

"I'm not sure I understand."

"You guys—GRU, NKVD, whatever—you all blab. Gossip. The word gets out, and then I'm really gonna be in for it."

"The word gets out . . . to whom?"

Metcalfe rolled his eyes. "My brother, who else? I swore up and down it was going to be just business. I wasn't going to go to any parties, I promised him. I made enough trouble last time when I . . . See, my brother, he's the serious one in the family, and he thinks I'm reformed. He thinks I'm on the wagon—a teetotaler. Let him think that. He swears he's gonna cut me out of the family business if he finds out I've gone back to my old ways."

"How absolutely fascinating," Kundrov replied. His perfunctory smile indicated that he didn't believe a word of it. He waved a hand at the dacha, as if to indicate all of the guests within. "And these people, none of them would take notice of your . . . *old ways?* None of *them* would talk?"

"I'm not worried about them. It's the damned chauffeur. This British guy my brother sent with me, allegedly to drive me around to meetings, act as my aide-de-camp. But in reality he's a ball and chain. *He's* the one I had to escape from."

"Ah. Well, you can count on my discretion," Kundrov said.

"Good to know," said Metcalfe. "I knew I could."

Lana cleared her throat. "If you'll excuse me, gentlemen, I must get back inside to Rudi. He'll think I've abandoned him."

An hour later, Metcalfe clambered into a Bentley driven by a second secretary in the British embassy that was filled with other guests returning to Moscow. The mood was boisterous, the banter loud and alcohol-fueled, the laughter contagious. As the car reached the end of the long, dark dirt road and was about to turn onto the paved highway, Metcalfe suddenly spoke up.

"*Damn* it, I left my briefcase back there!"

Several groans arose. Someone cracked, "No point in going back—you can be sure the NKVD boys have already cracked it open and stolen whatever's inside."

"Just pull over, if you don't mind," Metcalfe said.

"You're not *walking* back, are you?" a woman exclaimed.

"I could use the fresh air," Metcalfe said. "I'll catch the next car."

He got out and began walking slowly back toward the dacha until the Bentley had roared away. Then he stopped, looked around to make sure he was unobserved.

Abruptly he bolted off the path and plunged into the thick forest. He was certain that he had not been observed. Neither the gray-eyed watcher nor Lana's minder, Kundrov, had seen him.

If he was wrong—if indeed he was being followed—the consequences would be enormous.

He could not be too careful.

CHAPTER SEVENTEEN

Branches and needles crunched underfoot. As soon as he had gone far enough into the woods that he felt sure he couldn't be seen from the dirt path or caught by the headlights of a departing car from the path, he pulled out a flashlight and a military-issue compass. Holding the flashlight in one hand, he shone the light on the compass dial as he aligned the needle to magnetic north.

There was, of course, no map of the area available, so Roger had instead devised a grid using compass coordinates. Metcalfe knew that Roger would bury the transmitter in the woods here and would indicate its whereabouts by means of a simple system of markers. Sweeping the flashlight's narrow beam in an arc, he began searching for a dab of red paint on a tree trunk. The woods here were a dense collection of old birches, with peeling bark, and tall, slender pines. Outside the narrow beam of light, everything was dark, almost opaque. The night sky was overcast, a heavy canopy of clouds obscuring the moon. He glanced at his watch. The radium dial read almost two o'clock in the morning. The forest was not entirely silent; forests never were. The occasional gust of wind rustled the birch leaves and caused branches to creak; here and there small animals scurried. Metcalfe walked slowly, keeping his tread light, but there was no disguising his footfalls. At the same time, he remained alert for any sound out of the ordinary, any noise that protruded. Since he was in the vicinity of a dacha that belonged to the American embassy, it was reasonable to assume that the woods would be patrolled with some regularity by the guards directorate of the NKVD. Not in the middle of the night, presumably, but one could never be sure.

Where was the marked tree? It was possible, of course, that

Roger had somehow failed to establish the markers, that he'd been intercepted. A more likely explanation was the inaccuracy of either man's magnetic compass. Unless the instrument was calibrated with great care, a set of compass coordinates could be off by as much as several hundred feet. The compass was simply not meant to be as precise in a small plot of land as it was over a larger area.

At last he came upon a birch tree with a daub of red paint that had been freshly applied; it was still tacky. This was the outermost boundary marker that Roger had established, the first of a series of three such marked trees that would point toward the site at which he had concealed the bulky radio transmitter. Metcalfe checked the compass reading, recalibrated it, and then set out sixty degrees west until he came to the next red marker.

A crack echoed from a good distance away, perhaps a few hundred feet. He froze, switched off his flashlight, and listened. After a minute he reassured himself that it had been nothing out of the ordinary, nothing human. He turned the torch back on, moved it slowly from left to right until he struck another glistening patch of red paint on a tree trunk twenty-five feet north-northwest.

That was it. The final marker.

Metcalfe and Roger had arranged in advance how the transceiver unit would be concealed. The problem was that Roger could not know, until he'd reached the site, how he'd be able to do it. You never knew until you got there; improvisation was always paramount. Would there be hollow sections of trees? Or some sort of outbuilding, a shed or shack?

The answer had been scrawled in an alphanumeric code, which Roger had carved with a penknife at the base of the third marked tree. Metcalfe found the characters inscribed in small, crude block letters: C/8/N. That told him that the unit was located precisely eight feet due north from the tree. The letter C indicated the third of six possible arrangements: it was buried in ground and concealed with whatever natural objects were at hand. Metcalfe paced out eight feet and immediately spied the large, flat stone, mostly obscured by the underbrush. The casual observer would notice nothing. Metcalfe knelt and brushed away the pine needles, twigs, and dead leaves, then pried loose the rock. Directly underneath it was green canvas, the tarpaulin Roger had wrapped over the small leather suitcase, set into a hollow that he'd obviously dug out earlier in the day. Metcalfe pulled it out with great effort—it had been firmly wedged in place—and then, after dusting off the dirt and debris, opened the case. He was able to operate in the dark, for he knew the workings of the transceiver well.

Built into the suitcase, which weighed some thirty pounds, was a twelve-volt automobile battery and power supply pack, a headphone and antenna, and then the transceiver itself, a steel box about a foot square with a black wrinkle finish. This was a BP-3, the most sophisticated clandestine communications unit ever built. It had been constructed by a group of Polish refugees working, in complete secrecy, at Letchworth, thirty miles north of London. These Poles, a remarkable assemblage of telecommunications experts who had been trained by the Germans before escaping their country just ahead of the Nazi invasion, were civilian technicians who'd been hired to work for the British secret service. Charged with improving upon the unwieldy old Mark XV transceiver, which was so bulky that it took up two suitcases, they came up with a compact yet powerful two-way communicator constructed of miniaturized components. Its receiver was excellent; it had an output of thirty watts. Its enormous power permitted intercontinental communications. The workmanship was unexcelled. When Corky had handed the suitcase to Metcalfe in a church in Pigalle, in Paris, he had taken no small pleasure in the fact that he'd been able to obtain several of the first advance prototypes even before the British MI-6 had been able to get their hands on them. *This makes everything else obsolete,*

Corky had crowed. *All those other machines are now museum relics. But please, do guard it with your life. You can be replaced, but I'm afraid this device cannot.*

The instructions for operating the unit had been pasted under the lid of the black steel box, but Metcalfe had the procedure memorized. He paused for a moment to take in the sounds of the forest. He heard the faint rustle of the trees, a distant call of a nocturnal bird. But nothing else. His knees were now quite damp from the snow, and his legs were beginning to feel numb. This whole arrangement was uncomfortable—it would have been far easier if he'd been able to work somewhere indoors, but that was not an option—but there was no reason to make it more uncomfortable than necessary. He unfolded the green canvas tarpaulin in which the suitcase had been wrapped and spread it out on the ground. At least he'd be able to sit on a dry spot. He was hardly dressed properly for this errand into the woods: over his evening clothes he wore a black cashmere greatcoat. Not only was his clothing already soiled and torn from making his way through the dense foliage, but his very appearance limited his escape options, if escape ever became necessary. He was clearly a well-dressed foreigner skulking through the forests outside Moscow, which would be immediate cause for suspicion if he was caught; he would be unable to pretend to be, say, a local man, a hunter, a sportsman. He spoke Russian with an accent, but so did many citizens of the Soviet Union who came from any of the far-flung areas, so his accent would not necessarily attract scrutiny. It was the clothes that didn't fit.

In the back of his mind, Metcalfe began rehearsing a possible cover story, in case one became necessary. He looked like a visiting American, so he would *be* one. He was a weekend guest at the embassy dacha—Lana had said she and von Schüssler were spending the evening there, after all, so it wasn't implausible— and he'd simply gotten lost on a late-night stroll. Or perhaps he was coming from an assignation in the woods, he would say. There was a woman—a married woman, the wife of an embassy attaché. They wanted privacy, so they'd gone into the woods, and she'd already returned to the dacha. . . . His fevered mind spun version after version, trying each one out for the soundness of logic.

And simultaneously he worked at the urgent task at hand. From his front pants pocket he took a small black oblong with two prongs at one end: the crystal, which had been cleverly concealed in his suitcase back at the hotel room so that it appeared to be part of the locking mechanism. This crystal contained the encoded frequencies on which he would transmit and receive. It was dangerous to keep together with the radio unit, for if the suitcase had been discovered, the operational security would have been seriously compromised. You did not keep the key and the lock in the same place. He plugged the crystal into the Q socket on the lower part of the unit, then plugged in the headset and put it on.

Now he switched on the flashlight and set it down so that it illuminated the immediate area. He would have to work fast: he was sitting in an island of bright light in the middle of a black forest; he could now be seen for hundreds of yards or more. And if he was to be spotted, the circumstances could not be more incriminating. Arrest would be swift, execution in the basement of the Lubyanka a certainty.

He drew out from his breast pocket a pack of Lucky Strikes and a fountain pen. In the cigarette pack were concealed several small sheets of paper; he took one out. It was a one-time-pad sheet printed on a piece of nitrated rice paper so that it would catch fire instantly; it could also be dissolved in hot water, even swallowed if need be. He unscrewed the body of the fountain pen, in which was tightly furled a silk handkerchief measuring nine by four inches. He flung it open, pressed it flat against the canvas tarp. The entire silk square was covered with tiny groups of letters arranged in a grid.

These two items—the rice-paper one-time pad and the silk key—taken together made up the most sophisticated encryption system that had ever been developed. Known as the Vigenère table, it had recently been developed in London by Churchill's Special Operations Executive for use by agents in the field. The British were far ahead of the Americans in matters of codes and ciphers, Corky had often complained, because they took the necessity of espionage much more seriously. The genius of this system was that it was not only foolproof and fairly easy to use, but it was also unbreakable, even by the most powerful code-breaking machines. Each letter of the English alphabet was replaced by any of the other letters in a wholly random series. No pattern to the code could ever be discerned; the cryptogram could never be solved by the enemy even if the transmission was intercepted. Each key was used only once and then destroyed; the only duplicate was kept at the home station, and no key was the same. Formally this polyalphabetic substitution cipher was known as the "infinite incoherent key." Corky often called it the ultimate weapon.

Metcalfe turned on the power, then set the switch to Tune. He depressed a key, turned a knob marked with an arrow until a neon tube lit up. Moving another knob to Transmit, he selected the position that most brightly lit up the tuning bulb, indicating the frequency with the strongest signal. Now the transmitter was ready to operate.

He had composed and encrypted his message in advance, of course. It was an urgent message for Corky informing him of what had happened in Moscow, of the existence of the GRU "minder," Kundrov, who had been assigned to Svetlana, and asking for background on the man. Metcalfe also relayed to Corky the alarming degree of surveillance that had been placed on him, particularly the quality of the talent. He raised the question of whether his cover had somehow been blown. Finally, he wanted to give Corky his immediate assessment of von Schüssler, which echoed Amos Hilliard's—the German was no prospect for recruitment. But everything had to be abridged, condensed to the shortest possible format, using standard and other agreed-upon abbreviations. Printed on the silk master key was, in addition to the alphanumeric substitution grid, a series of code groups that represented commonly used phrases that might be employed by an agent in the field: "have arrived safely," say, or "safe house located." Further, Corky had issued another set of hyperabbreviated letter groups that stood for complex thoughts or long expressions.

Moreover, Metcalfe had to communicate not by voice but by Morse code. There was no choice. It wasn't simply a matter of the security of transmission, although that was certainly a factor. But more important was the fact that voice signals simply could not be transmitted more than a few hundred miles; such was the technology. Continuous-wave broadcasts—meaning Morse code signals—traveled five times farther.

Moving the lantern close, he read over the scrap of paper he'd slipped into the empty Lucky Strikes pack. The long series of letter groupings would look like gibberish to the casual observer, but it was not the casual observer he was concerned about. Skilled agents, such as Lana's minder or the blond NKVD man, would know immediately it was a code of some sort, even if they could never decrypt it. This slip of paper, along with the onetime pads and the silk key, were extraordinarily dangerous pieces of evidence if ever he was searched.

Move it, he told himself. *You're sitting here in a goddamned pool of light in a dark forest outside of Moscow. Every minute that ticks by adds to the risk of discovery.*

He began tapping the telegraph key, which was located at the bottom right corner of the transceiver's face. It was slow work: he was out of practice, not having had to operate a field radio in Paris, and the poor illumination made things still more difficult. Still, he managed to complete the transmission in little over a minute. It was addressed to home station 23-C, which automatically flagged Corcoran. The decoded message would be dispatched to him at once through secure channels. As soon as Metcalfe heard the code signaling receipt and acknowledgment, he removed his headset and switched off the transceiver.

He moved quickly now, extinguishing the light, disassembling the machine, and removing the crystal, then closing its case and rewrapping it in its canvas tarpaulin. He placed the bundle back into the hole, replaced the flat rock over it, and then, as thoroughly as he could, swept the detritus and organic matter from the forest floor in a pattern that looked undisturbed.

He heard the crack of a branch.

He froze, listened. He had no doubt that it was anything more than a chipmunk or squirrel, but still, it was always better to observe precautions.

Another crack, followed by the crunch of underbrush. And again.

It was not an animal. It was a human being. Someone was walking with difficulty through the dense forest, the labored steps seeming to come closer.

Now he was sure of it. There was no mistake.

Someone was approaching.

Metcalfe moved, as silently as he could, a few steps to his left until he was mostly shielded behind a pine tree. His heart was racing. He was standing just a few feet away from the transmitter, which he had just buried. But he could not be sure that he hadn't been observed placing the machine in the ground. How long, he tried to think, had his flashlight been on? Had that drawn the attention of whomever it was coming this way?

He realized, too, that if he was discovered here, it was likely that the transmitter would be discovered soon after; they would wonder what he was doing here, and a search would be conducted.

He had to run; he could *not* risk being found out. Not only was he standing a few feet away from a sophisticated piece of spy equipment, whose warm tubes would indicate recent use, but he had on his person other incriminating pieces of evidence.

There was the silk handkerchief printed with the cryptographic key, which he'd wadded up and stuffed into his jacket pocket; there was, too, the cigarette pack that held the rice-paper one-time pads. There was the transceiver crystal. All were unmistakable proof that he was a spy. *If I'm caught, I'm a goner for sure.*

Should he toss them, drop them to the ground, simply get rid of them? And then what? As soon as he took off running, he would be followed, and whatever he had dropped on the ground was likely to be found. Dropping them as he ran might just call attention to them. And the fact was, he didn't want to lose this vital equipment. The crystal was irreplaceable. Without it, he could no longer transmit to the home station. Without the one-time pads and the silk key, he'd be unable to encrypt his messages. He would be isolated in Moscow without a means of contacting Corcoran.

It was clear that he had no choice. He *had* to run—but as soon as he did, a pursuit would begin. For a moment he was frozen in indecision, running through his options, considering what made the most sense. He peered into the gloomy night, trying to see who it was who was approaching. That damned NKVD agent, the blond man with the pale eyes who seemed to find him no matter where he went? Or the GRU lieutenant, Kundrov, Lana's minder?

No. It was neither of those men. Now he could just make out, in the dim light, the approaching figure. He appeared at first to be a military man, in a loden overcoat and field cap. Then Metcalfe realized that the man was from the NKVD. He could see the epaulets, the insignia on the cap. Definitely from the Soviet security service, presumably from the NKVD's guards directorate, a separate department within the service whose officers were charged with protecting the nation's borders and secure areas.

A detachment from the NKVD would logically be assigned to patrol the area surrounding the American embassy dacha. The NKVD liked to keep all foreigners, especially Americans, under close surveillance, and a country house required particular attention. The security organs assumed that all diplomats were secretly spies—after all, most of the *Soviet* diplomats assigned abroad were spies, so why shouldn't every other country work the same way? Thus it was a matter of vital national security that a cordon of guards patrol the area surrounding the embassy property. Too, it was possible that these woods bordered some secure installation—the forests around Moscow were dotted with bases and institutes connected with the Red Army or the GRU or the NKVD.

But he hadn't expected a patrol at this time of night. And was it possible that there was a single guard? No, that made no sense. They made their circuits in patrols of two or three at the very least. At this time of night, their circuits would likely be infrequent, which was why Metcalfe had seen or heard nothing until now.

But if there was one sentry, there had to be others.

The guard continued to approach. He was barely into his twenties, but that didn't mean he was inexperienced. He was walking in the dark, without benefit of a torch, indicating that he was trained to circulate in these woods at night and knew the paths, the clearings. The Russian had an automatic advantage over Metcalfe, who did not. Seconds ticked by; Metcalfe could no longer stand here, hidden behind the trunk of a tree. If the guard came any closer, he would notice the interloper.

Suddenly a match was struck! Then, just as quickly, the match was extinguished.

The NKVD sentry had lit a match, but not for the sake of illumination, nor to light a cigarette. It was a *signal*—a signal to *others!* A rustling came from a good distance away: the tramping of boots against the ground. Metcalfe heard voices now, rapid phrases exchanged, their tone of voice indicating urgency. The other members of his team, summoned by the match strike, were running, crashing through the woods, not bothering to disguise their movements. They were converging on him!

Metcalfe spun around, vaulted through a narrow opening between two trees, scraping against the branches with a noise that was loud but unavoidable. He put on a burst of speed, running as fast as he could manage. He zigzagged from clearing to clearing, trying to look far enough ahead to make out an open path, but the night was too dark, the visibility limited. He could see no more than fifty feet ahead.

Shouts in Russian came from behind, instructions given from senior officer to junior. Though he dared not turn around, he could hear an alteration in the sound pattern that told him the men had split up, each taking a different path, hoping to anticipate any direction their quarry might take and thus intercept him.

No flashlights, though. Perhaps the men had no need of light, since they knew the woods. Or perhaps they didn't want to delay long enough to get out their torches. Whatever the reason, it was good for Metcalfe: the darkness was the best cover.

He remembered a little of the topography of the land here, though only what he had observed from his brief stroll around the dacha with Lana and on the short, interrupted drive leaving the party. He knew the forest undulated, that there was a valley—he had seen it from the backyard of the dacha—and his sense of direction told him that he was heading roughly in the direction of the valley. This was confirmed by the gradual downhill pitch of the land.

But how could he hope to outrun a team of experienced guards?

Perhaps he couldn't. But he would have to try. The alternative was frightening. If they managed to apprehend him and brought him to the Lubyanka, he would be imprisoned and there was absolutely nothing Corky or anyone else in the U.S. government could do for him. An American spy in Soviet Russia would be sentenced to prison, perhaps placed in the prison camps in Siberia—the dread gulag he had heard about—or, more likely, executed.

Impelled by terror, he ran as he had never run before, weaving through the trees, then into a clearing, veering off in an irregular, jagged pattern that he hoped would confound his pursuers.

Suddenly a shot was fired!

An explosion. A bullet splintered a tree trunk not five feet away. And then—another! This shot creased the birch tree barely a foot away. The forest was now filled with loud gunfire, the bullets whizzing by, one of them coming so close to his head that he could feel the gust of wind at his ear. He sprawled abruptly to the ground in order to confuse them, sprang forward on his hands and knees, then scrambled to his feet, running with his head down, moving this way and that in a crazy, jerky pattern. *A frightened man always reverts to the predictable,* Corky liked to say. *The easiest course, the shortest distance between two points.* So he would have to violate that natural, predictable course of behavior.

Another volley of shots, several wildly off but one alarmingly close. They seemed to be coming from three very different points; obviously, the men had split up, hoping to converge on him. At least one of the guards had the rare ability to fire with great accuracy even while giving chase. Just up ahead Metcalfe spied a rocky outcropping at the top of a slight rise. He headed toward it, hoping that the boulders and scree might make for temporary cover, obstruction against the gunfire. Bounding ahead, he then leaped into the air, landing painfully on the rocky ledge. He groaned, looked up, saw the gleam of ice in the faint moonlight. He was on the ridge of a deep ravine through which a creek ran, though it appeared now to be frozen, its banks covered with ice and snow.

The drop was a good twenty feet. To jump would be hazardous. But to turn back around would be even riskier, he realized. Another volley of gunfire pitted the ground, pinged against the boulders; the wild inaccuracy told him that he had succeeded in putting some distance between himself and his pursuers, who were now far enough behind that even from their various vantage points, they couldn't yet draw an accurate bead on him.

Perhaps they couldn't even see him; that was possible. He grabbed a sizable rock and hurled it as far as he could, back and to the right. It hit the ground with a thud and a loud rustle.

A volley of shots followed immediately, raking the trees and the ground where the rock had hit, indicating that his tactical diversion had been effective.

Then, without allowing himself to think—operating only out of an instinct for self-preservation—he leaped into the air, landing with a violent crash on the hard, icy riverbank, his legs tucked into his torso to minimize the impact. The pain jagged through his body as he lost his footing, hurling down the ice-cragged bank toward the river. Getting unsteadily to his feet, he stood at the edge of the frozen creek and tested it with an outstretched foot. It was solid, the ice at least several inches thick. He would be able to cross it. Gingerly he stepped onto the ice, then took another step—and immediately broke through, plunging into the semifrozen stream all the way up to his knees. He gasped. The water was extraordinarily cold, so much so that as he struggled along the streambed to climb back upon the icy surface his feet quickly became numb.

Gunfire echoed far behind him, seeming to indicate that the pursuers had been misled, were heading in the wrong direction. All it would take would be for one of them to climb to the ridge overlooking the stream and he would be spotted.

The frozen surface of the stream here was thin, breaking as he moved forward through the amazingly cold water. Just as he had almost reached the other bank, his right foot, which by now felt like an inanimate object, caught in something and he tumbled forward, landing facedown on the icy, craggy bank. Now his clothes were entirely soaked in the frigid water; he shivered as he tried to get up. His feet, which had lost all feeling, would not cooperate. They were deadweight, lacking in any mobility. Looking to one side he saw, twenty-five feet ahead or so, a pile of ice-glazed dead branches and leaves on the steep incline that led up from the riverbank, which appeared to have been blown down in a storm. Metcalfe crawled along the ground until he reached the pile, and then, with what felt like the last ounce of strength remaining in his body, he dived forward into it. The brittle branches gave way easily; he sank deep into it, buried in the detritus. His legs were buckling, trembling; he could not go on. He needed to rest. If he tried to keep running now, he would quickly be caught. He no longer had the endurance; his reaction time had slowed. Reaching up, he grabbed wildly at the dead leaves and branches and snow-covered loam, arranging them over himself so that he was well concealed.

Barely a minute or two later he heard running footsteps, the crescendo of shouts coming closer. Metcalfe could not tell where exactly they were coming from: the patrol squad could be on the ridge above, or they could have climbed down into the ravine, in which case they would see the broken ice on the frozen surface of the stream. That would point the way to where he lay hiding. Where he lay shivering, in truth, his body shuddering violently.

Then came a shout. How far away he could not tell. "He's over there—I *see* him!" It seemed to be the youngest of the group, the one who had first seen him in the forest. He was a country boy, a hick; his peasant speech betrayed him.

"What are you talking about?"

"There! Vasya, you simpleton, over *there!*"

"The rifle, idiot! Not the revolver!"

Had they spotted him, his greatcoat showing through the twigs? He cringed, braced himself. What could he do? If they were wrong and they were aiming in the wrong direction, the worst thing he could do would be to move from his blind, thereby attracting their attention. But if they weren't wrong—if one of them had indeed spotted him and was preparing to fire his rifle—then he was as good as dead. One well-aimed rifle shot to the head was all it would take.

"Okay," the young voice said.

Metcalfe was not a religious man, but he found himself praying to God that they were too far off to make an accurate shot. He squeezed his eyes shut, let his mind go blank. His heart raced.

And the shot exploded, echoing in the forest.

Nothing hit him or near him. Wherever the shot had been aimed, he didn't hear the impact. It must have been in another direction.

"You missed." An older voice.

"I saw it!" The younger man spoke. "I could see the shape, the outline. It was clear!"

"Idiot!" roared one of the older men. "That was a deer!"

"It was no deer!"

Another voice, the third member of the squad: "Artyem is right. That was a deer. Actually, I think it was a stag. But you missed."

"I know what a stag looks like!" the youngest one protested. "I hunted all the time when I was a boy."

"You're *still* a boy, and you just shot at a stag, and missed," one of the older ones said.

"Well, okay, maybe that was a deer," the young man conceded, "but I'm sure I saw a man. I know the difference between a man and a deer." His protests were met by jeers from the others.

It was clear from the young soldier's shakily defiant voice and the gibes of his comrades that the patrol was no longer convinced there had ever been a man fleeing through the woods.

"You enjoy your little hunting expedition, Sasha? After you dragged us twenty kilometers through this goddamned forest? I say enough sport for the evening. It's cold, and our shift is just about up."

"It's cold," another of the guards seconded. "The Order of Stalin is awarded to young Comrade Shubentsov for his brave attempt to track down and liquidate the counterrevolutionary stag, despite the resistance of its kulak supporters. Now, let's *go*."

———

For a long time—at least half an hour, though he lost track of time—Metcalfe remained buried beneath the twigs and leaves and snow before he dared to extract himself. He listened as the NKVD guards departed, talking noisily. Their gibes and jeers directed at the younger one, who had first spotted Metcalfe, were unceasing. It was likely that the young patrolman had indeed seen a stag and had taken a shot at it, which was a lucky break for Metcalfe. A stag had been running through the forest, not a fleeing man, they had come to believe. The sharp-eyed youngest member of the patrol, who had indeed seen Metcalfe, though only in silhouette and at a great distance, was no longer believed. Still, Metcalfe waited until he was sure that none of the patrolmen had remained behind. If another shift had taken their place, he heard no sign of it.

Meanwhile, though his limbs had grown stiff and uncomfortable, some feeling had returned to his feet. The brief respite had done him good. With considerable effort he managed to rise, shaking off the ice and snow and dead leaves. He was chilled and exhausted, but it was imperative that he get out of here. Fortunately, the night sky had cleared somewhat. Now there was some moonlight, which enabled him to orient himself. With the help of the compass and flashlight, he made his way through the forest toward the dacha, all the time alert for the sounds of a patrol. He would have to improvise a way to get back to Moscow, and the dacha was by far the most likely place to do that. There would be vehicles, which he could steal if he needed to; there would be guests to prevail upon for a lift back to the city. His reputation as a carousing partygoer would be useful in explaining away his shocking disheveled appearance: he had gone off with a girl, he could say sheepishly; he'd had way too much to drink, fallen down, passed out . . . A cover story could be devised and might well be believed. Certainly if the ambassador's wife was there, as she likely was since they had weekend guests, she'd be inclined to believe the most outlandish tales about him. She'd seen him leave, true, but it wouldn't surprise her to learn that he'd met up with a woman along the way. . . .

But then, as he neared the dacha, he came upon the stable he'd seen from the veranda. Here the embassy kept horses. And here he could sleep for the remainder of the night, no questions asked. He entered the barn quietly, trying not to wake the animals inside.

But he heard the grunts and nickers of the horses as he came in. A kerosene lantern had been left burning, presumably for the sake of the horses. It gave off a flickering yellow light. There were ten stalls but just three horses: magnificent Arabians, two black, one chestnut. One of them whinnied. These were beautiful but high-strung animals, and if he did not calm them, they would become distressed and perhaps awaken the sleeping guests in the nearby house.

One by one the horses began lifting and arching their necks, making soft, blowing sounds through their noses. Their ears were pricked up now, swiveling backward, listening. Metcalfe approached the first one he came to, not from behind, which would alarm him, but at an oblique angle at the rear. He spoke softly and calmly. The horse made a low, grunting noise as he began patting and stroking the animal's neck and withers, his sleek flanks; in a few minutes, the horse began to relax. His ears lolled to the front, and his lower lip drooped. The others began to calm down as well. Their breathing became regular, almost inaudible.

Bedding down on a bale of hay near the warmth radiating from the kerosene lantern, Metcalfe fell asleep. Sleep, badly needed, came quickly; it was deep, his dreams strange and fragmented.

A shaft of bright sunlight awakened him. It was early morning, and although he could have slept for hours more, he knew he had to get moving. He ached all over, the uncomfortable bed of straw exacerbating the bruises and sprains he had suffered during his flight through the forest. He was covered in dusty straw. He sat up, brushing the straw from his face, then rubbing his tired eyes.

There was a sudden groan of rusty hinges, and the stable was flooded with light. The door came open. Metcalfe jumped up, leaped into an empty stall, flattening himself against the wall. The Arabians whinnied softly, the sounds not of alarm but of greeting. They seemed to recognize whoever was entering.

Metcalfe did, too.

Dressed in riding clothes, a kerchief over her head: it was Lana.

CHAPTER EIGHTEEN

"Lana," he said quietly.

She blinked, surprised to see him but somehow not completely surprised. Before she could compose her face into an expression of disapproval, Metcalfe caught a fleeting glimpse of what looked very much like pleasure.

"Stiva?" She seemed to be attempting a coolness in her tone, a scolding. "But . . . we agreed, Sokolniki Park tomorrow at dusk."

"I guess I couldn't wait."

She shook her head, giggled despite herself. "Look at you! What happened to the best-dressed man in Moscow?"

He was a mess, he knew: there was straw in his hair and all over his coat and suit, and he smelled of horse. "You see what you've driven me to, *dusya?*"

"I'm going riding. It's one of my few pleasures these days."

"And your German boyfriend?"

She scowled. "He rarely gets up before noon. He won't even notice I'm gone. Everyone's asleep in the house, actually."

"Then you won't mind if I join you?"

She inclined her head. "I won't mind."

She saddled up deftly, Metcalfe no less quickly. His mother had kept horses and had seen to it that he had learned to ride not long after he learned to walk. But he was surprised that Lana had gotten so skilled at horsemanship; it seemed to be something she had picked up in the last few years. *Like so much that has changed about her,* he thought.

There was a horse trail that ran through the woods, a trail he hadn't noticed before. It had not been cleared in some time; they were whipped by small branches as they rode. Metcalfe allowed her to set the pace. When the path widened somewhat, she leaned forward, made a clucking sound with her mouth, squeezed her legs together. Her horse, the chestnut Arabian, increased his gait to a canter. She rode as if she'd been doing it all her life. The trail widened again, allowing them to ride alongside each other; but when it narrowed, she took the lead. Metcalfe turned his face up to the soft morning sun. It warmed him, soothed him. For a few moments, as they rode in silence, he was lulled by the rhythmic gallop. It was like old times again. The fear, the terror, the suspicion—all was left behind. He watched her lithe figure; she seemed to be an extension of the horse. The perfect features of her face, framed by her gaily colored head scarf, were beautiful in repose. The sadness that seemed to have overtaken her was gone. God, he loved her so!

After a while the terrain began to look familiar. He called out to her, got her attention, interrupted her reverie. He pointed toward the denser section of the woods, through which he had fled the night before. Four, maybe five hours earlier, but already it seemed like another day. She looked perplexed but followed him off the path. They slowed to a walk as they made their way through the trees.

After a few minutes, she called, "There is no path here!"

"I know."

"It will not be easy. We should go back to the path."

"I need to find something. It won't take long."

Soon he came upon a tree that had been daubed with red paint, and he knew where he was. "Wait here a moment." He dismounted and peered around for the patch of ground where he had strewn twigs and moss over the transmitter. His eye was immediately caught by an unexpected sight, something he hadn't seen before.

The ground had been cleared, scraped to the bare soil. The large, flat rock had been moved, exposing the pit that Roger had dug. The hole was empty. *The transmitter was gone.*

Metcalfe knew at once what had happened, and he was seized with terror. The youngest member of the patrol had gone back, retraced his steps. That had to be it. Goaded, perhaps, by the jeers of his elders, determined to prove that what he had seen had not been just a stag, he had searched the woods. The transmitter had been concealed well, but he had concentrated on the area where he had first spotted an interloper, and somehow he had found it. Triumphant, vindicated, he had taken it to his comrades, proving that he was right all along. And—if this was how it had happened—now the NKVD patrol knew that what they had chased through the forest had been no stag and no mere intruder but . . . a spy. A genuine spy, a discovery that would make their careers and would land like a bombshell in the NKVD's headquarters in the Lubyanka. A sophisticated transceiver of British manufacture! Proof that spies were operating in Moscow! Lights would burn through the night at the Lubyanka; urgent meetings would be held, frantic phone calls made, frenzied summonses.

Everything had suddenly changed. The NKVD would shift into high gear, searching for a spy—or a spy ring, for, like cockroaches, where there was one there were undoubtedly others.

It was not safe to be here, in this place where the transmitter had been found. Teams would be assigned to hide, lie in wait for the spy to return to this spot, just as a criminal is said to always return to the scene of the crime.

He had to get out of here at once!

Metcalfe raced back to where Lana and the horses waited. As he climbed back into the saddle, she must have noticed the strain in his face. "Darling, what's wrong?"

"Nothing," he said tightly. He tugged at the reins to get his horse moving back through the woods and toward the path. A few seconds later, he clarified: "Everything."

Lana stared at him, then nodded as if she understood. "Welcome to the USSR," she said with a grim, knowing smile.

As soon as they reached the path, they began circling back

toward the dacha, Metcalfe now taking the lead. Outside the stable they both dismounted, walking the horses back inside. Lana filled a bucket with water from a hand pump; her horse drank greedily. She pumped another bucketful and placed it in front of Metcalfe's horse, which drank as well. They knew her, trusted her. She removed her horse's tack, shook out the saddle before hanging it up, removed the bridle, and washed out the bit in a stream of water from the pump before hanging that up as well. She did all this quickly, expertly, all the time cooing softly to the horse, stroking him. She took a towel from a hook and rubbed the horse gently to restore the circulation in his back, then began grooming him with a soft-bristled brush. Metcalfe did the same. They worked in silence, but it was not an uncomfortable silence. It felt companionable, like old friends who did not need to talk. Once she had examined her horse's hooves for stones, she led him back to his stall.

As Metcalfe shut the stall gate, he noticed that she had come over to him, as if she had something she wanted to say.

"Lana," he began, but she placed a hand over his mouth, a quick touch, a request for silence. Her face was tilted upward to his, her eyes brimming with tears. She reached up with both hands this time, cupping his face. He wrapped his arms around her. Her lips parted as they touched his. He could feel the hot moisture of her tears against his face. She was trembling. He moved her hands down her back, fondling her, caressing her as they kissed with an urgency that surprised him. He pulled her in to him tight. Her hands kneaded the muscles of his back, of his buttocks, and he moved a hand around to her breast. Abruptly she pulled her mouth away from his. "Oh, God, Stiva," she said, her voice plaintive. "Take me. Please. *Love* me!"

Their bed was a horse blanket thrown hastily over a few stacks of hay. It was coarse and not particularly comfortable, but in the urgency of their passion neither noticed. They made love quickly and without speaking, disrobing only partially. And just as quickly they dressed, both of them fearful, without needing to say anything, that they might be discovered. As she dressed, Lana began humming a tune.

"What is it?" Metcalfe said.

"What is *what?*"

"That song. It sounds somehow familiar."

She laughed. " '*Comme ils étaient forts tes bras qui m'embrassaient.*' How strong were your arms that embraced me. A song that came into my head for some reason."

"It's pretty. Will we still meet tomorrow evening?"

"Yes, of course. Why not?"

"Rudolf—he won't be suspicious?"

"Please," she said fretfully. "I was feeling happy for the first time in a long, long while. Why did you have to mention his name?"

"What are you doing with him? I know you don't love him. I don't understand."

"There's so much you don't understand, Stiva."

"Tell me," he said. He placed his hand over hers.

She bit her lower lip. "I had no choice."

"No choice? You always have a choice, *milenki.*"

She shook her head slowly, sadly, and the tears returned to her eyes. "Not when you're a prisoner, *dorogoi moi.* Not when you are a hostage."

"What are you saying? How can this—"

"It is my father. He knows how I love my father, how I would do anything to protect him."

"Von Schüssler is threatening your father?"

"No, it is nothing so open. He . . . he has a document. A piece of paper that has the power to kill my father. To get my father executed and me arrested."

"Lana, what the *hell*—?"

"Listen to me. Please, just *listen!*" She took his hand in both of hers and held it tightly. "You know the name of the famous

Red Army general Mikhail Nikolayevich Tukhachevsky, the great Hero of the Revolution?"

"I've heard the name, yes."

"He defended Moscow in 1918, captured Siberia in 1920. A great, loyal military man. The chief of staff of the Soviet army. And he was an old friend of my father's. A few times we had dinner with his family. My father worshiped him. He had a photograph of himself with Tukhachevsky which he displayed prominently on top of the piano." She paused, drew in her breath as if steeling herself. "One night in May—it was three years ago, in 1937—I was asleep when I heard our doorbell ring. I thought it must be some prankster, some hooligan, some drunk, so I rolled over and put the pillow over my head. The ringing did not stop. I looked at my clock. It was after midnight. Finally the ringing stopped, and I was able to fall back to sleep. I had a big performance the next evening—we were doing *Sleeping Beauty*.

"It must have been an hour later when I was awakened again, this time by loud voices. My father's voice. I got up from my bed and listened. The voices were coming from my father's study. He seemed to be arguing with someone. I ran to his study but stopped just outside the door. Father was there, in his dressing gown, and he was talking quite agitatedly to Tukhachevsky. My first thought was that Marshal Tukhachevsky was yelling at Father for something, and I became quite angry. I stood there, eavesdropping. But I soon realized that Father was not yelling at him at all—he was angry, furious as I had never seen him before, but not angry at his friend Mikhail Nikolayevich. He was furious at Stalin. Tukhachevsky did not seem to be angry, though. His tone of voice was sad, resigned, almost mournful.

"I looked around the corner to see the two men, and I was shocked to see that Tukhachevsky's hair had turned gray. I had seen him two weeks earlier, and it was quite dark. Obviously something terrible had happened to him. I pulled back, careful not to be seen. I knew that if they knew I was there, that I was listening in, they would stop. And I had the feeling that whatever they were discussing was so serious, so dangerous, that my father would never tell me. He is always so protective of me, you know."

"Not because he doesn't respect you, *dusya*. But because he loves you."

"Yes. I've come to understand this, though for years it made me so angry that he insisted on treating me like a small child. So I listened to Tukhachevsky tell my father that Stalin and his NKVD had uncovered a huge plot within the army. He said the NKVD was tailing him, on Stalin's direct orders. The rumor was that Stalin had strong evidence indicating that a number of his top military officers were engaged in a secret conspiracy—a plot with members of the German High Command to carry out a coup d'etat against Stalin. And that among these plotters was . . . Tukhachevsky!"

"That's insane."

"Is it? I don't know the truth. I know that when my father and he spoke privately, they both agreed that Stalin was a dangerous man." She lowered her voice to a whisper. "My father loathes Stalin. This I know. He will not allow Stalin's name to be used in our house. Oh, in public he joins in all the toasts to the General Secretary. He praises Stalin to the skies when others are listening. He is not stupid. But he hates the man. And so did Tukhachevsky."

"What was the 'strong evidence' that Stalin had? Was that ever revealed?"

"Never publicly, no. But there was talk. Apparently a dossier was obtained in Prague from Czech intelligence, given to the NKVD. The dossier contained letters written by these Soviet military officers, letters to their German counterparts seeking to enlist their support in a scheme to overthrow Stalin. The signatures were verified, the seals, everything. One of the letters was signed by Marshal Tukhachevsky himself."

"He wrote such a letter?"

"Of course, he denied it. But he said it made no difference. He was convinced that he was about to be arrested, along with others."

"He was warning your father, then?"

"That may have been part of why he came. Father told him to write a letter to Stalin himself to clear up this misunderstanding. Tukhachevsky said he had done so already, but he hadn't received an answer. He said his days were numbered and he feared not only for his life but also for his family. He was a desperate man.

"The next morning, I asked my father who it was that had come in the night. He refused to tell me, of course. He said it was no concern of mine. But I noticed that he had removed the photograph of himself with Tukhachevsky. Later I found it hidden away in a drawer, wrapped in newspaper. And a few days later, Tukhachevsky and seven other high-ranking military officers were arrested. They were tried in secret—their trial lasted barely three hours!—and found guilty of espionage and treason against the motherland."

Her hands were squeezing his so tight that it was painful. But Metcalfe just nodded, listened.

"They all confessed," she said. "But the confessions were false. They were tortured, we later learned, and then told that the only way to save their lives—and, more important, their families' lives—was to sign confessions admitting to a conspiracy with the Germans. They were executed in the Lubyanka. Not in the cellar, by the way, but in the courtyard, during the daytime. NKVD trucks were brought in to rev their engines during the execution in order to cover up the sound of the shots." She paused for a long time, and Metcalfe said nothing. The only sound was the gentle breathing and nickering of the horses. "As they died," she continued at last, her voice cracking, "they shouted, 'Long live Stalin!' "

Metcalfe shook his head. He put his free arm around her shoulder, squeezed her tight.

"And of course," Lana said, "this was not the end but the beginning—of a cascade of blood. More than thirty thousand military officials were purged. Generals, army marshals, hundreds of division commanders, all of the navy's admirals."

"Lana, what does this terrible story have to do with you?"

"My father," she whispered, "was one of the few generals who were not arrested."

"Because he was not involved."

She closed her eyes. Her face seemed wracked with pain. "Because he was not caught. Or perhaps it was luck. These things happen, too."

"Not 'caught'? Are you saying your father was . . . a plotter against Stalin?"

"It seems scarcely believable. And yet he has often whispered to me of his loathing of Stalin. I have no choice but to believe."

"But he never *told* you he was part of any conspiracy, did he?"

"He never would! I told you, he is fiercely protective of me. One single word of his guilt and he would be summarily executed. Stalin does not give anyone the benefit of the doubt."

"Then what makes you so certain?"

Abruptly she broke away from his embrace. She stood up, walked over to the chestnut horse, and began absently stroking his flank. She was obviously avoiding something extremely painful. After a few minutes, without looking at Metcalfe, she began to speak.

"A few months ago I was invited to a party at the German embassy. It was a terribly extravagant affair, the sort the Germans like to put on, and of course they must always have the *crème de la crème* of Moscow society there, which means the famous actors and singers and dancers. To be honest, I only go to these things to eat. Really! I'm embarrassed to say it, but it's true.

"Well, a German diplomat came up to me and asked if I was the daughter of the famous general Mikhail Baranov."

"Von Schüssler."

She nodded. "Why did he want to know? I wondered. My

father now works in the Commissariat of Defense, and even
though his job is quite boring, quite bureaucratic, I must always
be careful whom I talk to; we are told there are spies everywhere.
He seemed to know all about my father's military career—far
more even than I knew. He said he wanted to talk to me in
private, that he had something to share with me that I would
find most interesting. I was intrigued, as he intended I would be.
We took our drinks to a corner of the room and sat down, away
from anyone else. Von Schüssler was clearly a cultured man, different from so many of the Nazi boors I've met. I didn't much
care for him—he seemed arrogant and self-absorbed, not at all
what you would call a charming man. But he spoke, in a very
casual and offhanded way, and I listened. He told me that an
old school friend of his who had gone into the SS had shown
him a most interesting, top-secret dossier concerning certain
highly placed members of the Soviet military. Some of the documents had already been obtained by Stalin, but there were
others."

"Oh, Jesus. Lana, *dorogaya.* How frightened you must have
been."

"He must have seen the fear in my face. I cannot help it—I
flush easily; I am not good at hiding my emotions. I said nothing,
pretended I didn't know what he was talking about, but he could
sense my terror. *Bozhe moi,* Stiva! My God. He said that there
were other letters in this dossier, names Stalin never knew about.
The SS, he said, liked to hold on to compromising evidence to
use when they had a use for it, as if they were trump cards."

"The bastard was threatening you."

"But nothing so *vulgar,* Stiva. Nothing so obvious. It was all
quite subtle and understated. Von Schüssler said he saw no reason why this damaging piece of information should be revealed
to the NKVD. What was past was past, he said. But didn't I find
it *interesting?* he said, so casually."

"However subtly he played it, he was obviously blackmailing
you."

"Ah, but you see, he only wanted to take me to dinner, he said. He said he found me quite interesting and wanted to get to know me better."

"That *bastard.*" Of course! It all made sense now. Metcalfe understood, and it sickened him.

"Naturally, I had dinner with him. And again the next night."

"You had no choice," Metcalfe said softly. "You couldn't refuse."

She shrugged. "I would do anything to protect my father. Just as my father would do anything to protect me. And if it meant spending nights with a man I find tedious and repulsive—well, in Russia people often must do far worse things to save their loved ones. People lie and betray and turn their dearest friends in to the NKVD. People go to the gulag; they're shot in the back of the neck. It is a very small thing, after all, for me to sleep with Rudolf von Schüssler. I would do far more, far worse, if I had to, to save my father."

"When I came to see you backstage at the Bolshoi . . . you were terrified, weren't you?"

She looked at him, and Metcalfe could see tears streaming down her cheeks. "Everywhere there are informants and gossips. If word had gotten back to him that my American lover was back in Moscow . . . I was afraid that jealousy might turn to rage. And he would carry out his threat. He would throw my father to the wolves of the NKVD. Oh, Stiva, I love you as life itself. I always have; you know that. But it cannot be. *We* cannot be."

Metcalfe barely heard her words. His mind was spinning, turning, like a kaleidoscope shifting shards of colored glass into one new pattern after another. Lana's father, a prominent general in the Soviet army, now retired from active military service but still working in the Commissariat of Defense. Her German inamorato, a man close to the Nazi ambassador, von der Schulenberg. An extraordinary chain of connections, links forged by ambition and coercion and power. A chain that bound his dearest Lana— but was it a chain that could also be *used?*

Was that what Corky had intended all along?

Metcalfe's pulse pounded. He stood up, came over to her, put his arms around her, comforted her. She went limp in his arms, seeming to dissolve into him, her body convulsed with deep sobs. Minutes went by. He held her; she wept. There was nothing he wanted to do more than hold his Lana, and in truth holding her was all he could do for her now; it was all she wanted as well. Then, still clinging to each other, she broke the silence. "I am like the Russian people themselves, you know, *moi lyubimi*. I am beyond help."

"Maybe not," Metcalfe said, his thoughts whirling. "Maybe not."

The symphony of odors almost overwhelmed the violinist, as it did so often when he was indoors, particularly in an unfamiliar place. He could smell the Nivea skin cream that the petty bureaucrat obviously used in place of shaving soap, his Obel pipe tobacco, the rosemary hair tonic he used in a sad and failing attempt to prevent baldness, though it was far too late for that. He could smell the consular officer's boot polish, which he recognized as Erdal brand; it took him back to his childhood and his father, a strict and orderly man who always kept his boots perfectly shined. His father bought canisters of Erdal shoe polish, which came with free collectible cards depicting zeppelins or gliders or, his favorite, prehistoric animals. He remembered with pleasure the beautiful color drawings of the diplodocus and the archaeopteryx and the plesiosaur, each cavorting in the primordial swamp. It was one of the very few happy memories of his childhood.

Less pleasantly—most of the smells that assaulted his sensitive nasal membranes were, alas, far from pleasant ones—he could smell the anxious bureaucrat's lunch, whose digestion was not progressing well. The man had consumed bockwurst and pickled cabbage, and he had obviously had an episode of flatulence in this office shortly before the violinist had arrived. It had largely dissipated, but not completely.

"How long a list could that be?" Kleist asked. "I am asking only for a list of British or American males who have arrived in Moscow within the last seven days. How many of them can there possibly be?" The violinist simply wanted to know if one Daniel Eigen had entered Moscow in the last few days.

It was entirely possible, of course—likely, in fact—that Eigen had entered under a different name. However the spy had entered the country, a list was a good starting point, though. It would shorten considerably the amount of time Kleist would have to spend going from hotel to hotel investigating these recent arrivals, making visual identifications.

Meeting with this man was a waste of valuable time. But the military attaché, General Ernst Köstring, with whom he properly should have been meeting, was out of the office for most of the day and had asked him to convey his request to this flunky.

The bureaucrat seemed to have one excuse after another at the ready. The man was a past master at the one skill that was paramount in the German Foreign Office: procrastination. For the last ten minutes he had improvised a veritable cadenza of reasons that he could do nothing. Kleist often encountered such an attitude in the Foreign Service, particularly when they dealt with the *Sicherheitsdienst,* whom they despised and feared.

Kleist did not particularly care that they despised the SD. That they *feared* the SD, on the other hand, was useful. So it was with this petty bureaucrat who postured at his little desk reeking of rosemary hair tonic and flatulence: *he dislikes me, but he fears me more.* These deskbound men, with their flabby asses and their flabby souls, disgusted him. They were frightened, resentful souls who felt superior to men such as the violinist, but they were nothing more than sparrows trailing in the slipstream of an eagle, mice who sought shelter with a lion. These virtuosos of the paper clip and the stapler: how ordinary was their existence, how drab their lives. They did not know, nor would they ever, the transcendence that Kleist, and his mentor, Reinhard Tristan Eugen Heydrich, knew: the transport of playing beautiful music, which could bring tears to the eyes of the listener. Or the similar transport of taking a life, which was another kind of music: measured, rhythmic, controlled, requiring not merely skill but instinct, *art.*

Kleist could not help but stare at the bureaucrat's throat, as the man gulped nervously and explained why it was *impossible,* how they could not ask the NKVD for such a list, how they did not, *could* not, cooperate with the Soviet intelligence service, who after all were working against them, suspicious of them, no matter *what* the stated policies were. . . . Kleist watched the bobbing of the man's hyoid bone, the thyroid cartilage of his larynx, the ligaments and tendons and soft fascia. It was so naked, so vulnerable. Briefly he imagined how it would feel to encircle the fleshy throat with a cold, high-tensile catgut E string and, gloriously, to snap it tight, to choke off this unending stream of *Scheisse,* all this bullshit! Kleist noticed the sharply pointed paper spike on the bureaucrat's desk and wondered what it would feel like to plunge it into one of this blabbermouth's eyeballs and into the soft tissue of his brain.

Something in the violinist's expression, some glint of his malevolent little daydream, must have suddenly come across to the bureaucrat, because Kleist could see the man's pupils shrink, his blinking become rapid, and all at once the desk man turned compliant.

". . . Which is not to say that we do not have our contacts here in Moscow," the man said hastily. "Bribes can be paid to the proper responsible authorities, our counterparts in the Soviet Foreign Ministry. They keep lists of all those who enter the country."

"Excellent," Kleist said. "When can I have this list?"

The bureaucrat swallowed, though he tried to cover his anxiety with a suave bravado. "I should think later this week we should be able to—"

"*Today.* I need the list *today.*"

The color drained from the man's face. "But of course, Herr Haupsturmführer. I shall do my best."

"And if it's not asking too much, I wonder whether you might find me a room here where I can practice my violin while I'm waiting."

"Certainly, Herr Haupsturmführer. Why don't you take my office?"

CHAPTER NINETEEN

"Great thundering Jesus, what happened to you?" roared Ted Bishop as Metcalfe entered the Metropole lobby. "You look as bad as I *feel*. Even worse than your hotel room after the YMCA boys got through with it!"

Metcalfe winked but kept walking toward the elevator. "You were right—these Russian girls can be wild."

"I don't think I ever said that." Bishop looked confused. "Hasn't really been my experience." He approached, shading his bloodshot eyes from the light, and confided: "Seems you've got an international following."

"How so?"

"Not just the Gay-Pay-Oo, or the NKVD buggers, as they're called these days. That's par for the course. Now you've got the Krauts sniffing around after you."

"Germans?"

"This morning a Kraut gentleman came by, asking the desk clerks for the names of any recent arrivals. Foreign guests who might have checked in within the last week."

Metcalfe stopped in his tracks, turned around, and tried to feign nonchalance. "Boy, the Nazis are already measuring Moscow for drapes, huh?" he attempted to joke. "Getting a bit too comfortable here, wouldn't you say?"

Bishop shrugged. "SD, from the look of him. *Sicherheitsdienst*, the SS security police, their intel types. But he wasn't making much headway with the desk clerk. Language difficulties, you know. That added to the fact that the Russkies don't much like questions, unless they're the ones askin' 'em."

"Did they give him what he wanted?" Recent arrivals? Foreign guests? Conceivably it could be a coincidence, but Metcalfe wasn't so sure. *Why a German?* he wondered.

"I took the bloke aside and had a nice little chat with him. You know how starved we are for news—thought he might know something about what the Krauts are up to, gossip, rumors, anything I could use. Very least it could be worth a line or two in my next dispatch. You know: 'According to one German visitor to this beleaguered capital . . .' People love that malarkey. Used all my ace interviewing skills. Had a good long talk."

"About what?"

"Fellow really knows a heck of a lot about music. Met Walter Gieseking personally. Elisabeth Schwarzkopf, too."

"Did he ask you for the names of guests?"

"Of course. Kept coming back to that."

"And did you help him out?" Metcalfe tried to keep the tone light.

"He said an old friend had asked him to look someone up. Said he didn't remember the exact name. Someone who just arrived from Paris."

"Well, that rules me out."

"Be that as it may. I'm a little better at *getting* information than giving it out, you know. Occupational hazard. Something about his story emitted the faintest odor of fish, I gotta say. Didn't remember the *exact* name? Please. Pull the other one; it's got bells on!"

Roger Martin was still asleep when Metcalfe knocked on his door. "Feel like going for a walk?" Metcalfe said.

"Not particularly," Roger groaned.

"Good. Let's go."

The two were followed out of the hotel by a new set of NKVD watchers, who immediately fell into the tail positions that Metcalfe was beginning to recognize as standard NKVD technique. One lagged behind at a distance; the other crossed the street and walked along at a parallel. They weren't amateurs, but they weren't good, either. Was there also another one somewhere in the vicinity, as yet undetected—the blond agent, who was virtually a Houdini by comparison with these two mediocrities? It was certainly possible. But Metcalfe was determined not to give any of the followers cause for alarm or suspicion. He and Roger simply needed to talk, out in the open and away from the hotel microphones. They would keep their movements regular, predictable.

To his observers, Metcalfe would appear to be taking a brisk morning stroll along the crowded avenue, a businessman taking a day off for some casual sightseeing; his voice, however, was anything but casual. Rapidly he went through what had happened, from the extraordinarily aggressive search of his hotel room, to the elusive, masterful tail assigned to him, to the alarming disappearance of the transmitter.

Roger's expression grew steadily graver; hearing about the stolen transmitter, he winced. "After all the trouble I went through to bury the damned thing," he said. "Unobserved, too."

"Is there any way you can assemble the relevant components? I've got the crystal; presumably the Morse key and other parts can be salvaged from shortwave radios—"

"Does that sound like a practical suggestion?" Roger broke in.

"I suppose not," Metcalfe admitted.

"Not something you could reasonably expect a feller to do, now, is it?"

"I guess it isn't."

"Right. Just so we're clear on that."

"We're clear. Absurd of me to suggest it. Can't be done. But there's got to be—"

"Then I'll do it."

Metcalfe smiled. "I knew you would, Scoop."

"Take me a day, maybe two."

"Of course. In the meantime, though, I need to reach Corky." Corky had to be told about the missing transmitter; otherwise, when his messages went unanswered, he would assume that something unfortunate had befallen Metcalfe.

"But how? We're cut off, until I manage to jury-rig a transmitter. *If* I manage to, I should say."

Metcalfe was silent for a long while, and at last he spoke. "There's a way Corky told me about. He told me to use it only as a last resort."

"I assume you don't mean the diplomatic pouch. It's slow—takes a couple of days at least. The only secure conduit for diplomatic communications that I know of is the telegraph. It goes over commercial lines, but it goes out in code."

"And it's not secure."

"Not *secure*? It's the most secure channel that exists! It's what the ambassador uses to communicate with the President, for God's sake."

"It *is* secure—from the *Russians*. But not from our own people. The enemies inside are apparently as dangerous as those outside."

"Jesus," Roger said. "So what does Corky recommend?"

"Apparently there's a secure telephonic hookup whose existence is kept secret even from most of the embassy staff. A scrambled, enciphered radio transmission relayed to a transmitter in Estonia where it's amplified, the signal sent over buried telephone trunk lines."

"*The black channel*," Roger whispered in astonishment. "Christ, I've heard rumors, but I thought that was just prattle."

"Evidently it's rarely utilized. Repeated use would risk Soviet scrutiny, so its use is reserved for emergency situations."

"Corky's man there has access?"

Metcalfe nodded.

"What's the urgency?"

"There's something wrong. Something *off* about the mission Corky sent me on here. Von Schüssler is about as far from a potential double agent as you can get, but Corky *must* have known that! His sources have to be far better than mine."

Roger looked pensive. "You're thinking there's something else going on here?"

"There's got to be. Otherwise it's a fool's errand Corky's sent me on, and that's not the way he works. He gets all his ducks in a row before he sends his men into enemy territory. He'd never have yanked me out of Paris for some speculative venture like this—it just doesn't make sense!"

"No," Roger said. "I suppose you're right. It doesn't *read*."

Metcalfe parted ways with Roger and circled back to the American embassy. On the way he passed a classical stone building that was marked with a brass plaque identifying it as the German embassy. He glanced at the building and thought of von Schüssler. All of the information he had collected on the diplomat, including their brief exchange at the American embassy dacha, formed a fairly consistent portrait of a careerist. Not brave or clever, neither an ardent Nazi nor an anti-Nazi activist.

So what was Corky up to? Why the hell had Corky sent him here?

Music spilled out of an open window at the side of the German embassy. It was frigid outside; whoever was inside must be a fresh-air freak, Metcalfe reflected idly. The music was beautiful, actually: a violin, played with impressive skill. What was the piece? he wondered. The name of the melody drifted into his head: *"Totentanz."* Dance of death. How like the Germans that was, that peculiar and sinister mixture of culture and carnage.

As he approached the American embassy, he noticed in his peripheral vision a quick motion. He turned, saw the familiar thatch of blond hair beneath a fur cap, the high Siberian cheekbones. The NKVD man who'd tailed him at Lana's apartment and had driven him to the dacha party. Now he had appeared, seemingly out of nowhere, at the embassy, as if knowing Metcalfe would be there. As if leaving for his inferior colleagues the chore of following Metcalfe from the hotel; this watcher was above that, beyond it. He seemed to *know* where his quarry was going.

Metcalfe whirled around, lurched toward the NKVD agent, but the man was gone. *Very well,* he thought. The watcher was pre-ternaturally gifted at anticipating Metcalfe's moves, but what, af-ter all, had he just learned? There was nothing out of the ordinary about an American businessman stopping into his own country's embassy. If this was pure psychological intimidation and nothing more—well, let them pull out all the stops. It would not work.

Amos Hilliard appeared in the small consulate reception area, looking disgruntled. He was obviously not pleased to see Met-calfe.

Metcalfe explained the reason for his visit. Reluctantly Hilliard assented. "The Keep," he said. "As in a castle's keep. It's jealously guarded, closely watched. I rarely use it myself. I'll have to come up with a pretext for my colleagues."

"I appreciate it," Metcalfe said.

"Tell Corky I want a raise," the diplomat replied.

A quarter of an hour later, Hilliard led Metcalfe through a rabbit's warren of locked corridors, ending at a steel door. This was, he explained as they walked, the most secure section of the embassy. There the diplomat methodically turned the dial on a large black combination lock. It took several minutes for Hilliard to unlock the door; it was obvious that he rarely entered this area.

Once they were inside the secure corridor, Hilliard pointed out a door marked ELECTRICAL CLOSET, where the junction boxes that powered the black channel were located, the telex and telephone cables fed in from outside. He stopped at an unmarked door that was triple-locked, the locks looking extraordinarily complicated. Behind the door was what looked at first glance like the interior of a telephone booth: a narrow, shallow space whose walls were steel-lined. In truth it was not much larger than a coffin. There was one metal chair. Mounted on a narrow steel ledge was an ordinary-looking black telephone handset, which sat on an over-size, bulbous base.

This was the secure communications module that Hilliard re-ferred to as the Keep. It was little more than a soundproof box, acoustically engineered using the most sophisticated methods available. Sound waves would not travel outside the enclosure. Once Metcalfe was seated, Hilliard shut the heavy door behind him and locked it.

Metcalfe could not suppress a panicky feeling of claustropho-bia. There was a small Plexiglas porthole in the door, through which Metcalfe could see Hilliard enter a small room directly across the hall, where he would monitor the operation, making sure nothing went wrong.

Inside the Keep, the air was dead and still. There was no ven-tilation—apparently another soundproofing measure—and it quickly grew hot as Metcalfe waited. Hilliard had initiated the black-channel contact by means of a highest-priority coded tele-gram; once the necessary links were in place, which required several minutes, an incoming call would be received.

Perspiration poured down Metcalfe's face. Suddenly there was a loud, shrill ring, like no telephone he had ever heard before. Metcalfe snatched up the receiver.

"Stephen, my boy," came Corky's unmistakable birdlike caw. Even on this secure connection, Corcoran was careful not to use Metcalfe's last name. It was somehow deeply reassuring to hear Corky's voice after what seemed like an eternity, even though it had been no more than a few days. "I take it there's some ur-gency. I was just enjoying a nice lunch." There was a strange hollowness to the connection, a metallic echo.

"My apologies," Metcalfe said stiffly.

"Have you been enjoying the ballet?"

"Did you receive my message telling you I've established con-tact?"

"Indeed. But what about the German?"

"A brief contact."

"Enough for an assessment?"

"I believe so."

"Would you say we have a turnable asset? A potential double?"

"I'd say no. And I'd say you knew that already."

Corky was silent for a few seconds. The only noise on the line was a faint white noise, a muted hiss. "The shortest path between two points isn't always a straight line," the old man replied.

"Why am I here?" Metcalfe raised his voice in irritation. "For Christ's sake, Corky, I don't think you sent me here, with all the risks involved, on a fool's errand. All right, so an old girlfriend of mine happens to have taken up with a complete mediocrity of a German diplomat—so what? Don't tell me you don't have a hundred better prospects for recruitment than von Schüssler! What the *hell's* going on here, Corky?"

"Settle down, Stephen," Corky said icily. "I wanted you to establish contact with your 'old girlfriend,' as you put it, and that you've done. Phase one has been accomplished."

"Phase one of *what?* I'm not some marionette, Corky. You can't pull the strings and assume I'll dance. *What the hell am I here for?*" He mopped his brow and neck with a handkerchief.

"Stephen, you'll be told what you need to be told, when you need to be told it."

"That's not good enough, Corky. I'm here in the field, risking my neck—"

"You are a volunteer, Stephen. Not a conscript. Any time you wish to go home, I'll be happy to make the arrangements. But as long as you're in my employ, operational security is paramount. This is a dangerous game we're all involved in. The nightmare of what happened to Paris station should serve as a reminder of that—"

"What's the next 'phase,' as you put it?" Metcalfe cut in.

A long, metallic hiss. The seconds ticked by. Metcalfe wondered briefly whether the connection had been severed when Corky replied, "Rudolf von Schüssler, like all of his colleagues in the German embassy, is there in Moscow to gather information about what the Russians are up to. Hitler has forbidden them to engage in any actual espionage, for fear of arousing Soviet suspicions. This, inevitably, makes their job just about impossible. The Nazis are desperate for intelligence on the Soviets, but they're unable to get it. I say we give it to them."

"Meaning what?"

"You will shortly be receiving a package of documents. You are to convince Svetlana to pass them to her German lover."

Metcalfe almost dropped the phone.

"Pass them on?" he cried.

"We have a confluence of factors here," Corky said. "Svetlana's father is a retired prominent Red Army general, a Hero of the Revolution, who works in the Commissariat of Defense."

"His job there is insignificant," Metcalfe objected. "A sinecure given to a lauded soldier. Purely bureaucratic. Lana told me—"

"Improvise, son. You can do better than that. Give him a promotion."

"You're asking me to *use* her. That's the real reason you sent me here, isn't it?" He'd guessed it, but he wanted to hear Corky speak the words.

"I'd put it differently. I want you to *enlist* her. I want you to use *von Schüssler*. To use him as a conduit, a channel through which to send information to the *Oberwehrmacht*. Strategic and tactical information, *intelligence* that will alter the decisions they make."

"Jesus, Corky, you're asking me to put her in an incredibly risky situation. I mean, she's a dancer, a ballerina, for God's sake! She's not a trained intelligence agent. She's not a spy—she's an artist."

"She's a performer, Stephen. Some of my finest agents have come from the theater."

"And if she slips, what do you think's going to happen to her?"

"Stephen," Corcoran said patiently, "need I remind you of the situation she's already in? For any Russian citizen to be involved with a foreigner is treacherous these days. But she's not any ordinary Russian. She's a prominent dancer, in addition to which her father is a general, and she's sleeping with a German diplomat. Forget the Hitler–Stalin pact—Soviet intelligence has to be watching her extremely closely."

Metcalfe flashed on her minder, Kundrov. *More closely than you realize,* he thought. But von Schüssler hadn't approached Lana for any reasons of espionage, he was sure. If his interest in her was connected in any way with her father's position, Lana had not seen it, even after months of his attentions. No, the German's motivation was carnal. She was a magnificently beautiful woman, which was reason enough for his interest in her. Moreover, she was a prima ballerina, hence a prize catch for him to brandish about. Insecure men like von Schüssler liked to enhance their reputations by showing off female baubles. Once he had blackmailed Lana by revealing the existence of Mikhail Baranov's name in a dossier that could get him executed at once, he had shown no further interest in the man.

"And what about her father?" Metcalfe persisted. "I'd be placing him at risk, too."

"Her father is—how do I put this tactfully—not long for this world. It's only a matter of time before he, too, is arrested, like most of his high-ranking compatriots in the Red Army."

"He's survived so far."

"His name is on a list. We happen to know this. The NKVD calls it *Kniga Smerty*—the Book of Death. Arrests have been proceeding in an orderly sequence. His time will come in a matter of weeks. Once he's arrested, Lana will no longer be a useful conduit for our disinformation, so the time is short. In any case, you think the NKVD doesn't already wonder whether she's a security risk as it is? She's already put herself in the stew."

"It wasn't voluntary," Metcalfe said, blotting his damp forehead. "She had no choice."

"Please. And let me remind you that we're watching the Nazis gradually devour all of Europe. Not so gradually, actually— they're taking huge gulps. The goddamn Nazi war machine has been blitzkrieging its way to the ends of the earth. We've never seen such a threat to the freedom of the world. France is defeated; Hitler has no enemies in Europe; England can't possibly hold out. If we have the chance to put a stop to it, it's our goddamned *obligation* to do so. *That's* what you're there for. There's nothing more important. And here I think the opportunity to do something about it has been placed in our laps. It would be sheer folly not to seize it. Worse than folly: it would be criminal neglect." Corky paused; Metcalfe was silent. "Are you there, Stephen?"

"And what would be in these documents you want her to pass on to von Schüssler?"

"These documents will paint a picture for the OKW, the *Oberkommando der Wehrmacht,* for Hitler and his High Command."

"What sort of picture?"

"Some painters use oil; others use watercolors. We will use numbers. Neatly stacked columns of digits. Estimates of troop strength, exact figures, equipment, divisions, numbers of men, locations of weapons depots. An agglomeration of data that will, to the green eyeshades at the *Wehrmacht* and eventually to Hitler himself, evoke a picture of the Red Army as vivid as anything by van Gogh."

"What *sort* of picture?" Metcalfe persisted.

"A painting of a bear, Stephen. But a cuddly one. A bear cub that has been declawed."

"You want her to pass on to von Schüssler fake documents that demonstrate how weak Russia is militarily."

"They'll be excellent forgeries, let me assure you. Stalin himself could not tell the difference."

"I have no doubt of that."

My God, Metcalfe marveled: it was brilliant and diabolical; it was perfect Corky. "If Hitler thinks an invasion of Russia is a cakewalk, he'll do it in a heartbeat," said Metcalfe. "He'll just kick down the door and go right in!"

"Do tell," Corky said, his voice dripping with sarcasm, audible even despite the odd acoustics of the connection.

"Jesus God, Corky, you're trying to trick Hitler into declaring war on the Soviet Union!"

Another long silence. The odd crackles, blips, and beeps continued, like the random noises of an ill-tuned radio. "Stephen, I've mentioned the Peloponnesian Wars, have I not?"

"Yes," Metcalfe snapped. "Athens survived only because its enemies began fighting each other."

"Athens *sowed* the discord between its enemies. They set one against the other. That's the real point."

"But you have no idea whether any of the documents will ever get to Hitler, do you? Think of how many links in the chain there are, how many opportunities for some skeptic in the Nazi bureaucracy to filter it out."

"True enough, Stephen, but if we only did the sure thing, we wouldn't do anything, now would we?"

"Granted."

"We know this: Hitler spends eight hours a day reading reports and memoranda and intel reports. He's a fiend for intelligence. He alone makes all the major decisions, and he does so based on the information he receives. And the only information he takes seriously is the stuff he receives from his espionage service. His trusted spies. Now, von Schüssler is no spy, but he's a supremely well-connected fellow. He has friends in high places."

Metcalfe's mind was whirling. His handkerchief was by now soaking wet and useless. He reached for another but didn't have one. "I'll do it on one condition."

"Excuse me?" Corky said incredulously.

"If anything happens to Lana—if she has reason to believe she's in trouble, that she's about to be arrested—I want you to guarantee me that you'll smuggle her out of Moscow." Now he wiped the stream of perspiration from his eyes with his palms. It was damned uncomfortable in here, and he didn't know how much longer he could last.

"Stephen, you know full well we don't do such things."

"I know full well we *do*. We've done it in France; we've done it in Germany."

"Extraordinary cases—"

"This is an extraordinary case, Corky. I won't involve her without that guarantee."

"We'll certainly do whatever we can to limit her risk, Stephen, but—"

"That's the deal," Metcalfe said. "Nonnegotiable. Take it or leave it."

Amos Hilliard sat at a teletype terminal directly across the hall, alert for any incoming messages that might require immediate attention. The black channel had been installed only recently, and like all new technology it was not completely reliable. It was a complex, even unwieldy fusion of international connections, a chain of links each of which was vulnerable to the vicissitudes of war. There were too many things that could go wrong. The best indicator of the steadiness of the transmission was the signal strength meter, inset into the console at which he was sitting. Both needles, indicating the strength of transmission and reception, remained stable, moving little. If either needle dropped, Hilliard was ready to leap into action if need be to restore the connection.

Metcalfe was taking longer than Hilliard expected. Whatever he was talking about with Corcoran, it was obviously a matter of some delicacy and complexity. Hilliard could only guess what the young man was up to in Moscow. He would not ask; Corky's sacred compartmentation proscribed that, but he couldn't help but wonder. He'd heard tell of young Metcalfe, a rich playboy who didn't seem quite serious enough to be one of Corky's boys, and this ballerina from the Bolshoi. He'd seen the two of them go off at the party at the dacha. It didn't take a rocket scientist to figure out that there was something going on between them. Then there were all these questions about von Schüssler. Obviously Metcalfe was trying to assess the German. Maybe he was using the girl to get at the Nazi. Maybe that was why Corky had sent somebody so callow. Maybe Metcalfe's experience in the field was not as important as his experience in the bedroom.

Hilliard glanced at the gauge and started. Both needles had dropped abruptly. The signal strength had, for some reason, plummeted. He leaped from the terminal and raced into the hall, his footsteps echoing throughout the corridor. Peering into the Plexiglas porthole inset into the Keep's steel door, he could see Metcalfe, drenched with sweat, chattering away. If he was still talking, that meant the connection hadn't in fact gone down at all.

So what could have caused the drop in signal strength?

Suddenly he went cold. Could it be—?

He hammered on the porthole with his fist until Metcalfe turned around, looking perplexed. Wildly Hilliard signaled to him to hang up, his index finger making a slashing motion against his throat. Metcalfe appeared to say another few words, then rapidly hung up the handset.

When Hilliard finally got the door unlocked, Metcalfe was on his feet, a sweaty mess. "What the hell—?" Metcalfe blurted out.

"A breach!" said Hilliard. "The last twenty, thirty seconds— how sensitive was the conversation? It may have been tapped into, overheard."

"*Tapped?* No, we'd already moved past the sensitive stuff; we were just tying things up. But how is this possible—*overheard?*"

Hilliard did not bother to reply. He spun around, began running down the hall, his footsteps clacking loudly on the terrazzo floor. The only other exposed nexus, Hilliard knew, was the electrical closet at the end of the hall by the entrance, where the ganglion of telephone cables was patched in, a temporary vulnerability that still hadn't been properly sealed off. Suddenly, all the way down the corridor, he could see the door to the electrical closet fly open. A dark figure emerged and immediately disappeared through the door at the end of the hall. Hilliard recognized the man: he was a junior embassy secretary, one whose allegiances Hilliard had always wondered about. Now, however, he knew. *The man had been listening in.*

For whom?

Hilliard ran to the electrical closet door, flung it open. There it was: a headset discarded on the floor by the man who had just left. Confirmation that Hilliard didn't need.

Metcalfe was now standing just outside the electrical closet. He saw; he understood what had happened.

"No more," Hilliard said. "The circuits are dirty."

"So much for the vaunted security of the black channel."

"The security of the black channel was designed to protect against the outside. The Soviets. Not against those within."

"Who was it?"

"A junior Foreign Service officer. Not important in and of himself, within the embassy hierarchy—"

"On whose *instructions?*"

"I don't know. And I doubt I'll be able to find out anytime soon. All I know is this, Metcalfe: There are a lot of players involved here. And when there are a lot of players, somebody's getting played. Next time you try to use the black channel, you may as well be broadcasting on Radio Moscow. Do yourself— and me—a favor. Leave by the service entrance, at the back. And no more, Metcalfe. Please. No more."

The violinist sat on a park bench facing the American embassy. The main theme to Schubert's quartet *Der Tod und das Mädchen* was running pleasantly through his head. He loved the way the angry, turbulent triplets of the opening gave way to the soothing, black-velvet D-minor cadences, the way the piece modulated from major to minor, the ominousness of the sweet melody. As he watched people entering and departing the main entrance, he attempted, unsuccessfully of course, to ignore the stomach-turning odors of Moscow. He had already learned them—the rancid stench of male sweat, astringent with vodka, the unclean females, the onion-foul breath, the cheap tobacco, the omni-present fug of boiled cabbage. He had not thought anything could be more repellent than the French, but he was wrong; the Russians were even worse. These smells had by now become background against which he would instantly recognize any for-eigner, whether he be American or British. Müller, his control in the *Sicherheitsdienst,* had strong reason to suspect that Daniel Eigen, a member of the clandestine espionage ring operating out of Paris, had gone to Moscow. And Reinhard Heydrich himself suspected that this Eigen might be involved in a high-level scheme, which had to be investigated. Anyone could eliminate Eigen, but very few SD agents had the skill to both investigate and, when necessary, kill at a moment's notice.

The French borders, even under German control, were porous. People could, and did, escape by any number of means. There were many English and British citizens living in Paris, many of them undocumented, unregistered, and deducing which ones might have gone missing in the last few days was simply impos-sible. Moscow, however, was much easier. True, a foreigner could enter here using a false passport, as was possible anywhere in the world, but it was much more difficult in Russia, where the scru-tiny was greater. And the number of foreigners entering Russia was minuscule. When he got the list later on today, he was sure it would not be a long one. Which was good; that meant the list of suspects was short and thus easier to investigate.

He had placed a fellow SD agent outside the British embassy as well. Between the two of them, it was not unlikely that they would spot their target. There was, after all, an excellent chance that he would visit his country's embassy; they all did.

A man in a tan overcoat strode out of the building. Could this be him?

Kleist stood up, crossed the avenue, and soon caught up with the man. "Pardon me," he said with a friendly look on his face. "We know each other, yes?"

But even before the man opened his mouth, the violinist knew he was not the target. Kleist could smell the particular array of animal fats that clung to the man's garb, the pork and goose, and then the overlay of paprika. He was a Hungarian, and his accent confirmed it.

"No, I don't think so," the man said. "Sorry."

"My apologies," the violinist said. "I thought you were some-one else."

CHAPTER TWENTY

At first, Metcalfe did not recognize the plump, dowdy woman with the *babushka* pulled tight over her head who was sitting on a bench in the gardens of Sverdlov Place. That was how well she had disguised herself. Obviously she had borrowed the costume from the Bolshoi, the padding strategically placed at various places around her body transforming her slender figure into a typically overweight Russian peasant woman of middle age.

Only once he had determined, at a safe distance, that it was indeed Lana did he stride past her bench. She did not seem to recognize him, did not even look at him.

There was a good possibility, he realized, that he was being observed; although he saw no signs of a tail anywhere, he had to assume that the blond NKVD agent with the pale gray eyes was concealed somewhere nearby, watching. Perhaps his every move was not being watched, but for all intents and purposes he would have to presume it was.

At their meeting at the stable he had given her detailed instructions setting up their rendezvous. Whenever they met from now on, he told her, they would have to employ the techniques of tradecraft—he had used the Russian term *po vsem pravilam iskusstva,* which literally meant "the rules of art."

She had responded with both fear and relief. The furtiveness terrified her, but she was grateful for Metcalfe's thoroughness as well, for it would protect her—and her father. And yet when Metcalfe explained the methods they would have to use, something had occurred to her, and she said, "How do you know so much about these things, Stephen? How do you know about these—these *pravily iskusstva?* I thought you were a businessman—but what kind of businessman knows how to act like a *spy?*"

He shrugged and replied, with a casualness that he hoped she found convincing, "I watch a lot of Hollywood movies, *dusya;* you know that."

Now, after he'd gone several hundred feet past her bench, he slowed his pace somewhat, as if uncertain of where he was going. At that point, he was overtaken by Lana, who was transformed not only in appearance but even in gait: she walked quickly but with a slight limp, as if afflicted with a touch of gout or perhaps some hip ailment.

As she squeezed past him on the narrow lane, she spoke quietly and rapidly: "Vasiliyevsky Alley is just off Pushkin Street." Then she moved ahead. He looked round the park uncertainly, seeming to orient himself, and then resumed walking, staying a hundred feet or so behind her at a fairly constant pace. He marveled at how different she looked, how she had mastered the walk of the impatient old lady. Leaving the park, she plunged into traffic, crossing Pushkin Street with an old woman's irritable fearlessness.

By going through this procedure they were, in the language of Corky and his trainers, "dry-cleaning" themselves, making sure that neither one of them had "grown a tail," or been followed. He watched her turn into the tiny Vasiliyevsky Alley; then he followed her there. She approached the wooden door of what appeared to be an apartment building, a row of doorbells on the left, next to each button a handwritten name set in a small brass frame. The building looked old and decrepit; inside, there was no lobby, just a stair landing. The building smelled of spoiled meat and *makhorka* tobacco. He followed her up two flights of creaky steps, covered in threadbare carpet, to an apartment door.

He entered a dark, close, and musty flat and closed the door behind himself. Immediately she threw her arms around him. Her padded shape felt strange and unfamiliar to his hands, but her face was as ravishingly beautiful as ever, her mouth warm and inviting, instantly arousing him.

She broke the embrace, pulled away. "We should be safe here, my darling."

"Who lives here?"

"A dancer. I should say, a *former* dancer. She rejected the advances of the rehearsal coach, and now she works as a cleaner at TASS, where her mother also works. Masha's fortunate to have a job at all."

"She and her mother are both at work?"

Lana nodded. "I told her I had . . . met someone. She knows I'd do the same for her, if she needed a private place, a—"

"A love nest, I think it's called."

"Yes, Stiva," she teased. "You would know what it's called."

He smiled uncomfortably. "Have you ever come here with von Schüssler?"

"Oh, no, of course not! He would never come to such a place! He takes me to his apartment in Moscow, and only there."

"He has another place?"

"In the country he has a grand house that the Russians seized from some rich merchant. The Germans are being treated very well these days. Stalin must be very concerned that Hitler see how serious he is about good relations."

"Have you ever been there? To von Schüssler's country house, I mean?"

"Stiva, I've told you already—he means *nothing* to me! I *despise* him!"

"This is not about jealousy, Lana. I need to know where you two meet."

She narrowed her eyes. "Why do you need to know this?"

"For planning purposes. I'll explain."

"He takes me only to his Moscow flat. The house in Kuntsevo is off-limits."

"Why?"

"It's a large and grand place, with staff, people who know his wife. He prefers to be discreet." She added with distaste, "He is a married man, you know. With a wife and children back in Berlin. Apparently I am to be hidden like a shameful secret. There he spends his weekends writing his memoirs, as if he had anything to say, as if he was anything more than a cockroach! But why are you asking me all these questions, Stiva? Enough about that beast! I have to see him tonight, and I'd rather not have to think about him until I have to."

"Because I have an idea, Lana. A way to help you." Hearing himself speak the words aloud sickened him. He was lying to her, using her. *Manipulating* her, more accurately. But it was killing him. "Does he ask about your father?"

"Very little. Only enough to remind me of what he knows about Father. The power he has. As if he needs to remind me! Does he think I can possibly forget? Does he think I don't remember this every second I'm with him?" She almost spit out: "Does he think I forget, that I'm swept away by his charms?"

"So it would not seem strange to him if you happened to mention that your father has recently been assigned to a new, important job at the Commissariat—a job that gives him access to a wide range of documents concerning the Red Army?"

"Why in the world would I want to say this?"

"To put an idea in his head."

"Ah, yes," Lana said with heavy sarcasm. "So he will ask me to steal documents from my father, is that it?"

"Exactly."

"And then . . . and then I shall *give* him these state secrets, is that your idea, Stiva?"

"Correct. Documents that reveal top-secret Soviet military plans."

She cupped Metcalfe's face with her hands as one would a silly child, and then she laughed. "*Brilliant* idea, my Stiva. And then shall I stand in the middle of Red Square with a megaphone and tell all of Moscow what I think of Stalin? Would you care to join me?"

Metcalfe continued, undeterred by her sarcasm. "The documents will be counterfeit, of course."

"Oh, and where shall I *get* these counterfeit documents?"

"From me. I'll supply them."

She pulled back, her eyes fixed steadily on his. "And he will discredit himself," she said slowly, no longer sarcastic, "by passing these documents to Berlin."

"Eventually, yes, he will discredit himself," Metcalfe conceded.

"And then he will be recalled to Berlin, and I will be free of him."

"In time. But before then, you'll be using him to save your country."

"*Save* Russia? How is this possible?"

Metcalfe realized that he was playing a dangerous, dishonest game with her, and he despised having to do it. By telling her only part of what he wanted her to do he was in effect leading her on, playing on her hatred of Nazism and her love of Russia, her hatred of von Schüssler—and her love of Metcalfe.

"You know there's no agreement, no piece of paper, that Hitler can sign that will stop him from doing whatever he thinks is best for the Nazis. He is determined to take over the world—he's never stopped saying that from his earliest days. It's in *Mein Kampf;* it's in all his speeches, all his remarks. He makes no secret of it. Any country that threatens him, he'll attack—and attack first. Including the Soviet Union."

"That's insane! Stalin would never threaten Nazi Germany!"

"I'm sure you're right. But the only way to make sure that *Hitler* believes that is to feed him information, intelligence, that assures him of that. Nothing else would he believe. Do you see? You will pass documents to Hitler, using von Schüssler, that *assure* Hitler that the Soviet Union is no threat to him, no risk to Germany. If Hitler does not feel threatened, he's less likely to act aggressively."

"Stiva, I've always wondered how much you tell me is true. You say you're a businessman, you speak Russian so well, you say your mother is Russian—"

"And she is. That much is true. And I am a businessman—sort of. Well, my *family's* in business—that's what brought me here in the first place."

"But not this time."

"Not entirely, no. I'm here to help out some friends."

"Some friends in intelligence."

"Something like that."

"Then it's true what they say about foreigners in *Pravda*. That you are all spies!"

"No, that's propaganda. Most are not." He hesitated. "I'm not a spy, Lana."

"You are doing this for love, then."

Was she being sarcastic again? He looked closely at her. "For love of Russia," he said. "And love of you."

"Mother Russia is in your veins," she said, "as it is in mine. You love her as I do."

"In some ways, yes. Not the Soviet Union. But Russia, the Russian people, the language, the culture, the arts. And you."

"I think you have many loves," she said.

Was there a flicker of comprehension in her face? In the shadows, it was impossible to say for sure.

"Yes," he said, drawing her close. He was roiled by passion and by guilt. "Many loves. And one." It was as close to the truth as he could express to her.

They lay on the narrow bed in this gloomy apartment of a stranger. Her arm lay across his chest, both of them sticky and sweaty, their breathing slowing now. Her face was down on the pillow; he stared up at the cracks in the plaster ceiling. Their lovemaking had brought him a sense of physical release but not an emotional one. He was still tense, perhaps even more so, and his guilt was swollen in his chest, creating a queasiness in his stomach, a sourness at the back of his throat. Lana had made love with her customary abandon, her eyes closed, her head thrown back. He wondered whether it had taken her away, even for a few minutes, from the terrible anxieties of her life. He didn't want to do anything or say anything to mar any serenity she might be enjoying. It was bad enough that he was misleading her as he was.

After a few minutes, she turned her face toward his. He could see the tension still there; it had not gone away.

"Do you understand about my . . . minder, as I call him?"

"The one I met at the dacha? Who follows you everywhere?"

She nodded.

"You seem quite comfortable with him. Is there something I don't understand?"

"I *seem* comfortable, yes. But I am terrified of him, of what he can do to me. Do you understand what he can do, what *they* can do? If they think I am meeting with an agent of American intelligence?"

"Of course," Metcalfe said, touching her flushed face with his fingertips, her silken skin.

"I wonder. Moscow is very different from the way it was when we first met. You cannot imagine the purges we have just been through these last few years. No one could believe the nightmare! No one who did not live here, as a Russian, and even *we* could not believe what was happening."

"It's not over, is it?"

"No one knows. It is less now than it was two years ago, but no one knows. This was the horrible thing, not knowing. Not knowing when a knock came on the door whether it was the NKVD coming to take you away. Not knowing when the telephone rang if it was terrible news. People just disappeared, no explanation given, and their family was afraid to say anything to anyone about it. If someone was taken away, sent to the camps or executed . . . you would *shun* their families. You would fear that the families of the victims were contagious—that you might catch this disease from them! An arrest in the family, it is like typhoid fever, like leprosy—you must stay away! And then they're always telling us to beware foreigners, because the capitalists are all spies. I told you about one of my dancer friends who got too friendly with a foreigner. Do you know what they say she is doing now, this beautiful and talented girl? She works in a camp in Tomsk, and every day she must chip out excrement from the frozen toilets with a crowbar."

"Innocence is no defense."

"Do you know what they say, the authorities, if you can get one to talk to you? They say, of course there will be the innocent victim, but what of it? When the trees are chopped down, the wood chips fly."

Metcalfe closed his eyes, slipped his arm around her.

"A neighbor of ours—a man with a pregnant wife—he was arrested; no one knows why. He was taken to Butyrki Prison, where they charged him with crimes against the state, and they ordered him to sign a false declaration. But he refused. He said he was innocent. So they brought in his wife, his pregnant wife, into the interrogation room. Two men held him down while two others threw his wife down onto the floor, and they beat her and kicked her, and she screamed and screamed, and he screamed at them to stop, but they would not." She swallowed. Tears were streaming down her face, dampening the pillow. "And then her baby was delivered, right then, right there. Stillborn. Dead."

"Jesus, Lana," Metcalfe said. "Please."

"So, my Stiva, if you wonder why I have changed, why I seem sad, you must know this. While you have been traveling the world and seeing women, this is the world I have been living in. This is why I must be so careful."

"I'll take care of you," Metcalfe said. "I'll help you." And he thought to himself, *What am I doing to her?*

CHAPTER TWENTY-ONE

"Ah, my poppy," cooed von Schüssler, "you don't seem to be listening to me."

He had been prattling on and on, as he liked to do, about the petty annoyances at his office, the colleagues who did not appreciate his brilliant ideas, the secretary who habitually came to work late, blaming the difficulty of public transportation in Moscow even though she lived not two blocks away. It was all the most tedious litany of complaints, all of which had just one common theme: none of these little people appreciated his greatness. Von Schüssler never divulged secrets. Either he was more canny than Lana gave him credit for or, as seemed more likely, he simply didn't really think about anything that didn't have to do with his own greatness.

"I suppose I'm a bit preoccupied," Lana said. They both lay on von Schüssler's enormous four-poster bed, which he had had sent over from Berlin. Von Schüssler was sipping brandy and gobbling marzipan as he blathered. He was wearing a silk smoking robe and (as she'd had the misfortune to glimpse a few times) nothing beneath it. His body odor—the German was not fastidious about his personal hygiene—was revolting. She felt the usual tightness in her stomach that she felt whenever she was around him, but tonight it was worse. She was dreading the moment when he slipped out of his robe, as she could tell he was about to do, and the sex act began. "Act" it was indeed, she reflected. But her anxiety was worse than usual tonight because of what she was about to do.

"You must be rehearsing your choreography in your head," von Schüssler said, stroking her hair as one would pet a dog.

"But you must leave your work at work, poppy. Our bed is a sacred place. We must not defile it with our worries about work."

She was tempted to ask him why he didn't observe the same rule, but she restrained herself. "It's my father," she said. "I worry about him so much."

"*Schatzi,*" von Schüssler replied tenderly. "Please, my little poppy. Not one word of the dossier will ever get to the authorities here! Haven't I assured you of that?"

She shook her head. "It's not that. It's the new job he's been assigned."

"Ah," von Schüssler said, settling back against a raft of pillows, no longer interested. "Well, then." He seemed to be waiting for her to change the subject so he could either return to complaining about the little people at the embassy or else, even worse, loosen the belt of his robe.

"They've moved him to a new position," Lana persisted. "A much more important position in the Commissariat of Defense Ministry."

Von Schüssler took another sip of brandy and reached for another marzipan. "Would you like one, my dear?"

She shook her head. "Father has now been put in charge of overseeing all Red Army expenditures. They have him reviewing all the expenses within the Commissariat, which means he must look over all the troop allocations, weapons expenditures—everything!"

Von Schüssler emitted only a bored grunt.

"It's an impossible job! He basically must read over the entire Red Army military strategy!"

Finally, a glint of understanding seemed to dawn in von Schüssler's watery blue eyes. And was that a hint of porcine greed as well? "Really? That's quite an important job, then, isn't it? He must be quite pleased with the promotion."

Lana heaved a great sigh. "All these documents he takes home, all these papers he must read late into the night! Those columns and columns of numbers—how many tanks and airplanes, how many ships, how many weapons, how many men . . . My poor father, they are working him to death!"

"You have seen these documents?"

"Seen them? They are spread all over our apartment—I trip over them! My dear father, he is a soldier, not an accountant; why do they make him do this?"

"But have you read any of them?" Von Schüssler was trying to appear casual, but he was not doing a very good job of it. "Do you, er, understand any of them, I mean to say?"

"Rudi, the writing on them is so tiny it makes *my* eyes hurt! My poor father—he must use reading glasses, and these papers give him such *headaches.*"

"So many papers all over the place," von Schüssler mused. "He must lose track of where they are, no? Is your father a very organized man?"

"Organized? Father?" She laughed. "When he was a commander of troops, there was no one more orderly. But when it comes to paperwork, he is a disaster! He's always complaining to me that he can't find this paper or that paper, have I seen it, where has he put it . . ."

"He would not notice if papers were missing, then." Lana could almost see the wheels in von Schüssler's mind turning slowly. "Very interesting, my poppy. *Very* interesting." The idea—it had become *his* idea, which was the crucial thing—had finally taken root in the arid soil of the German's mind. After a few seconds, he seemed to have made up his mind. He was not going to press her just now. He wanted to wait until after they had made love. No doubt he calculated that once he had made love to her, she would feel even more favorably disposed toward him, and then he would make his bold proposal. He reached for one end of the silk belt, whose loose knot sat astride his large belly like the ribbon on a gift. Her stomach clenched as he tugged at the belt and his robe came open, revealing the dark recesses of his crotch, where his minuscule organ was hidden somewhere beneath the tangles of pubic hair.

He placed his pudgy hand on her head as if to stroke her hair again, but this time he pushed at her head in a gentle, suggestive way, pointing her in the right direction. "My beautiful Red Poppy," he said. "My *Schatzi*."

For a few seconds she pretended not to understand what he wanted, and then she resigned herself to the inevitable. She had to keep in mind that she was now engaged in a mission larger than herself, a mission that from time to time entailed unpleasant chores, as did all important missions. She moved her face in toward von Schüssler's groin, and as she did so she forced herself to smile with anticipation and delight, a smile that she hoped would conceal her ineffable disgust.

The violinist entered the German consulate at Number 10 Leont'yevskiy Lane and gave his name. The receptionist, a middle-aged Frau with peroxide blond hair whose dark roots were showing, gave him a coy smile while he sat waiting for the military attaché. She seemed to find him attractive and seemed to believe that she herself was attractive, which might have been the case several decades ago. Kleist smiled back.

Lieutenant-General Ernst Köstring, the military attaché of the German embassy in the Soviet Union, was the man in Moscow who was nominally in charge of all German espionage activities within Russia, at least.

The German military attaché was in charge of local espionage activities against the Soviet Union. On the ground, at least, for he answered to several others above him in the *Abwehr* and ultimately his boss, Admiral Wilhelm Franz Canaris, the *Abwehr* chief.

But to call Köstring a spymaster was, to the violinist, a joke. He was an expert on Russian affairs, having been born and raised in Moscow, and he was fluent in Russian. But he lacked *Zivilkourage*. His dispatches were legendary for their vacuity. For years he had complained that he was unable to get any information out of the Russians, that they would not let him travel about the country without NKVD escorts. His reports contained no hard information about the Soviet army, nothing you couldn't get from reading the papers or watching the May Day parades in Red Square. Anyway, the *Abwehr* was famous for resenting the *Sicherheitsdienst,* the true spy agency. The *Abwehr* was threatened by the SD and realized that, in Hitler's eyes, they did not measure up.

Köstring, however, knew how the world worked. He knew that the violinist had arrived in Moscow with the personal blessing of SS *Gruppenführer* Heydrich; he understood that Heydrich was not a man whose enmity one wanted to incur. Reinhard Heydrich was brilliant and ruthless. Hitler once called him "the man with a heart of iron," which was from the Führer the highest praise, of course. The SD was a competitor agency, but Köstring knew enough to cooperate, or he would face a world of trouble. Simply by requesting a meeting with the military attaché the violinist was playing his strongest card. He would get the intelligence he needed. The petty bureaucrat he'd been fobbed off on could go straight to hell. Kleist had no time for that cowardly, excuse-making, farting nonentity.

The military attaché received Kleist politely. He was slim and dignified-looking, in his early sixties. He was a busy man and did not waste time with chitchat.

"I was not very pleased to learn of your arrival in Moscow," Köstring began. "As you know, since August of last year the Führer has forbidden the *Abwehr* to engage in any activities hostile to Russia."

"That is not my intent," Kleist snapped. He did not like the way this conversation was starting off.

"Admiral Canaris has issued a strict directive: nothing must be done to offend the Russians. The admiral is complying with the Führer's wishes, and so must I. German spies do not operate here. It is that simple."

Now Kleist understood why the mealymouthed bureaucrat

he'd met with earlier was so fearful. It was against official embassy policy to engage in undercover activities. Such cowards!

"As Goethe said, a lack of knowledge can be a dangerous thing," Kleist said. "Surely there are ways around such a prohibition. Particularly for a clever man such as yourself."

"On the contrary. I follow the letter of the law. That said, I understand that your commission comes directly from *der Ziege.*" He permitted the tiniest curl of a smile. *Der Ziege,* the Goat, was the disparaging nickname for Heydrich. It referred to the spymaster's high-pitched voice. He had been given this nickname in his college days and had been unable to shake it, and whenever he heard it, he still became furious.

Kleist did not smile. He let it be known, by the expression in his eyes, that he was not amused.

The attaché realized that he had made a slip. The gibe would get back to Heydrich. He hastened to repair the damage: "This assignment could not be more authoritative, unless it came from Himmler himself."

The violinist nodded.

"My boss and yours are good friends, you know. Canaris and Heydrich are neighbors; they play croquet together. Heydrich even instructed Canaris's daughter in the violin. I'm told they play music together." Unnerved by Kleist's silence, Köstring went on: "You all seem to be musicians, you men of the SD."

"Amateur," said the violinist. "And only a few of us. The list, please."

Köstring opened a desk drawer and drew out a sheet of paper, handed it to Kleist. The list of some twenty names had been handwritten in the strange Roman script of someone accustomed to the Cyrillic alphabet. Kleist read through the names. There were several officials of the Communist Party of the United States, a few left-wing artist types, including a Negro singer and a minor theater director. Some visitors from England's Fabian Society, a few men who were here with business aims. Along with names, there were dates of arrival and scheduled departure, passport numbers, the names and addresses of the hotels where they were staying. Conceivably, any of these people might be agents, here in Moscow under false names, or they could all be here legitimately. No matter: he would make the rounds of the hotels and learn what he could. This was, at least, a good start.

Kleist stood up. "I appreciate your help," he said simply.

"One thing," the attaché said, an index finger extended. "This we are most strict about. We do not kill Russians."

The violinist's smile was tight, his eyes cold. "I have no intention of killing any Russians," he said.

One of the front-desk clerks called out to Metcalfe as he entered the lobby, "Sir? Mr. Metcalfe? So very sorry, but you have an urgent message."

Metcalfe took the folded piece of paper the clerk handed him. *From Roger?* he wondered. *From Hilliard?* Neither, surely, would use the hotel desk clerk to pass on a message of urgency.

No. It was not a slip of paper from the clerk's message pad but a thick sheet of rag paper. At the top was engraved "People's Commissariat of Foreign Trade of the USSR." The message was a few typed lines:

> *Esteemed Mr. Metcalfe!*
>
> *You are hereby requested to report forthwith to the People's Commissariat of Foreign Trade for an urgent consultation with Commissar Litvikov. Your driver has already been instructed.*

It was signed with a bold flourish in fountain-pen ink by Litvikov's chief aide-de-camp. Litvikov, the commissar for foreign trade, was the man with whom he had met, the official who was sponsoring his visit to Moscow.

Metcalfe looked at his watch. It was late, after normal office hours, though Soviet officials kept strange hours, he knew. Something was up, something serious. Whatever it was, there was no avoiding it.

Litvikov's driver was waiting in the hotel lobby. Metcalfe approached him. "Seryozha," he said. "Let's get this over with."

Litvikov's desk was cluttered with telephones in various colors. Within the land of Soviet officialdom, the more phones you had on your desk, the more important you were. Metcalfe wondered whether one of these phones was a direct line to the General Secretary himself, whether Litvikov had that much power. Behind him were two large portraits, one of Lenin and one of Stalin.

The beetle-browed Litvikov got up from behind his desk as soon as Metcalfe was escorted in by his aide-de-camp. Litvikov was a tall, stoop-shouldered man with shoe-polish black hair and a ghostly pale complexion. Over the last decade, Metcalfe had seen Litvikov rise through the ranks of the department and had seen him transformed from an obsequious glad-hander to a harrowed, anxious presence. But there was something new about Litvikov: anger, indignation, a gladiatorial confidence mixed with fear, which Metcalfe found worrying.

Litvikov led the way over to his long conference table, which was covered in green felt and stocked with an armamentarium of mineral-water bottles that the commissar never seemed to offer. He sat at the head of the table, his aide to his right and Metcalfe to his left.

"We have a problem, Mr. Metcalfe." Litvikov spoke in English with an Oxford accent.

"The copper mine," Metcalfe put in. "I absolutely agree. This is a situation my brother and I have been discussing—"

"No, Mr. Metcalfe. It is not the copper mine. It is something far more serious. I have received reports of erratic behavior on your part."

Metcalfe's pulse quickened. He nodded. "Aleksandr Dmitrovich," he said jovially, "if your secret policemen are *that* interested in my romantic life, I wonder whether maybe they don't have enough to do."

"*No,* sir." He indicated a stack of yellow sheets, on the table to his right. They were stamped SECRET in red at the top. Surveillance reports, they had to be. "These reports suggest other explanations, Mr. Metcalfe. Explanations that raise serious questions about what you are really doing in Moscow. We are watching you extremely closely."

"That's obvious. But your NKVD is wasting a good deal of manpower on me. An innocent man has nothing to hide."

"Yet you act as if you have much to hide."

"There's a difference, Aleksandr Dmitrovich, between concealment and discretion."

"Discretion?" the commissar said, raising his eyebrows, his weary eyes full of fear.

Metcalfe pointed at the stack of surveillance reports. "I have no doubt that what emerges from all that laborious effort is a portrait of what is sometimes called a playboy. A dilettante. A rake. I'm aware of my reputation, sir. It's something I always carry with me, something I must always try to live down."

But the Russian was having none of it. "This has nothing to do with your—with what I believe is called 'catting around,' Mr. Metcalfe. Believe me—"

"Call it what you will, but when a foreigner such as myself, from a capitalist country, gets involved with a Russian woman in Moscow, the risks are borne entirely by the woman. You know this and I know it. I never kiss and tell, sir, and I always protect a woman's reputation. But here, the risks to any woman I might see go far beyond that of a besmirched reputation. So if the precautions I take seem suspicious to the NKVD, it is of no concern to me. I'm proud of it, frankly. Let them follow me everywhere I go." He remembered something that Kundrov, Lana's minder, had said, and added: "There are no secrets in the Soviet paradise, I'm told."

"Are you working with the Germans?" Litvikov cut in suddenly.

So that was it! Kundrov had seen him talking with von Schüssler at the dacha.

"Are you?" Metcalfe fired back.

Litvikov's pale face reddened. He stared at the table and toyed with his ancient fountain pen, dipping it into an inkwell but writing nothing. "Is that your concern?" he said after a long silence. "That we'll transfer our commercial allegiances to the Germans?"

"Why do you need to ask me that? You've already told me you see everything, you know everything."

Litvikov was silent again for several seconds. At last he turned to his aide. *"Izvinitye!"* he barked to the man, excusing him.

When the aide had left the room, Litvikov resumed speaking. "What I am about to say to you, Metcalfe, is enough to get me arrested, even executed. I am handing you this weapon in the hopes that you will not use it against me. But I want you to understand my situation—our situation. And perhaps once you understand, you will be more cooperative. I have long trusted your brother; I do not know you as well, but I can only hope that you are as trustworthy—as discreet, as you say. Because now it is not just trade that is on the line, but the lives of my family. I am a man with a family, Mr. Metcalfe. A wife and a son and a daughter. Do you understand?"

Metcalfe nodded. "You have my word."

Litvikov plunged his pen into the inkwell again, and this time he began doodling on the sheet of foolscap on the table in front of him. "Last August, a little over a year ago, my government signed a peace pact with Germany, as you know. Just one day before the pact was announced, *Pravda* published an anti-Nazi article about the persecution of Poles in Germany. For years, Stalin and all of our leaders had spoken out against Hitler and the Nazis. Our press was full of stories about how terrible the Nazis were. Then all of a sudden, one day in August—all of it stopped! No more anti-Nazi articles. No more anti-Nazi speeches. A complete U-turn. No longer do you read the word *Nazism* in our newspapers. *Pravda* and *Izvestiya* now quote from Hitler's speeches, favorably! They quote from the *Völkischer Beobachter*." Litvikov's doodles had become a back-and-forth series of lines, a violent scribble that was becoming a heavy blot. "Do you think this is easy on us, on the Russian people? Do you think we can forget what we have read, what we've been told about the atrocities of the Nazis?"

Metcalfe thought but did not say, *And what of* Stalin's *atrocities? What of the millions deported and tortured and killed in the purges?* "Of course not," Metcalfe said. "It's a question of survival, isn't it?"

"Does a rabbit seek out the *protection* of a boa constrictor?"

"And the Soviet Union is the rabbit?"

"Don't misunderstand me, Mr. Metcalfe. If we are attacked, we will fight to the death—and it will not be only *our* death. If we are invaded, we will fight with a vehemence the world has never seen before. But we have no interest in invading other countries."

"Tell that to the Poles," Metcalfe said. "You invaded Poland the day after you signed your treaty with Germany, am I wrong? Tell that to Finland."

"We had no choice in this!" the Russian said angrily. "It was a defensive measure."

"*I* see," Metcalfe said, his point made.

"My country has no friends, Metcalfe. Understand this. We are isolated. No sooner had we signed our pact with Germany than we began hearing about how Britain felt betrayed! Britain claimed that they had been 'courting' us, that they wanted us to join them in their fight against Nazi Germany. But how did they 'court' us? How did they woo us? They and the French sent a low-level delegation—a retired British admiral and a doddering French general—to Leningrad on a slow boat! It took them two weeks to get here. Not foreign ministers, but retired old military officers. This was a slap in the face to all of Russia. This wasn't a serious attempt at negotiating an alliance. Winston Churchill hates the Soviet regime—and he makes no secret of it. And who did he send over here as his ambassador, London's most important foreign posting after Washington? Sir Stafford Cripps—a radical backbencher, a socialist with no standing with the British government. What were we to make of this? No, Mr. Metcalfe, the signals from England were clear. They had no interest in an alliance with Russia." Litvikov's violent scribbling had torn through the foolscap. He let the pen drop.

"Yes," Metcalfe said, understanding. "The Kremlin really had no choice. So this agreement with Hitler—are you saying it's not a true partnership? It's a handshake, nothing more, to keep the enemy at bay?"

Litvikov shrugged. "I am a member of the Politburo, but that does not mean that I am privy to the decision making at the highest levels."

"You don't know."

"The questions you ask are not the questions one would expect from a playboy businessman."

"It's in my interest as a businessman to be very informed about politics. These days particularly."

"Let me tell you something, and I will let you draw your own conclusions. Last month, the Nazis quietly took pieces of Romania and made them part of Hungary. We learned about this only after it happened."

"A rift between Hitler and Stalin?" Metcalfe probed.

"There's no rift," the Russian said hastily. "We are whistling in the dark, Mr. Metcalfe. Who knows what this means? I only know that Stalin expects this agreement with Hitler to last a long time."

"Expects . . . or hopes?"

Litvikov smiled for the first time. His smile was the canny grin of a cynic who has seen it all. "My English is sometimes not precise enough. Perhaps *hopes* is the word I meant to say."

"I appreciate your candor. You can count on my discretion."
By speaking openly, even mildly critically, of the Kremlin, Litvikov was imperiling himself.

Litvikov's grin faded. "In that case, let me add to what I have
already told you. You may take this as a friendly warning."

"Emphasis on 'friendly' or on 'warning'?"

"I'll let you make that determination. Some of my colleagues
have long harbored suspicions about Metcalfe Industries. There
are those that suspect that it is not merely a capitalist combine,
which is reason enough for wariness on our part, but something
more. A front for foreign interests." His gaze was penetrating.

"I assume you know better," Metcalfe said, returning the gaze
with equal intensity.

"I know that you and your family are very well connected in
Washington and in leading capitalist circles. Beyond that, I know
very little. You should know that I have already alerted your older
brother that if repatriation of your properties is necessary, it will
be done."

"Repatriation?" Metcalfe knew what he meant but wanted the
threat to be explicit, thus addressable.

"Seizure of all Metcalfe facilities, as you well know."

Metcalfe blinked but did not react.

"This may not be of consequence to you, but I assure you,
your brother did not take the prospect well when I spoke with
him a few hours ago. Do you know the name James Mellors?"

"No. Should I?"

"What about Harold Delaware? Or Milton Eisenberg?"

"Sorry."

"I'm sorry, too, Mr. Metcalfe. All of them were American citizens. And all of them were executed by Soviet authorities on
espionage charges. They were not released or returned to their
native country. And do you think your government raised a fuss?
It did not. Larger concerns held sway. Broader matters of international relations. The United States government knew that these
men were guilty. They knew that we were in a position to prove

it, with written confessions. Nobody in your State Department wanted these confessions to see the light of day, so nothing was said. Comrade Stalin has learned from this. There is no longer any extraterritoriality. Comrade Stalin has learned that to extend a hand of help to the United States only attracts the jaws of rabid dogs. So there is no longer an outstretched hand. That hand is now a fist." Litvikov clenched a right hand into a tight fist. "Five fingers are collectivized into one fist. Lenin taught that the collective means the disappearance of the individual."

"Yes," Metcalfe said, trying to control his pounding heart. "And it's Stalin who's been overseeing the disappearance of a great *many* individuals."

Litvikov rose, trembling with anger. "If I were you," he said, "I'd watch that I didn't become one of them."

Sitting in a small park across the street from the Metropole, the violinist watched the hotel entrance using a pair of lightweight folding Zeiss 8 × 60 binoculars. He knew from his brief, unsatisfying interrogation of the front-desk clerks what the times of the shift changes were. He had been able to confirm that the set of clerks he had spoken with had left, replaced by others who did not recognize his face.

He folded the binoculars and put them away, then crossed the street and entered the hotel. He did not stop at the desk but immediately headed for the carpeted main staircase, his destination clear: he was just another foreigner going to the restaurant. No one stopped him, neither at the entrance nor in the lobby: he looked like a foreigner, and it was clear that he was coming to dinner. Most patrons of the hotel's restaurant were foreigners, after all.

He entered the main dining room, done in grandiose Art Nouveau style with gold leaf and columns and a stained-glass ceiling and a marble fountain that splashed water. Looking around, as if in search of a dining companion, he merely nodded and smiled at the headwaiter, ignoring him until the Russian moved on. Then, appearing to give up, not finding his companion there, he left the restaurant and went directly to the stairs. Four of the hotel's guests were on the list that the military attaché had given him. He did not need the help of any desk clerk now. He had their room numbers.

CHAPTER TWENTY-TWO

The Aragvi Restaurant was located on Gorky Street, just past
Central Telegraph. It was one of the very few decent restaurants
in Moscow, and Metcalfe and Scoop Martin were badly in need
of edible food. They had arranged to meet in front of the restaurant at seven o'clock in the evening.

But there was another reason that Metcalfe had decided to dine
at the Aragvi, a more important reason. It was here, at the men's
room, that Amos Hilliard had arranged to meet Metcalfe,
promptly at eight. The embassy, Hilliard had declared, was now
off-limits. Besides, the Aragvi had certain characteristics that
made it suitable for a furtive rendezvous. The restaurant was
bustling and always crowded, and there were always plenty of
foreigners in attendance. There were multiple entrances, Hilliard
had told him, permitting the diplomat to make an unobserved
appearance. Moreover, Hilliard knew the manager of the restaurant. "I've lost track of how much money I've dumped there,
and I don't mean on food. I've greased a lot of palms. That's the
only way you get reasonable service in Moscow."

Roger, however, was late. Generally he was punctual, but the
Brit was finding it a challenge to get around Moscow, to get
things accomplished. It was far worse, he'd moaned, than even
occupied France. At least there he spoke the language.

So Metcalfe was unconcerned that, after waiting a quarter of
an hour, there was still no sign of Scoop. Meanwhile, the line
snaking in front of the restaurant was growing steadily longer.
He stood out here in order to detect any surveillance, though so
far he saw none.

There was no sense in waiting any longer, Metcalfe decided. It was imperative that he be on time for his rendezvous with Hilliard; Roger would figure out, once he showed up, that Metcalfe was already inside. He walked up to the restaurant door, past the long line of waiting Russians, who sized him up from his attire as a foreigner and thus entitled to jump to the head of the line. A man popped his head out and waved Metcalfe inside without even asking his name. Metcalfe did not need to flash his American passport to gain admission; he had only to slip a twenty-dollar bill into the palm of the headwaiter, a strange-looking long-haired man in a long braided coat and pointed shoes. He wore pince-nez attached to a black ribbon around his neck.

The headwaiter led him to a table for two on a balcony overlooking the main dining room. Below, a band was playing Georgian love songs. He was served warm peasant bread and good butter and gray caviar. Metcalfe ate ravenously and drank several glasses of Borzhomi, Georgian mineral water, which was highly sparkling and strongly sulfurous. By the time the odd-looking headwaiter had come by for the third time to take his order—extra-attentive to this American who was likely to tip generously and in dollars, not in useless rubles—Metcalfe decided to order, for himself and for Roger. Clearly something important had detained him. When Scoop sauntered in, as indeed he would, to announce some coup he'd pulled off, at least there would be food on the table. Metcalfe ordered far more than either of them could possibly eat: *satsivi* and *shashlik* and beefsteak and pheasant.

The band began playing a Georgian song, "*Suliko*," which Metcalfe remembered from his last visit to Moscow. He associated it with Lana, just as he connected so much about Moscow with her. His mind was flooded with memories of her, thoughts about her; he could not help it. And he could not think about her without a sickening, agonizing sense of guilt. He had blatantly manipulated her into doing what she was now doing. Corky had devised a plan of breathtaking audacity, one that required a conduit who could only be Lana. If his plan succeeded, it would alter the course of the war. More than that, it would change history.

Compared to the fate of the earth, what was the fate of one person? But Metcalfe could not think this way; that was the kind of thinking that led to tyranny. That was what Hitler and Stalin believed: the destiny of the masses outweighed the rights of the individual.

And he loved her. That was the plain truth. He loved this woman, grieved for her situation, for the hand that fate had dealt her. He wanted to allow himself to believe that if his plan succeeded, she and her father would also be free. But he knew that the risks were enormous. Any number of things could go wrong. She could be caught, and if she was, she would be executed, a possibility too horrific for him to dwell upon.

He was surprised, when he next glanced at his watch, to see that it was just two minutes before eight. He got up from the table and made his way to the men's room.

Amos Hilliard was already there when Metcalfe entered. He was standing at a washbasin, washing his hands.

Metcalfe was about to speak when Hilliard put a finger to his lips, then pointed to a closed stall. Metcalfe looked, saw what appeared to be Russian shoes, with Russian trousers pooled over them. For a moment, Metcalfe was uncertain as to what to do; neither man had prepared for this eventuality. He went to the row of urinals and relieved himself. Hilliard kept washing his hands and watching the closed stall in the mirror.

Metcalfe finished, then flushed. But the Russian man remained in the stall. Was it a coincidence? Likely, Metcalfe decided, that was all it was. He went to the sink next to where Hilliard was still soaping his hands and caught the diplomat's eyes in the mirror, giving him a questioning look.

Hilliard shrugged. They washed their hands in silence. Metcalfe's heart pounded as he waited. If he and Hilliard happened to be arrested at this moment, they would be in serious trouble.

He knew that Hilliard had on his person the first set of forged documents that had been prepared by Corky's technical specialists and flown in to Moscow via the diplomatic pouch. If the

documents were found on either one of them, both would disappear into the gulag, if not executed. It was no wonder Hilliard
looked haggard and sullen. He knew what the risks were.

Finally a toilet flushed, and a Russian man emerged from the
stall. He looked at the two sinks, which were occupied by Metcalfe and Hilliard, and glowered at the two men as he walked
out of the rest room. Hilliard raced to the door, hands dripping,
and locked it.

Just as quickly he pulled a tightly wrapped package from his
suit coat and handed it to Metcalfe.

"This is only the first set," Hilliard whispered. "More to come."

"Thank you," Metcalfe said.

"Ordinarily, my upbringing would require me to say 'Don't
mention it,' or 'A pleasure,' or 'You're welcome,' but they'd all
be lies," Hilliard said. "I'm only here on Corky's orders, you
know that. If anyone else asked me to do this, I'd tell them to
go take a flying leap. I don't know what these documents are—
they're secure-sealed—but I'll be happy when you've left Moscow."

"As will I."

"All right, listen up, before some other soused Russian with a
bursting bladder tries to get in here. This is our last face-to-face.
From now on, we use dead drops."

"Good." That was safer anyway, Metcalfe reflected.

"Corky says you've got a great memory. Use it. Don't write
any of this down, you hear me?"

"I'm listening."

Fear and resentment seemed to have changed Hilliard.
Outwardly he was the same diminutive, soft-fleshed, balding,
bespectacled man. But inside the blunt-talking, charming Mid-
westerner, something had hardened. He was angry and deeply
frightened, and seeing the transformation made Metcalfe all the
more fearful.

"On the corner of Pushkin Street and Proyezd Khudozhestvennovo Teatra you will find two stores almost next to each other, okay? One is Store Number 19, marked *Myaso,* or 'Meat.' "

"Thanks," Metcalfe said, intending his sarcasm to be obvious. Hilliard surely knew he spoke Russian.

"The other is called *Zhenskaya Obuv.*" Women's Shoes. Hilliard didn't translate this time; Metcalfe nodded.

"The entrance to the building in between those two stores is unguarded, open twenty-four hours. On your right as you enter you'll see a radiator that's fastened to the wall by a metal bracket on one side. There's a gap behind it of a few centimeters. The next set of documents will be behind it."

"Not a good idea," Metcalfe said. "The documents are liable to catch fire when the radiator comes on."

Hilliard scowled. "This is Moscow, for Christ's sake. Two-thirds of the radiators don't even work, and this is one of those two-thirds. Believe me. And this is Moscow, so it won't get fixed for five years."

Metcalfe nodded. "Signal?"

"If I'm in the office, which I won't always be, you'll place a telephone call asking for me, telling me you've lost your passport. I'll reply that you've called the wrong office. If I've loaded the drop, I'll tell you to call back and ask for the consular division. If I haven't, I'll just hang up at that point."

"And if you're not in the office?"

"The fallback signal site will be a telephone at Kozitski Pereulok Number 2, Korpus 8, entry number 7. That's between Gorky and Pushkin streets. Got that?"

Metcalfe nodded again. "Kozitski Lane 2, Korpus 8, entry 7. That's fairly close to Yeliseyevsky's *gastronom.*"

"I'll recommend you to the folks at Baedeker when they get around to doing Moscow," Hilliard said astringently. "Entry 7 is between the entrance to Polyclinic Number 18 and a store labeled '*Ovoshchifrukty.*' " He didn't translate the Russian word for produce, fruits and vegetables. "This is four blocks from the drop

site, by the way. When you enter the building, you'll see a telephone on your left, mounted on a wooden board. The telephone's numbered 746, but there's only one phone there. On the
lower right corner of the board, where the veneer has broken off,
is a small area where you'll see doodles and scrawls put there by
people using the phone, so the marks you and I leave won't
attract undue attention. When I've loaded the drop, I'll signal
that by drawing a circle in red pencil. *Red* pencil, got it?"

"Got it."

"When you've unloaded the drop, you'll place a vertical line
in that circle. Is this clear?"

"Completely. The telephone's accessible twenty-four hours as
well?"

"Right."

"Have you built in any fake DLBs?" Metcalfe referred to dead-
letter box signals that were false, designed to mislead any who
might be watching.

"That's my business."

"Operational security is my business as well."

Hilliard gave him a fierce glare.

"Any emergency signal?"

Hilliard continued to glare.

"A capture signal—a signal warning me off, warning me the
channels are dirty, you've been intercepted?"

"If I've been intercepted, you won't find a ready-to-pick-up
sign. Simple as that. You won't hear from me again. Neither will
Corky nor any of my friends back home in Iowa or Washington,
because I'll be breaking rocks in Siberia, never to be heard from
again. Or shot in the back of the neck. Are we clear? So do us
both a favor. Dry-clean yourself. Don't get blown."

He turned and, without another word, unlocked the rest-room
door and left.

———

By the time Metcalfe returned to his table, his dinner—*their* dinner—had been set out. But still no Roger. The table was crowded with serving platters mounded with lamb shashlik and beef *chashushuli*, the meat dumplings called *khinkali*, the pheasant stew known as *chakhokhbili*. There were bottles of Tsinandali, a fine straw-colored Georgian white wine, and more bottles of Borzhomi mineral water. But Metcalfe was suddenly not hungry. He slipped a stack of bills under his plate and left the restaurant, trailing the headwaiter, who wanted to know if anything was wrong. Palming the waiter another twenty, he apologized, "Guess I filled up on bread."

He was tailed, of course, from the Aragvi back to the Metropole. He did not recognize the followers; the shift had changed, and the blond, pale-eyed expert was not among them. Or did not appear to be, anyway, for he might have been watching at a distance, undetected. The documents were in the breast pocket of his suit jacket, still sealed in their cellophane wrapper. It felt as if they were burning a hole in his chest. He tried not to think about what might happen if he was stopped by anyone and the documents were taken from him. Forged Soviet military documents—it would be impossible to explain them away.

At the hotel desk, he was not stopped by any of the desk clerks; Roger had left no message with them. He couldn't help but worry, but Roger was the least of his worries. He was a professional; he could take care of himself. There would be a reason for his absence. Lana was no professional; any number of things could befall her.

The *dezhurnaya* on his floor, a gorgon he had not seen before, greeted him with customary ill humor. She refused to hand over his room key.

"You took it already," she said accusingly.

"No," Metcalfe replied. "There must be some mistake." Unless Roger had taken his room key for some reason: perhaps to leave something in his room, whether a message or—

A transmitter! He had been working all day to assemble the components, and knowing Scoop, he had already built one by now and was waiting in Metcalfe's room to surprise him with it. Certainly he would not leave a transceiver unattended in a hotel room.

But his room was locked, and his repeated knocking met with no response. There was no answer in Roger's room, either. He returned to the *dezhurnaya*'s station. "My room is locked," he said sternly. This was the only way to deal with the sour-tempered floor ladies: answering imperiousness with imperiousness. "I need the key, and if you've given it to any unauthorized person, I'll have your job." He produced his passport. "Have you given my room key to anyone else?"

The *dezhurnaya* was stunned into silence. This was a woman who lived by the all-important Soviet notion of *poryadok,* order. There was a way to do things properly, and by giving out a room key to the wrong guest she had violated it. Scowling, she handed Metcalfe the key. "But bring it back!" she called out after him.

It could have been anyone, of course, who had taken his room key: NKVD, though they presumably had access to master keys; even someone from the American embassy. Only when he reached the door to his room for the second time did he recall Ted Bishop's words.

A Kraut gentleman. . . . He said an old friend had asked him to look someone up. Said he didn't remember the exact name. Someone who just arrived from Paris. . . . Something about his story emitted the faintest odor of fish.

A Kraut gentleman. A Nazi. *SD, from the look of him.*

Someone who had come from Paris to look someone up.

The destruction of the Cave, Corky's Paris station, had been only the beginning. Corky's network was being unrolled. Somehow they had traced him to Moscow.

What had happened to his friends at the Paris station could easily happen to him.

Someone was waiting for him in his room. Metcalfe was sure of it.

Waiting to finish the job of rolling up Corky's network. Waiting to kill him.

It was a *trap,* Metcalfe realized, a trap he would not step into. He did not have a weapon; entering the room was out of the question. There were other ways down to the lobby that did not necessitate passing by the foul-tempered *dezhurnaya* and engaging in time-wasting explanations. He raced down the service stairs, taking them two at a time. Crossing the lobby, he approached the front desk, a look of irritation on his face.

"This damned *key!*" he exclaimed, holding it up. "It doesn't work!"

"Are you sure you have the right key, sir?" asked the clerk. He took it, examined it. The room number was stamped on the key tag, as plain as day. There was no mistake.

"You turn it to the left, sir. Counterclockwise."

"I know *that.* How long have I been here? It's not working. Now, will you please send someone up with me to get this door open? I'm in a hurry."

The clerk pounded a bell, and a valet appeared from the luggage room behind him. There was a perfunctory exchange in Russian, and then the valet, a kid still in his teens, came up to Metcalfe, bowing bashfully, and took the key. Metcalfe followed him into the elevator. On the fourth floor they got out, walked past the *dezhurnaya,* who stared but said nothing, and down the corridor to Metcalfe's room.

"This is the room, sir?" the bellman asked.

"You try the lock. I've had no success." As he spoke, Metcalfe stayed behind the bellman. If the unnamed German was lying in wait inside the room, he would restrain from firing—if indeed he intended to dispatch Metcalfe by means of a firearm—once he heard the young man's voice. If a Nazi assassin was inside, he would be deterred not by any humanitarian considerations, such as the loss of an innocent life, but instead by practical ones. Unnecessary bloodshed was anathema to a professional killer, for it inevitably created far more problems than it solved. The young bellman would serve as Metcalfe's shield.

He drew back still farther as the bellman turned the key in the lock, beyond the line of sight of anyone stationed inside his room and thus outside of any firing line. He braced himself, coiled, prepared to leap out of the way, to run, the moment the firing began.

But the bellman had unlocked the door easily. Glancing at Metcalfe in bafflement, he pulled the heavy door open. Metcalfe felt his heartbeat accelerate.

"All right, sir?" the bellman asked. He hesitated at the open door, glancing into the room, then at Metcalfe. He obviously expected a tip, despite the official policy that frowned on gratuities as capitalist taint.

"I appreciate it," said Metcalfe. "I don't know why I couldn't get it to turn." He took out a five-dollar bill and came up to the young man from behind, clapping a hand on his shoulder jovially as he stood in back of the bellman and looked into the room.

It was empty. There was no one there.

The bathroom.

The bathroom door was ajar. He had left it open, and now it was nearly closed. That meant nothing, of course, because the room appeared to have been cleaned in his absence and the maid would have gone into the bathroom.

"Listen, as long as you're up here," Metcalfe said, "would you mind helping me lift something heavy? My back's killing me."

The bellman shrugged: *Sure, why not.*

"My damned suitcase is in the bathroom, so if you wouldn't mind getting it out of there, I've got another one of these for you." He handed the bellman the bill. This was a giant tip to the young man, and the prospect of another five-dollar bill was irresistible. The bellman crossed the room to the bathroom. Metcalfe hung behind, again positioning himself out of the line of fire.

The bellman pushed the bathroom door open, glanced into the bathroom, and said, "Sir? I don't see a suitcase—"

"Really? The maid must have moved it, then. Sorry."

But the young man was frozen in place, his eyes wide. He took a step forward into the bathroom and began to scream, "*Bozhe moi! Bozhe moi!*"

Metcalfe raced toward the bathroom, and then he saw what the bellman was staring at, his screams growing steadily louder.

The face that hung over the side of the bathtub was so purple and engorged, its eyeballs bulging and its purple tongue distended, that Metcalfe almost did not recognize it.

A gasp escaped his mouth as he rushed to the tub, touched Roger Martin's face, felt the clammy cold that told him that Roger was unquestionably dead and had been so for several hours. The serrated band that nearly bisected Roger's throat was horribly familiar.

Metcalfe had seen the exact same strangulation wound just a few days earlier, in Paris.

CHAPTER TWENTY-THREE

The bellman backed up out of the bathroom, his movements jerky, seeming involuntary. By now he had stopped screaming, but his face remained panicked.

Metcalfe, however, barely noticed. He was in a state of profound shock. *"My God,"* he whispered. What he saw before him was a horror, a grotesquerie, a vision that was unbearable.

Paris had happened again.

They had murdered Scoop.

There was no choice now, no question as to what to do. He had to get out of here before the bellman summoned help, before the Soviet authorities—read; the NKVD—were brought in and he was surely interrogated, locked up. Even in his stunned, grieved state, he could see the chain of consequences. The forged documents would be discovered, either on him or wherever he undertook to hide them, and no explanation he could come up with would satisfy the authorities.

Yet there was no explanation that could satisfy *him.*

Explanations, *understanding* of the horror, would have to wait. Swiftly he threw some clothes into the cheap cardboard suitcase he'd bought the day before. He turned and ran from the room.

Without a transmitter, there was no way to reach Corcoran, or at least no quick way. Even the famous black channel wasn't safe. The diplomatic pouch was probably not safe, either. The only remaining way to contact Corky was to ask Amos Hilliard to encode a message using the most secure cryptography available to him and dispatch a coded telegram. Hilliard would do it, though reluctantly.

Whichever way he did it, he *had* to get to Corky. The penetration of the network had now extended to Moscow, which indicated that the breach went alarmingly deep.

A thought struck him then. He tried to dismiss it as the delusion of a mind made frantic by seeing the murder of an old and close friend. But he felt it in the pit of his stomach and could not dismiss it.

Amos Hilliard?

Was it possible that Corky's own man in Moscow was rotten? Hilliard's words came back to him in a rush: *No one can be trusted.*

Was that an oblique reference to Amos Hilliard himself? Who else knew what Metcalfe was doing in Moscow, after all? If Hilliard was playing both sides, or several sides, as he accused his embassy colleagues of doing, then all he had to do was pass the word to . . .

But Metcalfe shook his head, dismissing the idea. It was ludicrous; he was seeing duplicity everywhere. Once you began thinking like that, you became crippled, paralyzed.

Still, the horrific reality remained: he had made Scoop Martin fly him to Moscow and had thereby gotten his old friend murdered just as surely as if he had done the deed himself. The fact that Roger had been in Metcalfe's hotel room when he was murdered indicated that Metcalfe had been the intended target. They had meant to kill Metcalfe. They'd gotten Metcalfe's hotel room number and had assumed that the person there was Metcalfe. Why Roger had been there was yet another mystery. If he'd been working on a transmitter and was planning either to surprise Metcalfe with it or to secrete it there . . . then where was it?

And if Corky's network had been penetrated and was being rolled up, agent by agent—first Paris, now Moscow—then it wasn't just Metcalfe who was in danger.

Lana was in danger as well.

The more Metcalfe met with Lana, the more she became a target. And once he gave her the forged documents he was now carrying, she became, by extension, a member of Corky's network, too, if an unwitting one. Now she was as much a potential victim as Roger or any of the men in the Paris Station.

It's bad enough that I'm using her, he thought. *But endangering her this way? This isn't something she signed up for. I volunteered for this work, knowing the dangers. Lana never did.*

Yet in some ways it was too late to turn back. She had already laid the groundwork with von Schüssler.

He'd have to protect her, avoid being seen with her. His public encounters with her in Moscow thus far could all be explained as a rich playboy's infatuation, his attempt to reconnect with a past love. And they had taken extraordinary precautions to avoid being seen meeting at her friend's apartment. These precautions would have to continue, even intensify.

Now, however, he had to use every method at his disposal to make sure he was not tailed. He had left the Metropole through a service entrance, one he had not used before. That had enabled him to avoid the drones, the low-level followers who sat waiting for him in the hotel lobby. But there were others, of course, including the blond NKVD man who seemed to turn up everywhere. So he would take extra measures. He would not be tailed.

He would make sure of it.

The cobblestone expanse of Red Square was bordered on its eastern side by an immense ornate building with a marble and granite facade, several hundred meters long. This was the *Gosudarstvenny Universalny Magazin:* GUM, the State Department Store, the largest shop in Moscow. Inside was an arcade three stories high that looked something like a turn-of-the-century railway station in London or Paris; it swarmed with people poking around the hundreds of shops. In bleak contrast to the extravagant architecture, however, the shelves were sparse.

The bustling crowds, combined with the innumerable nooks and crannies, stairways and passages, provided Metcalfe with an ideal place to lose any possible followers. Carrying his cardboard suitcase, he stopped into a series of shops, examining the phonograph records, the perfumes, the bad costume jewelry, the peasant shawls. The throngs closed in around him, swallowing him up, making the job of a watcher next to impossible. Anyway, there was nothing suspicious or peculiar about an American businessman visiting Moscow's most famous shopping gallery, and the narrow suitcase could have carried business files, for all anyone knew. He joined a mob making its way up an iron staircase, climbed up to the first balcony, where he was able to quickly survey the crowds. He saw no one.

Spotting a corner shop that was open on two sides, he entered, looking with great interest at a display of carved wooden toys and elaborately painted nesting *matryoshka* dolls. He picked one of the dolls up, turned its top half, and revealed a slightly smaller one inside. In all, there were six dolls concealed inside the outer one. It was a beautiful example of Russian folk art, and he thought Lana might appreciate it. It was also a good idea, he knew, to purchase something in order to establish a pretext for being here. While he stood in one line to pay for it, then another line to pick it up—Soviet bureaucracy had invaded even the shops in Moscow!—he glanced casually around. He did not recognize anyone, nor was there any discernible pattern of surveillance that he could make out.

Taking his purchase, he left the shop through the other side, then made an abrupt U-turn, as if he had spotted something of interest. He elbowed his way through the crowd, then climbed another set of stairs. The third level was less crowded. Striding quickly about a hundred feet, he then took yet another staircase back down to the second floor. He entered a men's room, where several men were standing at a trough urinal, two of them appearing to be drunk. He entered a stall, bolted the door, and then quickly changed into the Russian clothes that Corky had provided. The lining of the peasant jacket had been sliced open, but from the outside it would attract no attention. The shoes, pants, shirt, and jacket were all not only authentically Russian but also had been well distressed. They looked appropriately worn.

From the sounds of it, the drunken men had left; other men had come in. This was good. He donned the light brown wig, which fit tightly over his head, then daubed spirit gum over his chin, upper lip, and eyebrows; when it had dried, he carefully applied the scruffy goatee. It would have been far easier to do this standing before a mirror rather than seated on the closed lid of a toilet, but at least he had thought to bring a small shaving mirror to check that everything was in place. Next came the heavy, unkempt-looking eyebrows. He smeared a bit of dark makeup under his eyes, which accentuated the circles subtly, aging him dramatically. He could have been forty, a smoker, and a heavy drinker, a peasant who had lived a hard life like most Russian peasants.

He checked himself again, impressed by how different he looked. But he did not want to take a chance; he could go further, and he did. He inserted cotton wads into his mouth, tucking them inside his cheeks next to his upper teeth; this instantly transformed his face. The final touch was to insert specially designed metal nuts into his nostrils, which had been machined for the OSS with tiny breathing holes in them. They felt cold and uncomfortable at first, but they distorted the shape of his nose, made it flatter, more like that of a typical Russian peasant.

Glancing in the mirror again, he barely recognized himself. He peered through the cracks in the stall, saw that there was no one remaining who had seen him enter. Quickly stuffing his American clothes and shoes into the suitcase, he emerged from the stall, then went over to the washbasin, setting his suitcase down on the floor next to it. He washed his hands for a few minutes, then left the rest room, his suitcase remaining behind on the bathroom floor. Later on, some lucky Russian would find it, decide to steal it, and be pleasantly surprised to discover a good suit inside.

Glumly he ambled the length of the second-floor gallery. He had altered his walk, adding a slight limp, as if one leg were a little shorter than the other. By the time he reached the first floor, he was certain that no one was following him. He was a nonentity, a middle-aged Russian who looked like millions of others in Moscow. No one would give him the slightest notice.

Rudolf von Schüssler was annoyed at the interruption.

The prim, pinched-face security officer from the *Sicherheitsdienst* was sitting in his office asking all sorts of questions about any English-speaking people von Schüssler might have had occasion to meet in Moscow in the last few days. Von Schüssler had too much to do to waste his time being interrogated by a cop, but the ambassador had asked him to make time, so of course he'd agreed. Von Schüssler knew enough to stay on von der Schulenberg's good side.

"It is possible," said the man from the *Sicherheitsdienst,* "that one of these visitors is a dangerous spy."

The notion seemed ridiculous to von Schüssler, but he played along. "There are a great many Americans and Brits in this town," he said loftily. "Altogether too many, if you ask me. I was speaking to one particular simpering fool the other night, some prancing dandy, and I couldn't help reflecting—"

"His name?" the SD man rudely interrupted, leveling his cold gray eyes on von Schüssler.

Von Schüssler squinted, then slowly shook his head. "I can't remember just now. But if he's a dangerous spy, I'll eat my hat."

The SD man gave a malevolent grin. "And if he turns out to be the one, I may just make you."

Such vulgarity! von Schüssler thought. *Such impudence!* Von Schüssler found the man altogether repugnant, beneath contempt. Yet there was something about him that made his skin crawl; he couldn't put his finger on why. It was not a familiar sensation, but not a wholly unknown one, either. Von Schüssler tried to remember when he had felt like this before, and he recalled a time when he was an adolescent wandering through one of the outbuildings of the family's *schloss* outside Berlin. Yes, that was it: the shed was dark, filled with shadows, and he was reaching out for a coiled rope when suddenly he froze, stricken with a sense of primal alarm. And only an instant later did he realize what he had almost grabbed in the gloom: a snake. An enormous coiled snake.

That was what this man from the *Sicherheitsdienst* reminded him of.

A poisonous snake.

Metcalfe arrived at Lana's friend's apartment half an hour early and Lana was twenty minutes late, but it was not time wasted. While he waited, he took out a penknife and pierced the secure cellophane seal that encased the documents, then carefully took them out and examined them. They were impeccable. The paper was coarse and off-white and looked nothing like any paper manufactured in the West. The documents were typewritten, no doubt using a genuine Soviet typewriter, probably identical to the ones in use within the Commissariat of Defense. All of them were stamped with an official Commissariat stamp convincingly decayed from years of heavy use, in the purple ink they invariably used. The papers were all time-and-date-stamped, the dates ranging from a few weeks ago to today.

Some of them were even signed by the Soviet Commissar of Defense. Many were stamped TOP SECRET. Metcalfe had no doubt that the documents would stand up to the most stringent forensic examination in Berlin. He also had no doubt that they would be closely examined.

The thought struck him that if the documents were discovered to be fake, Lana would be killed. And not by the NKVD, but by the Nazis.

So the quality of the forgery was not just a matter of ensuring that Corky's scheme succeeded.

It was a matter of keeping Lana alive.

The top page in the stack was blank, presumably to conceal its contents from any handlers. As Metcalfe scanned the documents, he was impressed by how plausible they seemed, how detailed—and how extraordinarily misleading. Corky had briefed him a few weeks ago about the Soviet military, though at the time Metcalfe didn't understand why.

"Russia is a mammoth force," Corky had said. "The Germans don't understand that."

"Oh, come on," Metcalfe had scoffed. "Of course the Germans know it—why else would Hitler make a deal with Stalin? The Führer only respects strength. You don't make a deal with a weak man."

Corky had smiled. "Correct. But don't confuse what the Germans *think* with what they *know*."

Now, as Metcalfe read through the documents, he understood the illusion that Corky, the great illusionist, was creating. It was like looking at Georges Seurat's pointillist painting of *La Grande Jatte:* If you stood too close, you saw only the tiny, precise brush strokes of pigment. You had to stand back to apprehend the entire complex scene.

Anyone closely reading these documents would realize quickly how weak the Red Army was. It was a portrait that was entirely convincing because of its details. There were inventories, memoranda between the People's Commissar for Defense, Marshal S. K. Timoshenko, and the chief of the general staff, K. A. Meretskov, among scores of lesser officials, all of which contained lists, requisitions—a flurry of paperwork that told a story of a giant with feet of clay.

The Red Army, according to these forgeries, had only twenty cavalry divisions, twenty-two mechanized brigades—far fewer than the Germans believed. The famous Soviet strategic second echelon, particularly the Sixteenth and Nineteenth Armies and their mechanized corps, was simply a disaster; they lacked modern medium and heavy tanks. Soviet military aircraft were obsolete. The shortage of weapons and equipment was disastrous; the equipment the army did have was aging. Parts were in terrifyingly short supply: there were parts available to arm only 15 percent of the tank and armored units. There was no central military communications system; in any war, the Red Army would be forced to use nineteenth-century methods such as couriers and wires. In all, these documents told a story of an alarming deficiency that must, at all costs, be concealed.

It was not true.

Metcalfe knew enough to see that the thoroughly plausible picture evoked by these forged documents bore no basis to reality. The Red Army was going through an upheaval, he knew, but it was far stronger, far more modern—far more *powerful*—than the story that was told here.

"Weakness is provocative," Corky liked to say. Arrayed on the birch tabletop before him was a thoroughly convincing pointillist landscape of a feeble nation. Hitler's generals would see this and an opportunity, a brass ring that must be grabbed. They would decide to invade Russia; for Nazi Germany, there would be no question.

It was a brilliant deception.

As Metcalfe carefully restacked the papers, he glanced again at the blank top sheet. Strange: it wasn't an ordinary piece of foolscap but a creamy sheet of high-quality, high-rag-content British stationery of the sort that Corky favored. He inspected it closely. It bore the watermark of Smythson of Bond Street: Corky's favorite stationer. It also gave off the faintest odor of chemicals and peppermint. Pep-O-Mint Life Savers. Corky had handled this sheet of paper more than the others.

The chemical smell indicated something else entirely. Metcalfe took out a miniature vial of crystalline potassium ferricyanide, one of the items he usually carried on his person while in the field. He located a ceramic serving bowl in the kitchen, tapped out a small quantity of the chemical, and dissolved it in a few ounces of water. Then he immersed the blank sheet of paper in the solution. Within a few seconds the spidery indigo script appeared. Corky's distinctive handwriting.

He pulled out the wet sheet of paper, placed it on the kitchen counter, and began to read.

S—

Why do mirrors reverse left and right but not up and down? What happens when an irresistible force meets an immovable object? But such questions are child's play, my boy, and the time has come to put away childish things. Sooner than you can imagine, the questions will get harder, the answers harder still. Preserving civilization can be such an uncivilized pursuit. But then, someone must practice the dark arts, so that our apple-cheeked compatriots may enjoy the light. It was always thus. Remember: Rome wasn't built in a day. It was built at night. . . .

Herewith the materials for Operation WOLFSFALLE.

Remember, truth is a shattered mirror. Don't cut yourself on the shards.

—A

Metcalfe understood at once. He was accustomed to Corky's riddles. *Why do mirrors reverse left and right but not up and down?* But they don't reverse at all, Corky was always pointing out; they merely show what's in front of them. The confusion lies with the viewer.

What happens when an irresistible force meets an immovable object? The irresistible force, Metcalfe knew, was the Nazi war machine. The immovable object was the Russian bear. What would happen when the two met?

They would destroy each other.

And then there was the phrase Corky had used: "Operation WOLFSFALLE."

Die Wolfsfalle.

The Wolf trap.

Metcalfe realized at once the significance of the code name Corky had chosen. *Wolf* referred to Adolf Hitler.

Hitler often used the cover name Wolf in his early days. It was his pseudonym, his *nom de guerre,* probably because the name Adolf was Teutonic for "wolf." In 1924, shortly after his release from prison for his attempted coup, he took a room at the Pension Moritz in Obersalzberg, Bavaria, registering under the name Herr Wolf.

Wolf was the pet name that Eva Braun, Hitler's putative lover, called him. His deputy, Rudolf Hess, had even named his son Wolf in Hitler's honor. And then this past June, Hitler had moved his headquarters to an idyllic Belgian village, Brûly-de-Pesche, which Hitler promptly named *Wolfsschlucht,* or Wolf's gorge. This was the Führer's command post from which he oversaw the defeat of France. It was there that he stomped for joy when he learned of France's surrender. According to the very latest intelligence, Hitler's men had begun constructing a complex of heavily fortified concrete bunkers in Rastenburg, East Prussia, that would serve as his headquarters, his *Führer-hauptquartier.*

He had given it the name *Wolfsschanze:* the Wolf's lair.

The meaning of *Die Wolfsfalle*—the Wolf trap—was clear.

When Lana entered and saw him, she let out a scream. Only when she realized who it was did she laugh ruefully. "*Bozhe moi!* My God, Stiva, I didn't know you! Why are you dressed like that?" Then she caught herself, shook her head before he could reply. "Of course you are taking such precautions. I'm glad."

He embraced her, and as she kissed him, she shuddered. "Oh,

this beard—it feels like I am kissing Rudolf, and it is a terrible feeling. Please, you must remove that disguise at once!"

He just smiled. As much as he wanted to stay with her for as long as she could spare, he knew the visit would have to be brief. The more time he spent here, the greater the opportunity for exposure. He would depart momentarily; the disguise would be useful when he did. He gave her the *matryoshka* doll, which she received with delight, but very quickly her mood darkened.

"I'm frightened, Stiva."

He could see it in her face. "Tell me."

"Of what we are doing."

Barely able to suppress the acrid sensation of guilt that welled up, he said, "Then you shouldn't do it. If you're frightened, I don't want you to give von Schüssler these documents."

"No, you misunderstand. What you've asked me to do is to be brave. To do something for my father and for Russia both. The way Father fought for Russia with such bravery. You've given me a chance to be brave. You've given me a purpose."

"Then what are you frightened about?"

"I cannot fall in love with you again. You've given me the gift of your love, my Stiva. But there's no hope for us. We have no future together. It is like the ballet *Giselle*."

"How so?"

"Well, Giselle is a peasant girl who falls in love with a nobleman in disguise, who's pretending to be someone he's not. And then when she learns the truth, she knows she can never marry him, and so she loses her mind and she dies."

"Am I pretending to be someone I'm not?"

"Look at yourself!"

He chuckled. "You have a point. But *you* won't go mad, will you?"

"No," she said. "I can't. I have the gift of your love to live for."

"But it's not a gift, Lana."

She was looking at the sheaf of documents distractedly; it was clear that she was thinking of something else. "Yes, you're right," she said at last. "We are not *Giselle*. We are Tristan and Isolde."

"The two legendary lovers."

"*Doomed* lovers, Stiva. Remember that. They can never be together except in death."

"Fine. You're the fiery and beautiful Isolde, the magician and healer. And I am Tristan, the knight who loves her."

She smiled strangely. "Tristan is really working for his uncle the king. He betrays him, Stiva. He travels about under a false name—under the name Tantris, an anagram of Tristan—but she loves him anyway."

"He doesn't betray *her*, does he? He loves her—and he's just doing his duty."

"Yes. Love is always about betrayal and death, isn't it?"

"Only in the theater. Not in life."

Her eyes were wet. "The love potion in *Tristan* is far more dangerous than poison, Stiva." She picked up the package of documents and held it up before him as if showing it to him. "So tell me this, my knight: Are you loyal to your love . . . or loyal to your king?"

Metcalfe, abashed, didn't know how to reply. Finally he spoke impulsively: "I do love you, you know."

She gave him a sorrowful look. "That's what worries me most," she said.

CHAPTER TWENTY-FOUR

The shop was cluttered and dusty, its display cases filled with a jumble of silver, jewelry, and crystal. The shelves along its walls were lined with old plates and serving dishes, old busts of Lenin. It was neither an antiques store nor a pawnshop but something in between: a *komissiony*, a secondhand store located on one of Moscow's oldest streets, the Arbat. Its narrow aisles were crowded with customers who came to either pick up a bargain or raise desperately needed money by handing over Mama's treasured silver samovar.

Unnoticed among the raised voices and bustling were two men who sidled up next to each other, both examining the same icon. One appeared to be a Russian laborer in his thirties; the other was an older man in a foreign overcoat and a Russian fur hat.

"Almost didn't recognize you," Hilliard said under his breath. "All right. Just follow me out without speaking."

Shortly Hilliard made his way out of the shop, Metcalfe following behind. As they walked down Arbat toward Smolensk Square, the two men fell in alongside.

"What the *hell* is it?" Hilliard hissed. "If it's the second set of documents you're after, I told you I've set up a dead drop for this express purpose, and in any case, the courier won't be in until later in the day. I thought I also made it clear that face-to-face meetings were out!"

"A friend of mine was murdered today."

Hilliard glanced quickly at Metcalfe, then looked away. "Where?"

"The Metropole."

"The *Metropole*? Jesus. Where, in his room?"

"*My* room. I was the intended victim."

Hilliard let out a long, slow breath, and Metcalfe explained about Roger, who he was, his connection to Metcalfe, why he was in Moscow.

"What do you need?" Hilliard asked, his voice softening.

"Two things. One, I need to contact Corky immediately."

"You've *seen* how the black channel isn't safe, Metcalfe—"

"I know you have ways to reach Corky. I don't care whether it's a back door, smoke signals, or a goddamned message in a bottle: guys like you always have a way. You know the drill as well as I do—if a member of Corky's network is hit, he wants to be notified soonest."

"I won't let you back in the embassy to use our communications facilities, Metcalfe."

"I don't give a damn—you can do it for me. Tell him Scoop Martin's been killed the same way his Paris station guys were killed. Same manner of death: strangulation. And I'd send out that cable without delay."

"I will."

Then Metcalfe, remembering his doubts about Hilliard, added: "And I want a confirmation. Proof that Corky's received my message."

"How?"

Metcalfe thought for a moment. "A word. The next word on the list." Corky maintained a list of code words with Metcalfe, as he did with all active agents in the field, a list known to no one else but Corky and the agent in question. The list of words was drawn up by Corky and it was supposed to be random, though Metcalfe had his doubts about how random it was. Corky was too much of a puzzle lover to pass up the opportunity to impart meaning wherever he could.

"You got it," Hilliard said. "What's the other thing you need? You said there were two things."

"A gun."

From a pay phone Metcalfe called the Metropole and asked to leave a message for a hotel guest, Roger Martin.

The reaction would tell him a great deal. By now, of course, Roger's body had been found, and it was a certainty that all of the hotel's staff knew it. Very likely the police had been informed, certainly the NKVD as well. But the reaction of the desk clerk on duty would be a useful indication of the degree of alarm and suspicion—of whether they'd been instructed to keep a watch out for Metcalfe, to lure him, to *trap* him.

The clerk's voice faltered, the tension unconcealed. The clerk immediately switched into icy formality: "No, the hotel guest you are seeking is . . . is no longer at the hotel, I am sorry to say. No further information is available."

"I see," Metcalfe said. "Do you know when he checked out?"

"I have no idea," the clerk replied. "No idea. I cannot help you further." And he hung up.

Metcalfe stared at the walls of the phone booth, perplexed. That had been the frightened, genuine reaction of a hotel employee who didn't know how to respond. This told Metcalfe something: the clerk had *not* been briefed. If a cordon were in place, a trap—or if Metcalfe was simply wanted for questioning in connection with Roger's murder—the clerk would have been instructed to reply differently. He would have interrogated the *caller,* trying to find out what he could.

Very puzzling. This was not what Metcalfe had expected.

The hotel was located on Teatralnaya Square, close to the Bolshoi Theater, in front of which was a small park with benches. Metcalfe needed to stake out the hotel, but vantage points were few. He walked through the park, which was too exposed. It was not a place for him to take out his binoculars and survey the activity in front of the Metropole; there were too many passersby who might observe the suspicious sight of a man with binoculars.

Finally he settled on the columned facade of the Bolshoi. It was too early in the day; no one was entering or exiting the main entrance to the theater. He was able to stand in the shadows, unseen, staring through his binoculars at the Metropole.

He was not looking for anything so obvious as a visible cordon of NKVD troops around the hotel. Instead, he was hoping to discern any disturbance in the normal traffic pattern, the tiny, normally imperceptible signs that might indicate something out of the ordinary. The presence of NKVD or regular police in the hotel would, like the ripples on the surface of a pond into which a stone has been dropped, alter the normal pattern. One would see it in the furtive glances of those exiting the hotel, perhaps; the pedestrian who lingered a bit too long; movements that were too studied, too rapid.

But none of those signs were apparent. Everything seemed to be normal.

Strange. It was as if nothing had happened, and that bothered him most of all.

He circled back around the park and to the side of the hotel, the service entrance he had used earlier. Hesitating a moment, he entered the hotel. He passed the kitchen, whose double doors kept swinging open as workers came in and out with flats of dishes, crates of food, preparing for that evening's dinner.

Nothing out of the ordinary, so far as he could tell. No guards stationed here.

He kept going to the back staircase, which was also unguarded, and took the stairs to the fourth floor. Emerging at the far end of the corridor, he saw that it was dark, empty. He could see the *dezhurnaya* at her desk.

No one was coming or going. No policemen or plainclothes guards seemed to be stationed anywhere.

The hall was empty.

It was baffling. If there was no one waiting to grab him upon his return, that was one thing. But no one there, no police bustling about? No indication of a crime scene?

He felt in his pocket for the bulky room key. When he had run out of the room earlier, he had taken it with him without thinking. Now he was glad of it; that eliminated the need to ask the old gorgon at her station, thus alerting the hotel staff.

Then again, he might not need a room key. Not if his room was open, policemen or NKVD waiting inside.

Moving stealthily, he walked down the hall and took a right. Now he was a hundred feet or so from his hotel room.

The door to his room was closed.

That was something else he hadn't expected. The bellman had *seen* Roger's body; the normal procedure, in Russia or America or anywhere else, was for the authorities to secure the scene of the presumed crime, investigate in place.

He approached the door stealthily, standing just outside, listening.

Quiet.

Nothing inside, no voices as far as he could tell.

It was a risk, of course. He put the key in the lock, turned it, then pulled the door open, prepared to bolt if there was anyone waiting inside.

The room was dark, empty. No one was here.

Looking carefully around, Metcalfe strode quickly through the room to the open bathroom, bracing himself for the nightmarish sight of Scoop's body.

But there was no body.

Not only was there no body, but there was no trace of it. The bathroom was sparklingly clean. There was no indication whatsoever that there had ever been a body here just a few hours earlier.

It was as if the body had never been here at all. They had taken his body away and ordered the bathroom cleaned up, the crime scene expunged, but *why?*

What the hell was going on?

———

From another pay phone a few blocks from the hotel Metcalfe called the embassy and asked for Hilliard.

Hilliard answered his own phone, his voice gruff, almost a bark: "Hilliard."

"Roberts," Metcalfe said, the agreed-upon name. It was a given that the embassy phone was tapped.

There was a pause of ten, fifteen seconds. Then Hilliard spoke again. He said one word: *"Tain."*

"Repeat," Metcalfe said.

"Tain. Not *taint*, but *tain*." With that, Hilliard hung up abruptly.

Tain. That was the next word on the list Corky had given him. Confirmation that Hilliard had indeed spoken to Corky, given him the news.

Tain. A strange, rarely encountered word that referred to the metallic backing of a mirror; it was from the French word *étain*, or "tin."

Even the choice of word was classic Corcoran, who so loved words and phrases that were freighted with meaning. The backing of a mirror. It evoked that old conundrum Corky was so fond of: Why do mirrors reverse left and right, but not up and down?

And another: Truth is the shattered mirror. *Don't cut yourself on the shards,* he'd warned.

It was as if Corky had been warning him all along, simply by his choice of confirmation words. Metcalfe had entered a world of mirrors, a world fraught with dangers.

But Corky, even Corky, had no idea how fraught it was.

Rudolf von Schüssler reviewed the pages again. Amazing! Just amazing! The fruit of his own brilliance—it was immodest of him to say so, but the recognition of opportunity was itself the sign of the superior intellectual: the Führer himself had said no less. He had recognized the opportunity—the fact that his darling

Red Poppy had access to documents on the highest, most privileged levels. And the fact that she had given them to him: proof of her love for him. She was helpless, smitten, devoted to him; despite her toned ballerina's body, she was a frail creature. For in every way, she embodied the *Ewig Weiblich*—the Eternal Feminine. It was her nature to give, as it was man's to take. And soon Herr Hitler would be taking the empire that was rightfully his!

It would *make* von Schüssler's reputation. No, better, it would result in his *being recognized*. Recognized in turn. Recognized for what he truly was. He could picture the Knight's Cross being pinned on his fine navy tunic. What Ludwig von Schüssler had gained through brawn and sheer, frontal audacity, his descendant had secured through cunning, wiles—cerebral qualities, seemingly softer, but no less redoubtable for all that.

His heart was beating hard as he made his way down the corridor to Ambassador von der Schulenberg's office suite. Nodding curtly at some of his colleagues, bustling about with blasé looks, and barely turning his head, he recalled some of the condescending remarks he'd overheard from others in the Foreign Ministry, long before his Moscow posting. They'd look at him differently now. Information was what won wars! It was always thus—knowledge of oneself, knowledge of the enemy. And the greater the level of detail, the more valuable the knowledge. His eyes scanned the top page of the sheaf of documents, the neatly typed rows of numbers. No longer would the OKW have to speculate and surmise about the nature of the Soviets' military capability. Now they would *know*.

"I'm afraid Graf von der Schulenberg is occupied," said the fat-necked frau who served as the ambassador's own private Cerberus. Werner was always cordial to him, albeit with a slightly patronizing air ... but certain of those who surrounded him could seem almost brusque, verging on discourtesy without ever providing cause for formal complaint. One couldn't complain about a tone of voice, a quick eye roll, an expression of vague contempt: one would oneself seem foolish. Yet von Schüssler noticed these things. He noticed a great many things. It was precisely his capacity for observation and inference that had resulted in this—*this!*—the most valuable piece of intelligence that the Reich had yet received.

"Oh, is he now?" von Schüssler replied in the purring voice of absolute confidence. Occupied: it was how she always described him. It meant nothing: Was he in a meeting? Was he enjoying a glass of schnapps by himself? What was the point of saying he was "occupied"? Somehow she felt entitled to treat him with borderline rudeness. Well, that would soon change.

A quick on-off smile from the fat-necked Cerberus. "Occupied. Sorry, sir. I'll tell him you came by."

"Occupied or no, he'll want to see me," von Schüssler said. He knocked on the ambassador's office door himself, before turning the polished brass knob and letting himself in. The ambassador's office was large and stately, wood-paneled, its floor covered with the finest Oriental carpets. Soon enough, von Schüssler would be able to decorate his office in such a manner. Until now it would have seemed presumptuous. But after today, the proper, dignified decor would be only appropriate.

Count Werner von der Schulenberg was at his desk, hunched over a pile of bureaucratic forms, looking bleary-eyed and bored. A glass of brandy sat on one corner of his desk. He squinted in von Schüssler's direction. "Rudi," he said, sounding less than pleased. "What are you doing here?"

"I have something for you," von Schüssler said, his face crinkling into a smile. "Something that will interest you. Indeed, something that will fascinate the Führer himself."

PART THREE

Moscow, August 1991

Ambassador Stephen Metcalfe approached the leader of the commandos, the KGB Alpha Group that had ordered his limousine to stop. The street was dark, empty, the old buildings in this ancient part of the city looming above them ominously.

"Are you in charge?" he demanded.

The commando leader replied in Russian, a torrent of officialese. Metcalfe switched to Russian. Even half a century later, he had not forgotten Alfred Corcoran's rule number one: *When challenged by authority, you must always lay claim to a greater authority.* "What the hell do you think you're doing?" he barked. "You should have our license plate number, our names. God damn it to hell, we've been summoned by the chairman of the KGB himself, Vladimir Kryuchkov! All roadblocks were supposed to be notified!"

The commando's fierce expression gave way to one of confusion. The American's certitude, combined with his dignified bearing, intimidated even this trained killer.

Metcalfe continued, "And why the hell did the motorcycle escort never arrive?"

"I was not told anything about a motorcycle escort!" the commando shot back defensively.

Metcalfe knew that, because of the crisis, most communications were down. There would be no way for the KGB group to check back with their superiors. And in any case, Metcalfe's claim was too outrageous *not* to credit.

A moment later, Metcalfe and his Russian friend returned to the limousine, which was then escorted through the roadblock.

"You haven't lost your touch," the general said. "It's been over fifty years. A half a century." He reached out a hand and patted Metcalfe's breast pocket, feeling the large, bulky shape of the pistol. "Are you ready for this?"

"I don't know," Metcalfe replied honestly.

"Remember the old Russian maxim," said the general in a voice that crackled like old leather. "Fate makes demands of flesh and blood. And what does it most often demand? Flesh and blood."

CHAPTER TWENTY-FIVE

Berchtesgaden, the Bavarian Alps, November 1940

The small white-haired man got out of the black Mercedes and gave his driver a brief wave. He had piercing blue eyes, a pink complexion, and a kindly smile; he wore a navy-blue double-breasted uniform with brass buttons and a braided cap.

He was Admiral Wilhelm Canaris. As chief of German Military Intelligence, he was the grand master of all Nazi espionage. He had come to the Berghof, Hitler's retreat at Berchtesgaden, to present the Führer with some earthshaking intelligence he had just received.

He was escorted into the Führer's personal study, a large room with picture windows, sparely furnished, though the furniture that was here was oversize. There was a long sideboard that Canaris knew held Hitler's favorite phonograph records, mostly Wagner; there was, in fact, a bronze bust of Wagner here as well. There was an immense, and quite ugly, clock on the wall topped by a fierce bronze eagle. Two large tapestries on the wall concealed a movie projector on one side and a movie screen on the other.

In front of the huge stone fireplace, seated on chairs upholstered in red morocco leather, were four men, two on one side of the Führer, one on the other. They were clearly engaged in an animated, quite intense, discussion.

One man was the Commander in Chief of the German Army, Field Marshal Walther von Brauchitsch. The other was von Brauchitsch's chief of staff, General Franz Halder. Both were, Canaris knew, reasonable men; neither was a fanatic. They were not at the very top of the military leadership chain, but they were men Hitler trusted to discuss one of his most secret plans, a course of action opposed by many of his generals and about which he had been wavering for more than a year: the invasion of Russia. They were the first men whom Hitler had asked to draw up preliminary plans for the attack, the moment the French had surrendered, and they were men whose opinion the Führer trusted.

To Hitler's right sat a man of lesser rank but perhaps greater power. He was Colonel Rudolf Schmundt, and he was Hitler's chief adjutant for the *Wehrmacht.*

The men nodded at Canaris as he took a seat on the long and uncomfortably low sofa, which was the only place left to sit. Canaris listened to the argument, for that was what it truly was. One could never argue with Hitler, but one could make an argument *for* Hitler or argue in front of Hitler.

Schmundt, whom Canaris thought of as Hitler's alter ego, was speaking with banked fury. "Churchill has rejected our peace offers," he spat out, "and Stalin is now moving into the Balkans brazenly. Clearly, Churchill is pinning all his hopes on America and Russia entering the war."

"Correct," interjected von Brauchitsch.

"Therefore we must crush the Soviet Union by force," Schmundt continued, "and therefore eliminate the hope of Russia joining the war on behalf of England. And thus establish Germany as the master of Europe. The quicker we smash Russia, the better."

"You can't be serious," von Brauchitsch objected. "When was the last time you read your history? Do you want us to repeat Napoleon's mistakes and lose the war on the frozen steppes of Russia? Napoleon, too, failed to invade the British Isles. We will be destroyed if we attack Russia!"

"Have you forgotten that we defeated czarist Russia in the last war?" Schmundt shot back.

For the first time Hitler spoke up, in a low, almost inaudible voice. He had been listening, considering. The other men leaned forward to hear him. "And then we shipped Lenin to Russia in a sealed train, like a plague bacillus."

The other men chuckled politely. "That it was," said Hitler's adjutant. "But let the plague not spread. We cannot allow the Balkan peninsula to be Bolshevized. We cannot allow the Soviets to seize our oil fields in Romania—"

"What you're proposing is madness," von Brauchitsch interrupted. "It would mean war on two fronts, which must be avoided at all costs. None of us wants that. We should be *isolating* Britain. This requires *cooperation* with the Soviet Union."

"It *is* a one-front war! Britain is no threat—it's merely an annoyance," said Schmundt. "Britain is already defeated—we must make her admit it. Crush Russia, and England will give up—count on it!"

"You say 'crush Russia' as if it is a child's game," said Halder, "when the truth is that the Red Army is a colossus."

"The Russian 'colossus,'" replied Schmundt scornfully, "is a pig's bladder—prick it and it will burst."

"To attack Russia would be the sheerest lunacy," said Halder. "It would be suicide. We have no choice but to maintain the so-called friendship pact."

Canaris cleared his throat. "May I offer some pertinent information?"

There was silence, so he continued. "The *Abwehr* has received some valuable intelligence from Moscow." With a dramatic flourish, he produced from his briefcase a folder thick with typewritten documents, which he handed around, beginning with the Führer.

Hitler took out his reading glasses. The men were rapt in concentration.

After a moment, the Führer looked up. "This is genuine?" he exclaimed.

"My document experts confirm it, based on the paper, the ink, the stamps, the signatures, and so forth," replied Canaris.

"Mein Gott in Himmel!" said Schmundt. "The Red Army is a
house of cards!"

"What is the source?" asked von Brauchitsch suspiciously.
"One of your agents in Moscow?"

Canaris shook his head. "Getting intelligence in Moscow is
fiendishly difficult. It is easier for an Arab in a flowing burnoose
to walk unnoticed through Berlin than for a foreign agent to pass
through Russia. No, the source is a general officer high in the
Commissariat of Defense Ministry."

"A turncoat?" Halder said. "A traitor?"

"On the contrary," Canaris replied. "A loyal general who remains loyal. We have a source who is, shall we say, close to the
general."

"This source is reliable?"

"The source," Canaris said, "is of the sort who's the most reliable of all. Not a professional, but a civilian. A simple person
with no knowledge of intelligence games."

"A secretary, then," Halder put in.

"In fact, it is his daughter."

Schmundt looked up from the document. "The Bolshevik military is in ruins since the purges," he said. "But they are rearming—and quickly."

"In two years," said Canaris, "they will be powerful again."

"How soon can we attack?" Hitler asked of Schmundt.

His adjutant allowed himself a victorious smile. "After the winter. Early spring of next year. Certainly by June we will be ready."

Hitler stood up, and the others quickly followed. "Fate itself
has presented us with an opportunity," he proclaimed, "but we
must move quickly. I have not created this magnificent army only
to have it rot. The war will not end on its own. I want preliminary plans for a blitzkrieg against the Soviet Union drawn up at
once."

CHAPTER TWENTY-SIX

Moscow, November 1940

The dead drop location made Metcalfe uneasy. It was too exposed, too much out in the open; there was only one way to get to it and probably no alternative egress. He would not have chosen this location, but he had no choice; Amos Hilliard was the control in this instance, and he had selected it.

There was one advantage to the drop site, though, and that was that it was easy to stake out. Metcalfe was able to observe pedestrian traffic patterns, watch those who entered and left the women's shoe store and the meat shop on Pushkin Street as well as the building in between, see anyone who seemed to loiter for too long in the area. Dressed in his peasant outfit, his *telogreika* and a large backpack filled with various tools, he passed easily for a laborer; he attracted no attention.

For a long while he watched intently, allowing his mind to stray to thoughts of Lana. So far things had gone according to plan, and her initial fear seemed to have dissipated. She had given von Schüssler the first load of documents, telling him that she had selected them at random from her father's briefcase and his study at home. They meant nothing to her, she'd said; they were all numbers, incomprehensible, and terribly dull. But he had not found them dull at all, Lana said. He had been most excited, more excited than she'd ever seen him before.

Von Schüssler had explained to her the procedure, for after all, he believed that he was running this operation. He would take the papers to the German embassy, where a Photostat would be made of each sheet, and then he would immediately return the originals to her. It was important, he insisted, that her father never notice any of the papers missing, so she would have to follow a very strict procedure. She would take the papers only at night, when her father had retired, and call von Schüssler to let him know she had them. Then she would meet him at the apartment, give him the documents, and he would immediately bring them to the embassy to have them photocopied. He would return to the apartment right away and give her the originals back, and she would return to her father's apartment and replace them before he awoke in the morning. Obviously there were many factors that might alter the plan. Most nights Svetlana had to perform at the Bolshoi and thus couldn't steal any documents. But on her off nights, it was most important that she stay at her father's apartment to see whether he had brought any new documents home.

Von Schüssler also sought to reassure Lana that what she was doing was a good thing. Lana had recalled his reassurances with a grim humor. "The more our two countries know about one another," he'd said, "the longer this peace between us will last. You are doing a wonderful thing, not only for my country but for yours as well."

After an hour of watching and contemplating, Metcalfe was as certain as he could be that there was no surveillance. He strode quickly up to the unguarded entrance of the modest apartment building between the two shops. The small lobby was dark and empty, the green-painted radiator fastened to the wall on the right just as Hilliard had described. He reached behind it—it was cold, as Hilliard had promised—and his fingers touched something. He pulled it out: it was a thick green envelope, its color a perfect camouflage.

This contained, he knew, the second set of documents, prepared by Corcoran's documents experts and dispatched via the diplomatic pouch. He stuffed it inside his peasant *telogreika* and walked out as quickly as he could without attracting suspicion. Just a few blocks away was the signal site, where he would indicate with a red pencil that he had successfully unloaded the drop.

But as he emerged from the building, an abrupt movement from across the street attracted his eyes. Metcalfe turned to look and saw a familiar face. He did a double take.

It was the pale-eyed, blond NKVD man, and he was coming at him at a quick stride, not even bothering to keep his normal discreet distance. It was as if the agent *knew* Metcalfe had just serviced a dead drop, knew he had incriminating documents on his person!

He could not be caught now. He could not be apprehended, not with the documents on him. They would be cause for immediate imprisonment followed by execution, without even the pretext of a trial. The operation would be unmasked, and the subsequent investigation would lead to Svetlana; she, too, would be executed.

Metcalfe's heart raced, and he broke into a sweat. The consequences would be inconceivable! He spun to his left, raced down Pushkin Street, and saw in the reflection of a store window that the blond man was running after him. Metcalfe stopped abruptly, reversed direction, lurched off to his left again, zigzagging crazily through the square. The blond man followed, mirroring Metcalfe's jerky movements, equally heedless of the pedestrians in his way.

The NKVD man was coming after him. This was no longer a matter of surveillance; he had shifted to a brazen attempt to grab Metcalfe.

Good Christ, no! This couldn't be allowed to happen.

Spinning once again, Metcalfe vaulted into a narrow alley between two ancient-looking ramshackle brick buildings, and he ran at top speed.

The blond man had not been tricked; he followed Metcalfe into the alley, but his pace, oddly, had slowed. Was the NKVD man tired already? How could it be? Metcalfe glanced back over his shoulder, saw a broad gray-toothed smile on the blond man's face. *Why?*

Immediately up ahead, the alley took a jog to the right; Metcalfe sped up, practically jumping around the corner, and then he understood the reason for his pursuer's smile.

It was a dead end.

The J-shaped alley did not go through to the next block. It ended right here.

He was trapped.

He froze, turned back, saw the blond man advancing on him slowly, his pistol drawn.

"*Stoi!*" the man shouted, his deep voice echoing: Stop!

"Hands up, please." The blond man had switched to English.

He was several hundred feet away, too far to fire accurately—and *would* he fire? It seemed unlikely. You did not stalk your prey for so long in order to kill it. He wanted to ask questions, wanted a full interrogation, Metcalfe was sure.

In one sweeping motion Metcalfe pulled out the weapon Hilliard had given him and pointed it at the NKVD man, who smiled. "Not a good idea, Comrade Metcalfe. There is no sense to run."

"Oh, is that right?"

"This is not your city. I know these streets much better than you. It is important always to know what you do not know."

"I'll keep that in mind."

"This will be much easier if you cooperate. We will talk."

"What are you going to arrest me for?" Metcalfe said. "The crime of being a foreigner in Moscow?"

"We know much more about you than you think," the man replied.

Metcalfe looked desperately around at the crumbling brick walls of the building that bounded the courtyard into which the alley had dead-ended. There was no fire escape. Neither were there any footholds on the building's facade, any ledges to grab hold of, as he might have done in Paris.

Yet to be trapped with the forged documents was unfathomable.

He would have to toss them, but *where?* There was *no* place, damn it, no place where the blond man couldn't retrieve them.

There was an old copper drainpipe that ran down the length of the ancient stone building. It did not look sturdy, but it was all there was.

"All right," Metcalfe said, still pointing his weapon. "You stop right there, and maybe we can make an arrangement."

The man stopped advancing, but he kept his gun extended in a two-handed firing grip. He nodded.

Suddenly Metcalfe fired, just over the Russian's shoulder. The agent ducked out of the way, firing back instinctually, but missing Metcalfe by a dozen feet. *Deliberately* missing him.

A split second later, taking advantage of the momentary chaos, Metcalfe shoved the weapon into the waistband of his trousers and then leaped toward the drainpipe, grabbing hold with both hands, scaling it quickly. "If you know anything about me," he shouted, "you know I'm not going to get caught!" The copper pipe was indeed rickety, and as he pulled at it, it came away from the brick wall. But still it remained attached at the top and in several places along the brick face of the building. Shoving with his feet against the brick, he pulled himself up the length of the pipe until he was three-quarters of the way up the tall two-story building.

Bullets pitted the brick on either side of him as the NKVD man fired warning shots. "There's no place to go!" the Russian shouted. "The next shot will be a disabling shot. It will strike *you,* if you don't stop and climb down!"

Metcalfe continued climbing, but there came a pause in the firing; he heard the Russian eject an empty cartridge, the metal clattering to the ground, and then reload. Metcalfe reached the top of the building, grabbed at the cornice, but it came away in his hands, the old plaster crumbling like piecrust. He reached for the copper gutter, which seemed more secure, and used it to pull himself up onto the flat roof, just as another round of gunfire exploded against the parapet. The Russian was now firing *at* him! These were not warning shots any longer.

The building was perhaps twenty feet wide, a mess of tar and rubble, vent pipes sticking up irregularly here and there. He ran to the opposite edge, losing his footing on the icy surface, slipping just feet from the drop-off. Below was a narrow street crisscrossed with tram tracks; a fire escape on this side was a welcome sight. From behind he could hear the NKVD man's retreating, echoing footsteps. The Russian had obviously deduced Metcalfe's only escape route and was running down the alley, out onto Pushkin Street, and then around the building to the avenue that intersected it. But why was the agent operating alone? These men inevitably operated in teams, and certainly a team would have made all the difference right now; with a team in place, they could easily have trapped Metcalfe! He was grateful but puzzled all the same that this particular NKVD man, by far the most skilled of all those assigned to him, was a lone wolf. No, he realized: the NKVD man was no lone operator. He was simply ahead of his team. Others would join him.

Metcalfe leaped to the top of the rusted iron fire escape and descended it by rappelling along its grating; in a few seconds, he reached the street and raced along the tram tracks. In a few hundred feet, the narrow street joined a broader avenue. He looked wildly from side to side for the best route just as he heard running footsteps from behind.

Just up ahead was the entrance to an underground passageway. He ran toward it. It was a pedestrian pathway beneath the street, a recent appearance in Moscow with the advent of the automobile. He took the steps two at a time, propelling himself through the crowd, then spotted the entrance to the Metro.

He had never taken the Metro—it was another thing that hadn't been here on his last visit—but he knew that if it at all resembled the one in Paris, the Metro would provide a profusion of branching tunnels that would enable him to lose his pursuer. It was a risk, but everything was a risk now, and nothing compared to the danger of being apprehended with the forged documents on him. As he raced through the ornate marble-walled entrance toward the turnstiles, he searched for trash cans where he could toss the packet of documents; none was in sight.

There was a long line waiting at a booth by the row of turnstiles; another line, moving more rapidly, of people waiting to pass through the turnstiles. Were they buying tokens? He had no idea whether entrance required tokens or coins or what, and he had no time to find out. Looking from side to side, he saw two uniformed officers, both of them women, and he decided to chance it. Racing past the lines, he leaped over the turnstile; behind him came shouts, the shrill blowing of a whistle. He had no doubt that the NKVD man was close behind as well, but he couldn't take the time to look back.

He raced past marble columns, mosaic walls, crystal chandeliers: the beauty staggering, wholly unexpected. The People's Palaces, Stalin had called the Metro, and Metcalfe could see why. He entered an archway from which a crowd was surging. It was an escalator that was moving up; he forced his way onto it, going the wrong way, ignoring their angry protests, muscling his way down the astonishingly steep, fast-moving steel steps. It was choked with people, hard to maneuver, but he could hardly turn around and head back the way he came—not with the NKVD agent so close behind. He vaulted ahead, colliding with the on-rushing masses, trying to force his way down the escalator. It was slow, *too* slow!

The sounds of running and whistle blowing told him that his pursuers were close behind. There was more than one now; the blond NKVD man had been joined by others. Desperate to advance through the impossibly thick oncoming crowd, he noticed the handrails on either side, roughly two feet wide. Could he jump up onto the railing and run down? But the path was obstructed by a cylindrical light every few feet, an ornate sconce that provided illumination to the dim tunnel.

There was no choice. He leaped up, jumped onto the steel

railing, crashing into a glass tube, shattering it. Screams were everywhere. The railing was steep; it was impossible to get a foothold. He slid down, smashing lamp after lamp, until he was finally able to grab the low, vaulted ceiling to steady himself, allowing him to crab-walk down to the bottom of the escalator, though he could not avoid crashing against the glass sconces.

Finally he leaped to the floor, just missing a seated blue-uniformed security guard, a harridan who jumped aside and began screaming at him to stop. Metcalfe kept going, now almost oblivious to the madness he had incited.

The train from which the crowd had poured was still there. A sequence of four tones sounded over a loudspeaker, indicating that the train was about to leave. He raced toward it, propelling himself into the nearest wagon just as the doors shut.

He collapsed onto the floor, ignoring the shocked expressions of the passengers. An old man and a young child, presumably his grandchild, backed away, the man throwing his arms around the boy.

But he had made it. The train began moving rapidly. The NKVD man, he assumed, had been left behind at the station. Still, he would have to assume that there were emergency procedures in place. There would be telephone hookups between stations or perhaps radio transmissions; the NKVD agent, who was nothing if not resourceful, would have phoned ahead to arrange for others to be in place at the next stop.

When he got up, however, he saw that he had not lost the blond man at all.

He was there, in the next compartment, and he was trying to force the door between the two wagons, which was meant to open only in an emergency. Christ! It was as if the damned agent were tethered to him! Metcalfe could see the man turn around, run toward the far end of his compartment, calling for an official—a conductor, perhaps, or a *militsiyoner*. Was there one in that compartment? Or in the next one down?

Suddenly, with a squeal of brakes and a rush of air, the train came to a stop midtunnel. The walls on either side were black.

Somehow, the NKVD man had gotten the officials to halt the train, obviously to trap Metcalfe. Or had he simply pulled the emergency brake cord?

But Metcalfe did not intend to make it easy for them. He ran to the doors, inserted his fingers between the rubber gaskets, and tried to pull them apart. But they were stuck. The door-opening mechanism was intended to keep the doors closed between stations; there seemed to be no way to pry them open, no matter how hard he tried. The young boy, watching him from his grandfather's lap, started crying. A man began shouting at him, waving his hands crazily.

He tried the windows and had more luck there. They opened; he was able to slide one all the way down. Climbing up on the leather seat, he reached out into the blackness. There was a space of several feet. He grabbed hold of the ceiling-mounted straps and used them to pull himself up, then thrust his legs through the open window. He dropped to the ground painfully, a longer fall than he expected, landing on ballast.

But he was out of the train. And now . . . now what?

The shouting continued, crescendoing, as he sidled along the tunnel wall. The only illumination came from the dome lights inside the train, but it was enough to highlight the regular niches set several feet deep into the walls, presumably used by Metro workers to protect them from the passing trains.

He remembered the flashlight in his backpack, reached behind him, and pulled it out. He switched it on, and suddenly there came an explosion. Metcalfe dived forward in the darkness as a fusillade of bullets pitted the tunnel walls inches away, the sound reverberating in the tunnel. He turned, saw the blond man firing from the next car down, his Tokarev angled out the window. The NKVD man had obviously gone beyond wanting to bring him in; now he wanted Metcalfe dead. He was not going to allow Metcalfe to escape.

There was not enough room to duck to either side. Between the stopped train and the brick wall was two feet or so. Metcalfe could only flatten himself against the ballast. But the gunfire continued, steadily, rhythmically. Metcalfe grabbed his pistol from his waistband and, his left hand steadying his right, began firing back. He squeezed off two shots, but the blond man had pulled back into the compartment.

Another noise began: the sound of the train's engines powering up. The train had begun to move again. Metcalfe leaped to his feet and out of the way of the train's wheels, his back flat against the tunnel wall. He could feel the rush of air; he flinched as the accelerating steel passed inches from his face. For the time being he could not move. Flat against the tunnel wall, he was vulnerable, a stationary target. He raised the gun, gripped in his right hand, and with barely a few inches of space attempted to aim it at the passing car. But he was unable to position the gun in time. He saw the pale gray eyes of his pursuer, saw the pistol aimed dead at his face through the glass of a window a few feet away, flickering in the kaleidoscopic light of the tunnel. This was the end, he thought to himself in that split second: *I can't move, can't defend myself. But I can't let this happen!* And abruptly he slid down against the brick wall, his shoulders bracing his body, keeping himself from pitching forward into the train. It all happened in the space of a second or so: he saw the blond man smile, squinting one eye, firing; he saw the white-orange muzzle flash, and as he slid, he felt the bullet slice across his shoulder, the pain agonizing.

In a moment, it was all over. The train had passed, and he had crumpled to the ground, on the tracks. He reached for the wound, felt the stickiness of blood under his thick peasant jacket. It felt as if the bullet had creased his shoulder: the wound was painful, the blood flow heavy, but it was not grave. The important thing was that he was still alive. He felt for the package of documents inside the jacket; the stiff crinkle of the cellophane told him they were still in place.

He would have to escape some way, but how? The distance between Moscow's Metro stops could be as much as two thousand meters; despite the pain, he could walk through the tunnel to the next station if he had to, but he knew that would be a mistake. His pursuer had seen Metcalfe shot, but he would not likely assume that Metcalfe had been killed. That would be a careless assumption, not characteristic of an agent who seemed to be as canny and thorough as he did. The man might well have gotten off at the next stop to wait for Metcalfe to emerge, or else to lead a search party through the tunnels. This would require shutting down the trains temporarily, but the NKVD certainly had that authority. No, it would be dangerous for Metcalfe to return to the last station or go to the next one, where he would have to assume that searchers would be posted.

He was trapped.

Yet he could not stay here, either. There had to be another way out. He continued along the narrow ledge, alert for the distant sound of an oncoming train, shining his flashlight along the tunnel walls and ceiling, looking for an air shaft, something, *anything* at all. The tunnel curved to the right, and then he saw that the tracks branched off. No, that wasn't quite right, he saw as he approached; there was a newly laid section of track that came off the main run, a switch that wasn't yet operational. As he rounded the bend, he saw that the secondary set of tracks led to another tunnel, but this one was still under construction. Its walls were only partially bricked in, earth still visible in certain areas, reinforced by steel girders.

This was indeed promising. A tunnel under construction was likely to lead to an entrance used by its workers, probably a shaft down which workers were lowered. He turned into the unfinished tunnel and was immediately assaulted by a sulfurous stench. A sewer conduit was probably nearby. He saw a few discarded vodka bottles on the ground. These could not have been left by workers; was it evidence of vagrants living in the tunnels, seeking temporary refuge? If so, that might indicate that there was indeed another way out.

He must have walked for half an hour, his pace slowed by the throbbing pain in his shoulder. He was weakened by the loss of blood. He would have to get medical treatment, but where? Obviously, going to a Soviet hospital was an impossibility, with all the questions that would be asked, all the reports filed. Roger had been trained as a paramedic—but Roger, he remembered with a pang of grief, was dead. That left only Lana. Perhaps when he got the documents to her she could arrange for the assistance of a doctor.

The farther he went along the tunnel, the more finished it appeared to be. Obviously it was being built from the outside in. By now the walls were fully bricked in, the tracks laid. The sequence of work puzzled him, but then, so did most things Soviet.

But then the tunnel came to an abrupt end at a tall set of heavy steel doors. The surface was flat, smooth, with no knob or handle, no way to force the doors open. Clearly this was a security measure, designed to keep out trespassers, accessible only with the right keys. He examined the doors for a good five minutes, but it was hopeless. There was no way out of here.

Frustrated, weary, and in pain, he turned around and headed back the way he came. Now he was trapped more than ever, the only way out the main tunnel, which meant heading toward one or the other of the stations where men waited. Had he not been wounded, he could probably have attempted to wait them out, to hide in the crevices of the tunnel for hours, even days. But he was continuing to lose blood, and he would not be able to endure this cold for much longer.

He needed a plan, damn it, but what?

For a moment he thought he heard voices, and he stopped to listen. Yes, there *were* voices. From where?

He was still hundreds of meters from the main tunnel. Did

that mean that a search party was headed his way, trapping him in this blind alley?

But no! The voices were not coming from up ahead; they were coming from somewhere to his *right*. How could that be? To his right was nothing but brick wall and . . .

And another set of steel doors, he noticed: an access hatch, actually, built into the brick wall. It was something he had not noticed when he had first walked by, because the hatch was low to the ground, camouflaged, it appeared, by dark paint the color of the surrounding bricks, obscured by girders. Metcalfe stopped in front of the steel plate, knelt down, placed his ear against it.

Definitely voices.

But not shouts, not barked orders: not the cadences of a search party. It was the low murmur of conversation. What was on the other side of this hatch? Perhaps it was a way out, Metcalfe thought; in any case, it was his only possibility.

The hatch was not painted, he realized; it was covered in rust. It was made of iron, with a handle and latch on one side; it appeared to be ancient, far older than the surrounding brick. He carefully turned the latch, then slowly pulled it open. It gave a rusty squeak, and he stopped. Then he resumed opening it, even more slowly, this time silently, until it was open just enough for him to be able to see inside. He felt warm air.

What he saw astonished him.

In the flickering light from a fire he saw what appeared to be an immense, elaborate hall with walls and floors of green marble. The opening through which he peered was some ten feet off the floor; an iron ladder led all the way down. The chamber was several hundred feet square, its ceiling almost twenty feet high. At the far end was a raised dais. Behind it, built into the wall, was a tall crèche displaying a large white marble bust of Joseph Stalin. A small bonfire was burning in the middle of the room. Around it huddled three seedy-looking, shabbily dressed men. On the floor nearby, blankets had been placed.

Were they vagrants? What were they doing here? And more important: What was this imposing, grand hall?

One of them looked up, pointed at him, and shouted, "Seryozha!"

Suddenly something slammed into Metcalfe from behind, crashing into his neck. Metcalfe spun, saw his attacker, a wild-eyed bearded man wielding a crowbar. He lunged, slamming all his weight against the attacker, knocking him to the ground as he wrested the crowbar out of the bearded man's hands and then cracked the man's forehead against the floor. His attacker let out a bloodcurdling scream. Metcalfe jammed his knee into the man's abdomen, forcing the breath out of him.

"Who are you?" Metcalfe demanded. "You sure as hell don't look like NKVD."

The bearded man moaned. "NKVD? I'm no goddamned Chekist, like you! Or are you a goddamned cop?"

He heard the clatter of footsteps on the iron rungs of the ladder; he whirled around to see one of the seedy-looking vagrants from the marble hall pointing a small antique revolver at him, a nineteenth-century Galand. "Get off of him, Chekist, or I'll blow your head off!" the vagrant roared.

Metcalfe pulled out his Smith & Wesson and aimed it nonchalantly while maintaining his grip on the bearded man. "Put that old musket down," Metcalfe said, "or you're liable to put your own eye out."

The vagrant standing on the iron ladder kept pointing his gun, but it shook in his hand. "Let Seryozha go!" he cried.

"I'll let Seryozha go, you put down that damned toy, and we'll talk. Now, I need your help. I'm not a Chekist, or I'd have a Tokarev, not a Smith & Wesson. You can see the damned blood on my shoulder."

Metcalfe could see the vagrant's resolve waver. He went on, "I'm trying to *hide* from the damned *militsiyoneri,* and it looks to me like you've got room in there for one more."

"But *who* are you?"

A few minutes later Metcalfe was seated around the fire with the four Russians. The one named Seryozha had a nasty bruise on his forehead.

Metcalfe had removed his quilted jacket and was compressing his bullet wound with a scrap of dirty bedsheet provided by the man who had aimed the antique revolver at him, who seemed to be the leader of this motley group. Metcalfe told them he was visiting from the Ukraine; he told them a tale of an attempted robbery gone bad, an escape from the Moscow police that led him into the Metro, into the tunnels.

"And you?" he asked. "How long have you men been living down here? And what *is* this place anyway?"

"This is a bomb shelter," said the first man, who gave his name as Arkady.

Metcalfe looked at him skeptically. "With all this marble?"

"Why should the leaders suffer?" Arkady lit a cigarette. He offered one to Metcalfe, who demurred. "It is part of the Metro-2 complex," he said. "The *spetztunnel.*"

"The special train just for the emergency use of the Party elite," Metcalfe said, nodding. He had heard rumors, seen vague intelligence reports out of Moscow, of a secret metro system built to take Kremlin leaders to an underground town fifty miles away.

"In the classless society, some are more equal than others." Arkady's smile was mordant.

"Is there more than one bomb shelter down here?"

Arkady and the other men laughed. "It is a wonder all these tall buildings they are building don't fall into the earth," said a gray-bearded professorial-looking man in a long shabby black overcoat, "with all the digging that goes on down here. There are maybe twelve levels below ground, far below the Metro tunnels, hundreds of meters deep in some places. A huge network of bunkers and secret tunnels for Stalin and his gang. And all of this built by slave labor!"

"I thought it was all done by Komsomol volunteers," said another in a dry tone of voice.

More laughter. "The Komsomol volunteers were just for the newspaper photographs," said the professor. "The tunnels were actually dug in the frozen ground by prisoners with shovels and pickaxes."

"Come, the czars have been digging under the city for centuries," Arkady said. "Ivan the Terrible had a torture chamber built deep underground beneath the Kremlin, and then he had the diggers killed to conceal its existence. His grandfather even had his priceless library, his collection of medieval Hebrew and Byzantine scrolls, buried somewhere down here in an Egyptian-style sarcophagus to keep it safe, and it's never been found."

"The famous Lost Library of Ivan the Terrible, they call it," said the professor. "Because Ivan the Terrible discovered it, then had it concealed again. And our own Ivan the Terrible, Stalin—they say there are mass burial sites far beneath Moscow as well. The millions of Russians he has executed had to be put somewhere, after all."

"But the bomb shelters that Stalin had built," Metcalfe said. "How long ago did he have them constructed?"

"He started in 1929," Arkady replied. "And he continues to have them built."

"Stalin expects Moscow to be attacked."

"Of course."

"But this treaty with Nazi Germany—?"

"Stalin is always expecting a war! He's always expecting to be attacked. He talks about capitalist encirclement, about the enemies that would strangle the Bolshevik infant in its cradle."

"So if the Germans attack—"

"He will be prepared," Arkady replied. "Know this about Stalin. He is always prepared for war. He never trusts his allies. He trusts only himself. But why do you ask these questions? What kind of a thief are you, who's so interested in wars and attacks?"

Metcalfe deflected the question with a question of his own. "And who are you? Forgive me for saying it, but you're not—you're all far too well spoken to be . . ."

"Bums? Vagrants?" said Arkady. "But we are bums, you see. In this society, we cannot hold jobs; we cannot live in apartments. We are fugitives."

"From what?"

"From the NKVD. All four of us—and there are surely dozens more like us hiding in underground shelters like this—are hiding from the persecutors. The secret police."

"You've escaped them?"

"We've escaped before they could get to us. We were called in to the Lubyanka, or we were warned that they were coming to arrest us."

"For what?"

"For *what?*" scoffed Seryozha, the wounded one. This was the first he had spoken since he had attacked Metcalfe. "They arrest people at random now. They arrest for no reason, or for the slightest reason whatsoever. You say you are from the Ukraine? Are you saying it's different there?"

"No, no," Metcalfe said hastily. "It's the same. But I need your help. I need help getting out of here without being caught. There must be a way! I, too, am evading the NKVD."

"You are a political refugee as well?" the professor asked. "A fugitive?"

"In some ways," Metcalfe answered vaguely. Then he paused, reconsidered. "Yes. I'm a fugitive as well."

CHAPTER TWENTY-SEVEN

The cement courtyard was small and desolate, much like the run-down building that surrounded it, located in a seedy area in the southwest of Moscow. Discarded newspapers swirled around the courtyard; heaps of trash lay all around. No one cleaned the courtyard; barely anyone ever looked at it. Even the word *courtyard* was far too grand for this sad little patch of concrete, at the center of which was a cast-iron sewer grate.

No one saw the grate turn, no one saw it lift up, and no one saw the solitary figure quickly emerge from it, having swiftly ascended the iron ladder that led from the drainage tunnels far below. The man replaced the grate, and within a minute he was gone.

No one saw him emerge. No one saw him disappear onto the streets of the rough working-class neighborhood.

Approximately ninety minutes later, an old truck loaded with firewood pulled into another courtyard in a much more presentable section of Moscow. It was a cranky old GAZ-42 truck, belching fumes; it rattled loudly as it idled by the delivery chute at the rear of the handsome stone building on Petrovka Street.

The driver and his assistant got out of the truck's cab and began shoving into the chute split firewood, which landed loudly in a large hopper in the building's basement. The delivery of firewood had not been scheduled, but in the dead of this very cold Moscow winter an unscheduled delivery of fuel would hardly raise any questions. Once a convincing quantity of wood had been unloaded from the truck, the second man, the passenger-assistant, entered the basement of the building through the delivery entrance and began stacking the wood neatly. The driver came around to the basement entrance and cleared his throat; his passenger then slipped him a wad of rubles, far exceeding the cost of the firewood, but enough to reimburse the driver for the trouble of making this unscheduled stop.

Had anyone been watching—though no one was—they would have been puzzled to see the driver hop into the truck and drive away, leaving his assistant still toiling away in the basement.

Two minutes later, Metcalfe left the basement and walked up several flights of stairs to the familiar leather-padded door, where he pushed the buzzer and waited. His heartbeat sped up, as it always seemed to when he came to Lana's apartment. But this time it was more than anticipation, it was fear. He had gotten here without being observed, thanks to Seryozha, the man he had tackled to the ground in the Metro tunnel, and his truck driver friend. But coming to this apartment was still a risk. It was also a violation of his agreement with her never to come here again.

He heard the heavy tread, and when the door opened he was unsurprised to see the weathered face of the cook/housekeeper.

"*Da? Shto vyi khotite?*"

"*Lana, pozhaluista. Ya—Stiva.*"

The old *babushka*'s squinting eyes seemed to recognize him, but she indicated no familiarity. Instead, she closed the door and disappeared into the recesses of the apartment.

A minute later, the door opened again, and this time it was Lana. Her eyes flashed with some combination of anger and fear and something softer—tenderness? "Get in, get in!" she whispered.

As soon as she had closed the door behind him, she said, "*Why*, Stiva? Why are you here? You promised me—"

"I've been shot," he said quietly. Her eyes widened in shock, but he continued in a calm tone, "It's a minor wound, but it needs to be treated. It's already infected, and it's just going to get worse."

In truth, the throbbing in the wound had grown worse, limiting his mobility somewhat. Seeking professional medical help was not only out of the question; it was probably unnecessary. Lana had a first-aid kit, she said; she would take care of him herself. "Shot! Stiva, how?"

"I'll explain. It's nothing to worry about."

She shook her head in disbelief. "Shot!" she repeated. "Well, my darling, we will have to work fast. Father is usually home from work forty-five minutes from now." She told her housekeeper to take the rest of the day off. Then Lana led him through a comfortably furnished room lined with books, a remarkable eighteenth-century Turkmenistan flat-weave on the floor: one of the family's few remaining heirlooms, she explained.

"Come, into the kitchen, and I'll take care of your wound." The kitchen was small and smelled of kerosene. She put a kettle of water on the stove, and while she waited for it to boil, she stripped off his filthy *telogreika,* then gingerly peeled away his shirt, which adhered to the dried blood. He winced as she pulled at the cloth. Lana made a clucking sound. "It does not look good," she said. She made some strong black tea, which she served in glasses; to sweeten it she offered a plate of gummy chunks of sugary candies to stir in instead of sugar. "Here, you drink this while I gather my surgical instruments. Are you hungry, my darling?"

"Famished."

"I have some piroshki with meat filling, some cabbage soup, a little salt fish. This is all right?"

"It sounds perfect."

While she bustled around, ladling cabbage soup from a pot on the stove, taking food from string bags that hung from the outside of a window that gave onto an air shaft, he watched her. This was another side to Lana he hadn't seen before, a domestic, nurturing aspect that was so different from the fiery diva, the beautiful dancer-artist. It seemed peculiar, yet wonderful, that all these aspects could coexist in one person.

"This must seem a terribly small apartment to you," she said.

"Not at all. It's beautiful."

"You've told me about how you were brought up. The wealth, the many houses, the servants. This must be a sad little place to you."

"It's warm and comfortable."

"We are very lucky to have our own apartment, you know. There are just the two of us, my father and I. The city authorities could put us into one of those foul communal apartments. We were afraid that would happen after Mother died. But because of his military record—because Father is a hero—they grant us this privilege. We have a gas stove and a gas water heater in the bathroom—we don't have to go to the public baths like most of my friends."

"He's a Hero of the Soviet Union, isn't he?"

"Twice. He also received the Order of Victory."

"He was one of the great generals." He took a spoonful of the soup, which was hot and delicious.

"Yes. Not the most famous, not like Marshal Zhukov or his old friend Tukhachevsky. But he served under Tukhachevsky, he helped capture Siberia from Kolchak. He helped defeat General Denikin in the Crimea in 1920."

Metcalfe studied a photograph of Lana's father, and he found himself speaking. "You know, I have friends in Moscow—old friends, highly placed in various ministries, people who tell me things. And I'm told that the NKVD keeps what they call a *kniga smerty*—a book of death. A sort of list of persons scheduled to be executed—"

"And my father is on it," she interrupted.

"Lana, I didn't know whether to tell you, how to tell you."

"And you think I don't know this?" Her eyes flashed with anger. "You think I don't *expect* it—that *he* doesn't expect it? All of the men of his rank, all of the generals, they have all come to expect the knock on the door. If not now, then tomorrow. If not tomorrow, then next week, or next month."

"But von Schüssler's blackmail—"

"His time will come when it will come. It is not for me to hasten its arrival. But he is resigned to it, Stiva. He waits for the knock on the door. When it finally comes, I think he'll actually feel relieved. Every morning, I say good-bye to him for the last time." She began rinsing the wound, then began dabbing at it with iodine and cotton batting. "Well, I don't think this needs stitches—thank God, because I can barely sew my stockings! I wouldn't want to sew your skin, my darling. You know, it's terribly ironic, isn't it?"

"How so?"

"Or maybe it's fitting. I can't help thinking of Tristan and Isolde again. My darling one, remember, it was a wound that drove Tristan into the arms of his Isolde. She had to nurse him back to health."

Metcalfe gritted his teeth as she taped the wound closed. "She was a magical healer, just like you." He took a sip of the strong tea. "Unfortunately, as I recall, it was a mortal wound he suffered, wasn't it?"

"Twice he was wounded, Stiva. The first time in a battle with Isolde's betrothed, whom he kills, but his wound won't heal. Only Isolde, the magical healer, can save him, so he seeks her out. And when she realizes that Tristan has murdered her fiancé, she attempts to take revenge on him—but then their eyes meet, and the weapon falls from her hand."

"Just like life, huh?" Metcalfe retorted sarcastically. "Then Tristan is wounded again, in another duel, but this time Isolde can't save him, and they die together, in eternal rapture. In the world of ballet and opera, that's called a happy ending, I believe."

"Of course! Because they can no longer be separated, foolish one! Their love is now immortal."

"If that's a happy ending, give me tragedy," he said, taking a bite of the piroshki. "Delicious."

"Thank you. Tragedy is what we live with every day here," Lana said. "Tragedy is commonplace in Russia."

Metcalfe shook his head and smiled. "Your point?"

She batted her eyelashes in a deliberately theatrical gesture of faux naïveté. "I'm not *making* a point, Tristan. I mean, Stephen. Only that Tristan's real wound is deeper, within him—it is his own sense of blood guilt. *That* was the wound that could never heal."

"Now I'm *sure* you're trying to tell me something," Metcalfe said. His tone was bantering, but he felt a twinge that had nothing to do with his gunshot wound.

"In Russia, guilt and innocence are as mixed up as loyalty and betrayal. There are the guilty, and there are those who are capable of feeling guilty—and they are not the same."

Metcalfe gazed at her curiously, swallowed hard. There were depths to her, he realized, that he had only begun to fathom.

Lana gave a small, rueful smile. "They say the human soul is a dark forest, you know. Some are darker than others."

"That's so Russian," Metcalfe said. "Tragic to the marrow."

"And you Americans love to deceive yourselves. You're always convinced that no matter what you do, something good will come of it."

"Whereas you tragic Russians seem to think that nothing good can ever come of anything."

"No," she said sternly. "All I know for certain is that nothing ever goes according to plan. *Nothing.*"

"Let's hope you're wrong about that."

"You have more documents for me, yes?" she said, noticing the secure-sealed packet inside his jacket, which lay inside out on the kitchen table.

"The last set," Metcalfe said.

"Last? Won't he wonder why the stream has dried up?"

"He may. Maybe you should feed these to him slowly, a few at a time."

"Yes. It's more believable that way, I think. But what do I say when they finally stop?"

"You express bewilderment. You say you have no idea why he's not taking them home anymore, but you can't ask him, of course. You speculate that perhaps security has been tightened, and he's not permitted to take classified documents out of the office any longer."

She nodded. "I have to become a better liar than I am."

"Sometimes it's a necessary skill. Terrible but true."

"There's an old Russian saying that goes, If you fight a dragon for too long, you will become one."

"There's an old American saying that goes, Any fool can tell the truth; it takes talent to lie well."

She shook her head as she walked from the kitchen. "I must get ready to leave for the theater."

Metcalfe took his penknife and slit open the cellophane package. There was no note from Corky here. He perused the documents, skimming them quickly, wondering as he did whether Lana even looked at the documents she passed on. She was far brighter and more discerning than he'd given her credit for.

And if she did read them closely? What would she see? Metcalfe had assured her that all the notes and secret communications were pieces of a puzzle that would show the Nazis how weak—therefore, how *docile*—Russia was. She would see in the documents what she been *told* to see, wouldn't she?

Was she politically astute enough to see that the opposite message was actually being communicated: that Russia was defenseless and thus an inviting target for a German invasion? He worried about that. Yet she had said nothing to indicate she felt she was being misled. It was a risky game Corky had sent him to play, risky on multiple levels.

He riffled through the papers quickly, and then something

caught his eye. It was a page of what looked like garbage, meaningless strings of letters and numbers. A code, he saw at once. He looked closely, saw the groups of five numbers and the identifier that started the transmission, and he recognized the code.

It was a particular Soviet cipher, the SUVOROV code, named for the great eighteenth-century Russian general. It was also a code that the Germans had *broken*, Metcalfe knew. Finnish troops had discovered a scorched Russian codebook in the Soviet consulate in Petsamo and had passed it to the Nazis. The British, from analyzing German traffic, were able to confirm that the Nazis had indeed cracked the code. The Russian military, however, had no idea.

Metcalfe understood at once why so many of the WOLFS-FALLE documents were in the SUVOROV code. It was a Corky masterstroke. Documents that were encrypted would automatically be more intriguing, and somehow more credible, to the Nazis, the code bolstering the illusion of the seriousness of their content.

Most of the papers, therefore, Metcalfe could not read. But he scanned those in plaintext, and quickly he realized that something was different about this batch. The last set had portrayed a Red Army that was surprisingly weak and vulnerable but trying to rearm.

This second set "revealed" the *reason* for the rearmament. The *details* of the planned Soviet rearmament were here, and the details told an alarming story in shocking detail.

There were orders for the immediate production of tens of thousands of superadvanced tanks, far heavier and more powerful than anything the Germans had, heavier even than the Nazis' Panzer IV. High-speed tanks capable of moving a hundred kilometers an hour—and, according to their specifications, they were designed not to operate off-road but on the good roads of Germany and Western Europe. Twenty-five thousand of these tanks were to be finished by next June.

There were orders—*counterfeit* orders, made up by Corky's

team—for the development of the most advanced offensive weapons systems, including aircraft, rockets, and bombs. Orders for the mass production of airborne assault transport gliders. These weren't weapons meant to defend Russia against a possible attack. They were *offensive* weapons. And they, too, were to be ready by next June. The orders were emphatic about this deadline.

And more. Urgent top-secret memoranda between two highly placed Red Army generals, General A. M. Vasilevsky and General Georgi Zhukov, made reference to something called Operation *Groza*—Thunder. Operation *Groza*, he read, had been presented to Stalin and the other members of the Politburo in September, a few months ago, under conditions of utmost secrecy.

Memorandum by memorandum, document by document, Metcalfe pieced together the details of this fictional "Operation *Groza*," just as he knew Nazi intelligence would do. By the beginning of next July, according to the plan, the Red Army would have twenty-four thousand of its new tanks on its western border.

The border with Nazi Germany.

Over the next several months, there was to be a secret, yet massive, buildup of Red Army troops on Russia's western frontier. Other orders had gone out for the training of airborne assault troops—almost a *million* paratroopers, trained to attack Germany behind enemy lines.

Operation *Groza* was not a set of plans for the defense of Russia. It was a detailed outline for an offensive war against Nazi Germany.

And Operation *Groza* set a date for a preemptive attack against Nazi Germany: July of 1942.

It had been laid out in a secret speech by Stalin to top military officers barely one week earlier. Copies of the speech had been circulated among the top Red Army leaders, according to these documents.

Documents that Metcalfe had to keep reminding himself were fake.

A copy of this fictional Stalin speech was included among the WOLFSFALLE papers, and it was so authentic in tone that Metcalfe wondered whether it might possibly be genuine.

Comrades! it began:

> *Operation Groza has been approved. Our war plan is ready. Within eighteen months, in the summer of 1942, our lightning strike on the fascists will commence. But it will be merely the opening blow, comrades, a wedge for the overthrow of capitalism in Europe and the victory of Communism under the leadership of the Soviet Union!*
>
> *The capitalist ruling circles in all the countries of Europe will, as a result of their mutually destructive war, become weak and unable to challenge the glorious rise of socialism throughout Europe and the world. It is our honored duty to liberate the peoples of the world!*

Metcalfe read with astonishment mixed with increasing outrage. It was the sheerest madness, but at the same time it was brilliant. It was entirely notional, entirely made up, yet at the same time it was entirely plausible.

And it was yet more evidence, if any were needed, of Corky's deception. Not just of Hitler—but of Metcalfe. *These documents will paint a picture,* Corky had said.

What sort of picture?

A painting of a bear, Stephen. But a cuddly one. A bear cub that has been declawed.

Corky had lied to him about the nature of the false documents, just as he'd lied about the real reason he was sending Metcalfe to Moscow. The old spymaster had told him his mission was to assess von Schüssler as a potential target for recruitment when his mission was something else entirely: it was to use Lana to pass on these doctored papers to von Schüssler. And then Corky had deceived him, brazenly, once again, by concealing the true intent of the WOLFSFALLE documents. They didn't show a cuddly bear cub at all. They portrayed a rapidly rearming military power that was planning a massive secret strike against Nazi Germany.

A couple of sets of perfectly forged documents passed from the daughter of a Red Army general to an ambitious Nazi diplomat. That was all it would take to propel the Nazis into launching an attack against the Soviet Union—an attack that would surely spell the end of Nazi Germany.

Metcalfe's indignation quickly gave way to worry: If Lana read these documents, wouldn't she realize that he hadn't been honest with her? She thought she was passing on documents that would assure the Germans that Russia wanted only peace. Yet these did the opposite. These indicated that Moscow intended to attack Germany first.

What would she do—*if* she did read them? Would she refuse to hand them to von Schüssler?

Well, it was a risk. He had no choice now. Corky had manipulated him into this, and he would have to manipulate her into it as well. He could only hope that she would not have the time to read them, that she wouldn't be inclined to do so.

He hoped she would simply pass them over to the German.

"Stiva," she called out.

She was wearing a black leotard and a loose, large white smock over it; her face was made up, lipstick freshly applied. "You look magnificent," he said.

"And you are silly," she said with a toss of her head.

"You don't just look magnificent, you *are* magnificent. You're a remarkable woman."

"Please," she chided. "You give me far more credit than I deserve." She reached for the packet of documents.

"Be careful not to handle them," Metcalfe said. "Handle as little as possible."

"Why?"

Why? he thought. *Because if you don't handle them, maybe you won't look at them. And if you don't look at them, then maybe you*

won't see how you're being lied to. No, not "being lied to"—how
I'm lying to you. How I'm manipulating you, betraying you.

But he replied, "Apparently the wizards who've forged these
documents have also somehow managed to put fingerprints on
them. Fingerprints belonging to the top Soviet military leaders.
So that if the Nazis do a fingerprint analysis, these papers will
pass muster, seem totally authentic." Metcalfe was making this
up entirely, but it sounded plausible. The lies were convincing,
but telling them to her made him ache.

"Ah," she said. "How very clever."

"Lana, listen. You've been tremendously brave. What you've
done—I know how hard it's been. But there's a reason for everything. So much depends upon what you've done. So much hangs
in the balance."

"These papers so dense with figures and mysterious words,
you'd think nobody could read them."

"Yes."

"And yet each contains something powerful. Like the philter
that Isolde's maid prepares, right?" She laughed.

"Not exactly," he said uneasily.

"You mean these papers are not designed to produce a deep
and abiding love between our fearless leader and the leaders of
the Third Reich? They won't produce an intoxicating affection
for Russia in the hearts of von Ribbentrop and Heydrich, Himmler and Hitler?"

Metcalfe gazed at her curiously and swallowed hard. There
were depths to her, he realized, that he had only begun to fathom.
"You said you know nothing of these things. But you seem to
know a little bit more than 'nothing,' my *dusya.*"

"Thank you, my darling. And you, too—we both know a little
bit more than nothing. But wasn't there an English poet who
warned against a 'little learning'? I sometimes wonder whether a
little bit more than nothing is more dangerous than nothing at
all. But then, I would, wouldn't I? Since I know almost nothing."

Her smile was cryptic. "Come, my darling. Now it is I who have something to show you."

"I like the sound of that," Metcalfe replied. He followed her out into the living room and was surprised to see a Christmas tree in one corner adorned with homemade decorations and fruit. "A Christmas tree?" he remarked. "Isn't that against the law, in this godless paradise? Didn't Stalin ban Christmas?"

She smiled, shrugged. "It's not a Christmas tree, it's a *yolka*. We just put a red star on top, and then it's no longer called a Christmas tree. It's a pagan custom anyway, decorating fir trees. The Christians just took it over. We don't have Santa Claus, either; we have *Dyed Moroz,* Father Frost."

"And this?" he said, pointing to a varnished burlwood case on a side table. It was lined with green baize and had two intricately tooled, perfectly matched dueling pistols set into the recesses. The walnut half-stocks were ornately figured, carved with acanthus leaves and fluted pistol grips; the octagonal twist steel barrels were engraved with images of fire. "Those must be a century old," he said.

"Older. It's my father's greatest treasure—dueling pistols that they say were used by Pushkin."

"Extraordinary."

"You see, our leaders tell us they are creating the New Soviet Man, that we are all new, washed clean of history, washed clean of the bad old traditions and the corruptions of ancestry. But they're still here, these family roots. They still anchor us. Little things that get passed along from generation to generation. They give us a sense of who we are, these things—what is the English word, such a beautiful word? A poetic word. It sounds like something woven from our breath, from the very air . . ."

Metcalfe laughed. *"Heirloom?"*

"Yes, precisely!"

"If there's poetry in that word, you put it there."

"Heirloom," she said slowly, treating the word carefully, as if it were itself a fragile antique. "My father has a number of these—*heirlooms,* his own secret treasures he's so proud of. Little treasures he has held on to, not because they are valuable, but because so many of his ancestors were so careful to pass them down to him. Like this Palekh music box." She gestured toward a black lacquered box with a beautiful multicolored firebird on top. "Or this fifteenth-century icon of the Transfiguration." It was a painted wooden panel measuring maybe four by five inches, showing Jesus in glowing robes, being transformed into a radiant spiritual apparition in the presence of two disciples.

"And someday all these will be yours."

She looked pensive. "Nothing of value is ever really ours. They are ours only for safekeeping."

"But I don't see any of your things, Lana. You must get many gifts from your many admirers. Where do you keep them?"

"That's what grandmothers are for. Grandmothers who live far away from here. Grandmothers who live in Yashkino."

"Where's Yashkino?"

"A small village in the Kuznetsk Basin. Many hours on the train from here. They call themselves 'provincials born and bred,' and that is a boast, not an apology."

"With Russians, sometimes it's hard to tell the difference. But at least you have a safe place for your own heirlooms-to-be."

"You seem to be imagining Aladdin's cave. My treasure consists of one gift in particular, from one admirer in particular—although it remains a treasure beyond compare."

"There you go again—now, tell me, Lana, is that a boast, or an apology?"

"Does it matter?"

"It's just that you're starting to make me jealous."

"Don't be. The gift of your love is what matters to me more than anything." She drew him near. "My Stiva, ever since we first met, what you've given me—it matters more to me than you can know. More than you'll ever know."

"Lana, I—"

The phone rang abruptly. She looked startled. She let it ring several times before she decided to pick it up.

"*Allo?* . . . Yes, this is Lana." Her face went pale. She listened, interjecting a few syllables from time to time. After a few moments, she thanked the caller and hung up.

"That was my friend Ilya, the stagehand," she said. She was flustered, even appearing to be frightened. "He spoke to me in the kind of code we have for speaking on the phone. Ilya says that Kundrov, my minder, has been at the Bolshoi today, asking many questions about me. And about my friend, the American."

"Go on."

"But there were others as well. From the NKVD. They are all looking for you. They use the word *spy*."

"Yes," Metcalfe said nervously. "All Americans are spies."

"No, this time it is different. Orders have been given to find you and, if they find you, to take you in."

"Threats," Metcalfe tried to assure her. "Hollow threats."

"Why, Stiva? Do they know about this—about all of this?" She indicated with a wave of a hand the documents she was taking with her for her meeting later with von Schüssler.

"No, they don't."

"You wouldn't deceive me, Stiva. Would you?"

He embraced her, unable to continue lying. "I must go," he said. "Your father will be here any second."

CHAPTER TWENTY-EIGHT

"Ted?"

"Yes?"

"Do you recognize my voice?"

There was a long pause. "Yes, I think I do. Bloody hell, man, what's going on?" Ted Bishop's voice sounded different—muted, tense. It was the voice of a frightened man. Metcalfe was calling from a telephone kiosk several blocks from Lana's father's apartment on Petrovka. The British journalist worked out of the Metropole; thus he was almost always there.

"Later," Metcalfe said abruptly. "I need your help."

"You're telling *me*. This place is swarming with YMCA boys."

"I need you to grab some things from my room. You can get in, right? You've known the staff there for years; someone can let you in."

"They've known me for years, doesn't mean they like me. Familiarity breeds contempt, and all that. But I'll see what I can do."

"I appreciate it. Let me call you back in a few hours with a place to meet."

"Speaking of phone calls, you've been getting a bunch of urgent messages from someone—they've even been giving 'em to me, in the dining room, in case I saw you. Someone named 'Mr. Jenkins'? Bloke sounds desperate."

"Mr. Jenkins"—that was Hilliard. "Got it," Metcalfe said. "Thanks."

"All right—uh, listen, do yourself a favor, and don't come back here. You understand what I'm saying?"

Metcalfe hung up and immediately placed a call to Hilliard at the U.S. Embassy. He identified himself as Mr. Roberts, but before he had a chance to say that he'd lost his passport, Hilliard interrupted.

"Jesus Christ, where the hell have you *been?*" Hilliard said in a low, trembling voice, some combination of fear and anger. "What the *hell* have you been up to? You've been burned, do you know that?"

"Yes."

"They're out for blood, man. You've got to get the hell out of Dodge, you understand me? You're in sanction now. You've been called out of play."

Metcalfe went cold. He had to get out of Moscow, out of the Soviet Union, immediately. He had been burned; he was now designated for either arrest or an immediate kill. Corky had passed on the order that he was to be exfiltrated out of the country at once.

"I'll need support." Meaning false papers, visas, plane tickets. Documentation that only Corky could provide.

"Obviously. The good Lord has provided, but He wants you to move fast. Like yesterday. Understood?"

"Understood." Hilliard's manner of referring to Corcoran might have been, at another time, amusing. It wasn't now.

"And as for me, I'm feeling a hankering for *satsivi*. In half an hour or so." With that, Hilliard hung up.

Metcalfe rushed from the telephone booth.

The violinist observed the small, balding, bespectacled man leaving the main entrance of the American embassy. The man was, he knew, a minor functionary in the embassy, a third secretary. He was also, according to the intelligence that had been provided him, an agent of American intelligence.

As he tailed the American, the wind shifted, and he caught a whiff of Barbasol. The man had freshly shaved, using an American brand of shaving cream.

Yes. This man would lead him to his target. He was sure of it.

The gun weighed heavily beneath Amos Hilliard's suit coat. He was not used to wearing a gun, disliked its heft, and he hated what he was about to do. But it had to be done. Corky had been adamant about it. The encoded message had been unambiguous.

Metcalfe is a risk to the mission, therefore a risk to the fate of the free world. It is a sad necessity, but he must be eliminated.

The young agent had accomplished what he'd been ordered to do. But he'd been blown. Moscow was crawling with goddamned NKVD and GRU agents who were on the verge of grabbing the fellow. They'd get him; it was only a question of when, how soon. Corky couldn't possibly exfiltrate Metcalfe in time. And once they got him, they'd interrogate him as only the Russians could, and Metcalfe would crack; there was no doubt of it. The entire operation would be exposed, and Corky could not—would not—allow that to happen. Far too much was at stake. It must not be jeopardized by a single human being.

Hilliard wondered at times like these whether he was truly cut out for this job. This sort of thing was truly the worst part of the assignment. He sort of liked Metcalfe, but that wasn't the main thing. He knew that Metcalfe was one of the good guys, one of the white hats. The young fellow was no traitor. But Corky had issued the order, and Hilliard had no choice. He had a job to do.

Metcalfe arrived at the Aragvi Restaurant seven minutes ahead of schedule. "In half an hour or so" meant thirty minutes precisely; Hilliard was as exact with language as he was punctual. The customary line that snaked out the front of the restaurant wasn't there, because it wasn't yet dinnertime; this made it easier for Metcalfe to observe the comings and goings. As he staked out the front and side entrances of the restaurant from his vantage point on the steps of Central Telegraph on Gorky Street, he recalled that he'd promised to call Ted Bishop back with a rendezvous site. But that would have to wait until after this meeting. The ache in his shoulder had lessened, though he could still feel the throbbing of a minor blood vessel.

Amos Hilliard entered the Aragvi by the back stairs, where he knew he would not be noticed, and met his way through the dark passage to the men's room.

He was surprised, and a little unnerved, to find that someone was there. A man was standing at the sink washing his hands vigorously with soap and water. Well, no matter. Hilliard would wait. Once the guy had left, he would take out the Smith & Wesson revolver and screw the sound suppressor into its specially modified threaded barrel. He would double check to make sure the chamber was loaded.

Stephen Metcalfe would arrive, expecting to receive false documents and instructions on how to leave Russia furtively. The last thing he would expect was for Hilliard to whip out a revolver and fire several silenced rounds into his head.

Hilliard hated having to do this, but there really was no choice.

He hesitated, glancing at the man at the washstand who kept washing his hands with a remarkable thoroughness, working up a foam that Hilliard thought wasn't possible with that shitty Soviet soap.

There was something naggingly familiar about the blank-faced man with the aristocratic features and the long, delicate fingers. He wondered whether he'd seen the man's face somewhere before. Just recently, he thought; could it be? But no. It was just his nerves.

Then the man at the sink looked up, and their eyes met, and Amos Hilliard felt a sudden, unaccountable chill.

At exactly one minute before the designated rendezvous time, Metcalfe crossed Gorky Street and strode up to the restaurant's service entrance. It was unlocked, naturally, given the frequency of deliveries of food and other supplies; he was able to enter undetected and walk through the deserted restaurant to the men's room where he had met Hilliard just a few days earlier.

There seemed to be no one in here, and he hesitated for a moment, unsure whether to lock the door, as Hilliard had done last time. Best not to, he decided; Hilliard was late. He briskly walked through the room, checking the stalls, and in the last one he saw Hilliard.

Hilliard's shoes and trousers, to be more precise. There was no mistaking the diplomat's tweed pants and brown leather brogues; they unquestionably belonged to Amos Hilliard and not to a Russian.

Strange, he thought. Why was Hilliard on the can rather than waiting out here by the sinks, as he had last time?

"Amos!" he called out, but there was no reply. "Amos," he said again, more concerned.

He pulled at the stall door, which swung slowly open.

Jesus *Christ!* What he saw sickened him, stunned him, caused him to sink to the floor. No, not *again!* Amos Hilliard sat on the toilet, his head slumped back, his darkly bloodshot eyes staring at the ceiling, a bloody discharge coming from his nose and mouth. His throat had been nearly severed just below the larynx. The ligature mark, a razor-thin furrow, was scarlet and pronounced; it indicated that the weapon had been some kind of thin, strong wire. The diplomat had been strangled, garroted in exactly the same way as Scoop Martin and the members of the Paris station.

No! Hilliard must have *just* been killed, minutes ago—he could not have been here long. Five minutes? Even less, maybe?

Metcalfe touched Hilliard's crimson face. It was at a normal body temperature.

The killer had to be nearby.

Metcalfe raced out to the door, then hesitated. The murderer might be waiting for him on the other side of the door, the deserted restaurant affording him temporary shelter, enabling him to stand there, ready to pounce.

Metcalfe crashed his foot against the door, causing it to swing open. He hung back, crouched to the side of the doorjamb, watching to see if any figure jumped from the shadows, garrote in hand. No one did. He leaped into the hall, torquing his body from side to side, ready to jump if he had to. But no one was there. Still, the killer could not have been gone for much more than a minute or two.

He ran down the nearest staircase, bounding down the steps two and three at a time, nearly crashing into a waiter bearing a tray. Metcalfe glanced at the slight, uniformed waiter, sizing him up quickly, rejecting him as the possible killer.

A gust of cold air in the hall told him that the exit to the street had just opened, moments ago. Someone had either come in or gone out, though this was not the way Metcalfe had entered the restaurant. *The killer.* It was possible, in any case. Had he left through this door?

Stealthily he pushed the steel door open a crack, taking care not to make a sound. If the killer had left this way and was walking—so as not to appear suspicious to others on the street—not running, then he could not be far. He would be within sight. If there was even the possibility of an element of surprise, Metcalfe wanted to preserve it. He slipped through the narrow opening, gently pushing the door closed behind him, satisfied that he had not made a noise.

He was at the rear of the building. Large steel trash bins overflowed with malodorous food garbage. He looked around, but there was no one here.

Whoever it was who had murdered Amos Hilliard had vanished.

Metcalfe knew he had to leave at once, but to go where? He couldn't return to the Metropole. The fact was, he'd been burnt. He'd been observed servicing a dead drop; the NKVD knew he was engaged in clandestine activities. He had to get the hell out of Moscow as soon as possible. But that was far easier said than done. In this totalitarian state, where everyone was watched and borders were heavily guarded, it was as difficult to leave as it was to enter. Among his papers at the Metropole had been several sets of passports and other bogus identification, but they had surely been seized by the NKVD by now. By far the most prudent, most logical course was to contact Corky and have him proceed with the exfiltration Hilliard had mentioned. To do it right required coordination, horse-trading at a high level. The sort of thing that Corky, who worked in mysterious ways, was expert at arranging. An exfiltration was not something that was done by a lone agent, except in the direst emergencies.

He wanted to take Lana with him. It wasn't safe for her here any longer, given her involvement. He had promised himself that he would protect her; now, he needed to bring her out.

In order to set the plan in motion, Corky had to be contacted, and for now the best way to reach Corky seemed to be through Ted Bishop. Metcalfe, after all, could not place an international telephone call except from his hotel, and returning there was out of the question. In Moscow one could not place an overseas call from a telephone booth. Amos Hilliard was dead. He had no transmitter.

That left only Ted Bishop. Bishop, as a foreign correspondent, was expected to place long-distance calls regularly, perhaps even daily, whether from his hotel room or from Central Telegraph. So Bishop could place a call for him, to one of the emergency numbers in London or New York. Simply by speaking a few meaningless-sounding words, once the phone was answered,

Bishop would alert Corky without knowing what he was doing or whom he was speaking to.

And there were other ways for Bishop to help, if he was for some reason unable to place a call. It was the BBC radio broadcasts that Metcalfe used to listen to in Paris that gave him the idea. Coded messages, in the form of personal greetings, were broadcast during each evening's BBC news—messages that alerted agents in the field, their true meaning opaque to all other listeners. *Why not use news dispatches in the same way?* Metcalfe decided. He mentally drew up a plan for an innocent-sounding dispatch that Bishop might plausibly send to his newspaper, the *Manchester Guardian.* It would be, say, a review of a concert, a performance—maybe even the ballet. But certain emergency phrases contained within the bland-sounding dispatch—coded language that Corky had formulated, which would easily get past the Soviet censors—would reach Corky, come to his attention, alert him to what was going on, what needed to be done. This method wouldn't be as quick as an emergency telephone call to a prearranged number in London or Washington, which was the preferred method.

Of course, Metcalfe couldn't level with Ted Bishop, couldn't tell the journalist the truth about who he was, what he was doing here in Moscow. He'd craft a plausible lie about how the Soviet authorities were preparing to arrest him because he was a wealthy businessman, as part of their ongoing campaign to discredit foreign capitalists as spies. That's all Ted Bishop needed to be told. Given the Englishman's apparent anti-Soviet bias, that was probably all it would take.

After all, Metcalfe reflected, he'd lied to someone far more important to him, someone he cared about—no, *loved*—deeply. Lies were beginning to come far too easily to him.

Still, the English journalist remained a question mark in Metcalfe's mind, his loyalties unclear. For now, Metcalfe would have to assume that no one was to be trusted. He would have to be exceedingly cautious with Bishop.

Quietly, with a casual lope, Metcalfe took the path around to the far side of the Aragvi, unseen by the police. He found a phone booth a few blocks away in front of a shabby-looking storefront infirmary, the Central Moscow Clinic Number 22. The clinic was dark, closed; no one was observing him. He called the Metropole and asked for Ted Bishop.

Number 7 Gorky Street was the massive, imposing Central Telegraph building, completed in 1929 in the grand Soviet architectural style. Its interior was equally imposing; it was designed to convey the solidity of a central bank or at least an important government institution, which it was. Here Muscovites waited in long lines to send telegrams to friends and relatives in distant reaches of the Soviet Union, to mail packages or buy postage stamps, to place international calls from stuffy booths. Still, despite its amazingly high ceilings and columns and granite, despite the immense hammer-and-sickle emblem of the USSR on the wall, it retained the gloomy aspect of all Soviet bureaucracies. Metcalfe stood in the shadows of an alcove, waiting for Ted Bishop.

As he watched a middle-aged man place a phone call from one of the booths, he saw how closely monitored telephone calls were. You had to show either a passport or an identity card, fill out a form, pay in advance, and then there was no doubt that someone was listening in to your call. He considered, then rejected, the option of placing an international call himself to one of Corky's emergency numbers. His false Russian identity papers would not permit him to place an international call; for that, he'd have to use either his true identity, which was now far too risky, or his Daniel Eigen passport, which he had to assume was compromised as well. No, Ted Bishop would have to place the call for him. He could do it without arousing undue attention.

Finally, precisely on time, the rotund journalist entered the massive doors, carrying Metcalfe's leather bag, looking around anxiously. Metcalfe hung back, watching, waiting to be sure that no one had followed Bishop in. While Bishop walked all the way into the center of the rotunda, peering around the interior, Metcalfe stayed concealed in the dim alcove, watching the front doors to make sure there were no others trailing in the reporter's wake. Others following Bishop—or working *with* him.

Metcalfe let another minute go by. Bishop began pacing back and forth, a scowl of irritation on his face. Finally, when it appeared that Bishop was about to leave, Metcalfe slowly emerged from his concealed alcove.

But Bishop, who hadn't yet seen Metcalfe, appeared to be signaling to someone, flicking an upraised index finger steadily. Metcalfe froze, stayed put, watched.

Yes, Bishop was definitely gesturing to someone. But whom?

And then Metcalfe saw whom Bishop was gesturing to.

At the far end of the lobby, beside a long row of what looked like bank-teller windows, a door opened, and a blond man came out.

A blond man with pale eyes. His NKVD pursuer strode up to Ted Bishop and began speaking rapidly in what Metcalfe could hear was Russian.

Metcalfe felt his insides turn to ice. *Oh, Christ! Ted Bishop was rotten.*

It suddenly came to him in a sickening headlong rush: The insatiable, jovial, journalistic curiosity, the searching questions. The anti-Soviet rants that concealed darker allegiances. The drunken scene in his room, when Bishop had rushed to the bathroom to vomit. That must have been a ruse, a pretext to go through Metcalfe's belongings, which included certain spy paraphernalia, the hollow shaving brush and cream, the multiple false identity papers. Bishop must have searched them while he was in the bathroom pretending to be sick and had thereby discovered the truth about Metcalfe. Perhaps he had been tipped off by the NKVD, after its agents had torn apart Metcalfe's room. Perhaps he was doing a follow-up search for the NKVD.

Anything was possible. The reporter had been in Moscow for years, tolerated by the authorities. Deals must have been struck, compromises made. Or worse. Foreigners occasionally were recruited by the NKVD; Ted Bishop was one of them.

Know all your exits, Corky said. But Metcalfe hadn't had the time to do so. The press of time had caused him to omit the very security precautions he most needed to observe.

Walking quickly along the perimeter of the lobby, keeping to the shadows until he reached the front doors, Metcalfe waited until a couple approached, arguing loudly, and slipped through the doors close behind them.

Then he accelerated his pace until he was running down Gorky Street. He had to reach Lana at the Bolshoi and warn her.

Unless it was already too late.

CHAPTER TWENTY-NINE

The Bolshoi Theater's facade was illuminated dramatically, but all was quiet in front, which told Metcalfe that the ballet was well under way. He circled around to the rear of the building until he located what appeared to be a stage entrance. It was locked; he pounded his fist on the door until it was opened by a tall, lanky, balding security guard with gold spectacles. He wore a navy-blue blazer whose patch read STATE ACADEMIC BOLSHOI THEATER SECURITY, with the same legend sewn on the visor of his navy-blue cap.

The security guard's wariness abated somewhat when he saw the man standing before him.

Dressed in a physician's white coat, a stethoscope around his neck, and carrying a black leather doctor bag, Metcalfe made a convincing Soviet physician. His disguise was completed by his haughty, even imperious gaze.

It had been a simple matter to break into the shabby-looking clinic. The infirmary's security was practically nonexistent; the lock had given way to a few seconds of work with the lock pick. He had quickly spotted the coat closet and grabbed one of the spare white coats, then found a stethoscope and black bag in a supply closet nearby. All told, it had taken him no more than five minutes.

"Yes, Doctor?"

"I'm Doctor Chavadze," Metcalfe said, figuring that the Soviet Georgian name might explain his slight accent. "I've just been called to attend to one of the dancers who's performing tonight."

The guard hesitated. "Which one?"

"How the devil should I know. One of the leads, I'm sure, or else they wouldn't have called me out of my dinner party. Apparently this is a matter of some urgency—a stress fracture. Now, please have me escorted to the dressing rooms at once."

The guard nodded, opened the door wider. "Please, come this way. I'll get someone to take you there, Doctor."

A young, scruffy-looking teenage stagehand with a pubic mustache escorted Metcalfe through a series of dark, squalid corridors in the Bolshoi's backstage labyrinth. The stagehand whispered, "We go up three levels and then stage left," and then he spoke not a word; the performance was under way. Metcalfe could hear the orchestra playing Tchaikovsky's music; he recognized a theme from act two of *Swan Lake*.

Compared to the grandeur of the Bolshoi's public spaces, the backstage was surprisingly grubby. They went past reeking toilets, down creaking low-ceilinged corridors with missing floorboards, around rusting catwalks and ladders. Dancers in costume, their faces caked with makeup, huddled and smoked. As they passed near the stage, Metcalfe heard the haunting strains of the oboe and the harp and the swelling tremolo strings of Tchaikovsky's score, and he recognized the beautiful melody of the act two pas de deux. A shaft of ghostly pale blue light lay across the backstage darkness; Metcalfe stopped and found himself looking directly at the stage and a section of the house.

"Wait," he said, grabbing the stagehand by the shoulder. The teenager looked at him, bewildered that the doctor wanted to catch a glimpse of the performance.

The stage set was magical and glowing: a moonlit lake, a painted backdrop of a lake and surrounding forest, several large prop trees—and in the center was Lana. Metcalfe watched, transported.

Lana was Odette, the swan queen, costumed in a close-fitting white tutu that emphasized her tiny waist, fringed with feathers and tulle; her hair was up in a tight chignon, and on it a white

feathered headdress. She looked delicate and vulnerable, astonishingly birdlike. She was dancing with Prince Siegfried, while
around them spiraled the cygnets, which then spun offstage, leaving just Odette and Siegfried. He gracefully hoisted her, set her
down gently, his hands tight around her body; she embraced him,
arching her swan neck intimately against his, and Metcalfe felt a
ridiculous pang of jealousy. This was a dance, no more; it was
her work, her job, the prince merely a coworker.

"All right," Metcalfe said. "Let's go to her dressing room. I'll
wait for her there until intermission."

"I'm afraid you really shouldn't be here," came a quiet voice
in English with a Russian accent.

Metcalfe turned, surprised—could this be the taciturn stagehand?—and then saw who was speaking. He recognized the
blond hair, the pale gray eyes.

The NKVD man. He stood a few feet away, pointing a pistol.

"Yes, it is you," the NKVD agent said, his voice barely audible.
The young stagehand watched in terror. "For a moment I didn't
recognize you, but you are nothing if not resourceful. Well, if
you've come to watch Miss Baranova perform, you should have
purchased a ticket like everyone else. Guests are not permitted
backstage. Come with me, please."

Metcalfe smiled. "A gun is useless," he replied, "unless you're
willing to fire it. And I doubt you want to fire a gun in the middle
of the pas de deux. It will shatter Miss Baranova's concentration
and detract from the spectators' enjoyment, will it not?"

The agent nodded, his face impassive. "I'd much rather not
have to fire, but given a choice between letting you get away and
disrupting the performance . . . well, I really have no choice."

"You always have a choice," Metcalfe said, backing away slowly.
He felt the weight of his pistol in his breast pocket, but it was
not reassuring: by the time he reached for it, the Russian would
have squeezed the trigger. Something about the NKVD man's
composure told Metcalfe that the Russian would not hesitate to
fire.

"Keep your hands at your sides," the Russian commanded.

Metcalfe's eyes shifted to the left, taking in the rigging, the system of pulleys within his reach. High above them a pair of lead sash weights dangled, anchored in place by means of ropes that were tied to iron hooks. He moved his hands behind his back and backed up a few feet as if intimidated by the agent. "Don't shoot," he said, putting a slight quaver in his voice to indicate fear. "Just tell me what you want."

The *rope!* It was there; he was able to grasp it! Slowly removing his knife from his back pocket, unseen by the Russian, he placed the sharp blade against the taut rope and sliced once, twice, keeping his movements subtle.

The NKVD agent allowed the faintest curl of a smile, which looked more like a sneer. "Your act doesn't fool me. You can't continue to run; there are no exits. I suggest you come along quietly."

"And *then* what?" Metcalfe said.

Finally the blade sliced all the way through the rope, which jerked out of his grasp. The lead sash weights swung in an abrupt downward arc from high above, toward the blond man. The Russian heard the swish of air, glanced up, and jumped to the side just as the weights rushed at him, just missing him by inches. But he was off his stride, no longer poised in a firing stance, his weapon no longer pointed at Metcalfe. The young stagehand let out a yelp and ran off.

Metcalfe lunged, not away but toward the blond man. He crashed into the NKVD man, knocking him to the ground, pinioning him against the floor as he slammed his knee into the Russian's stomach.

A sudden babble of loud voices erupted from the main hall. The orchestra had stopped playing; it was pandemonium! But Metcalfe couldn't look to see what happened. The blond man was fighting back, torquing his body up, his powerful arms struggling against Metcalfe, but the wind had been knocked out of him. Suddenly something hard struck the back of Metcalfe's head, so forcefully that he could taste blood. It was the agent's gun: the Russian had managed to free his right hand and swing the weapon at him.

Metcalfe grunted, then slammed his knee into the NKVD man's stomach, even harder, and at the same time wrenching the gun out of his hand. He struck the Russian with it, in his temple, with such force that at first he thought he might have killed him.

The blond agent's body went slack, his arms dropped to the floor, and the whites of his eyes showed. He was unconscious—but for how long?

Now the shouts were coming from all around. Men were coming at him, members of the crew, racing to tackle the intruder. Metcalfe jumped to his feet, saw that he was cornered!

He spun to his right, ran toward a metal ladder, and climbed up it. It led to a bridge constructed of metal pipes and wooden planks, directly above the stage. As he reached the bridge, he pulled the ladder up, keeping the others from chasing him up here. He ran across the bridge, and for the first time he saw what had happened when he'd sliced the rope and unharnessed the sash weights. No wonder the music had stopped, the theater was a cacophony of panicked voices. He had dropped a heavy black fire-safety curtain in front of the stage, thus cutting off the performance without warning; the audience had assumed that fire had broken out somewhere in the theater, and many were rushing to get out!

The bridge led to another catwalk. Metcalfe raced along the narrow catwalk until he reached a hatch that led to some kind of a wooden access panel. The shouts from below grew louder, more frenzied, as the members of the crew attempted to catch the intruder in the doctor's white coat who had rung down the curtain in the middle of *Swan Lake*. The panel swung open. Metcalfe entered and was immediately plunged into total darkness. He felt his way along a low-ceilinged, narrow tunnel—a walkway, presumably. The voices, the shouts from the stage below, were muffled. He stumbled along the hall, his hands in front of him to protect himself from unseen obstructions.

A crack of light along the floor indicated another door; Metcalfe stopped, felt for the frame, then the handle of a crude wooden door. He turned the knob, pulled the door open, and he was in a dimly lit corridor that looked vaguely familiar. Yes! He remembered it from the last time he had gone backstage to find Lana. He had walked this way before. In a moment he had oriented himself, reversed directions before turning a corner and finding himself in the long row of dressing rooms. The third one down, marked BARANOVA, S.M., the door open a few inches.

He ran toward it, heard voices within. She was there! Dressed in her white swan outfit, the feathered headdress still atop her hair, speaking with a ruddy-cheeked young crew member.

"There is nothing," the man was saying to the prima ballerina. "It is a false alarm—a malfunction of the backstage equipment, it must surely be."

"This is crazy!" Lana replied. "It's never happened before! Where's the director, the stage manager? Someone must make an announcement!"

She looked up, gaped. "Stiva!" she shouted. "What are you—?"

"Quick, Lana. Listen to me!" He looked from the assistant to Lana, his eyes questioning.

"It's all right, Stiva. This is Ilya, my friend. The one who warned me?"

"No, I'm sorry, Lana. We have to talk alone." He gestured toward the door; Ilya nodded, looking abashed, and left the dressing room.

She rushed up to Metcalfe, embraced him. Her stage makeup was thick, her eyes kohl-lined, but it did not detract from her beauty. "Why are you here? You are dressed—I see you must have gotten in here as a doctor, but you should not have come here! Stiva, what is going on?"

"Lana, everything's too risky! I'm leaving the country, and I want you to come with me."

"*What?* Why do you say this?"

He told her quickly about Ted Bishop, about the NKVD agent who'd seen him at the dead drop. "Connections have been made. They know about me, they've seen me retrieving the documents. They know about my connection to you. It's far too easy to connect us two, and I can't have that; I *won't* have that!"

"Stiva!" Lana blurted out. "Everything is a risk here, everything I do. I chose to do what I did not because you forced me but because I believed there is a good reason, because good will surely result from it—for the motherland as well as for my father. And no, I will *not* go with you, do you understand? Now, please— you must get out of here."

"I don't want to leave without you."

Lana looked frightened. "No, Stiva, I can't leave Russia."

"It's not *safe* for you here."

"I don't live here because it's safe. It's my home. It's in my blood."

"Lana—"

"*No,* Stiva!"

It was useless to argue with her; it was infuriating! Metcalfe removed his white doctor's coat and stethoscope, shoving them into the empty black doctor's bag. "If you won't come with me, I need a way out of here where I won't be seen, and I'm afraid too many people have seen my face. They're going to be searching everywhere. Any minute they'll be up here."

"Wait," she said. She opened the door, stepped out into the hallway. Metcalfe could hear her speaking with someone not far away. She returned a minute later. "Ilya will help you."

"You trust him?"

"With my life. And so with yours, too. He knows all the secret ways out of here, and he drives the prop truck, so he can take you out of Moscow."

"But where?"

"There's a warehouse on the outskirts of Moscow where the Bolshoi stores its larger props, scenery that's not in use. Where sets are built. There's someone on duty there, but he can be bought easily—and cheaply."

Metcalfe nodded. "There's a place for me to hide there?"

"Plenty of places. For a couple of days at least."

"I won't need that long. I just need a place to work from, to figure out my next step."

There was a knock at the door, and Ilya entered, shoving a large face mask, hood, and black robe at Metcalfe. "This is one of Baron von Rothbart's masks," he said. "A spare. It's the one he never uses."

Metcalfe took it, impressed. "The evil genius. The sorcerer who keeps Odette imprisoned as a swan. Good idea. It's the only plausible way for me to be walking around here with my face hidden."

Ilya smiled gratefully. "Anything for a friend of Lana's. Now, Lana—Grigoriev wants to resume the performance immediately."

"Stiva," said Lana, drawing near to him again. She put her arms around him. "I don't need to tell you I'd rather be with you than down there, onstage."

"That's where you belong," Metcalfe said. "Onstage."

"Don't say that!"

"But you do," Metcalfe said. "I mean no disparagement. It's where you're most alive."

"No," she said. "I'm most alive when I'm with you. But this"—she indicated her costume, then the dressing room they stood in—"all this is part of me, too. We'll see each other again soon, my Stiva. Ilya will take good care of you." She kissed him on the lips, then rushed from the room.

The hall outside the row of dressing rooms was now bustling with various costumed performers rushing toward the stage. Someone, apparently in charge, was clapping her hands and chiding the dancers to move along quickly. Through this chaos Ilya was able to move unnoticed with Metcalfe, who wore the elaborate face mask and black robe. To all observers Metcalfe appeared to be the character named the Baron von Rothbart; the chief risk was that the real von Rothbart might appear, though fortunately he did not.

Then Metcalfe saw a pair of security guards among the flow of performers. They were surveying the passing faces, shouting out questions. Metcalfe passed within a few feet of one of the guards, bracing himself to be stopped and interrogated, but it was almost as if he were invisible. The guards paid him no notice. The mask he wore not only hid his face, but it conveyed a legitimacy to his presence here. He was a performer, therefore not to be stopped.

The risks of exposure seemed to diminish once the two had turned a corner to an unused section of corridor Metcalfe hadn't seen before, which led to a steep back stairway. Ilya gestured with a flick of his hand. They entered the dark staircase and descended quietly.

But another security guard entered the stairway from the level below. He put out his hand to stop them.

Metcalfe's stomach clenched.

"Hey, Volodya!" called Ilya in a jovial voice. "What the hell's going on here?"

The security guard knew Lana's dresser! "We're looking for an intruder wearing a doctor's coat," the guard said.

"Doctor? Haven't seen one, sorry," Ilya replied. "But if my friend here doesn't get to the stage in thirty seconds, I'm out of a job." He continued down the stairs, Metcalfe following close behind.

"Just a minute!" the guard shouted after them.

Ilya turned around. Metcalfe froze.

"You promised you'd get me two tickets for the performance this weekend," the guard said. "Where are they?"

"Give me a little more time," Ilya said. "Come on, Baron, we got to get going." He continued down the steps, Metcalfe immediately behind.

At the bottom of the stairwell, Ilya led the way through another maze of passageways until they reached a steel hatch. He fiddled with a bolt, finally succeeding in yanking it open. "Livestock entrance," he said.

"Livestock?"

"Horses, bears, sometimes even elephants when we do *Aida*. The filthy beasts don't use the stage entrance, believe me. Not the way they drop dung all over the place."

Metcalfe removed his mask. They raced through a long brick tunnel that smelled strongly of animal excrement, the cement floor covered with straw. It ended in a covered loading dock, where several vans were parked, each of them painted with the words STATE ACADEMIC BOLSHOI THEATER. Ilya ran to a wide set of double doors and unlocked them, then pushed them open. Outside, traffic roared by. Then he leaped into the cab of one of the vans. Metcalfe raced to the rear of the van, pulled open the door, and climbed in. The compartment was loaded with giant painted canvas sets, but he was able to squeeze in, then close the door behind him.

The engine turned over feebly, then came to life. Ilya revved it repeatedly, and then the vehicle started to move.

Metcalfe sank to the rusty steel floor, which vibrated as the van accelerated. The smell of partially combusted fuel was overpowering.

He settled back for the long ride to the outskirts of the city. Although it was completely dark, the image of Lana in his mind glowed, luminescent. He thought of the way she had dismissed his warning, the way she had kissed him and then run off. Her bravery, her impetuousness. Her passion.

And how she had refused his offer to get her out of the country. He was disappointed, deeply so, but at the same time he understood. She could not leave her father, could not leave her homeland. Not even for her Stiva. Her ties to her country were stronger; that was the grim truth.

Suddenly the van came to a stop; the engine shut off. It could not have been five minutes since they'd left the Bolshoi. What had happened—had Ilya been pulled over? The engine had not died; it had been shut off. He would not shut off the motor at a traffic light. Metcalfe listened for a signal of some sort, for voices. But there was nothing.

He stood, climbed behind one of the tall canvases to conceal himself in case the van was searched. Standing between two canvas sets, he waited.

Abruptly the door to the van opened and the interior was flooded with a strange yellow light. Metcalfe stood perfectly still, hoping that if the van was being searched, the inspection would be quick, cursory. Any searcher would see stage props from the Bolshoi, be satisfied, then close the van door, and they could safely resume.

Why? he wondered. *Why had they been stopped?*

"He's back there!" a voice called.

Ilya's voice; Metcalfe recognized it.

Several more voices, followed by the hollow footfalls of someone climbing onto the van's steel floor. Metcalfe froze. He heard the voice again, the voice that had to be Ilya's: "Believe me, he's in there."

But it couldn't be Ilya! And if it was, who was he talking to?

The canvas set was yanked away, exposing Metcalfe. Two men shone flashlights at him. Two men in uniforms. Bolshoi uniforms? Were these security guards?

No. He recognized the uniforms, the coiled snake and dagger emblem on the epaulets. But it made no sense!

The two men grabbed him, pulled him out. Metcalfe saw at once that there was no use in struggling: the van was surrounded by uniformed officers. Ilya, smoking, was talking to a few of them, his casual pose indicating that he hadn't been waylaid. He hadn't been pulled over. These were people he knew, or at least people he seemed comfortable around, men he was *cooperating* with.

The van was in a courtyard, an area he recognized only from photographs. A place he thought he would never actually see in person.

Handcuffs were placed on his wrists; he was shoved forward, surrounded by a phalanx of uniformed men.

"Ilya," Metcalfe shouted. "Clear up this misunderstanding!"

But Ilya was already climbing back into the driver's seat of the van. He threw his cigarette onto the concrete surface, then gave the men a friendly wave before he started the engine and drove off.

Metcalfe was pushed, dragged along by the guards, into an arched entrance whose yellow bricks were sickeningly familiar.

He was in the headquarters of the NKVD.

In the Lubyanka.

CHAPTER THIRTY

To call it a nightmare would be inaccurate: nightmares always contain the tiniest kernel of realization that they are but dreams, that one can and will awake and be free of the horror. Metcalfe knew this was no nightmare. It was reality, *his* reality, the most horrific thing about it that there was no way out. In the last year working for Alfred Corcoran's organization, he had been in quite a few frightening situations. He had come close to being discovered, had evaded detection or arrest on numerous occasions. He had been shot, nearly killed. And then he had witnessed murder, the deaths of people he cared about deeply.

But all of it paled to insignificance now.

He was in a cell in the infamous Lubyanka prison; he was in another world, where escape was impossible, where the skills that had gotten him out of so many difficult situations could no longer help him. He had no idea how long he had been in this cell: Was it ten hours? Twenty? There was no way to keep track of time, no rising or setting of the sun, no schedule, no regularity.

He was in a narrow, solitary underground cell, unheated and frigid. He lay on a hard iron bed whose mattress was no more than an inch or two thick and reeked of innumerable prisoners before him. There was a coarse gray woolen blanket no more than four feet long, which just covered his feet and knees and not much more.

Metcalfe was exhausted beyond exhaustion, but he couldn't sleep: there was a bright electric light in the cell that never went out and slatted iron blinds that admitted tiny slits of electric light from somewhere outside. They didn't want him to sleep; exhaustion, physical and mental, was their objective. Every half-minute or so, the metal disk that covered the spy hole on the door slid open and an eye peered in. Whenever he pulled the short blanket over his face, a guard slid open the spy hole and barked at him to uncover his face. Whenever he turned to the wall, a guard would bark at him to turn back.

The cell was so cold he could see his breath. He couldn't stop himself from shivering. He had been forced to undress, his clothes removed and slit open with razor blades, all metal buttons removed, his belt taken away. His body was searched. He was ordered to take a shower but was given no towel with which to dry himself. He had to put his ruined clothes back on his wet body, and he was then marched across an icy courtyard to another part of the building, where he was fingerprinted, his photograph taken, front and profile.

He knew a fair amount about the Lubyanka, but what he knew was nothing more than the dry, dispassionate stuff of briefing books, of intelligence reports, and the occasional whispered rumor. He knew that the oldest building in the Lubyanka complex had once been, before the Revolution, the headquarters of the All-Russian Insurance Company. He knew that the Cheka, the first incarnation of the Soviet secret police, had converted it into offices and interrogation chambers and prison cells.

He knew that it was a death factory, that important prisoners were executed in the cellar of Number 1 Dzerzhinsky Street, the most secretive of the connected Lubyanka buildings. He had been told that when a prisoner was about to be executed, he was led into a chamber in the cellar, where a tarpaulin was spread on the floor and a bullet administered to the back of his head from an eight-shot Tokarev automatic pistol, either just as he entered the room or as he faced the wall. The executioners were paid well, were always male and usually illiterate, and their work was said to take a toll: alcoholism and suicide ran rampant among the men who fired the shots.

Immediately afterward, the body was taken away to be buried in a common grave. A woman came in to mop up. Death was certified by a doctor employed by the NKVD, the death certificate the last piece of paper placed in a victim's file. Unless the victim was famous, his relatives were always told that the executed man had been sentenced to ten years in prison with no right to correspondence, and that would be the last the relatives would ever hear.

All this he knew, but what he *didn't* know was far greater. Had he been betrayed by someone—or had the NKVD simply decided it was time to bring him in? He'd been seen at the dead drop; his hotel room had been searched; his transmitter had been found. There were a dozen reasons to arrest him.

But why had it been *Lana's* friend, her dresser and crew member, Ilya—a man she seemed to trust implicitly, a man who had warned her that agents were searching for her—who had brought him here?

It was possible, certainly, that Ilya was an informer, a low-level collaborator with the NKVD like so many people in Soviet life. The secret police would get a hold on someone—a threat against a family member, the discovery of a petty dishonesty—or simply offer a token regular payment. It didn't take much to co-opt someone. The NKVD was suspicious of Metcalfe, knew that he regularly visited Lana: it was logical for them to hire or subvert Lana's trusted assistant, to order Ilya to bring Metcalfe.

But was it possible . . . was it at all possible that Lana had betrayed him?

She would do anything to protect her father. If pressure had been placed upon her—great, unendurable pressure—was it so far-fetched to imagine that she might have cracked, gone along with the NKVD?

And then he reminded himself: *Why is it so inconceivable that Lana might have deceived you . . . when you yourself have been deceiving her?*

He didn't know what to think. He was so deeply exhausted that he could no longer think clearly.

There was a loud metal clanking, and the lock on his cell was unbolted. Metcalfe sat up and braced himself for the unknown. Three uniformed guards entered, two of them pointing their weapons. "Stand," the lead guard said.

Metcalfe stood, watching the three carefully. Not only was he outnumbered, but even if he managed to wrest the gun away from one of them, even if he put the gun to the head of one of them, seized a hostage, he knew he would never get out of here. He would have to cooperate until an opportunity arose.

"What time is it?" he asked.

"Hands behind your back," the same guard shouted.

He was marched through a dark hall to an iron door with a small grate in the center, which turned out to be a small, primitive elevator. His face was pushed against the elevator wall. The door clanged shut, and the elevator rose.

It opened on a long corridor with a long Oriental runner on a parquet floor and light-green-painted walls. The only light came from white glass globes that hung down from the ceiling.

"Look straight ahead only," the lead guard commanded. "Hands behind your back. Do not look to the side."

Metcalfe walked, a guard on either side of him and one behind. Out of the corner of his eye he saw they were passing a long series of offices, some of them with doors open, men and women working inside. Every twenty or so paces stood another uniformed guard.

He heard the repeated tap of metal against metal, then saw that one of the stationary guards was tapping his key against his belt buckle. A signal of some sort.

Suddenly he was pushed toward the wall and into a niche the size of a telephone booth. Someone of importance was passing by, or at least someone they did not want him to see.

At last they came to a large, dark-stained oak door. The lead guard knocked; after a few seconds it was opened by a small, pale-haired man of ghostly pallor. He was a secretary/receptionist of some kind, an aide-de-camp whose office was the antechamber to his superior's office. His desk bore a typewriter and several telephones. Papers were signed, a copy given to the leader. Metcalfe watched in silence, unwilling to betray any emotion, any anxiety about where he was being taken. The aide-de-camp knocked on an inner door, then lifted a hatch set into it.

"Prisoner 08," he said.

"Come," a voice responded.

The aide opened the door, standing back as Metcalfe was escorted in by the lead guard; the others stayed behind, standing stiffly in a military position.

This was the spacious office of someone of high rank. The floor was covered with a large Oriental carpet; the furniture was dark and massive. Against one wall stood a tall combination safe. A massive desk, topped with green baize cloth, was piled high with folders and a battery of telephones. Behind it stood a slender, delicate-looking man with a high, domed forehead, a balding head, and round frameless spectacles that magnified his eyes grotesquely. He wore a crisply pressed gray uniform. Without moving from behind his desk he extended a spidery hand, making a quick gesture. The guard turned on his heel and departed from the room, leaving Metcalfe standing there alone.

The bespectacled man bent over his desk, sorting through papers for several minutes as if Metcalfe were not there. He pulled out a thick folder, then looked up at Metcalfe, saying nothing.

Metcalfe recognized the time-honored interrogation technique: silence tended to make the inexperienced subject uncomfortable, anxious. But Metcalfe was not inexperienced. He was determined to remain silent as long as his interrogator refused to talk.

After a good five minutes, the bespectacled man smiled and said, in perfect British-accented English, "Would you prefer to speak in English?" He then switched to Russian: "Or in Russian? I understand you speak our language fluently."

Metcalfe blinked. English might give him an advantage, he thought. Perhaps it would deprive the NKVD man of the ease of nuance, a subtlety of expression that only a native speaker possesses. He replied in English, "It's of no consequence to me.

As long as we can speak freely and openly. Do you have that authority, Comrade . . . ? I'm afraid I didn't catch your name."

"I didn't, as you Americans say, throw it. You may call me Rubashov. And 'Mr.,' not 'Comrade'—we are not comrades, after all, Mr. Metcalfe. Sit, please."

Metcalfe sat on one of two large green leather couches positioned close to Rubashov's desk. Rubashov, he saw, did not sit. He remained standing. Behind him hung three framed portraits, of Lenin, of Stalin, and of "Iron Felix" Dzerzhinsky, the infamous founder of the Cheka. Rubashov's head appeared to be flanked by the portraits, as if it were part of the gallery.

"Would you like a glass of tea, Mr. Metcalfe?"

Metcalfe shook his head.

"It really is superb tea. Our chairman has it brought in from Georgia. You should have some, Mr. Metcalfe. You need sustenance."

"Thanks, but no."

"I am told you haven't eaten the food you've been given. I'm sorry to hear that."

"Oh, is that what it was, food?" He recalled the tin plate of watery tripe soup that had been thrust at him, along with a stale hunk of black bread. How long ago had that been? How much time had passed since he'd been thrown into his solitary cell?

"Well, this is not exactly a spa by the Black Sea, although there's no limit to the length of your stay, hmm?" Rubashov strutted out from behind his desk and stood facing Metcalfe, his arms folded across his chest. His tall black leather boots were polished to a mirrorlike finish. "So, you are a most skilled operative. There are not many who can evade our agents the way you did. I am most impressed."

A quick denial was, of course, the response the interrogator wanted. But Metcalfe said nothing.

"I hope you understand the situation you're in."

"Absolutely."

"I'm glad to hear it."

"I understand that I've been kidnapped and imprisoned illegally by agents of the Soviet secret police. I understand that a serious miscalculation has been made that will have ramifications far beyond what you may imagine."

Rubashov shook his head slowly, sadly. "No, Mr. Metcalfe. No miscalculation. All 'ramifications,' as you put it, have been considered. We are a tolerant nation, but we do not tolerate espionage conducted against us."

"Yes," Metcalfe said calmly. " 'Espionage' seems to be the charge you like to throw around whenever someone decides a visitor is inconvenient, isn't that the case? Someone, let's say, in the Commissariat of Foreign Trade doesn't like the terms of a deal that has been struck with my family's firm, and—"

"*No*, sir. Please don't waste my time with your pettifoggery." He pointed a tendril-like index finger at the heaps of folders on his desk. "These are all cases on which I am the lead prosecuting investigator. You see, I have much work and not enough hours in the day to do it. So let us, as they say, get right down to brass tacks, Mr. Metcalfe." He strutted to his desk, retrieved a piece of paper, and handed it to Metcalfe. The investigator reeked of pipe tobacco and sour perspiration. "Your confession, Mr. Metcalfe. Sign it, and we can be done with our work."

Metcalfe looked at the paper and saw that it was blank. He looked up with a sly smile.

"Just sign at the bottom, Mr. Metcalfe. We will fill in the details later."

Metcalfe smiled. "You seem like an intelligent man, Mr. Rubashov. Not a crude man, like whoever made the foolish decision to arrest a prominent American industrialist whose family has friends in the White House. Not a man who wishes to be responsible for a diplomatic incident that is about to spiral out of control."

"Your kind words warm my heart," the investigator said, leaning back against his desk. "But diplomacy is not a concern of mine. It is not my portfolio. My job is simply to prosecute crimes, then to decide the sentences and see that they are carried out. We know far more about you than you might imagine. Our agents have observed your activities since you arrived here in Moscow." Rubashov held up the thick folder. "Many, many details. And they are not the activities of a man whose purpose here is truly business."

Metcalfe cocked his head to one side and arched a brow. "I am a man, Mr. Rubashov. I am not immune to the charms of your Russian girls."

"As I said, Mr. Metcalfe, please do not waste my time. Now, your comings and goings in Moscow intrigue me. You seem to get around rather easily, and rather widely."

"I know the city well."

"You were seen retrieving documents on Pushkin Street. Are you denying you were there?"

"Retrieving documents?"

"We have photographs, Mr. Metcalfe."

Photographs of what? he wondered. Of him taking the packet from behind the radiator? Of him slipping the packet into his coat? Without knowing how much they had seen, he didn't know how much to admit to.

"I'd be curious to see these photographs."

"I'm sure you would."

"I deal in documents all day long. All this paperwork is the bane of my existence."

"I see. And is it customary for you to run when approached by agents of the NKVD?"

"I think it's a good idea for *anyone* to run when they see the NKVD coming, don't you? Isn't that a reputation you're proud of—that you strike fear into the hearts of even the innocent?"

"Yes," the Russian said with a mild chortle. "But even more so, the guilty." The wan smile faded from his face. "You are aware, I'm sure, that it is a criminal violation for a civilian to carry a gun in Moscow."

"I carry a gun for protection," Metcalfe said with a shrug. "There is a criminal element here, as you know. And we prosperous foreign businessmen are easy marks."

"This is not a casual matter, Mr. Metcalfe. For this alone, you face a rather long prison term. And believe me, you do not want to spend time in a Soviet prison." He turned around and stood before the portraits of Stalin, Lenin, and Dzerzhinsky, as if taking inspiration from them. Without turning back, he said, "Mr. Metcalfe, there are people in this organization—men far more highly placed than I—who wish to see you executed. We have evidence, far more evidence than you may realize, of your espionage activities. We have enough evidence to send you to the gulag for the rest of your life."

"I wasn't aware you people needed evidence to send people away."

Rubashov's magnified eyes stared. "Are you afraid to die, Mr. Metcalfe?"

"Yes," Metcalfe replied. "But if I lived in Moscow, I wouldn't be. In any case, if you really have enough of this trumped-up evidence to send me away, then why are you talking to me?"

"Because I wish to give you an opportunity. To make a deal, shall we say."

"A deal."

"Yes, Mr. Metcalfe. If you provide me with the information I seek—confirmation of various details concerning the organization you work for, your objectives, names, and so on—well, you may well find yourself on the next train home."

"I wish I could help you. But there's nothing to tell you. I'm sorry."

Rubashov clasped his hands. "Well," he said. "It is I who am sorry." He stepped to his desk and pressed a button. "Thank you for your time, Mr. Metcalfe. Perhaps you will feel more inclined to speak freely the next time we get together."

The door to the office flew open, and the three guards stormed in as if they had been waiting for their cue.

He was immediately taken to another part of the building, where the corridor was all white and brilliantly lit. A guard pressed a button on the door to a room that was marked INTERROGATION CHAMBER THREE. Armed NKVD soldiers inside opened the door to an all-white room, gleaming tiles on the floors, walls, even ceiling. Metcalfe saw that five guards were waiting for him bearing rubber truncheons. The door was shut.

He said nothing, for he knew what was coming.

The five men converged on him, wielding their truncheons. It felt as if he was being kicked, hard, in his stomach, in his kidneys, only ten times worse; pinpoints of light sparkled before his eyes. He struggled only enough to protect his vital organs from the brutally hard blows. But it was insufficient. He collapsed to the floor, his vision blurred.

The beating continued; fortunately, he passed out, the pain beyond endurance.

Cold water was thrown on him, reviving him, bringing him back to his state of excruciating, ineffable pain. Then the beatings resumed. He spit blood onto the floor. Blood pooled in his eyes, ran down his cheeks. No longer was his vision blurred; now it was oddly segmented, like a motion-picture projector whose film was slipping its sprockets. Flashes of light alternated with a maroon-stained field of vision. He wondered if he was going to die here, in this gleaming white-tiled room, his death certified by some anonymous Soviet staff doctor, his body tossed into a common grave. Even in his delirium—a crazed, segmented hysteria that alleviated the unbearable pain of the truncheon blows— he thought about Lana. He worried about her, wondered if she was safe, whether they had brought her in for questioning as well. Whether she would remain safe, or whether her day would soon come and she would before long be in the white-tiled room, blood streaming from her scalp, her nose, her eyes.

That was what did it for him: that image of Lana having to

endure what he was now going through. He couldn't permit it. *If there's anything in my power,* he commanded himself, *I must use it to protect her, to keep her out of this nightmarish place. If I die here, I'm not protecting her.*

I must live. I must stay alive somehow.

I must talk.

He put up a crumpled hand, a crooked index finger. "Wait," he moaned. "I want—"

The guards stopped, on a signal from the man who seemed to be their leader. They watched him expectantly.

"Take me to Rubashov," he croaked. "I want to talk."

Before they brought him back to Rubashov's office, however, they took special pains to clean him up. It wouldn't do to have him seeping blood all over the chief investigator's Oriental carpet. He was stripped, pushed into a shower, then handed a fresh gray uniform to put on. He was barely able to raise his arms, the knifelike pain in his side was so great.

But Rubashov, it seemed, was in no hurry to see him. Metcalfe recognized this tactic as well. He was kept standing in the hallway outside the investigator's outer office for what seemed an eternity; he longed to sit; he had to force himself to remain standing. Metcalfe knew that the beating in the interrogation chamber was only a prelude to other techniques. Often the prisoner was made to stand against a wall for days on end without sleep. The prisoner soon came to crave death. Only two guards accompanied him this time, an implicit recognition that he was too weakened, too enfeebled, to pose much of a physical threat.

At last he was shown in. The pale, ghostlike assistant was gone, his workday presumably ended, replaced by another young man, who looked even more furtive. Papers were signed, then the inner door was opened, and Metcalfe was escorted in.

———

Whenever the violinist spoke with SS *Gruppenführer* Reinhard Heydrich, he was keenly aware of what an extraordinary privilege it was to have such a mentor. Heydrich was not only a virtuoso violinist, but he was also a brilliant strategist. That he had personally selected Kleist for this mission was a testament to the assassin's talents.

He did not, therefore, like to disappoint Heydrich. He got right to the point, as soon as the scrambled telephone connection had been made and Heydrich had picked up.

"I have as yet been unable to learn what the American is up to," he said. He quickly recounted—because Heydrich had little patience for extraneous details—how the American's associate, the Brit, had refused to talk even under great duress and had to be killed. He related how the diplomat Amos Hilliard, who had led Kleist to a scheduled rendezvous with the American, had unfortunately recognized Kleist—perhaps from one of Corcoran's face books—and had to be eliminated as well. After which, of course, with a body in evidence, Kleist had had to beat a hasty retreat.

"You acted properly," Heydrich reassured him. "The diplomat would have blown your cover. Moreover, each member of the ring you are able to rid us of is a gain for Germany."

The violinist smiled as he glanced around the German embassy communications room. "That raises the question, sir, of whether it is time to eliminate the American as well." Kleist did not dare suggest the great frustration he felt that he had not yet been allowed to finish off the American once and for all.

"Yes," Heydrich replied quickly. "I think it is indeed time to shut down this spy ring. But a report has just come in that the American has been taken into the Lubyanka for questioning. There he is almost certain to die—the Russians may do our work for us."

"Another fisherman has hooked the fish," Kleist said, disappointed. "And if they don't complete the task?"

"Then it will fall to you. And I have no doubt whatsoever that you will succeed."

This time, Rubashov was seated behind his enormous desk, his head all but obscured by the towers of folders. He appeared to be writing something; after a few minutes he finished, set down his pen, and looked up.

"You had something you wished to say, Mr. Metcalfe?"

"Yes," said Metcalfe.

"Good. I knew you were a reasonable man."

"You have forced me into this."

Rubashov stared, his magnified eyes fishlike. "We think of it as persuasion, and indeed, it is only one of many forms of persuasion we employ."

Blood was pooling in his mouth; Metcalfe spit it onto the carpet. Rubashov's eyes flashed with anger.

"A shame. You see, it would have been better—far, far better—for you not to hear what I am about to tell you." *When challenged by authority, you must always lay claim to a greater authority. If you learn nothing else from me, learn this.* Alfred Corcoran.

Rubashov's brows arched above his rimless spectacles.

"Of that I have no doubt, Mr. Metcalfe," the investigator said gently. "You would much prefer not to tell me the truth. But let me assure you that you are doing the right thing. The difficult thing, yes, but you are a brave man."

"You misunderstand me, Rubashov. What I am about to tell you, you will wish you had not heard. You see, it is not easy for a businessman such as myself to operate in Russia. Accommodations must be made—*inducements* at the highest level, shall we say. *Arrangements* made in great secrecy, discretion observed scrupulously." Metcalfe raised his hands with difficulty, turned his palms up to indicate the grandeur of the room. "In this fine office you are blissfully unaware of the workings at the very top—

at the level of the Politburo—which is how it should be. Matters of state at the highest level are always matters of states*men,* Rubashov. And statesmen are but *men,* after all. They are human beings. Human beings who have desires. Human beings who have greed, avarice—wants and needs that, in this workers' paradise, must always be kept private. Wants and needs that must be taken care of by discreet, well-connected individuals. And that is where Metcalfe Industries comes in."

Rubashov stared, unblinking, betraying no reaction.

"And certainly you will understand that any . . . accommodations my company has made on behalf of the very highest officials in your government must remain entirely secret. So I will not tell you about the Western appliances we have secretly shipped to a house in Tbilisi and in Abkhazia—houses that belong to the mother of your boss, Lavrenty Pavlovich." He used the name and patronymic of Beria, implying familiarity; it was a little-known fact that Beria had provided his mother with two houses in Soviet Georgia and had furnished them expensively. But Rubashov would know; Metcalfe had no doubt of that.

Rubashov shook his head slowly, his reaction cryptic. Metcalfe continued, "When it comes to himself, of course, your Lavrenty Pavlovich is considerably more extravagant. You will never hear from me about the magnificent little sixteenth-century Tintoretto that hangs in the dining room of his town house on Kachalova Street." Few, if any, knew where Beria lived, but Metcalfe, who had been briefed, was able to call that detail to mind. "Somehow I doubt you have ever been invited to Lavrenti Pavlovich's house for dinner, and even if you had, I suspect you wouldn't even have appreciated the glory of that little gem. The chairman of the NKVD is a refined man with exquisite tastes; you are but a *muzhik.* And you will never hear from these lips about how Lavrenti Pavlovich raised money for this purchase by selling Russian church artifacts and icons abroad—a transaction handled with complete discretion by Metcalfe Industries."

The investigator was no longer shaking his head. His face had paled visibly. "Mr. Metcalfe," he began, but Metcalfe cut him off.

"Please, ask Beria about this. Pick up the phone right now and call him. Ask him, too, about the icons that were removed from the Church of Christ the Savior in Moscow. Please, go on and call him. *Ask* him."

Metcalfe returned Rubashov's look with a blank-faced stare. Rubashov reached the tendrils of his right hand toward the bank of telephones and picked up the receiver of a white one.

Metcalfe sat back against the couch and smiled. "Tell me something, Mr. Rubashov. Was it your decision to arrest me? Or were you following orders from above?"

Rubashov held the receiver against his face. A faint nervous smile played about his lips, but he did not reply. Neither did he dial the phone.

"It is now clear to me that either you are conspiring against Beria . . . or you are being used as a tool, an instrument, by his enemies within this organization. Which is it?"

"Your insolence will not be tolerated!" Rubashov exploded, the receiver still to his ear. His anger—helpless anger, it seemed to Metcalfe—was a good sign.

Metcalfe continued as if Rubashov had not said anything. "Of course, I'm sure you imagine that you can simply make me disappear and your problems will disappear as well. Well, I'm afraid you underestimate me. I have family attorneys on retainer in New York who keep some particularly damaging documents in a safe, to be released publicly if I do not contact them by a certain prearranged time. The scandal that will result will be enormous. The names of the men in Moscow with whom Metcalfe Industries has dealt secretly over the years, men even more highly placed than Chairman Beria—well, these are not names you will want to have any part of blackening. One name in particular is not a man one wishes to upset." Metcalfe turned his head and looked straight at the portrait of Stalin on the wall. Rubashov turned to see where Metcalfe was looking, and then a look of unmistakable terror crossed his ashen face. It was an expression

Metcalfe had never seen on the face of a ranking NKVD officer.

"That would be tantamount to signing your own death warrant," Metcalfe went on. He shrugged. "Not that it makes a difference one way or another to me. After all, you did force me to talk, isn't that right?"

Rubashov pressed the button on the side of his desk to summon the guards.

Berlin

When Admiral Wilhelm Canaris had finished his briefing, the men around the conference table were thunderstruck. They met in the main conference room of the new Chancellery, which had been built to the Führer's specifications by his favorite architect, Albert Speer. Outside, a blizzard was raging.

In an alcove above them was a marble bust of Bismarck. None of the men in the room, not even Hitler, knew that it was in fact a replica of the original bust that had sat in the old Chancellery for years. When the original was moved to the new headquarters, it had been dropped and it broke at the neck. Speer had secretly commissioned the sculptor to create an identical replacement, which was then steeped in tea to give it the patina of age. The architect considered the accidental destruction of the original to be an ill omen.

The men at the table were all the topmost leaders of the Reich. They were all here to debate the merits of the prospective invasion of the Soviet Union, which was still in discussion. There remained a good deal of opposition to attacking Russia. Men like Field Marshal Friedrich von Paulus and Field Marshal Wilhelm Keitel and General Alfred Jodl had all argued that their forces were overextended in other theaters of war.

The old arguments had been assembled. They must not enter this quagmire. Instead, they should neutralize Russia, keep it at bay, make sure it did not interfere.

But the intelligence out of Moscow had changed all that.

The atmosphere in the room was electric.

Operation *Groza* had changed everything. Stalin was secretly planning to attack them. They must move first.

The first objection came from the head of the Reich Main Security Office, SS Gruppenführer Reinhard Heydrich. "How can we be sure this intelligence is not a plant?" he asked.

Admiral Canaris watched the tall, sinister-looking security chief with the long, bony nose and the reptilian eyes. He knew Heydrich well. They were social friends, of a sort. Heydrich, a talented violinist, often played chamber music at the Canaris home with Frau Canaris, who was also a violinist. Canaris knew that the younger man was a barbarous fanatic, never to be trusted. Raising an objection like this was just the sort of thing Heydrich would do. He wanted to demonstrate before the Führer his superior understanding of the espionage business.

"My people have examined the documents thoroughly, and I would invite you to have your staff do the same," Canaris replied equably. "You will find that they are genuine."

"I simply question why it is the NKVD has not yet discovered this leak," Heydrich persisted.

Field Marshal von Paulus said, "But we have seen no other evidence that Stalin is planning such an attack. We have seen no mobilization, no deployments. Why would the Russians do us the courtesy of attacking?"

"Because Stalin wishes to seize all of Europe," Jodl said. "That has always been his desire. But it will not happen. There can be no more question that we must launch our *Präventiv-Angriff*— our preventive attack—on Russia. With eighty or a hundred divisions, we will defeat Russia in four to six weeks."

CHAPTER THIRTY-ONE

The streets were dark, covered in a newly fallen blanket of snow, the late-night traffic sparse, the sounds muffled. A street clock told Metcalfe it was one o'clock in the morning. Just up ahead lay the Krymskaya Embankment and then the imposing Krymsky bridge, spanning the Moscow River, the longest suspension bridge in all of Europe, built just two years earlier.

As Metcalfe approached, he saw a solitary figure standing in the middle of the bridge, on the pedestrian walkway. A female figure clad in an overcoat and a head scarf. It was Lana; he had no doubt. His heartbeat quickened; he couldn't help it. He quickened his pace as well, through the frigid night air, but he could not run, not yet; his legs and rib cage ached fiercely. The ravages of the beating had only begun to subside. The wind knifed through his wretched ruined clothing, which was little more than rags.

Chief Investigator Rubashov had ordered his immediate release, all paperwork expunged. All of his possessions were returned to him, with the exception of his gun. But Metcalfe felt no sense of victory; he felt nothing but a hollowness, a numbness.

The Moscow River was still and flat, the full moon broken into a million shards along its surface. Moonlight glinted off the bridge's silver chains and iron beams. The occasional car or truck passed over the bridge, making it tremble.

The walk seemed interminable; she seemed so far away, and he could barely get his limbs to move. Lana stood with her back to him, looking over the water, seemingly lost in thought. An hour or so earlier he had placed a call to the Bolshoi from a public telephone kiosk. When she heard his voice, she gasped,

then cried out: "My dearest, my darling, where have you been?"
Terse words were exchanged, cryptic phrases employed, a rendezvous site established without revealing the specifics to anyone
who might be listening in.

He was ashamed that, in a moment of weakness, he had suspected her of complicity in his arrest. It simply could not be. If
she had betrayed him, then how could he believe in the immu-
table physics of the world? How could he believe in the law of
gravity, in the existence of the sun and the moon?

She turned, saw him trudging across the bridge, and suddenly
ran toward him. When she got close enough to see his face, she
screamed, then threw her arms around him.

He groaned, "Hey, careful, there."

"What have they *done* to you?" She loosened her embrace, held
his pain-wracked body gingerly. She kissed him, and for a long
time he was enveloped in her arms; he smelled her perfume, felt
the warmth of her mouth. He felt oddly *safe,* though he knew
there was nothing at all safe about being with his love in Moscow.
"Your face—" Sobs convulsed her body. "Stiva, they beat you!"

"They call it persuasion. They told me the Lubyanka isn't a
spa, and I learned they're right. But it could have been far worse.
And I was lucky—I survived."

"It *was* the Lubyanka! I didn't know where you'd gone—I
asked Ilya; he said he'd been stopped, that the police had
searched the van and found you, arrested you. He said he
couldn't stop them, he didn't know what to do. He seemed so
terrified; I felt so bad for him. Friends of mine went to the police,
demanded to know what had happened to you. But the police
claimed not to know what I was talking about. After three days
a friend went for me to Lefortovo Prison, and she was told they
had no such prisoner. But everyone lies here; I didn't know,
couldn't find out, the truth. You've been missing for five days! I
thought you'd been sent away, maybe executed!"

"Your assistant is a *stukach*," Metcalfe said, using the word for
informer.

Her eyes widened, and for a long moment she did not speak. "I never suspected it, or I would never have let him go near you, Stiva, you must believe me!"

"I do believe you."

"So many questions over the years, so many strange little details, now make sense. Things I ignored. He sometimes sells tickets on the outside, illegally, yet he never seems to be very careful about it. So many insignificant things I overlooked, when I should have taken them as clues!"

"You couldn't have known. How long has he worked for you?"

"Several months he's worked as my dresser and assistant, though we've known each other for years. He's always been very friendly. Four or five months ago he began spending more time around me, helping me out, doing me favors. One day he said he wanted to be reassigned as my assistant during performances, if I was interested, and of course I—"

"Was this after you began your relationship with von Schüssler?"

"Well, yes, just after, but . . . Yes, of course, it could be no coincidence. The authorities wanted to keep a close watch on me, and they planted Ilya on me to do that."

"Von Schüssler's a German diplomat, an important potential intelligence source, and you're a nationally renowned performer. The risks and the potential were too great for the NKVD not to assign someone."

"But Kundrov—"

"He's GRU, military intelligence—a rival agency. Each wanted its own source; each works in a different way, the NKVD more covertly. But Lana—listen to me. I need to ask you again; I want you to think about this seriously, because I know it's a big decision. I want you to come with me."

"No, Stiva. That I cannot do—we've talked about this. I never will. I won't leave my father, I won't leave Russia. I can't! You must understand!"

"Lana, it's never going to be safe for you here."

"This is my home, this terrible place that I love."

"If you don't come with me now, they'll never let you leave."

"No, Stiva. That's not true. In just a few days they're sending my troupe to Berlin on a friendship mission to perform for the top Nazi leadership. We will always be allowed to travel outside the country."

"And you'll still be a prisoner. Berlin is no less a prison than Moscow, Lana."

There was the metallic click, the unmistakable sound of a gun's safety being released. Metcalfe spun toward its source. Even in the darkness, the pale eyes and blond hair were horribly familiar, as was the expression of triumph in the NKVD man's face as he pointed his weapon at Metcalfe. He had approached stealthily, his footfalls covered by the sound of traffic rattling the bridge and by the lovers' absorption in each other.

Metcalfe instinctually reached for his own weapon, then realized he had none. It had been confiscated in the Lubyanka.

"Hands in the air," the NKVD man said. "Both of you."

Metcalfe smiled. "You're off the reservation. Or no one's bothered to inform you. You might want to speak with your superiors before you make an idiot of yourself. Rubashov, for example—"

"Silence!" roared the secret policeman. "Your lies about Beria may have intimidated a weak, cowardly careerist such as Rubashov, but fortunately, I report directly to Beria's office. Hands up, *now!*"

Metcalfe and Lana both complied. "So you *do* intend to make an idiot of yourself," Metcalfe said. "You persist and persist, making a personal mission out of this, refusing to accept the error of your ways. You seem to forget that you are but a lowly street agent. You know nothing about matters far above your level. It's no longer your own career you're destroying with your pigheadedness. Now it's your very life."

The Russian made a spitting sound, indicating derision and hostility. "You lie creatively, and brazenly—but sloppily. I was the one who found your transmitter. Buried in the woods southwest of Moscow, near the American embassy dacha."

Metcalfe's expression displayed only bland, amused skepticism, but his mind reeled. Rubashov had made no mention of a transmitter! If he had known, he would have mentioned it; why had he not?

"Yes," the gray-eyed agent resumed. "A small detail I withheld from my report to Rubashov. A fact held in reserve for later use—I've never trusted that ass-kissing swine. But the transmitter has been examined by our special technical section, and I've seen the results. Constructed by the British secret service for agent field communications. Not the sort of communication needed by any businessman." He shifted his gun a few inches, toward Lana's chest. "But extremely useful for transmitting military intelligence obtained from the daughter of a Red Army general."

"No, it's not true!" sobbed Lana. "It's a lie! I'm not conspiring against the government!"

"Step away from each other! This time, the only way either of you will leave the Lubyanka is in a pine box," the NKVD man said.

"She's mine," came another voice. Metcalfe turned, saw the red-haired GRU man approaching from the other direction.

"Kundrov!" Lana shouted. She actually seemed relieved to see her GRU minder. "You watch me, you *know* me—this monster hurls all kinds of insane accusations!"

"Yes," Kundrov replied calmly, addressing the NKVD agent. "I know the woman. She's been assigned to me. You know the procedures, Ivanov. This arrest is the responsibility of the GRU, as the originating agency."

The NKVD man shifted his pistol back toward Metcalfe, the glacial expression on his cruel face wavering not a bit. "You will take the woman into custody," he replied. "I'll take the American spy."

Kundrov had taken out a pistol as well and was pointing it at Lana and Metcalfe. "It's more efficient for you to take both in at once," he said coldly. "So long as the proper credit is assigned in the reporting documents."

"Agreed," said Ivanov, the NKVD man. "Credit will be divided, the arrest mutually agreed upon. The resources of both state organs will be needed, after all, to investigate the conspiracy. An American spy is the chief responsibility of NKVD, but the leaking of vital Red Army secrets is a matter for Military Intelligence."

"Wait," Kundrov blurted out. "This American is far too cunning, too skilled a liar. The legal process is wasted on him."

The other Russian looked at Kundrov, a smile of understanding appearing on his face. "Wasted, yes."

"Our rules specify the procedures to be followed when a detainee attempts to escape."

"No!" screamed Lana, realizing what Kundrov was saying.

"Yes." The NKVD man smiled. "The American insisted on evading arrest, as he has done repeatedly."

There was a look of absolute resolve on Kundrov's face as he cocked his Tokarev, the look of a man who would do what he had to do and not look back. The star on its Bakelite grip glinted in the moonlight. "Let's finish off this troublemaker now," he said quietly as he pulled the trigger.

Lana screamed just as Metcalfe arced his body to one side, throwing himself toward her, catapulting her to the steel surface of the bridge and out of the line of the GRU man's fire.

Two explosions came from Kundrov's gun, two rounds swiftly fired, but they missed, *both* shots! Lying on top of Lana, shielding her with his body, Metcalfe watched with incomprehension as the NKVD agent suddenly toppled backward against the low steel railing of the bridge, his lifeless body plummeting off the side of the bridge. There was a splash as the body hit the water. Kundrov had shot his NKVD comrade! He had missed them, both shots piercing the other man's chest! How could it be?

Metcalfe stared at Kundrov, realized at that moment from the look in the GRU man's face: *It was no accident!* He had not missed at all. *He had aimed for Ivanov!*

"There was no choice," Kundrov said, reholstering his pistol. "His report would have done you in, Svetlana. You and your father both."

Lana's screams had turned into low, whimpering sobs as she, too, stared at her minder. "I don't *understand!*" she whispered.

"An act of murder can be an act of kindness," he said. "Go . . . now! You must get out of here at once, Svetlana Mikhailovna, before others arrive and the situation gets even more complicated. Quickly. The shots will bring others. Go on home." There was a tenderness in the GRU man's voice, a tenderness and, at the same time, steel.

Metcalfe got to his feet slowly, and Lana did the same. "But Stiva—my Stiva—what will you do with . . . ?"

"He must get out of Russia," said Kundrov. "Too many are after him, and there's no turning back now. Listen to me, now. Go. Run! You cannot stay here!"

Lana looked at Metcalfe in bewilderment.

"Yes," Metcalfe said. "You have to go, *dusya.* Please." He put his arms around her, squeezed her, kissed her firmly on the lips. Then he pulled away. "We will see each other again. Just not here, in Moscow. Run, my darling. Run."

Still stunned, Metcalfe sat in the passenger's seat of the GRU man's M-1 sedan. With his cruel mouth and strong nose, Kundrov seemed the picture of arrogance as he maneuvered the vehicle through the streets of the city. But his voice belied his manner: there was something cultured and even gentle about the man.

"It's possible no one saw Ivanov's body go into the Moscow River," he said, "but I doubt it. We can only hope that whoever witnessed it will do the proper Soviet thing and keep their mouth shut. Fear of the authorities, fear of unintended consequences— they usually convince people to mind their own business."

"Why?" Metcalfe interrupted.

Kundrov knew what he meant. "Why did I do what I did? Perhaps because I care for Miss Baranova more than I should."

"You could have bargained with Ivanov to let her go."

"They never let go. This is why we call them the *shchelkun-chik*—the nutcracker. Once they have you in their grip, they can only squeeze you harder."

"It's no different with you. With your people. That's not a sufficient explanation."

"What is the American expression, 'Don't look a gift horse in the mouth'? This is a gift horse."

"We have another expression, passed down from Virgil, 'Beware Greeks bearing gifts.' "

"But you are not a Trojan, and I am not a Greek. You think I am the enemy because I work for the GRU."

"It's the reality."

"The reality as you see it, perhaps. As an American asset placed in Moscow, you would naturally see things in such black-and-white terms."

"Call me whatever you like. You know better." Metcalfe noticed that they were pulling up near the train station.

"I do know better, and we have no time to argue. You imagine that those of us who work in Soviet intelligence are somehow blind to what goes on around us? That we see less than you outsiders can see? Such arrogance amuses me—you are the blind ones. We who work within the black heart of the system know the truth better than anyone else. We see how things work. You see, I have no illusions. I know that I am but a screw in the great guillotine. My mother used to tell me an old Russian maxim, 'Fate makes demands of flesh and blood. And what does it most often demand? Flesh, and blood.' One must never forget this. Maybe someday I will tell you my story. But for now, there is no time."

Kundrov shut off the engine and turned to look at Metcalfe. His eyes blazed as fiercely as his red hair. "When I return to GRU headquarters, I will compose a report stating that I shot and wounded you while you were escaping. It will be understood that when it comes to foreigners, an outright kill is considered the last resort. Therefore, you are somewhere at large. I can delay submission of my report for several hours, but after that your name will go on a border-guard watch list. For me to do anything more than that is to put myself at great risk."

"What you've already done is considerable," said Metcalfe quietly.

Kundrov glanced at his watch. "You will buy a ticket for the Leningrad train. When you arrive in Leningrad, you will be met by a very ordinary-looking peasant couple who will ask you only if you are Cousin Ruslan. You will greet them formally, shaking their hands, and they will take you to their truck. They will not want to talk to you, and you should honor their reticence."

"Who are they?"

"Part of the underground. Good people who work on a collective farm, who have their own reasons for doing what they do."

"Which is what, exactly?"

"From time to time, and only occasionally, they serve as intermediaries in a chain of smugglers—smugglers not of goods but of human cargo. People who must escape from the Soviet Union quickly and safely. They will drive you to a village very close to the border, where others will take over. Please understand: they are risking their lives to save yours. Treat them well, observe complete discretion, and do what they say. Cause them no trouble."

"You *know* these people?"

"I know *of* them. A long while ago I came across these people, learned about their activities, and I had a choice. Add another few bodies to the pile of millions already executed . . . or overlook them, let them go, let brave people continue to do brave things."

"Fighting the system you are defending," Metcalfe goaded.

"I don't defend the system," Kundrov shot back. "Heroes are in short supply in the Soviet Union, and they are getting fewer by the day. We need more of them, not fewer. Now, you must go, quickly, or you will miss the train. And then there will be no saving you."

PART FOUR

Moscow, August 1991

Ambassador Stephen Metcalfe was dreading this meeting, more than he had ever dreaded any meeting in his life. He touched the pistol concealed in his jacket pocket, the steel cold against his fingers. As he did so, he remembered his old Russian friend's words: *Nobody but you can get close to him. He's better protected than I am. Only you can get to him.*

With his old friend at his side and flanked by a detail of uniformed guards, Metcalfe walked down the still, dark hallway. They were inside the Kremlin, in the epicenter of Soviet power, a place Metcalfe had visited dozens of times. But there were many buildings within the walled fortress called the Kremlin, and Metcalfe had not been in this particular building before. This building, which housed the Presidium of the Supreme Soviet, was located in the northeast corner of the Kremlin complex. It was in this neoclassical columned building that the head of the Soviet secret police, Lavrenti Beria, was arrested in 1953 after attempting a coup d'etat after the death of Stalin.

Fitting, thought Metcalfe grimly.

Here, in this very building, is the office of the man most Moscow insiders consider to be the most powerful in all of the Soviet Union, more powerful even than Gorbachev–or rather, more powerful than Gorbachev used *to be.*

A quiet man of unassuming demeanor named Stepan Menilov. A man Metcalfe had never met but had only heard of. Menilov was the power behind the throne, a career apparatchik who held levers of power most didn't even know existed. He did more than hold the levers of power, however; he was said to play them like a great church organ. Within his shadowy dominion, he wielded his baton of influence, orchestrating the complex interplay of instruments with the adroitness of a virtuoso. He was the Conductor. The *Dirizhor.*

Menilov was the Secretary of the Central Committee of the Communist Party of the Soviet Union and the Deputy Chairman of the all-powerful Defense Council–a body that oversaw the KGB, the Foreign Ministry, the Defense Ministry, and the Interior Ministry. The chairman was Gorbachev—but he was now indisposed, a prisoner in his lavish seaside villa in the Crimea.

Now Stepan Menilov was in charge.

Metcalfe's old friend had briefed him on Stepan Menilov. He was fifty-seven years old, a hard-liner and weapons expert who had been raised by his great-grandmother, and then an uncle, in a tiny village in the Kuznetsk Basin, and had quickly climbed the ladder of Soviet industry, had become the Central Committee Secretary in charge of the military-industrial complex, had been awarded the Lenin Prize for his faithful service to his country.

But what Metcalfe had not been prepared for, when the door to Menilov's office suite swung open and the man himself emerged, was the man's appearance. He was tall, rangy, and extraordinarily handsome—not at all the way one expected a behind-the-scenes operator to look. He moved with an unusual grace and poise, shook Metcalfe's hand firmly. He asked the general to remain in his outer office. He would speak only to the American.

As he took his seat facing the *Dirizhor*'s large, ornately carved mahogany desk, Metcalfe found himself, uncharacteristically, at a loss for words. Prominently placed atop the desk, he noticed, was the black case that held the Soviet nuclear launch codes.

"Well, well, well," said Stepan Menilov. "The legendary Stephen Metcalfe. An emissary from the White House, above reproach, above partisan politics. Carrying a message, I have no doubt, from the Oval Office. A message that can later be disavowed if need be. A conversation that can be denied. It's quite clever, really—this displays a level of subtlety that I had not thought you Americans were capable of." He spread his hands as he leaned back in his high-backed chair. "Nevertheless, I will listen to what you have to say. But let me first warn you: I will do no more than listen."

"That's all I ask. But I'm not here on behalf of the White House. My mission is not official in any sense. I simply want to speak very directly, and in the strictest confidence, to the only man who has the power to stop the madness."

"Madness?" said Menilov curtly. "What you're seeing in Moscow today is an *end* to the madness, finally. A return to stability."

"An end to reform, you mean. An end to the remarkable changes that Gorbachev was bringing about."

"Too much change is dangerous. It brings only chaos."

"Change can indeed be dangerous," Metcalfe said. "But in the case of your great nation, by far the most dangerous thing would be *not* to change. You never want to return to the terrible old days of the dictatorship. I've seen the days of Stalin; I've seen the terror. They must never be allowed to come back."

"Ambassador Metcalfe, you are a great man in your own country. You are a lion of the American Establishment, which is the only reason I've agreed to see you. But you *cannot* presume to tell us how to conduct our affairs."

"I agree. But I can tell you what the consequences will be of this coup d'etat that you and the others are leading."

Stepan Menilov arched his brows in that peculiar expression of skepticism and defiance so familiar to Metcalfe. "Is that a threat, Mr. Ambassador?"

"Not at all. It's a prediction, a warning. We are talking about going back to an arms race that has already broken your country. The deaths of hundreds of thousands of your countrymen in proxy civil wars around the globe. Perhaps even nuclear disaster. I can guarantee you that Washington will do everything in its power to shut you down."

"Really," said the Conductor coldly.

"Really. You will be isolated. Trade, which you so desperately need, will plummet. Grain sales will end. Your people will starve, and the unrest that will result will plunge Russia into a turmoil you cannot imagine. I have just spoken with the national security adviser to the President of the United States, so although I'm not here on any official mission, I do speak with authority, let me assure you of that."

The *Dirizhor* sat forward and placed his hands atop his desk. "If America thinks it can exploit a moment of disarray in the Soviet leadership to *threaten* us, you are making a grave error. The very instant you make any move against us, anywhere in the world, we will not *hesitate* to use everything at our disposal—every weapon in our arsenal."

"You misunderstand me," Metcalfe interrupted.

"*No,* sir, you misunderstand *me.* Do not misinterpret the turmoil in Moscow for weakness." He gestured toward the nuclear suitcase. "We are *not* weak, and we will stop at *nothing* to defend our interests!"

"I don't doubt that, and we have no interest in testing your resolve. What I'm suggesting is that it's not too late to back away from the precipice, and only you can do it. I'm proposing that you call the other members of your

Emergency Committee and tell them that you are withdrawing your support for their junta. Without you, their plans will shrivel up."

"And *then* what, Ambassador Metcalfe? Go back to the chaos?"

"You can never go back. Everything has changed now. But you can help lead true, peaceful change. Listen to me, damn it: you cannot sit on a throne of bayonets."

The man known as the Conductor only laughed. "You say you know my country. But what you *don't* seem to know is that in Russia, the most dangerous thing is chaos. Disorder is the greatest threat to our welfare."

"It will take enormous courage for you to back down," Metcalfe persisted. "But if you do, you can count on our support. You will be protected—I promise you that. You have my word."

"Your word!" scoffed Menilov. "Why should I believe you? We mean nothing to each other—we are as two submarines passing in the ocean."

"So it would appear. And yet neither of us is in the business of trusting appearances. Let me tell you a story."

"I think you have been doing nothing *but* telling me stories since you got here. And I've heard them all, Mr. Ambassador. I've heard them all."

"With all respect," said Metcalfe, "you haven't heard this one."

CHAPTER THIRTY-TWO

Bern, Switzerland, November 1940

The Swiss capital, far quieter and less cosmopolitan than its better known sisters, Zurich and Geneva, was built on a steep promontory of rock, a natural geological fortress, surrounded on three sides by a moat that was the River Aare. The oldest section of the city, the Altstadt, was a maze of cobblestone streets and narrow arcades. Just off the Casinoplatz, in the Altstadt, was Herrengasse. Number 23 was the last in a row of fourteenth-century houses, an old burgher's mansion whose backyard descended gradually to the banks of the Aare in terraced vineyards. High above one could see the Bernese Oberland mountains.

This was where Alfred Corcoran had taken up residence. It was his new base of operations, now that wartime espionage was shifting into a new level of activity.

Metcalfe's journey across the Finnish border had been harrowing. He had been met at the train station in Leningrad by an elderly couple, as Kundrov had promised, who had dropped him off in the woods outside the city. There, twenty minutes later, a truck had pulled up, the driver demanding a stiff price before he would even shut off his engine. The truck was laden with a dozen hot-water tanks destined for Helsinki: commerce continued even in wartime. One of the tanks had been cleverly modified, with holes bored at the top and bottom for air, a removable panel for air intake, the top cut off with a hacksaw. It had reminded Metcalfe far too much of a coffin. Still, entrusting his fate to a man he had never seen before in his life and never would again, Metcalfe had gotten into the hollow steel tank, and it was welded shut.

The inspection at the Soviet-Finnish border had been cursory. A short while later, the truck came to a stop, and then the driver

had demanded an additional hundred rubles to let Metcalfe
out—"for my trouble," he insisted.

Metcalfe paid.

Very few flights were departing from Malmi Airport, in Helsinki, to Bern, Switzerland, but a rich businessman with good
connections, who was willing to pay the price, could always strike
a deal.

Now, on Herrengasse in Bern's Altstadt, Metcalfe, following
Corky's instructions, approached the back entrance to the town
house, which was hidden among grape arbors. Visitors, he saw,
could enter and depart unseen.

He rang the bell and waited with apprehension. It had been
only a few weeks since he had last seen Corky, in Paris, but it
felt like years. He had gone to Moscow as Daniel Eigen, really—
the cover that had become his true identity: the trivial playboy,
cavalier in his personal dealings, carefree in the midst of the war's
travails. But Daniel Eigen was no more. Not just because the
cover was blown. But because the persona no longer fit. The
murder of a close friend, the betrayal of a lover—these things
could not help but change a man.

His attitude toward his old mentor had changed, too. He had
followed orders, had drawn Lana into Corky's scheme, had misled her. He had done what he'd been told to do. But he could
no longer follow Corcoran's orders unthinkingly, blindly.

The door opened; a housekeeper let him in. She was a ma-
tronly woman with her hair in a tight bun, Swiss by the look of
her. She asked his name, nodded when he gave it, then showed
him into an airy, spacious sitting room with tall windows and
two large fireplaces. In one of them a wood fire was burning;
before it sat Corky, in a wing chair. He turned as Metcalfe entered.

Corcoran looked even paler, even more wizened, than he had
just weeks before. Had the stress of the war, of Operation
WOLFSFALLE, aged him so much? The pressures of losing his
field agents, his crown jewels, as he called them? The rumors

about his health seemed to have some basis in truth: Corky did look ill, markedly worse in a matter of weeks.

"Stephen Abernathy Metcalfe," Corky announced, his voice high, crackly yet firm. "You never cease to amaze me." There was a ghost of a smile on the old man's face as he rose to his feet. A cigarette burned on an ashtray next to him, the plume of smoke curling in the air.

"Should I take that as praise?" replied Metcalfe, approaching and shaking Corcoran's hand. "Or reproach." The smell of Pep-O-Mint Life Savers arose from Corky's tweedy suit as strongly as the odor of cigarette smoke.

Corky paused contemplatively. "Both, I think. I wasn't sure you would make it here."

"It wasn't easy arranging a flight out of Helsinki, I've got to say." He seated himself in a brocade-covered chair on the other side of the fire.

"Oh, that was the least of my concerns. I'm speaking of Moscow. Far too many things went awry." Corky had turned toward the fire again and was poking at it with an andiron. There was something about the fire, something primitive, elemental, that set Metcalfe at ease. The aging spymaster was a staunch believer in theatrics, in stage setting; Metcalfe had no doubt that Corky had chosen this house, with its fireplaces, its churchlike medieval architecture and comfortable furnishings, its location on a cobblestoned street in the Altstadt, for its utility in making visitors feel comfortable, inclined to confess all sins to the father-confessor.

"And even more things went exactly as you planned," Metcalfe said, feeling his anger rise. "Not that you ever bothered to tell me what the plan was."

"Stephen—" Corcoran began, warningly.

"Was it really necessary to lie to me about why you wanted me to go to Moscow in the first place? And then to lie about the documents you wanted Lana to pass to von Schüssler? Or maybe it's just that lying is second nature to you. You can't help it."

"I know it must have been hard for you," Corcoran said, very quietly, staring into the fire. "What there was between you two—it was rekindled, wasn't it? The thing that made it so difficult for you was the very thing that ensured she'd do what you asked of her. You want to know why I lied to you? That's why, Stephen. That's precisely why."

"You're not making sense."

Corcoran sighed. "If you had known you'd be using her in this way, you'd never have been able to win her back. Only authenticity could fan the flame of love. I lied to you, Stephen, so you wouldn't have to lie to her. At least, not at first."

Metcalfe was silent for a minute, his mind reeling. He didn't know what to say. He had to let go of his anger, which was preventing him from thinking clearly.

"Stephen, you don't know the half of what's going on. Things are far more dangerous than you realize."

"I find that hard to believe, Corky. I was there. I was in the goddamned *Lubyanka,* for Christ's sake!"

"I know."

"You *know?* How the hell—? Don't tell me you have a source in the *NKVD!*"

Corky handed Metcalfe a sheaf of papers. Metcalfe examined what appeared to be an intelligence intercept. He read it through quickly, confused. It was a detailed report of Metcalfe's interrogations within the Lubyanka, including a partial transcript of his exchanges with his NKVD investigator.

"What—what the hell is this, Corky? You have a source in the Lubyanka?"

"I wish we did. No, alas, we have a source at one remove."

"What does that mean, 'at one remove'?"

"I'm speaking somewhat facetiously. We have been successful of late in intercepting *Abwehr* agent transmissions. What you have in your hands is a transcript of one of those intercepts."

"Meaning that the *Abwehr* has an asset within the Lubyanka?"

Corky nodded. "Apparently a very good one, too."

"*Jesus!*" Metcalfe spun away from the fire and stared at Corky. "So does that mean they know about our connection to Lana?"

"Evidently not. Nothing more than your casual acquaintance with her. Not your tradecraft involvement with the girl. *That* would have come up, most certainly. Serious doubts have been raised about the WOLFSFALLE documents, but not for that reason."

"What do you mean, 'serious doubts have been raised'?"

"The operation hangs in the balance, Stephen." Corcoran took a long drag from his cigarette and looked into the fire. "Hitler's generals are deeply divided about the wisdom of invading Russia. There are those who have always wanted to do so, though they're a fanatical minority. A large segment has been won over by the WOLFSFALLE documents. They are pushing for an invasion as early as May of next year—before the Red Army can launch any preemptive strike. But there are others within the Nazi High command who see any invasion of Russia as sheer madness— utter folly. These are the levelheaded generals, the ones who seek to restrain Hitler's insanity. They remind their colleagues about Napoleon's ill-fated attempt to invade Russia in 1812."

"But if Stalin is planning to attack them first, as our documents tell them, how can they justify doing nothing?"

"They justify inaction by casting doubt on the intelligence itself. It's a natural response."

"Casting doubt? Have the documents been exposed as fakes?"

Corcoran shook his head slowly. "I have no indication of that. The documents are really first-rate counterfeits, I must say. No one within the Nazi leadership, to our knowledge anyway, has any reason to suspect that the papers were created by the Americans. But they say it's not impossible that they have been cooked up in Moscow, by the Russians."

"That makes no sense! To what end? To get the Nazis to invade them?"

"Don't forget, there are elements within the Soviet leadership whose hatred for Stalin runs so deep that they pray for a Nazi invasion—they see Hitler as their salvation. Those elements are particularly strong among the Red Army."

"They'd wreck their own country to eliminate Stalin? Insanity!"

"The point, Stephen, is that there are serious reasons to doubt the bona fides of the WOLFSFALLE documents. Especially if one *wants* to doubt them, if one sees any potential invasion of Russia as a quagmire, which it certainly would be. So questions are raised. Certain German military leaders argue that if the NKVD is so good, why have they not caught this woman, this general's daughter who is passing top-secret papers to von Schüssler?"

"But as long as the documents seem authentic—"

"Doubts continue to be raised," Corky replied, his voice steely. "And these doubts, combined with the quite reasonable, logistical arguments against a blitzkrieg strike at Russia, are beginning to gain the upper hand. Time is against us. Unless something more is done—something that confirms the authenticity of the documents—our plan is doomed."

"But what more is *possible?*"

"The source must be unimpeachable," Corky said after a pause.

"The source . . . ? The source is a daughter of a Red Army general—a general whom the Nazis know to be a secret conspirator against Stalin!"

"A secret conspirator against Stalin," Corky echoed with a sarcastic twist, "who just happened not to be caught and tried?"

"It's the hold that von Schüssler has over Lana! He has the evidence."

"The spy business, my son, is a wilderness of mirrors. Learn it now, before it's too late. Mirrors reflecting other mirrors."

"What the hell are you talking about?"

"In April of 1937, Joseph Stalin received a dossier from Prague containing evidence that his chief of staff, Marshal Tukhachevsky, as well as his other top generals, had been plotting with the German High Command to carry out a coup d'etat against Stalin."

"Obviously. That was the basis for the treason trials, the massive purges that followed."

"Yes. Thirty-five thousand military officials shot. The entire leadership of the Red Army, on the eve of war. Rather convenient for the Nazis, no?"

"*Convenient . . . ?*"

"Surely you don't imagine that we're the only ones capable of forging documents, Stephen. Hitler's intelligence chief, Reinhard Heydrich, is a formidable opponent. Truly a brilliant man. He knew how paranoid Stalin is, how willingly he'd believe that his own people were plotting against him."

"You're saying the evidence against Tukhachevsky was *forged?*"

"Heydrich enlisted two of his deputies, Alfred Naujocks and Dr. Hermann Behrends, in an ingenious deception operation. He had his SD documents experts forge thirty-two documents—correspondence between Tukhachevsky and other Red Army leaders with the top mucketymucks in the *Wehrmacht*. Seeking their help in ousting Stalin."

"Jesus *Christ!*" Metcalfe gasped. "Forged?"

"Heydrich had the documents planted well. Dr. Behrends carried the documents to Prague and sold them—*sold* them, mind you, for millions of dollars—to Soviet agents there."

"Tukhachevsky was framed? Is that what you're saying?"

"The Revolution, like Saturn, devours each of its children in turn. My point is that Heydrich knows the truth, because he engineered the lie that manipulated Stalin into decapitating his own military. He knows that Tukhachevsky wasn't guilty, and so he knows that General Mikhail Baranov is no conspirator, either."

So the grip that von Schüssler had on Lana was a fraud! Metcalfe could not wait to tell Lana the truth. But his elation dissipated quickly as soon as he realized the implications of this revelation. "So the bona fides of Lana's father remain in doubt," he said.

"Everything remains in doubt." Corky exhaled twin plumes of white smoke. "Including the fate of *Die Wolfsfalle*. Unless we're willing to burn our own agent. A sacrifice that will save the operation—and, dare I say it, save the world at the same time."

Blood drained from Metcalfe's face. "I don't understand."

"But I think you do understand," Corky said, his voice quiet, barely audible. He continued poking at the fire, unwilling to meet Metcalfe's eyes.

"Spell it out for me," Metcalfe said fiercely. "I'm slow."

"You're anything but slow, Stephen, but you seem to want me to speak the words aloud. If that's what it takes, I'm willing to do so. Svetlana Baranova must be caught by the NKVD. She must be arrested. It's the only thing that will convince the Nazis that the documents she's been passing on are genuine."

Metcalfe leaped up, stood directly in front of Corky. Pointing an index finger at his mentor's face, he rasped, "Any means to an end, eh, Corky? Is that it? If a human being gets in the way, becomes a hindrance, you won't hesitate to hurl her to the wolves? Even a woman who acted so bravely on our behalf, put her own life in jeopardy—"

"Spare me your school-rector sanctimony. I'm talking about the survival of Europe, the United States—the survival of democracy upon this planet. I don't need any lectures from you about operational ethics." Corcoran's heavy-lidded eyes were dead calm.

"*Operational ethics?* Is *that* what you call it?" Disgusted and speechless, Metcalfe returned to the chair and sank down. He resumed staring at the fire. "To have her arrested is madness!"

"Yes, well, as Lord Lyttelton said, 'Love can hope where reason would despair,' hmm?" The amber firelight seemed to pencil in the creases in the old man's face.

"What do you know about love?"

"I'm a spy, Stephen. What I know about is despair."

"How about reason?"

"That, too. Reasons to despair, mainly. Believe me, I understand the woman is a dilly. But you know what? World peace— well, *that's* a dilly, too. Saving the planet from being devoured by the fascist armamentarium? A real beaut. Preventing the Third Reich from engulfing civilization? Now that's a cool drink of water."

"Stop it," Metcalfe said stonily.

"You took the words out of my mouth." Corcoran's eyes were unblinking.

"You never change, do you, Corky?"

Corcoran inclined his head a few degrees. "I sense that you've changed, though."

Metcalfe shrugged. "Have I? Maybe it's the world that's changed."

"Stephen, Stephen. Why do you still not understand? The world hasn't changed. The world hasn't changed at all. And it won't change—not until we change it."

Metcalfe put his hands over his face. The wheels in his head began to turn rapidly. There had to be a way! After a moment, he looked up from the fire, resignation seemingly in his face. "What do you intend?" he asked tonelessly.

"Tomorrow afternoon, the Bolshoi Theater's leading ballet troupe is arriving in Berlin—a friendship delegation sent by Moscow. They'll be performing at the Staatsoper. Probably take their tired old production of *Swan Lake* out of mothballs again for those undiscriminating Germans."

"Lana will be there."

"And her Nazi lover, von Schüssler, as well. A little home leave, visiting the old homestead, I'm sure. A well-placed tip to the NKVD is all it should take. The NKVD will arrest her, and the Germans will witness it. And all will be right with the world. I'm terribly sorry, Stephen."

"And she'll tell the NKVD the truth."

"Will she?" Corky said without interest. "At that point, it really makes no difference. She can protest all she wants, but once the Nazi High Command hears that she's been arrested, the WOLFS-FALLE plan will be salvaged."

"You wish it were that simple," Metcalfe said, carefully controlling his voice. "No. I have a better idea. You get me into Berlin and I'll—"

"You'll restring the marionette."

"Something like that."

Corcoran peered at Metcalfe for several seconds. "You want to say good-bye to her, is that it?"

"Allow me that," Metcalfe conceded. "And I promise I'll do my best."

Corcoran shook his head slowly. "Forget about it. You're going back to Bar Harbor. You're going to spend afternoons sailing to the Cranberry Islands with a Tom Collins in one hand and a lovely blond girl recently graduated from Westover in the other. And you're going to put all this behind you."

"God*dammit,* Corky—"

"Don't be like that. You've already earned our everlasting gratitude." Corcoran displayed a quick, chilly smile, like a magician flashing a face card from a trick deck. "But let's be practical. All the covers you had are blown. Putting you back in the field is a risk I won't take."

"But I will," Metcalfe replied.

"You don't understand, do you? The risks aren't to you alone. They're to all of us—the remnants of the Registry—to the very operation itself."

"I think I'm in a better position to decide."

"Stephen, please. The failure is mine. I taught you many things—"

"Everything I know. I'd be the first to say it."

"But I never taught you something truly crucial: humility. I thought life would teach it to you, but apparently I was wrong. No, Stephen, you don't get to decide. The stakes are far greater than even you could grasp. Your usefulness has come to an end. Go back home. A great playground awaits. Put the horrors behind you. And leave the rest to your elders."

Metcalfe was silent for a long while. "Fine," he said at last.

"Ship me back home. But let me tell you what you can expect to happen when you do. I don't know what your sources are telling you, but I know the woman, and I've spent a great deal of time with her recently, and I happen to know that she has a soft spot for von Schüssler."

Corky was taken aback. "You never gave me to believe anything of the sort!"

"Maybe you think you understand a woman's heart better than I do. All I know is what I can sense. I think she feels a little sorry for the German—she may even have feelings that run deeper than that."

"Meaning *what*, exactly?"

"Meaning that there's a real danger that Lana may compromise the mission—tip off von Schüssler that he's been set up. That's all it would take, and all our efforts will be for naught."

"That can*not* be allowed to happen," Corcoran snapped.

"Indeed. And I promise I'll do everything I can to keep it on the rails. I know how to control her." He looked at Corcoran with a fierce determination. It was crucial that Corky believe what he was saying now. Far too much hung on it.

Corcoran's stare was like an X ray; he seemed to be trying to penetrate into Metcalfe's soul. After a full minute, he said, "Chip Nolan is staying at the Bellevue Palace. He can set you up with all the papers you need."

Alfred Corcoran sat staring into the fire and smoking. He had been surprised, and truth to tell not a little annoyed, to discover that Stephen Metcalfe was still alive. Amos Hilliard had been killed before he had been able to eliminate the security risk that was Metcalfe.

But Corcoran prided himself on being an infinitely pragmatic man. He'd always believed that successful operations required constant improvisation. So be it. Metcalfe's assessment of the

Russian ballerina was probably correct. Let him go to Berlin and make sure that Operation WOLFSFALLE stayed on track. Perhaps it was better that things worked out this way.

His Swiss housekeeper entered the room with a silver tray and poured him a cup of steaming hot tea.

"Thank you, Frau Schibli," he said. He was so cautious about his arrangements here in Bern that he'd even asked Chip Nolan to run a background check on this poor hausfrau. One couldn't be too careful.

He reached over to the telephone, dialed the Bellevue Palace, and asked for Chip Nolan's room.

The Bellevue Palace was set high above the Aare River on Kochergasse, its views sweeping, magnificent. Nolan's suite was no less spacious or magnificent, a fact Metcalfe didn't hesitate to point out to the FBI man. "J. Edgar Hoover must give you guys a pretty healthy per diem," Metcalfe needled the small, rumpled man.

Chip regarded him warily, his hazel eyes seeming to cloud over. "Mr. Hoover recognizes the importance of expanding the Bureau's worldwide intelligence work . . . James. That's your name, right? James?"

For a moment, Metcalfe was confused, then he remembered that the FBI man was not fully in the loop, that Corky's sacred compartmentation dictated that he not learn the true identities of Corky's agents.

"Close enough," Metcalfe said.

"Like a drink?" Nolan said, moving to the bar. "Whiskey? Gin? Or maybe you'd prefer *vodka,* after your visit to Mother Russia, huh?"

Metcalfe glanced over, saw the leering smile on the FBI man's face. "Nothing for me, thanks."

Nolan poured himself a Scotch on the rocks. "You been over there before, right?"

"Russia, you mean?" Metcalfe shrugged. "A couple of times."

"That's right; it's coming back to me now. You speak *Rooskie,* don't you?"

"A little."

"Like it?"

"Like what? Russia?"

"The socialist utopia. What's that some guy said, 'I've been over to the future, and it works'?"

"If that's the future," Metcalfe said, "we're all in trouble."

Nolan chuckled, seemingly relieved. "You can say that again. But the way Corky talks about the Russians sometimes, you'd think he's maybe getting a little soft on 'em."

"Nah, I just think right now he fears the Nazis more."

"Yeah, well, that supposed fear has turned far too many patriotic Americans into Reds."

"No one who's seen Stalin's Russia firsthand—I mean, really *seen* it, seen what that system does to human beings—is going to end up a Communist."

"Bravo," Nolan said softly, tipping his glass toward Metcalfe. "Tell *that* to your Social Register friends."

"Like who?"

"Corky's boys. I've met a number of them by now, and all they seem to care about is Hitler this and Hitler that, the Nazis, fascism . . . It's as if they haven't given a thought to what happens if Uncle Joe gets his way. If the Kremlin takes over, there sure as hell won't be any Social Register, believe me. Those dandies'll be planting radishes in Novosibirsk." He set down his glass. "All right, you've got to get over to Berlin, I understand, but your old Paris cover's been blown, right?"

"I assume so. In any case, I'm not going to take a chance."

"Berlin, huh? You're playing with the big boys now."

"What makes you say that?"

"You think the NKVD's tough, wait'll you get a load of the Gestapo. They don't fuck around."

"I got a load of them in Paris."

"Paris was kindergarten, James. Paris is nothing. In Berlin, the Gestapo's in charge. Lemme tell you, you're going to have to watch your ass over there. You're not going to be running around and bedding dames."

Metcalfe shrugged. "My assignment is pretty straightforward."

"Which is?"

"My assignment?"

"Can't help you unless you give me details."

"Remember Corky's sacred principle."

"Compartmentation can get you killed, James. Look at how many of Corky's boys have already bit the dust in the last month. All because he kept them isolated, unconnected. I'm in and out of Berlin all the time—I can help you there."

Metcalfe shook his head. "I appreciate the offer, but I just need cover papers."

"Suit yourself." Nolan unlocked an armoire and drew out a leather portfolio. "I've always said you wanna hide in plain sight. Okay, so you're an American banker based in Basel. William Quilligan." He handed Metcalfe a dog-eared American passport. Metcalfe opened it, found his own photograph inside and several pages of stamps indicating a couple of years of transatlantic journeys, mostly between New York and Switzerland. "You're with the Bank for International Settlements, sort of an international consortium that does a lot of business with the Germans. The Reichsbank's your bank's largest client. There's a fair amount of banking that you guys do on the Q.T. with Germany, gold shipments and the like."

"You're saying the bank launders money for Nazi Germany."

Nolan gave Metcalfe a sharp look. "All its operations are legal, conducted under Swiss laws of neutrality. Hey, the bank's president is a Harvard man, just like you."

"Yale, actually."

"Yale, Harvard, whatever. Anyway, the guy goes to Berlin pretty often, meets with the Reichsbank's president, Walther Funk, but he can't make it this time, so you're basically serving as a glorified courier. Hand-delivering some financial instruments that need to be signed and handed back to you."

"Whatever gets me to Berlin."

"Yeah, well, I suggest you do whatever you have to do and don't fuck around. You're not in some Errol Flynn flick anymore."

An hour and a half later, Metcalfe was on a train from Bern to Basel, en route to Nazi Germany.

CHAPTER THIRTY-THREE

The streets of Berlin echoed with the sound of soldiers marching in formation, their hobnailed boots clacking loudly; there were black-uniformed SS officers all over as well, some brown-clad storm troopers, a sprinkling of Hitler Youth in their dark blue uniforms and high boots. When Metcalfe had last passed through Berlin a decade or so ago, it was a high-spirited city, ringing with laughter. Now the Berliners were stolid and expressionless, well dressed in their ulster overcoats, yet colorless. The women, once so pretty, had become drab as well in their cotton stockings and low-heeled shoes, devoid of makeup, which was discouraged by the Nazis.

His overall impression was one of darkness. It wasn't just the normal dreary Berlin weather, the shortness of the days at this time of winter. No, it was the somber mood combined with the *Verdunklung*, the blackout. He had arrived at the dark railroad station two hours late and had taken an ancient, rattling cab, operated by an equally ancient cabdriver, to the Hotel Adlon on Unter den Linden. There were no street lamps, the only illumination coming from the slitted crosses of the traffic lights where Unter den Linden met Wilhelmstrasse and from the occasional flickering of flashlights carried by pedestrians, who pointed them downward, flashed them off and on like fireflies. The interiors of the trams and buses that passed by were cast in a ghostly blue light, making their passengers look like apparitions. The few cars that drove by had their headlights hooded. Even the Adlon, which used to blaze brightly and welcomingly, had dark curtains drawn across its entrance, concealing the brightly lit lobby within.

The city had had a facelift since the Nazis had taken over, and it was hardly an improvement. Hermann Göring's Air Ministry building on Wilhelmstrasse, Joseph Goebbels's Ministry of Prop-aganda—Nazi architecture was grim, monumental, and intimi-dating. A number of huge concrete *Flakturmen,* or flak towers, had been built around the city. Berlin was a city under siege, at war with the rest of the world, and its citizens did not seem to share the martial enthusiasm of their leaders.

Metcalfe was surprised when the hotel's desk clerk handed him a block of food ration coupons, allowing him so many grams of butter or bread or meat. The clerk explained that you couldn't eat in restaurants without them and it made no difference if someone else was taking you to lunch or dinner. You couldn't eat in Berlin without ration coupons.

Metcalfe arranged with the hotel's concierge to get tickets to the special performance of the Bolshoi Ballet this evening at the Staatsoper, just down Unter den Linden. While he was unpacking in his hotel room, the telephone rang. It was a Reichsbank of-ficial, contacting him just as Chip Nolan had said he would.

They met in the hotel lobby. He was an obese middle-aged man with plucked eyebrows and a shiny bald head named Ernst Gerlach. He wore a well-cut gray suit; on his lapel was a large white button on which was emblazoned a red swastika. He was a midlevel officer at the Reichsbank, though he conducted him-self with a certain arrogance that seemed to imply that he con-sidered Metcalfe—William Quilligan—a lackey he had been saddled with receiving and entertaining.

"Have you been to Berlin before, Mr. Quilligan?" Gerlach asked as they sat in overstuffed chairs in the bar.

Metcalfe had to think for a brief second. "No, this is my first time."

"Well, it is not the best time to visit. It is a time of great hardships for the German people, as you have no doubt seen. But with the leadership of our Führer, and the help of important financial institutions like your bank, we will prevail. So, shall we have a drink?"

"Just a cup of coffee for me."

"I do not recommend that, Mr. Quilligan. The coffee these days is *ersatz*. The National Socialist coffee bean, as it is called—well, the slogan used in the advertisements, you know, tells us that it is 'healthy, strength-giving, tasty, indistinguishable from the real thing!' What the advertisements don't tell you is that it is swill not fit to drink. How about a pony of good German brandy instead?"

"That would be fine." Metcalfe slid a large sealed manila envelope across the table toward the banker. He wanted to get the business over with as quickly as possible so that he could head over to the Staatsoper. There were far more important things to do than listen to this corpulent midlevel Nazi hold forth. "All the financial instruments are in here," Metcalfe said, "along with complete instructions. They need to be executed and returned to me at your earliest convenience."

Gerlach looked mildly surprised at Metcalfe's impertinence. Business was to be conducted only after the social niceties were observed. To launch into business dealings this early was somewhat rude. But the German quickly recovered. He shifted smoothly into a florid and somewhat patronizing oration about the difficulties of doing business these days, with the war on. "Only your bank and the Swiss National Bank," he said, "have remained steadfast friends of Germany. And I assure you that we will not forget it when the war is over."

Metcalfe knew what Gerlach was really talking about: every time the Nazis had invaded a country—from Poland and Czechoslovakia to Norway, Denmark, and the Low Countries—they would loot the country's treasury, seize its gold reserves. The only foreign banks that would cooperate in this grand theft were the Bank for International Settlements and the Swiss National Bank. As a result, the Nazis had thousands of tons of stolen gold on deposit in Bern and Basel. The BIS was even paying Germany dividends on the looted gold and was selling some of this seized gold to purchase foreign currency, all to fund the Nazi war machine. The value of the BIS to the Nazis was that the Basel-based institution could never be closed down. The Nazis' plunder was safe in Switzerland. It could not be confiscated.

This was an outrage, and Metcalfe listened with growing furor as the glib, imperious official spoke about rescheduling interest payments on terms more favorable to the Reichsbank, about letters of credit and depository receipts and earmarked gold in London being transferred to Basel, about transactions in Swiss gold marks. But Metcalfe played his part, listening meekly, taking down Herr Gerlach's instructions, promising to communicate them to Basel at once.

"Let me take you to dinner tonight," Gerlach said. "Although I must warn you that today is *Eintopftag*—one-dish day. Unfortunately, this means that all restaurants, even Horcher's, the finest restaurant in all of Berlin, must serve a hideous stew. But if you're willing to put up with this culinary insult . . ."

"It sounds lovely," Metcalfe said, "but I'm sorry to say that I have plans tonight. I'll be attending the ballet."

"Ah, the Bolshoi. Yes, indeed. The Russians send their pretty girls to dance for us, hoping to win us over." He gave a feral smile. "Let the Russians cavort for us. Their time will come. So, that is just as well. Another night will be better. If you are free for lunch or dinner tomorrow, I shall take you to Horcher's or Savarin's, and we can dine on lobster and other such unrationed delicacies, hmm?"

"Wonderful," Metcalfe replied. "I can't wait."

Thirty minutes later, having at last freed himself of the odious Nazi banker, Metcalfe entered the Staatsoper. One of the world's great opera houses, it had been built in the eighteenth century under Frederick the Great in classic Prussian style, though it was meant to resemble a Corinthian temple. It was one of the grandest architectural masterpieces among a parade of wonders including the Pergamonmuseum, the Altes Museum, and the Staatsbibliothek, ending at the Brandenburg Gate.

The interior was high rococo, its entrance glittering, tiled in black-and-white marble. The patrons were no less glittering, and markedly different from the Berliners on the street. Though evening attire was officially discouraged, the operagoers nevertheless were dressed in finery, men in suits or uniforms, women in ball gowns, silk stockings, their faces and their jewelry glinting. French perfume wafted by, Je Reviens and L'Air du Temps. Everything French, which was in such short supply in Paris, was here in abundance: the spoils of war.

Metcalfe needed to contact Lana tonight somehow. He knew nothing of the security arrangements here, how protected the Bolshoi troupe would be. Somehow he would have to get word to her. Kundrov, her minder, was likely to be here: he might be the best intermediary. Perhaps Kundrov would be in the audience: it was likely, in fact. He would have to search the audience, search for Kundrov—unless Kundrov found him first.

"Herr Quilligan!" An imperious voice he recognized at once. He turned and saw Ernst Gerlach, the Reichsbank official, and Metcalfe understood at once. Gerlach must have been assigned to keep tabs on "William Quilligan." The Nazis were every bit as suspicious of foreign visitors as were the Russians. Once "Quilligan" had turned down Gerlach's invitation to dinner, Gerlach had probably chosen—or been ordered—to go to the Staatsoper in order to maintain a watch. It was unsubtle, like all police-state surveillance, and Metcalfe was not going to make it easy for the banker.

Gerlach had moved in so close that Metcalfe could smell the soaplike aroma of the Underberg herbal digestive on the man's breath. "Why, Herr Gerlach! You didn't mention you had tickets to the ballet!"

The imperiousness faded as Gerlach scrambled for a plausible explanation. "Ah, well, the pleasure of watching the Bolshoi is, I'm afraid, a poor consolation for the far greater pleasure of your company," Gerlach said, looking uncomfortable.

"You're too kind, but still, I had no idea—"

"Daniel! Daniel Eigen!" A female voice. Metcalfe felt a sudden jolt. Daniel Eigen—his Paris cover name! Oh, God, it should hardly have been surprising, given the flow of Nazis between Berlin and Paris, that someone who knew him as the Paris-based Argentine playboy would turn out to be here!

Metcalfe did not turn to look, even though the voice was loud, exuberant, not to be ignored. And plainly directed at him.

"As our Führer says, even the most elaborate plans must sometimes be adjusted to the current realities," Gerlach said stiffly, attempting to regain his dignity.

Now Metcalfe needed to break away from the banker as quickly as possible. The woman who knew him as Daniel Eigen was approaching closer, moving through the crowd with astonishing swiftness, and was just a few feet away. She could no longer be ignored; she *would* not be ignored. He saw her in his peripheral vision, recognized her at once. A slightly faded beauty draped in ermine, the sister of a Nazi official's wife. The name came to him: Eva Hauptman. A woman he had befriended and bedded while she was in Paris with her sister and her important brother-in-law. The brother-in-law had been recalled to Berlin, taking with him his coterie, including Eva Hauptman. Metcalfe had assumed he'd never see her again.

Oh, *Christ!* The heavily perfumed woman reached out a bejeweled hand, tapped him on the shoulder. He could not ignore her any longer. He turned and looked at her blankly. She was with a female friend, another German woman who had been with her in Paris as well. The friend was smiling bashfully, eyes gleaming rapaciously, and Metcalfe could only assume that Eva Hauptman had whispered excitedly to her friend all about the Argentine businessman she had befriended in Paris, and why, here he is!

Metcalfe looked puzzled and turned back to Gerlach. "Well, how nice to run into you again," he said. "We must take our seats."

"Daniel Eigen!" the ermine-draped woman scolded, blocking his egress. "How . . . how *dare* you!"

Gerlach stared in perplexity combined with a glint of amusement. "This woman is talking to *you*, Herr . . . Quilligan."

He could not ignore the woman; she was too insistent, too *adamant*. He looked at her, eyes narrowed, expression phlegmatic. "No, I'm afraid you have me confused with someone else."

"What?" the woman spluttered. "I have you *confused?* . . . Perhaps I have you confused with a gentleman, is that it? Herr Eigen, *nobody* treats Eva Hauptman like a common *tramp!*"

"Madam," said Metcalfe firmly, "you are mistaken. Now if you'll please excuse me."

He shook his head, rolled his eyes at the banker, who was staring aghast. "I think it's this common face of mine," Metcalfe said. "I get that alarmingly often. Well, if you'll excuse me, I should use the WC. The first act is quite long."

Metcalfe turned swiftly and pushed through the crowd as if heading urgently toward the men's room.

From behind him he heard the furious woman shout, "And you call yourself a *man!*"

In reality, he had spotted a nearby exit to the street; he had to remove himself from here immediately. Gerlach didn't believe Metcalfe's protestations, and Eva Hauptman surely didn't, either. The problem was Gerlach, of course; he would report his suspicion that William Quilligan was not who he said he was. In one chance encounter, Metcalfe's cover had been blown.

Metcalfe had to get out quickly. Later in the evening he would return, once the performance had started, and search for Kundrov. The door opened outward, a side entrance to the theater that was probably locked from the outside. He pushed it open and stepped outside, into the cold night air, flooded by a sense of relief. A close call had been averted.

He heard the noise a split second before he felt the cold, hard
steel press against his left temple.

"*Stoi!*"

Russian. *Freeze.* He heard, *felt* the magazine slide into place,
ready to fire.

"Don't move," the Russian continued. "Look straight ahead;
do not look to either side."

"What is this?" Metcalfe demanded.

"*Don't* speak, Metcalfe!" the Russian hissed. "Or Eigen. Whatever your name is, *shpion!* Directly in front of you is a car. You
will walk slowly down these steps to the car. Do you understand?"

Metcalfe did not reply. He stared straight ahead. The Russian
knew his name. He was NKVD; that much Metcalfe was convinced of.

"*Answer!*" the Russian rasped. "Do not nod your head."

"Yes, I understand."

"Good. Move slowly. I will keep this pistol against the side of
your head. The slightest pressure on the trigger, and it will fire.
Any sudden moves, and your brains will be on the sidewalk. Do
you understand me?"

"Yes," Metcalfe said. Adrenaline surged through his body; he
stared straight ahead at the black sedan parked at the curb maybe
twenty-five feet away. He calculated his options; there seemed to
be no solution, no exit. The Russian was not making an idle
threat: any small jolt to his trigger finger would cause the gun
to fire.

"Place your hands in front of you. On your stomach. *Clasp*
them together! *Now!*"

Metcalfe did so. He walked slowly down the side steps of the
Staatsoper, looking straight ahead all the while. He could see little
in his peripheral vision beyond a dark shape, a hand gripping a
gun.

Maybe when he reached the car he could try to grab the Russian's hand, wrest the weapon out of his hand. Or maybe when
the Russian got behind the wheel of the car, unless he insisted

that Metcalfe drive, which would present other opportunities. Maybe. He would have to go along and hope there was another opportunity later to escape . . . or to negotiate for his release. What did they want? To question him, *interrogate* him?

Or to kidnap him, take him back to Moscow?

Back to the Lubyanka, this time for good?

He kept walking, feeling the muzzle pressing into his temple painfully hard. He heard the shuffling of the Russian's shoes as the NKVD man kept pace.

There was no way out this time.

A scrape on the pavement.

A shoe. Suddenly another sound: the clattering of a gun against the sidewalk. The pistol was no longer pressed against his temple! He dared to turn his head, and he saw his abductor slumped to the ground, head flung backward, foam gathering at his mouth, his noise. The Russian's eyes had rolled up into his head, showing only the whites; he made a peculiar gargling, choking sound, gagging as the foam spilled forth from his lips.

His assailant was dying before his eyes, but how?

Metcalfe spun backward, trying to understand what had just happened.

What he next saw explained everything.

Chip Nolan.

The FBI man stood there, a syringe in his right hand. He held up the hypodermic needle. "Ye olde Mickey Finn," he announced. "Chloral hydrate. Injected into the neck, it works fast— and it's deadly. This Commie bastard's not waking up. Ever."

"Jesus!" Metcalfe exhaled. "Thank God you were here—my God, what are you doing in Berlin?"

Nolan smiled thinly. "Compartmentation, remember? Didn't I tell you to watch yourself?"

"You warned me about the Gestapo. You didn't say anything about the NKVD."

"I didn't think you needed to be warned about those bastards. Thought you'd seen for yourself what they can do. They're sick sumbitches. I don't mind spilling a little Russian blood on German soil." He kicked at the NKVD man's body. The man was dead, limp, his face gray.

"I owe you one, man," Metcalfe said. "I was done for."

Chip ducked his head modestly. "Just stay out of trouble, James," he said, pocketing the syringe as he ambled off. His voice was barely audible over the loud rumble of army trucks, carrying ordnance and matériel down Unter den Linden toward the Brandenburg Gate.

Metcalfe looked around for a moment to orient himself, still dazed and flooded with relief. He raced back to the side of the Staatsoper building, leaving the Russian's corpse there, determined to place as much distance between it and himself as possible.

A figure was standing on the steps, at the exact place where the Russian had sneaked up behind him and put the gun to his head. Metcalfe unholstered his own weapon.

Then he recognized the man. It was Kundrov, a cryptic smile on his face. As Metcalfe approached, Kundrov said, "Who was that?"

"The guy with the gun? I figured you'd know—he's one of your countrymen."

"No, not the *shchelkunchik*."

"He's one of mine."

"He looks familiar. I've seen the face somewhere. Maybe in one of our face books. Well, if he hadn't gotten there, I would have had to kill my second *shchelkunchik* in a week. Not good for my reputation. The NKVD prefers to reduce its payroll its own way."

"They like to do the executions themselves."

"Correct. You are here to see Lana again. You could not stay away from her. Even if it endangers her."

"It's not that. I need your help."

The Russian lit a cigarette—a German brand, Metcalfe noticed. "You would trust me enough to ask my help?" Kundrov said, exhaling twin ribbons of smoke through flared nostrils.

"You saved my life. And Lana's."

"Miss Baranova is another situation entirely."

"I'm quite aware of that. I wonder if you know you're actually in love with her."

"You know the Russian proverb, I'm sure: 'Love is evil. You can fall in love with the billy goat.'"

"Lana is no billy goat." The Russian was evading; let him evade, Metcalfe thought. Honesty was not always the best policy.

"Most assuredly not. She is a remarkable woman."

"A phrase I've used to describe her more than once."

"I am her minder, Metcalfe. Nothing more. I cannot help it if my proximity to her has made my assignment more difficult, but I have no illusions about her. She has always seen me as her jailer—more cultured, more civilized, perhaps, than the average, but a jailer nonetheless."

"She's not a woman who can be caged."

"Nor owned," Kundrov countered. "The help you're seeking— it must be for Miss Baranova."

"It is."

"I will do anything to help her, I think you know that."

"It's why I'm here."

Kundrov nodded, took another drag from his cigarette. "It is a foul habit, but so much more pleasant when the cigarette is German, not Russian. Even the fascists make better cigarettes than we."

"There are more important things to judge a country by than its cigarettes."

"True. Certainly there are more similarities than differences between Germany and Russia today."

Metcalfe cocked an eyebrow. "I'm surprised to hear you say that."

"I told you in Moscow. I know the system from the inside out. I know its evils far better than you can even guess at. That is why it doesn't surprise me that you want me to help Miss Baranova to defect."

Metcalfe was unable to conceal his astonishment.

"But I don't think she wants to," Kundrov said. "There is too much that binds her to Russia. In some ways, the woman *can* be caged."

"She's talked to you about this?"

"Never. She doesn't need to."

"You understand her."

"I understand the tug in both directions."

"You understand the desire to escape from the Soviet Union?"

"Understand? I feel the desire myself. I would even make it a condition."

"A *condition?* . . . For *what?*"

"For helping you, helping Miss Baranova. It would be my price."

"*You* want to defect? Is *that* what you're saying?"

"I have information, a good deal of information, about GRU, about Soviet intelligence, that could be most useful to the American government. To whoever it is you work for. I can be of enormous use to you."

Metcalfe was staggered. But there was nothing in Kundrov's expression that suggested a gambit, an attempt to test Metcalfe. Kundrov was entirely serious. "Why? Why would you *want* to?"

"You ask me that seriously?" Kundrov threw his cigarette butt onto the ground and took out another cigarette, lighting it with a small brass lighter. His hand was unsteady; the man was nervous. "You, who have seen what our great tyrant has done to one of the greatest countries in the world, would ask me why I want to leave? You, who have witnessed at firsthand the terror, the paranoia, the dishonesty, the cruelty? I turn the question back to you: Why do you not understand the need to escape such a prison?"

"But you're one of the jailers!"

"Sometimes even the jailers are not there voluntarily," Kundrov said softly, almost in a whisper. "When I was in my early twenties, my father was taken away. He was imprisoned. Don't ask me why; you should know by now that there often are no reasons at all. But I went to look for him, I inquired in every office in Moscow until I found my way to the GRU headquarters on Arbatskaya Square. And there I was myself imprisoned, beaten, and tortured." He pointed to a pale white scar that ran along the side of his mouth. The sneering expression that Metcalfe had noticed before in Kundrov's face: it was not truly a sneer, but a deformation of his mouth, a narrow scar. "I was finally released on the condition that I myself go to work for the GRU." He nodded at Metcalfe's incredulous expression. "Yes, quite a few of us were 'recruited' that way."

"And your father?"

"He died in prison, actually," Kundrov said offhandedly. "They say he suffered a heart attack. I never learned the truth."

"My God," Metcalfe whispered. He had long assumed that the privileged servants of the Soviet system were spared its cruelties. But obviously no one went unscathed.

"I don't need to tell you stories about friends and colleagues of mine in the GRU, about what happened to them. A new GRU chairman is named; he brings in his own lackeys, promotes his own people, and they in turn hurl accusations against their enemies, who are then purged. It is an endless cycle of arbitrary cruelty, a sickness. You know of the ancient Gnostic symbol of the *ouroboros,* the serpent-dragon that swallows its own tail— which simultaneously gives life to itself yet devours itself. This is the tyranny of the state. The revolution devours itself. The Russian Revolution gave birth to Lenin, the monster that the world considers a savior, who created the gulag, the prison camps— and he gave birth to another kind of monster, Stalin. And he will in time give birth to some other monster, and the cycle will continue ad infinitum. And the machinery of terror that Stalin uses to maintain his rule—it consumes itself; it devours the Russian people as it gives birth to an endless cycle of terror. The machinery feeds on the people it terrorizes; it cannibalizes its own. You say I'm one of the jailers. I tell you, as I told you in Moscow, that I am but one of the screws in the guillotine."

"But you helped me to escape. You know the underground network of partisans who smuggle people out—you could have defected anytime you wanted to!"

"Oh, you think so? Alas, no. When an ordinary Russian escapes, the rulers shrug their shoulders; they don't care. When one of the jailers escapes, they will stop at nothing to hunt him down. NKVD squads are dispatched to assassinate anyone of their own who dares to defect. Without a patron—without protection from a Western government—I would be dead in a matter of days. As I've just said, I can be of great use to your employers."

Metcalfe was silent for a long moment. This was no ruse; Kundrov was entirely serious. His hatred for Stalin's Russia was genuine; it was something he had obviously thought long and hard about for years. Finally, Metcalfe spoke. "In Moscow, you can be of greater use to your own people."

"Only if I survive," Kundrov replied with a sardonic smile. "But for me, it is only a matter of time before I, too, get the bullet in the back of the head."

"Look how long you've lasted, how you've risen through the system."

"I have the chameleon-like ability to appear quite loyal to the tyrants who employ me. It is a survival mechanism."

"It's an ability that will serve you well."

"It's an ability that destroys the soul, Metcalfe."

"Perhaps, if it serves only the purpose of survival. But if it furthers another goal, maybe not."

"Now it's my turn to ask you what *you're* saying."

"Don't you understand? What happens to Russia if everyone like you leaves? What happens to the *world?* It's men like you who can change the system from within—who can prevent Stalin's Russia from destroying the planet!"

"I've told you, Metcalfe, I am but a screw in the guillotine."

"You may be a minor functionary now, but in five years, ten years, you could be one of the leaders. One of the men who help shape the direction of the state."

"If I survive. If I'm not shot."

"No one knows how to survive in the system better than you. And Joseph Stalin cannot last forever, though it sometimes seems as if he will. In time, he will die—"

"And another Stalin will take his place."

"Another leader will take his place. Whether it's another Stalin or a reformer—who's to say? Maybe someone like you. Maybe you! My point is, if you defect—if you come to America, or to Britain, or wherever in the free world remains free when this goddamned war is over—you'll be just another Russian émigré among hundreds of thousands. But if you remain in Moscow—if you keep your views to yourself, if you work within the system— there's a chance! A chance that you'll make a difference, that you'll change history. A possibility that you'll prevent the machinery of terror from destroying the planet. The world needs men like you in Moscow—good men, honorable men, *sane* men, damn it! Do you remember what you said to me in Moscow? You said that heroes were in short supply—that Russia needed more of them, not fewer."

Kundrov had turned around, facing the Staatsoper building. He stood there in silence for so long that Metcalfe thought he had stopped listening, but at last he turned back, and Metcalfe saw something different in the Russian's face. The proud, almost haughty expression was gone, replaced by an unexpected vulnerability, a haunted look in his eyes. "Have I a choice?" he asked.

Metcalfe nodded. "I wouldn't refuse your request."

"That's not what I mean. I suppose I really *have* no choice. To defect would be, for me, but a foolish fantasy."

Metcalfe understood what the Russian was saying. He had been listening all the while; he had made up his mind.

"Tell me what you want me to do for Miss Baranova," Kundrov said.

CHAPTER THIRTY-FOUR

Ernst Gerlach was a loyal and devoted employee of the Reichs-bank, but he distrusted the jackbooted police officers, the *Schutz-polizei* and the *Kripo* and the Gestapo, who liked to round up men of his sexual persuasion and send them to concentration camps. He'd been spared so far, perhaps because he was a valued, even irreplaceable worker and perhaps because he had highly placed patrons or perhaps for both reasons—or maybe it was just good fortune. In any case, he didn't like to press his luck. He went out of his way to avoid attracting the attention of the jackbooted thugs.

Still, this was trouble—and it was the sort of trouble that could come back to bite him in *der Arsch* if he was not careful. That woman, who seemed to be a perfectly respectable German woman, if a tad overdressed and overly made up, had called Herr Quilligan by another name. She had called him Daniel Eigen. Quilligan had denied it, insisted there was some mistake, but then he had darted off. His behavior was suspicious.

Gerlach realized that he had not yet had a chance to examine the documents Herr Quilligan had presented. What if this was some sort of bank fraud? More to the point—and a truly serious concern—what if this American who called himself William Quilligan was in actuality an American agent who was taking part in an operation against the Reichsbank? The Americans and the British were always trying to seize Germany's foreign assets; what if "Quilligan" was trying to obtain signatures, account num-bers, all the information needed to appropriate Reichsbank funds?

There were any number of Gestapo and *Schutzpolizei* agents at the opera house this evening. But he decided the best course of action was to call one of his superiors at the ministry. He located a telephone booth in the *Zuschauergarderobe* downstairs. Obviously it was too late to call the office; he called his immediate boss at home, but there was no answer. He called his boss's boss, Klausener, who was only one rung down from the director and dealt quite a bit with the Bank for International Settlements. Klausener was obviously in the middle of a dinner party, and he was furious at the interruption. "I've never heard of any flunky named Quilligan!" Klausener shouted. "Why the hell do you bother me? Call Basel; call the police, Hosenscheisser!"

After Klausener hung up, Gerlach muttered to himself, *"Ach! Verdammter Schweinhund!"* What a moron. He couldn't call Basel, where it was too late, and besides, placing an international telephone call was complicated these days.

Finally he strode up to one of the black-uniformed SS officers who were loitering outside the entrance to the hall. His stomach constricted as he approached, but he reminded himself that, in his gray suit and tie, he looked utterly dignified.

The SS man was in black, head to toe: black tunic, black leather buttons, black tie, black breeches, and black jackboots. On his right forearm were the letters *SD,* enclosed in a silver diamond. The three plaited parallel silver threads on his shoulder tabs and the badge on his collar patch indicated that he was an SS *Sturmbannführer.*

"Forgive me for disturbing you, Herr Sturmbannführer, but I need your assistance."

Frau Eva Hauptman noticed that her best friend, Mitzi-Molli Krüger, was acting a bit superior. The box in which they sat, which belonged to the Hauptmans, seemed positively cavernous without their husbands. Maybe that was why she was paying more attention to Mitzi-Molli than she might normally have. Mitzi-Molli's air of superiority rankled her, and the worst thing about it was, Eva couldn't say anything about it. She knew what Mitzi-Molli was thinking—she'd known the woman long enough, since finishing school in Hannover. Mitzi-Molli had taken pleasure in Eva's humiliation. She was always jealous of Eva anyway—of Eva's beauty, even her choice of a husband—so it must have given her no small pleasure to see her friend embarrassed that way. Imagine, that cad had pretended not to know her! He couldn't have forgotten her—in Paris they'd had a brief but ardent affair, and Eva Hauptman was a vixen in bed: men did not forget her.

No, Daniel Eigen hadn't forgotten her, of course—but why had he pretended not to know her?

Maybe he was here with another woman—that would explain it—yet she hadn't seen him talking with a woman. He was talking to some boring-looking *Tunte,* with not a woman in sight.

Eva began thinking about how to let Mitzi-Molli know about Daniel Eigen's rakish reputation. Eigen, she would explain to Mitzi-Molli, must have been embarrassed to see her, given how passionate their relationship had been; surely he was still in love with her, and no doubt he was at the ballet with another woman. That was why he had acted so strangely!

As she was about to turn to Mitzi-Molli and casually, ever so casually, say a few words about Daniel Eigen, the door to the box opened. The women turned to see a black-uniformed SS man standing there.

The SS men always made her uneasy, even though her husband was highly placed in the Reich. They were arrogant, drunk with power, and they really didn't know their place. She had heard far too many stories of people from good families, well-connected society people, who had been taken in to the SS headquarters in Prinz-Albrechtstrasse, never to return.

The SS man pointed at her and began speaking, rudely and without even introducing himself. "Can you come with me, please," he said.

"Excuse me?" Eva replied in her haughtiest voice.

"We need to clear something up."

"The ballet is about to begin," Eva said. "Whatever you want, it can wait until later."

"It's a matter of utmost urgency," the SS man said. "You greeted a man in the lobby—an American."

"He's not American, he's Argentine. What about him?"

Nazi Germany's security service, the *Reichssicherheitshauptamt,* was divided into seven distinct departments. One of them, Department VI—in charge of foreign intelligence and counter-espionage—was so large that it had its own headquarters building, a modern four-story building located at Berkaerstrasse 32, at the corner of the Hohenzollerndamm.

Less than one hour after SS Sturmbannführer Rudolf Dietrich placed an urgent call from a special SS call box on Unter den Linden, in front of the opera house, a senior official knocked on the door of the chief of Department VI and entered the corner office. Both men worked long hours, but the department chief, SS Oberführer Walter Rapp—at thirty-two, the youngest department chief in all of the SS—seemed never to leave his office. Rapp prided himself on his attention to the smallest detail. He read every intelligence report, vetted all major expenses, even ran his own agents. He was said to have an ear up to every wall.

The junior man, SS Standartenführer Hermann Ehlers, spoke quickly, because he knew that his chief had little patience for interruptions. When Ehlers had been speaking for no more than a minute or two, Rapp broke in.

"This American—if he was exposed by SD Paris, why was he in Moscow?"

"I've searched the card files myself, and I don't know much more than bits and pieces, sir. I know he killed several of our men in Paris after his *réseau* was eliminated."

"His real name?"

"Stephen Metcalfe. He works for an American espionage ring founded by a spymaster named Corcoran."

"Corcoran's name I know." Rapp sat up, now intent on the junior man. "I have my own lines into Corcoran's ring. What do you *know* about what he was doing in Moscow?"

"Very little. But I have the summary here of the agent report dispatched by our asset in the Lubyanka. The NKVD detained Metcalfe and put him through a lengthy series of interrogations."

"And?"

"The interrogations were not successful. Metcalfe was released."

"Why?"

"I can only read between the lines. He seems to have manipulated his investigator, led him to believe that he was working for Beria."

"Is he? Was he?"

"That's very likely a lie he concocted, though Beria has not been asked directly. No one dares. The point is, his is a case that is of personal interest to Gruppenführer Heydrich, a matter of the highest priority."

"*Heydrich?* How do you know this?"

"The SD agent assigned to eliminate Metcalfe is a favorite of Heydrich's, a fellow violinist and a ruthless bastard—"

"Kleist, surely. It can be no one else. And the American still lives?"

"Heydrich wanted the American flushed out, followed, his business in Moscow investigated. But now, of course, Heydrich wants the American out of the way."

Oberführer Rapp thought for a moment. "Call him in. If what I hear about Kleist is accurate, I have a feeling he'll be happy to complete his assignment. Does Metcalfe have any known contacts here, any acquaintances?"

"There is a banker. A *Tunte,* a queen, named Gerlach."

"A sexual connection?"

"No. Gerlach is the one who reported his suspicions about Metcalfe. The American arrived in Berlin earlier today under the cover of a banker with the Bank for International Settlements in Switzerland. He met with Gerlach a few hours ago."

"He's staying where?"

"The Adlon. We've already had his room searched. Undercover Gestapo agents have been stationed at the Adlon waiting for his return."

Rapp grunted an acknowledgment of Ehlers's fast work. "He will be seeing Gerlach again?"

"Presumably. Gerlach will cooperate, of course."

"Other known contacts?"

Ehlers hesitated for a moment. "I ran a thorough cross-check," he said with scarcely concealed pride, "and Metcalfe's name came up in another card file. Apparently a minor Foreign Office diplomat in Moscow named von Schüssler filed a routine contact-with-foreigner report. He encountered and had a brief conversation with Metcalfe. Von Schüssler was also questioned by Kleist in Moscow."

"Really? I know of von Schüssler—at least, of the Schloss von Schüssler."

"So he's a rich man."

"Extremely. He's in Moscow, you say?"

"Actually, he's on leave for a few days here in Berlin."

"*Most* interesting coincidence. Perhaps there's nothing in it, but this is a lead that must be explored. I'd like you to contact this Kleist and send him around to von Schüssler's residence at once."

"Yes, sir."

"We must cover all possibilities. It goes without saying that a matter of top priority to Gruppenführer Heydrich is of top priority to us, too. The American will not leave Berlin. It's as simple as that."

CHAPTER THIRTY-FIVE

The Schloss von Schüssler was nestled in the thick, dark pine forests about thirty kilometers northwest of Berlin. It protruded from a mountaintop, with its battlements and conical turrets of ancient stone, its steep red stone roof and ancient white stone walls, looking precisely like the fourteenth-century castle-fortress it was. Centuries ago, the von Schüsslers had been Free Knights of the Empire, a status greater than any noble title, though the title of *Graf,* or count, was bestowed upon one of Rudolf von Schüssler's illustrious ancestors in the early nineteenth century. The estate had been in the family for centuries, and though it had not served as a true fortress since medieval times, its fortifications remained intact.

Kundrov had given Metcalfe directions to the von Schüssler family estate. While the Russian made preliminary arrangements, Metcalfe had bought a car off of a downtrodden-looking German several blocks from Unter den Linden. The German had been parking his beat-up Opel Olympia when Metcalfe had approached and, in his best, most colloquial German, had offered close to a thousand Reichsmarks, far more than the vehicle was worth. Money was tight in Berlin these days; the German seemed surprised at the generosity of the offer and had hastened to turn over the keys. Only when Metcalfe was driving up the mountainside to von Schüssler's *schloss* did he see why the German had been in such a hurry to sell his Opel. Not only was the car underpowered, but it had all sorts of transmission problems; the car shivered and shuddered as it climbed the mountain to the *schloss,* to an extent that Metcalfe feared he wouldn't make it.

On the way he managed to buy a pair of Zeiss binoculars for

bird-watching as well as some Tyrolean-style clothing, all loden-green and gray boiled wool. By the time he arrived at the *schloss*—parking the Opel in the woods, out of sight—he was attired as a bird-watcher. It was early evening, however: not a plausible time of day for any legitimate birder. But his cover was better than nothing, and as long as he didn't linger, he would have time to conduct a brief surveillance. Ideally, if he could enter the *schloss* undetected, he could find a place to hide and then meet up with Lana later in the evening.

But after circling the *schloss,* he determined that the obstacles to penetration were formidable indeed. The stone walls were high and smooth, and inside the walls roamed trained German shepherd guard dogs. The fortress mentality was probably more a matter of style than of necessity. It was the way rich Germans liked to live, a symbolic display that had practical uses in wartime. Metcalfe attempted to scale the walls at one point, which set off the dogs, who obviously smelled him. Rather than risk alerting the castle's caretakers—von Schüssler himself was still at the Opera House, but he would have staff in residence—Metcalfe dropped back to the ground and returned quickly to his car. But he had seen enough to know that climbing into the grounds would be difficult to the point of impossibility. At the main entrance to the *schloss* were massive tall iron gates, where more German shepherds, and even more Doberman pinschers, growled menacingly as he drew near. Only authorized vehicles would be permitted to enter. Not far from the main *schloss* building was a brick carport where a stunningly beautiful Daimler saloon was parked. It obviously belonged to the master of the house. As Metcalfe watched from behind a broad oak tree, he saw a man emerge from the side of the *schloss,* dressed in the livery of a chauffeur. He stopped for a moment, seeming to observe the dogs growling.

Metcalfe tensed. The driver must have been alerted by the disturbance. If he came to investigate, Metcalfe would have to run through the woods without being seen. But he waited to see what the chauffeur would do.

The uniformed man pulled out a small silver whistle and blew into it. Immediately the dogs stopped their growling. Metcalfe breathed a sigh of relief. The driver must have assumed that it was some animal that the dogs were growling at.

A few minutes later, Metcalfe returned to Berlin, driving down Unter den Linden to the Staatsoper, then pulling around to the rear of the building. He did not have to wait long before von Schüssler's Daimler—ivory with black trim, its tall radiator grille distinctive, its interior cream leather and walnut burl—pulled up near the stage entrance. After a few minutes, the liveried driver, the same one Metcalfe had seen calling off the dogs at the *schloss*, got out of the car. He lit a cigarette. Leaning against the building, he smoked placidly, waiting for his employer and his employer's lady friend.

Kundrov, who made it his business to know Lana's whereabouts at all times, had told Metcalfe that the chauffeur had earlier brought Lana and von Schüssler's bags to the *schloss*. Kundrov also reported that von Schüssler was inside the Staatsoper, standing by the dressing rooms, bearing an armful of poppies. Hearing that, Metcalfe was embarrassed by his feelings of jealousy. It was ridiculous, of course; she detested the man. But still . . .

He checked his watch. The performance should be just about over by now. Lana would emerge, probably with von Schüssler, and together they would get into the Daimler. The trick was for Metcalfe to catch her eye first, let her see him without von Schüssler seeing him as well. He had to get a note to her, somehow arrange a rendezvous. He had considered and rejected the idea of giving the driver a note to hand to her—the chauffeur worked for von Schüssler, so he would be loyal to the German and might instead give any such note to his employer. No, the only way to get a message to Lana safely was to hand it to her himself as she exited the theater.

Unless . . . There were other ways. A delivery boy could run up, hand her a bouquet of flowers, a note inside. Yes. That could work. He looked around and noticed that the chauffeur was walking toward the stage entrance. Why? To greet von Schüssler there? Metcalfe hadn't noticed anyone coming out; had the driver seen something Metcalfe hadn't? Then he overheard the driver speaking to the guard attending the stage door. A snatch of German floated toward him: *"die Toilette."*

Metcalfe looked at the unattended Daimler and made a snap decision.

It was an idea, perhaps a crazy idea . . . but if it worked, it would solve the problem of how he and Lana could meet.

He raced toward the rear of the Daimler, pushed the trunk release, and lifted the lid. The roomy trunk was empty, lined with carpet, and immaculate. There weren't any bags, because Lana and von Schüssler had already sent them ahead. The only thing in it was a folded blanket.

He looked around; no one was in sight.

If he did this, he would have to move fast . . . *now!*

He climbed into the trunk, then pulled the lid closed. The latch snapped shut, and he was in darkness. He rolled over to one side of the compartment, reached for the blanket, pulled it over him.

If everything went well . . . *if* . . . the trunk would not be opened: there was no reason for anyone to open it. Until they reached the *schloss* and von Schüssler, Lana, and the driver got out. A few minutes later, once he was sure there was no one around, Metcalfe would open the trunk from the inside and climb out. It was a bold maneuver and risky, yet it was the best way to reach her.

If everything went well. *If* the trunk was not opened.

And if it was? He had a gun, provided for him by Chip, and would use it if he had to.

He felt around the pitch-black interior of the trunk, shifted his body until he could reach the top of the trunk lid, feeling for the trunk-release lever.

There was nothing there.

Only smooth enameled steel.

There was no trunk release! He was flooded with panic. How the hell was he going to get out of here? *He was locked inside!*

Metcalfe could smell the fuel exhaust from the idling car, the gases filling the space in which he was coiled. People could pass out, even die, from breathing a car's exhaust fumes.

He ran his hands frantically over the trunk's interior, searching desperately for a lever, a knob, anything that would pop open the trunk. But there was nothing—nothing but smooth steel.

Christ on a raft!

He was trapped!

The violinist parked his car by the circular drive and walked slowly toward the *schloss,* taking in the medieval architecture with a gimlet eye. It was impressive, to be sure, but he had seen much finer.

The news that his prey was in Berlin—had come to Kleist's hometown!—was an invitation, a provocation, impossible to resist. The violinist did not like to leave business unfinished.

He rang the bell, and the mammoth wooden door was opened by a wan gray-haired manservant.

"Herr Kleist? Darf ich Sie bitten, nährer zu treten?" The head butler, who had already been told to expect the SD man, asked him to enter in the excessively formal manner that one would use with a tradesman. It was a deliberate snub, but Kleist ignored it.

"Is your master here?" Kleist asked.

"No, sir, as I told your boss—"

"He's not my boss. When are you expecting von Schüssler?"

"Graf von Schüssler is not expected for two hours. He is in Berlin, at the opera house."

"Have you had any visitors?"

"No."

"Are von Schüssler's wife and children in residence?"

"No," the butler answered huffily. "They are on holiday in the mountains."

The violinist paused for a moment, took in the dank, fungal odors of the old castle, the fetid smell of ancient stone mixed with the must of decomposing organic material. On top of it was the smell of cleaning fluids, of silver polish and furniture oil, and a faint trace of a female perfume. The only male smells were that of *der Hausdiener* and the ammoniac, perspirant smell of a laborer. Not von Schüssler. The female smells were not strong, indicating that the family members were indeed absent, had not been here for several days.

He returned to his car a few minutes later, discouraged. This was a blind alley. Maybe the American would attempt to contact von Schüssler later on or tomorrow. That was theoretically possible, of course.

Then, as he opened the car door, a gust of wind came his way, bearing a plume of odor that arrested his attention.

Very faint.

His nostrils flared. Someone had been here within the last few hours. Someone wearing brand-new woolen clothing, brand-new leather, fresh from a clothing store. Not too many Berliners had new clothing. One wore what one had. He turned his head to catch another draught of the scent. Male, that he was certain of. And not a German: not that beery, barley, potato odor that most German men gave off. He detected a secondary note of soap— not a scented soap, not deodorant soap exactly, but something clean, foreign.

Ivory soap. Yes, he was sure. It was an American. Wearing brand-new woolen—*boiled-wool,* in fact—clothing and brand-new leather boots. The smell of Alpine, perhaps Tyrolean clothing. Being worn by an American.

He carefully shut the car door and returned to the *schloss.*

The servant was not happy to see him again.

"You have had no visitors," Kleist said ponderously.

"You asked me that already, and I told you: none."

Kleist nodded. "I see you have guard dogs on the property. Was there any disturbance earlier this evening?"

"No . . . well, yes, I suppose there was, but that doesn't necessarily mean—"

"You had a visitor. Someone who visited the perimeter of the grounds, at least. Quite recently. And he will be back."

SS Oberführer Walter Rapp, chief of the *Reichssicherheitshauptamt*'s Department VI, stared at Hermann Ehlers.

"Kleist is certain that Metcalfe was there?" he demanded of the younger man.

"So he says."

"The servants say so?"

"Apparently not."

"Then what does he base this on?"

" 'Trace evidence' is all he would say. But he says he is absolutely certain."

" 'Trace evidence,' " Rapp muttered, reaching for the phone. "Well, one thing there's no shortage of is Gestapo agents," he said. "I want a team assigned to the *schloss* at once."

The Daimler was moving.

Two minutes ago, he had heard voices close by, one of them Lana's. His heart lifted to hear it, it alleviated somewhat the panic he felt at being locked in the trunk.

Then came the sound of a car door being opened, then closed. He braced himself for what might come next: the trunk. It was almost humorous to consider which was worse: being locked in here for the foreseeable future or having the chauffeur discover him. If the latter happened, he would have no choice but to lunge at the chauffeur and subdue him, but that would mean trouble.

The vehicle accelerated with a deep-throated mechanical purr.

Lana and von Schüssler were sitting a few feet away, in the passengers' compartment. They were speaking, but he could make out nothing beyond a murmur. He thought of what he was going to tell her, what he was about to *ask* her, and he wondered how she would react. She was a brave woman and practical, but she could be unpredictable. What he was about to suggest to her was a scheme that was brazen to the point of seeming ridiculous.

It was dangerous as well.

But it was the only way to save both *Die Wolfsfalle* and Lana.

The Daimler's engine strained at a lower gear, and the car felt as if it was climbing a hill. They were nearing the *schloss;* they must have reached the steep stretch of road just before the gates of the castle. Then the car slowed: probably they had arrived at the gates and were waiting for them to be opened. He heard other voices now, shouts from nearby. There seemed to be a number of men at the gates; Metcalfe wondered what was going on. But after a moment, the car resumed, more slowly. Presently it stopped, and a door was opened. He heard von Schüssler's unpleasantly grating voice, then Lana's lilting, sensuous voice. He heard their footsteps scrape on the gravel, then the door slam.

But the engine was not shut off. The car kept going at a slow pace, a brief distance longer, before it stopped again, and this time the motor was switched off. Had the car entered a garage?

He waited in silence, in the absolute darkness of the trunk. There was a low, tuneless whistle, then the car doors opened, and closed, again. Was the driver cleaning up? After a few more minutes, he heard the scuff of the driver's shoes against the pavement, heard the jingling of the car's keys being hung up, and then there was silence.

He waited.

Five, ten minutes—he couldn't keep track of time. He wanted to make sure the chauffeur was nowhere nearby before he moved, before he attempted to figure out some way to free himself from this claustrophobic steel chamber.

Finally, enough time had gone by. He felt the entire expanse of the trunk lid, patiently, but there still was no internal release knob or lever. There were cables and wires tucked into the corners, but none of them popped open the trunk.

The sense of panic that he had felt earlier had returned in force. His heartbeat thudded in his chest; he was short of breath; his mouth was dry.

There *had* to be a way out of here, damn it!

He thought of Lana, who'd been sitting just feet away, so close he could almost touch her. And then an idea came to him.

So close he could almost touch her.

He felt around until he found a small compartment that contained an emergency tool kit, which was used for changing tires. He pried it open. Inside were screwdrivers, a tire pressure gauge, pliers, and lug wrenches. Using the slotted screwdriver, he lifted the carpet liner, peeling it back until most of the rear section of the trunk compartment was exposed down to its bare sheet metal. As he expected, he felt several bolts that fastened a detachable panel in place; working quickly, he was at last able to loosen the rectangle of steel, slide it away, and reach the rear-seat assembly. It was not meant to be accessed from the trunk side, but by reaching around through the coils and struts he managed to loosen the bolts enough to push the rear seat forward.

Twenty minutes after he had begun, he was in the backseat of the Daimler, at last free of the trunk.

The car had been parked in some sort of carport, not a closed garage. It was a rudimentary brick structure, open at one end, allowing in the moonlight. He got out of the backseat quickly, the interior dome light flashing on, then off, but only for a second or two. Was there anyone around to see the light go on? He remembered the voices that had accosted the car as it entered the estate. Looking out through the open end of the carport, he was able to see the tall iron fence a few hundred feet away and down the hill. Just outside it were the shifting silhouettes of men. Guards? He heard the crunch of boots against gravel, the testy whine of dogs straining against their leashes. The guttural growl of other dogs—the German shepherds and Doberman pinschers he had seen earlier, roaming restlessly inside the fence—chuffing warningly at the men and their leashed dogs.

A match flared up, struck by one of the guards as he lit a cigarette, and in that brief moment of illumination Metcalfe saw that these were not guards at all.

From their uniforms he could see at once that they were Gestapo. A detachment of guards from the Gestapo was patrolling the main gates.

Why?

They had not been here earlier. Von Schüssler, a minor functionary in the Foreign Office, did not merit the sort of protection that might be given to a high-ranking official of the Reich. Why were they here? Metcalfe's thoughts whirled. Von Schüssler had just arrived in town, accompanied by Lana. Did the *Sicherheitsdienst* know Metcalfe was here as well? Did they know of his connection to Lana—and suspect that he might come here to find her?

It was possible—anything was possible—but it seemed unlikely. The Gestapo was here to watch for someone either leaving the *schloss* or entering. Which was it?

They were outside, not on the grounds, he realized. They were not searching the estate; that meant they were waiting for someone to arrive.

For me, he thought. *Could it be?*

He had to get into the *schloss* without being seen by the Gestapo team. The main house was perhaps a hundred feet away, the path more or less exposed. He could see lights in several rooms on the top floor. One of the rooms glowed with a pinkish light, and he knew that had to be Lana's: she sometimes liked to drape a red silk scarf over her bedroom lamp, he remembered.

The Gestapo agents were looking for arrivals, not someone within the gates; if he moved silently through the darkness . . .

But what about the dogs? They seemed to be gathered by the gates, whimpering at the Gestapo's dogs. Perhaps they were poorly trained, or more likely they had been trained—like their human counterparts, the Gestapo—to watch for intruders from *outside,* not those *within* the grounds.

He stepped quietly out of the carport. Spying a low yew hedge that bordered the circular drive, he dropped to the ground and crawled on his hands and knees along the lawn. When the hedge ended, he pulled himself across the grass on his belly. In short order he had reached the castle. He loped around toward the back of the building, searching for a service entrance of some sort.

He found it without trouble: a narrow wooden plank door that was unlocked. The *schloss* was so well guarded, surrounded as it was by walls and gates, defended by prowling dogs, that there was no need to lock the servants' door. He pulled the door open slowly, cautiously, wary of any squeaky hinges.

He did not hear the thump of paws against the earth until too late.

There was a sudden, terrifying growl, deep and throaty. Instantly the body of a Doberman crashed into him as it sank its teeth into his woolen coat, tearing wildly at the fabric in a furious attempt to attack the meat of his upper arm. A jagged lightning bolt of pain shot up and down his arm when the dog's fangs broke the skin.

Metcalfe kicked at the ferocious beast, torquing his body to loosen its monstrous jaws. The door was half-open; he jumped into the entrance, at the same time slamming the door, slamming it repeatedly on the dog until finally, with an angry yelp, it released its grip.

He raced into the dark hall, his adrenaline pumping. Far down the corridor, a crack of light appeared under a door. He had to get out of here before a servant, alerted by the noise of the dog attack, came out into the hall. Several doors lined the hall, though he had no idea where they led. He tried the first knob, then the second. The third turned. The door gave onto a narrow staircase. He shut the door behind him, descending the steps to a dank basement.

Despite the darkness he saw that he was surrounded by hundreds of bottles of wine, Rhinehessens and Moselles. He was in von Schüssler's wine cellar. Backing himself into an alcove, he waited.

When no one came down within the next few minutes, he calculated that he was safe. He glanced at his watch: it was twenty minutes before midnight. He would wait another hour down here. By then, it was more likely than not that Lana and von Schüssler would have gone to sleep. Only then would the servants go to bed as well. It was too risky to go looking through an unfamiliar house.

But the clock was ticking. If Kundrov had succeeded in arranging his part, no more than six hours remained.

For all that needed to be done, that was not enough time.

CHAPTER THIRTY-SIX

An hour later, Metcalfe stole silently through the darkened hallways of the top floor of the *schloss*.

The floor plan was typical of medieval German castles, Metcalfe realized quickly. The ground floor was for the servants; on the first floor was a chapel, and a great hall with a mammoth refectory table; on the second were the living quarters. Each floor, however, was divided into several wings. It became clear that one wing, with tiger skins on the floors and hunting trophies mounted on the walls, belonged to Rudolf von Schüssler. Metcalfe walked through it quietly, past what seemed to be the master's bedroom. At the end of the hall was his study: Metcalfe caught a glimpse of a book-lined room and heavy furniture.

Another wing was the domain of von Schüssler's children. Yet another, which obviously received less use, was for visitors.

That was where Lana had to be.

Everything Metcalfe knew or had observed about von Schüssler told him that he and Lana would be sleeping separately here, in the familial estate, with its air of baronial propriety. Lana, in fact, would likely insist upon it.

A crack of light was visible under one highly polished chestnut door. The light's reddish hue told him that this was Lana's room. She was inside, her scarf-draped lamp on; perhaps she was reading.

But was she in fact alone?

Outside the door was a linen-covered butler's tray, on it a crumpled linen napkin, a crystal glass, a silver water pitcher, a single flute of champagne, empty. One of each, he noticed.

She was here, and she was alone.

He turned the brass knob, opened the door slowly.

He heard her voice. "Rudi? Is that you?"

Metcalfe did not reply until he stepped into the room and shut the door behind him. The room was all sumptuously carved wood, a coffered ceiling, heavy embroidered draperies. Lana was sitting in the middle of an immense canopy bed, surrounded by pillows, looking as radiant as the first time he had seen her on-stage. In her pink-silk negligee, her raven-black hair cascading around her swan neck, she was magnificent. Her face lit up; she let out a gasp, threw out her arms as he ran to her.

"Stiva, *zolotoi!*" she cried. "I thought I'd never see you again!"

"You can't get rid of me that easily," Metcalfe replied, then kissed her on the mouth, long and ardently.

When he pulled away, he saw that she was crying. "How did you get in here? How did you get to Berlin?" She lowered her voice to a whisper. "*Why* are you here?"

"I heard you were dancing tonight. You know I never miss your performances when I'm in town."

"No," she said, shaking her head, dismissing his attempt at levity. "It's about the . . . the documents. It's serious—I can see it in your eyes, Stiva." Her voice became urgent, frightened. "What is it? Is there a *problem?*"

Metcalfe would no longer lie to her; he had lied to her far too much. "*Dai ruchenku,*" he said, taking hold of one of her soft, scented hands in both of his. He sat down on the bed beside her and began to speak quietly. "It's not safe for you to stay in Moscow. I want you to come out."

"To defect." Her eyes were wide, glistening.

"This is probably your last chance. They're not likely to let you out of the country again."

"Stiva, *golubchik*, I've told you: Russia is my *rodina*. My motherland. It's who I *am*."

"It'll *always* be your *rodina*. It'll *always* be part of who you are. Lanushka, it'll always be there, a part of you. That won't change. But at least you'll be alive, and free!"

"Freedom," she began bitterly.

Metcalfe cut her off. "No, Lana. Listen to me. You don't know freedom. No one who was born and brought up in a prison can understand freedom."

" 'Stone walls do not a prison make,' " she quoted, " 'Nor iron bars a cage . . . If I have freedom in my love.' "

"But you *don't* have freedom in your love, Lana. Not even that!"

"My father—"

"That's a lie, too, Lana."

"What are you talking about?"

"There was no plot. That was all manufactured 'evidence,' planted by the Nazis to gut the Soviet military. The SS knew how paranoid Stalin is about traitors, so they forged correspondence that implicated the Red Army's top leaders."

"That's impossible!"

"Nothing's impossible, Lana; nothing's beyond the paranoid imagination. Your father may secretly detest Stalin, like any sane man does, but he never plotted against him."

"You *know* this?"

"I know it."

She gave a sad smile. "It would be nice to think that he was safe now."

"No," Metcalfe agreed. "He's living on borrowed time."

"Do you remember my father's dueling pistols?"

"The ones that once belonged to Pushkin."

"Yes. Well, he once told me that during the time when people fought duels, there were probably a hundred thousand people who owned dueling pistols. Yet how many duels were actually fought in all those years? Maybe a thousand. The point of owning a pair of dueling pistols and displaying them prominently, he said, was to warn your potential enemies not to challenge you because you were prepared to fight."

"Your father is prepared to fight?"

"He's prepared, yes—but to die," she whispered.

Metcalfe nodded. "Innocence has never been a defense in the workers' paradise," he said fiercely. "The terror machine sets one innocent man against another, doesn't it? It puts an informer in every apartment building; no one knows who's 'informing,' who's reporting 'disloyalty,' so no one trusts anyone. No one trusts their neighbor, their friend, even their lover."

"But I trust you," she whispered. Tears were streaming down her cheeks.

Metcalfe didn't know how to answer that. He, who had lied to her, manipulated her, didn't deserve her trust, and it sickened him. Her *trust* sickened him now, her goodness. Now tears came to his eyes: hot, burning tears of frustration, anger, compassion. "You shouldn't trust me, either," he said, his eyes closed.

"Is that what you've come to believe? Is that what your world has done to you? Your world of freedom—it has made you trust no one, either? Then what makes your 'free' world any better than my prison, with its gold bars?"

"Lana, *milaya*, listen to me. Listen to me carefully. What I'm about to tell you—I want you to know the truth. I don't care what you'll think of me after—no, that's not true; I *do* care what you think of me! But you should know the truth, and if it ruins everything, so be it. If it ruins the operation, if it makes you never want to see me ever again, so be it. I can't have this lie on my conscience anymore. You deserve more, far more."

She was no longer looking at him. She sat next to him on the bed, seeming to shrink into herself. He still held her hand, but it seemed to have gone cold and damp. Something inside of him had turned icy as well, but it was not the ice of a man who was past caring; it was the frozen interior tundra of a man who felt alone and frightened, a lost child. "I want to tell you about the operation I've led you into," he said. *Why am I saying this?* he wondered. *Why am I doing this?* He had come here with the simple intention of persuading her to defect, of taking part in one last, breathtakingly bold operation that would simultaneously save her and save Operation WOLFSFALLE. But now . . .

something inside had given way: a compulsion to tell the truth to this woman he never wanted to live without. "The documents I've been giving you. The ones I told you would convince Hitler and his men that Russia's intentions were peaceful—"

"I know," she interrupted. She had opened her eyes, but she was staring at the floor. She looked deeply weary. "I know the truth, *dorogoi* Stiva. I know what was in those papers."

"You read them."

"Of course I read them. You underestimate me, *milenky*. A Russia that poses no threat to Hitler would be an engraved invitation to Hitler to invade. Men like Hitler—and like Stalin—despise weakness. It does not reassure them. It provokes them. If Hitler believed that Russia was weak, he would send his armies in to Moscow and Leningrad, he would have taken us over long ago. No, the only thing that has kept Hitler from declaring war against Russia is his fear that Russia is too *strong* an adversary. I know this."

He was stunned. He wanted to look into her eyes, but she kept staring at the floor as she continued: "But you want Hitler and Stalin to go to war. That's the real objective. Your documents tell Hitler of Stalin's plans to attack Germany *first*. Hitler's men, if they believe the truth of these documents, will have no choice but to launch an attack."

He turned, took her face in both of his hands. "Dear God," he breathed. "You've known this all along."

"And I approve, Stivushka. I think it's dangerous, and daring, but it's also brilliant. It's the only hope. If Hitler attacks us, believing that we are weak, he will be led to his own grave. Yes, Stiva, I've known this from the beginning."

"You're a beautiful woman, the most beautiful woman I've ever met. And the most remarkable woman I've ever met."

"Then tell me this," she said solemnly. "And you must tell me the truth: Does the NKVD believe that I'm passing Soviet military secrets? Is that what you've come here to warn me?"

"No. Not yet. But it's only a matter of time before the NKVD

begins to suspect you. The *Abwehr*—German military intelligence—has an asset within the Lubyanka. There are leaks in both
directions. No secret is truly safe."

"An 'asset'?"

"A spy. Someone who's working for them, informing for them,
reporting to them."

"Spies among spies!"

He nodded. "The Germans have begun to suspect that the
documents have come to them too easily. They wonder if it's a
Soviet plant."

"And you think their—their 'asset' in the Lubyanka will raise
questions about me."

"It's possible. There's always leakage, in any operation that involves more than two persons. It's always a risk."

"But that's not your chief concern. You are concerned that the
operation will fail."

"How ruthless you must think I am."

"I'm not a child," she snapped, turning to him suddenly with
eyes wide. Her expression was fierce. "I thought you'd figured
that out about me by now. We both know what's important. We
both know that the fate of the free world is more important than
the life of any ballerina."

Her words were chilling. "Maybe I want too much," he replied
gently, "but I want to protect you at the same time that I save
the operation."

"How is that possible?"

"Kundrov."

"*Kundrov?* What do you mean?"

"If you give us the go-ahead, Lana, Kundrov is going to report
you to his higher-ups."

"*Report* me," she said. "I don't understand."

"He will report his suspicions that you, the daughter of a renowned Soviet general, have been passing military secrets to the
German diplomat you're in love with. It will be a thunderbolt in

Moscow; it will surge to the highest levels. The GRU will call in the NKVD on this, and orders will be issued at once."

She nodded, a terrible understanding dawning in her face. "When I am arrested, the Germans will learn of it through their spy in the Lubyanka. Then Hitler's men will see that this was no Soviet plant. They will be persuaded that the documents are authentic." She shrugged; her tone was casual, but she could not hide the strain, the fear. "The execution of one insignificant ballerina is surely worth it if it means the end of Hitler."

Metcalfe grabbed her with both hands, wresting her face toward his. "*No!* I would not sacrifice you!"

"I would be sacrificing myself," Lana replied coolly.

"Listen to me! You will *not* be arrested. You know how these things work. The NKVD will not arrest you on German soil. They will lure you back home, tell you that you must return at once. There's an emergency, they'll tell you. Perhaps something with your father. They will use some pretext, some ruse. They will put you on the first train out of Berlin, and once you reach Moscow, *then* they'll arrest you."

"Yes, yes," she agreed. "That is indeed how they'll do it."

"But you won't get on that train! You'll defect—they'll think you were tipped off, that you figured out the truth and you chose instead to defect. You chose life over execution—it's entirely reasonable."

"And how will I defect?"

"All you have to do is say the word, Lana, and I'll place a call to Switzerland. The British Special Operations Executive and the RAF operate a fleet of small, light monoplanes—Lysanders—that are used to parachute agents into Nazi-occupied territory. Occasionally to make pickups as well."

"They fly into German airspace?"

"They know the capabilities and schedules of Nazi antiaircraft defenses. They fly in low and fast enough that the Nazi defenses don't have time to react. These planes have already made dozens of flights like this. But the timing is extraordinarily tricky. The whole thing requires a high degree of coordination. Once we request a plane, we have to be ready to meet it, signaling at a designated rendezvous site outside of Berlin. If everything doesn't happen with perfect timing, the plane won't even land. It'll circle around and return to Tempsford Airfield in Bedfordshire. And then the window will slam shut."

"The window?"

"Once Kundrov has transmitted his report about you to Moscow, we'll have only one opportunity to get on the plane. If we miss it, the NKVD will grab you. And I won't have that."

"And Kundrov?"

"We've already spoken about this. He's already arranging his end of the rendezvous. All I have to do is call Bern, and once I know the Lysander is being dispatched, Kundrov will make his report to Moscow. The authorities in Moscow will coordinate your arrest with the NKVD presence here. The machinery will be set into motion. It'll be unstoppable. There'll be no turning back then."

"You trust him?"

"That's the same question he asked of me. He saved your life and mine." Metcalfe recalled Kundrov's request to defect. "I have other reasons to trust him as well. But Lana—this is up to you."

"Yes."

"I want you to think long and hard about this. It may sound terribly risky, but I think it's even more risky for you to return to Moscow, where it's only a matter of time before you're arrested."

"I said yes, Stiva."

"You realize that things can still go wrong?"

"I told you, I'm not a child. Nothing in life is guaranteed. Nothing in *our* world is safe. Not anymore. Leaving my father— this will tear me apart, my darling. But I have said good-bye to him for the last time, just as I do every morning. So I'm telling you yes."

Both of them were silent for a minute or two.

"I need to place two calls. One to Kundrov, who's waiting for my call." He pulled out a scrap of paper on which he'd scrawled the number of a telephone booth in central Berlin. "The other to Switzerland. Von Schüssler's a diplomat, which means the Foreign Office provides him with the kind of telephone line with international access that few other Germans have."

"There's a telephone in his study. He placed a call to the German embassy in Moscow shortly after we arrived here."

He glanced at his watch, something he realized he had been doing with increasing frequency this evening.

"All right. We have five hours, even less. If all goes according to schedule, once I call Kundrov, he will call Moscow. The wheels will turn quite fast; Kundrov will see to it. You will then be called, very likely within the hour, by someone from the NKVD—only he will pretend to be someone high up in the Bolshoi Theater administration, someone you've never heard of. You will be told that your father has been stricken ill, that your presence is required in Moscow, as your father's legal guardian. You will be instructed to arrive at the Berlin Ostbahnhof to board the Brussels-Moscow train, leaving Brussels at nineteen-thirty and making a brief stop in Berlin at four-oh-two in the morning."

"And then?"

"And then Kundrov will arrive at the *schloss* and take you to the pickup site. It's an abandoned movie lot outside of Berlin that's currently being used as a decoy—a fake town, designed to fool Allied forces, to divert their bombing runs from Berlin. There's a large field there that's large enough for a small craft to land. Apparently, since it's deserted, it's the most secure location within sixty kilometers of Berlin. Now, in order for this plan to have a chance of working, the plane cannot enter German airspace until *after* you've received the call from the NKVD but well before you're expected at the Ostbahnhof. Records will be scrutinized later, after the fact. Everything must seem plausible. It must appear that you received this call, that you were suspicious and talked to your handlers—"

"My 'handlers'?"

"The people you work for. I'm sorry. These are words from my world, not yours."

"But how do you know you will be able to arrange for a plane on such short notice?"

"The people I know have an enormous amount of influence. If it turns out an emergency flight can't be arranged, we'll postpone it until one can. Kundrov won't make his report to Moscow until he's sure we can get a plane."

She paused, seemed to consider something. "And what if the plane is brought down by the German air force—or shot down? And the NKVD is already planning to seize me."

"I don't like to think that way, Lana," Metcalfe said after a pause.

"You must always prepare for the worst."

"Sometimes you don't have a choice. You hope for the best."

"That's a very casual attitude when you're talking about the fate of someone's life. Or even the fate of the world."

"There's nothing casual about it. I'm an American—I'm an optimist."

"And I am a Russian, and therefore I'm a pessimist. Only one of us can be right."

"But soon, my darling, you'll be an American yourself. Listen, the time is growing shorter as we sit here talking. We must move, and fast. We must run. If everything works right, by this time tomorrow, my darling, we'll both be in a place where we can finally stop running."

CHAPTER THIRTY-SEVEN

Metcalfe stood by the door, the same one through which he had entered the *schloss,* and watched for any trace of the guard dogs. There were none in the vicinity; they had probably returned to their customary stations alongside the gates and stone walls of the property. Too, the Gestapo patrol, having failed to apprehend Metcalfe, was gone, presumably reassigned. In one quick dash he made it to the carport, where, without needing to switch on the light, he located the Daimler's key on its hook.

The car started up quietly. He pulled out of the carport and down the drive to the main iron gates, which were locked. He pulled the Daimler to a stop. Several German shepherds and Dobermans loomed in the darkness, peering at the car, their eyes glowing yellow. They stood, several of them emitting low warning growls. Obviously they were unsure of what to do, since they recognized the automobile, if not the driver. But once Metcalfe got out of the car to open or unlock the gates, even assuming he could do so, the dogs would scent him, identify him as an interloper, and pounce. Even if he defended himself with his gun, the noise would alert the servants, perhaps von Schüssler as well.

The dogs began surrounding the car, whining softly, growling. They seemed curious, puzzled about this strange driver in the familiar car. There were five, six of them now, all standing at attention, all staring with ferocious intensity.

It was a standoff. Any moment, one of the dogs would start barking, then they all would, and von Schüssler's servants would be awakened. In order to unlock and open the gates, he *had* to get out of the car. There seemed to be no alternative, and the clock was ticking. The schedule was set; it was irrevocable. There was no time to waste!

A gleam of silver caught his eye.

A thin metallic tube was resting in a small compartment in the dashboard. He reached for it: it was a whistle.

A dog whistle.

He remembered seeing the chauffeur use it to call off the dogs several hours earlier. Putting it to his lips, he blew hard. It produced only the faint sound of air being forced out, the whistle sound emitted at a frequency audible only to dogs.

Suddenly the growls stopped. The dogs backed away a good distance from the car, then sat obediently.

Tentatively he opened the car door, the whistle grasped in one hand in case he needed it. He got out, walked over to the gates, and was relieved to see the large iron key still in the lock. Picking the lock would not have been complicated, but he had just saved five minutes.

And he needed every minute.

Guided by the Berlin map that Chip Nolan had provided him, he drove as fast as he dared, not wanting to attract the attention of the Orpo, the *Ordnungspolizei*.

As he drove he mentally rehearsed the arrangements he had made with Corky and Kundrov. The normally unflappable Corky was surprised to hear Metcalfe's voice on a direct trunk line from Berlin. "Good heavens, boy, where are you calling from, the Führer's private office?" he'd said. He greeted Metcalfe's request with a long silence. Metcalfe had expected Corcoran to raise any number of objections to the plan, but to his surprise, the older man did not. He didn't even complain about being awakened in the middle of the night. He had only one objection: "This is not like calling for a cab, Stephen. I have no idea what the flying conditions are, the visibility." The aging spymaster set down the phone for a few minutes, and when he returned, he said, "A

Lysander will be departing momentarily from the RAF fighter base at Tangmere, on the English Channel coast, arriving at three A.M. You have no idea how many chits I had to call in to pull this off." He specified the precise location that he had selected for the pickup and rattled off a series of instructions.

As soon as Metcalfe hung up, he called Kundrov at the pay-phone number the Russian had given him. They spoke for no more than a minute; both men knew what had to be done.

"I will call Moscow now," Kundrov said. "But once I make this call, it's irrevocable. There will be no going back."

Now, as Metcalfe approached the pickup site, he was astonished. Corky had prepared him, but it was staggering nonetheless.

It appeared to be a vast complex of buildings arrayed in horseshoe formation around a large, open grass field. In the center was an immense concrete hangarlike building with a corrugated steel roof; to either side were smaller brick buildings. Smoke plumed from their many chimneys. Scattered around the buildings were fuel tanks and waste barrels. It appeared to be an industrial facility of some kind, probably a giant munitions plant.

In fact, it was a stage set. Although the building at the center was real, the structures to either side of it were all fake, the barrels and tanks and trucks probably bogus, too.

This was the location of a defunct movie studio, a huge lot that had been expropriated by the Nazis and turned into a decoy fire site. Hitler's men had swiftly constructed dozens of such sites around Germany in the last few months—fifteen in Berlin alone. They had been inspired, some said, by the British, who during the recent Battle of Britain had set up five hundred dummy cities—airfields, shipyards, and bases, built in remote areas of plywood and corrugated metal, designed to lure the Nazis into bombing these fake installations rather than real cities. The strategic deception had been a great success, causing the Nazis to squander valuable time and matériel and thus reducing the damage inflicted upon population centers.

The ancient Chinese tactician Sun Tzu had proclaimed, "All

warfare is based on deception," and the Nazis had taken this principle seriously. In Berlin, the Lietzensee, the lake between the Kurfurstendamm and Kaiserdamm, was a useful guide for incoming bombers targeting the city center, so the *Luftwaffe* had confounded enemy radar by covering the lake with enormous timbered floats that resembled, from above, residential buildings. They had dressed lampposts up as fir trees, strung camouflage netting along the Charlottenberger Chaussée from the Tiergarten to the Brandenburg Gate, decked out with green cloth strips to look like forest. Bogus government buildings were put up in the vicinity of the Ostkreuz S-Bahn station to fool Allied reconnaissance aircraft pilots into believing it was the Wilhelmstrasse.

But no decoy site in all of Germany was as elaborate as this.

The Brandenburg Studios had been founded in 1921, when the German film industry was at its peak and a serious rival to Hollywood. Such legendary stars as Marlene Dietrich and Pola Negri and such talented filmmakers as Fritz Lang and Ernst Lubitsch had all worked there. Shortly after the Third Reich came to power and seized control of the film industry, banishing all "non-Aryans," the Brandenburg Studios went out of business. The Nazis appropriated the gigantic lot, which had been used to film westerns and biblical epics. The mammoth soundstage, located in the concrete building at the center, was filled with stage sets and props that had accumulated over the almost two decades of the Brandenburg Studios' history. That had been left alone; the sets where so many classic German movies had been filmed were now gathering dust.

But the deception experts in the *Luftwaffe* had created, on either side of the soundstage, a series of false brick buildings, turning the whole site into an astonishing replica of a weapons-manufacturing complex. Even the artificially generated smoke that poured from the chimneys—smoke intended to attract enemy aircraft—was convincing. The optical illusion was nothing short of brilliant.

This area immediately west of Berlin had been well chosen to fool the British fighters, for it was close to where so much of Germany's military-industrial manufacturing facilities were located. Siemens's Kraftwerk West facility was nearby, as were the AEG plants, Telefunken's radio-communications factories, the Alkett tank-production facility, and the Maybach engine factory. Berlin was ringed with the industries that were feverishly churning out the components of the Nazi war machine.

The site was, of course, deserted, as were all Nazi decoy fire sites. This made it one of the most secure locations in Berlin for Metcalfe, Lana, and Kundrov to meet. Far more important, though, was the open, snow-covered field, several hundred yards square, which had been the old studio back lot. It was an area large enough for the Lysander to land and take off comfortably; the small craft needed no more than two hundred yards.

The three-quarters moon was bright in the sky, which was fortunate; it would provide adequate illumination for the pilot, Metcalfe thought. RAF photographic reconnaissance already had detailed aerial photographs of Berlin; this decoy site was, in fact, well known to British intelligence. After all, the RAF had made more than forty bombing sorties over Berlin since August and, with each raid, was improving its accuracy.

Still, there were procedures that had to be followed in order to ensure that the pickup went off without a hitch. Corky had dispatched Chip Nolan to assist Metcalfe with the landing. The FBI man would bring an assortment of needed supplies, including flashlights to be used to send the prearranged recognition signal to the pilot in Morse code. If the Lysander pilot didn't see the flashed signal on the ground, indicating that all was safe to land, he would simply pass by without touching down and return to England. Nolan would also bring flares, presumably from a cache stored in Berlin by the anti-Nazi underground. Three flares, Corky had instructed, were to be set down on the landing field in the shape of a large L to mark the landing path. The pilot would land the monoplane at the first flare, then turn around approximately one hundred and fifty yards down between the other two. He would keep the engine running—the chances of the Lysander stalling and then being unable to start back up were too great. All in all, the plane would be on the ground no more than three minutes, assuming all went well.

But that assumption seemed an increasingly untenable one. There was just too much that could go wrong, far too many human variables.

The entire fake armaments facility was enclosed by a low chain-link fence, which had been placed there not for security but for the sake of appearance from above. Metcalfe drove the Daimler through one of the open gates and parked in a macadam lot in front of the concrete soundstage building.

Surveying the area to make sure there were no unexpected visitors, he got out and approached the soundstage, inside of which he was to meet Chip. He passed one of the fake brick buildings. Even from a few dozen feet away, the painted bricks looked real. Rows of windows had been painted on the plywood facade, enhancing the illusion. The structures had been built with walls and roofs, cut-out doorways, a few cut-out windows, the effect remarkably realistic.

He glanced at his watch. Chip should have arrived by now.

He walked around the soundstage to the front entrance, which faced the open field. A voice—Nolan, he recognized—called out to him from inside the building.

The FBI man was holding a wooden crate, standing in front of an amazingly realistic replica of a Berlin street, a long row of nineteenth-century building facades along a fake cobblestone street lined with streetlights, a mailbox, an outdoor café. Metcalfe instantly recognized the set from a classic Marlene Dietrich film.

"Hey, there you are!" Metcalfe called out. "Right on time. I'm glad you're here. This is not going to be easy."

He looked around the interior of the building, marveling. It was as large as a European railroad station, but it was crowded with sets in long aisles, some collapsed and stacked up, many simply abandoned in place, as if the filming of a dozen movies had been momentarily interrupted. There was a line of crazy German expressionist houses, tilted every which way, windows painted on at random angles, like something that might have been used in the filming of the classic silent film *The Cabinet of Dr. Caligari.* The interior of a sophisticated Manhattan apartment. A miniature Swiss chalet set against a painted backdrop of the Alps. The storefront of a bakery, KONDITOREI painted on the plate glass in gilt Gothic letters, its windows heaped with shellacked pastries. The rooftops of London done almost life-size.

Chip gave a modest smile. "Well, you know what they say at the Bureau. Neither snow nor rain nor heat nor gloom of night . . . No, wait a minute—that's the post office." Nolan's eyes were warm but watchful as he set down the crate.

"Anyway, I'm glad you're here."

"Are you?" Nolan smiled. "Gotta respect that principle of compartmentation and all. But sometimes keeping your colleagues in the dark is the most dangerous thing of all."

Metcalfe shrugged. "Could be."

"You know, I only found out about the rendezvous from the home office about an hour ago. And the thing is, I've got some real worries about operational integrity here. Our security seems to have been compromised on a high level."

"You mean you've only just figured that out? After Corky's already lost . . ." Metcalfe trailed off. The aging spymaster was always intent upon partitioning information, within and without the Registry. "Look, is there something you have to tell me? Then tell me now." He glanced at his watch and tried to figure out what piece of country the Lysander would be flying over just then. The nerves in his body felt stretched taut.

"You're misunderstanding. I think you have something to tell *me.*"

"I'm not following."

"I think there are a lot of things we can put together, the two of us, if we compare notes. But you've got to put your cards on the table. For starters, what are you doing in Berlin?"

"I think you know." He gestured around them. "An exfiltration."

"Yes, but *why?*"

"It's complicated, and there really isn't time to get into this right now, okay? Let's just say it involves a Russian asset."

"A Russian asset, right." Nolan took a step closer, his face grimly intent. "And you're running this Russian asset."

Metcalfe shrugged uneasily. "In a sense."

"Or are the Russians running *you?*"

"What the hell are you talking about?"

"I need to know what they've told you, my friend." Nolan spoke in a level tone.

"I don't follow." Metcalfe didn't bother to hide his bewilderment.

The FBI man watched him stonily; Metcalfe knew the look. It was the look of a professional interrogator who knew the power of a watchful silence. "Look, I saw you and your GRU friend together. Kundrov, right? Outside the opera house? You think I don't know you're working with him?"

"*Working* with him, did you say? Boy, have you got this all wrong. He's working with *us*—helping *us* out, at considerable risk to himself!"

Nolan emitted a short, derisive laugh. "You know the story about the guy who finds a rattlesnake on a snowy mountaintop. Rattlesnake says, 'I'm freezing here, I'm starving here. Take me down to the valley, and I promise I'll never harm you. I'm not like the others.' The guy does just that. Soon as they reach the valley, the snake bites him on the ass. Guy says, 'But you promised!' Snake says, 'Hey, you knew what I was when you picked me up.' "

"Hey, thanks for the wildlife tip. But if we don't get the flares in exactly the right position, and I mean right away—"

Nolan talked over his protests. "I'm just saying. You can't trust anything they tell you. Everything has a purpose, and the purpose is always manipulation. To sow discord. To turn people against their real friends." Nolan paused. "So what did he tell you about me?"

"What?" Metcalfe's bewilderment gave way to a surge of annoyance. He glanced at his watch again. "We didn't talk about you. Why would we have?" A moment after he spoke, he remembered that Kundrov had, in fact, asked about Nolan. *I've seen the face somewhere. Maybe in one of our face books.*

"No reason," Nolan said equably. "Hey, I'm just a flaps-and-seals guy—'peek and ye shall find,' right?"

"If you're thinking *I'm* the security breach . . . that's just *crazy*, all right?"

"Calm down, kid." Nolan continued to scrutinize Metcalfe's face, and after a few long moments he gave the younger man a wink and a smile, as if his suspicions were allayed. "I just had to know for sure."

"Listen, are you going to help me or not?" Metcalfe said, biting off the words.

"Then again, the whole art of espionage is getting people to do your dirty work without them realizing it. The Russians are masters at that. Here's the thing. In the past few weeks, I've learned about this spy ring. Very formidable, very covert. It's operating all through Europe, and even in the US of A, and it's completely compromising the integrity of American foreign policy. A Stuka dive-bomber over Washington couldn't do more damage."

"*Christ,* Chip, are you sure about this?"

"Sure as shooting, my friend. But we've been making progress against it. Rolling it up. Deadheading the bastards, one after another. Soon as I learn another name, we act. There's just too goddamn much at stake to pussyfoot around. I'm talking about a cell-based network of highly placed Americans and Europeans, many of them from old, established families, some of them belonging to the inner circles of power. It's an incredible feat, really."

"But if the Soviets put this ring in place . . ."

"I didn't say they did. They didn't have to. You gotta remember Comrade Lenin's favorite question: *Who benefits?* When you're the beneficiary of a spy ring like that, it doesn't matter who's in charge of it."

"How come Corky never mentioned this?"

"Maybe because he's part of it." Nolan winked and took a step toward Metcalfe. "And you're part of it, too."

Blood pounded in Metcalfe's ears. "Do you have any idea how *insane* you sound? There's no *time* for your paranoid fantasies. And the next time you feel like making accusations, I suggest you—"

"What you gotta appreciate is, I watch the traffic signals. I know the patterns. Believe me, I'm plugged in five ways to Sunday, in ways you can't even imagine. Russian intelligence cracks a code my friends in the *Sicherheitsdienst* assured me was unbreakable, and suddenly the GRU sends their guy to Berlin to rat me out. Next thing I know you're on the phone to Corky, who contacts me with some *cockamamie* pretext about showing up at the Brandenburg decoy site with flashlights and flares." He shook his head slowly, a disgusted smile on his face. "Sorry, I'm not buying it. I'm not in the market for any more of Corky's bullshit. Let's just be clear about that, *James*—or should I say *Stephen?*"

Metcalfe was thunderstruck. *My friends in the* Sicherheits-dienst. Recognition dawned suddenly, with a terrifying rush.

Nolan was the traitor.

It had been Nolan all along.

"Jesus Christ!" Metcalfe cried. "You're the one—you're the one who burned them all!" His mind was reeling.

The gun—a Colt .45—had somehow materialized in Nolan's hand before Metcalfe had even noticed it. It was pointed directly at Metcalfe's forehead.

The telephone rang, its bell strident and jarring.

Lana Baranova, lying in bed, watched it ring, dreading the call, the *knowing* making it all the more terrifying.

After three rings, the phone was answered, presumably by a servant, and there was silence. She lay trembling. She was packed and ready.

A few minutes later came a knock on her door.

"Yes?"

The door opened slowly. Eckbert, one of Rudi's footmen, stood there in a bathrobe, his hair uncombed. With an awkward bow he said, "*Entschuldigen Sie,* madam. I am sorry to disturb you, but there is a telephone call for you."

"The guys in the Paris station . . . There's no way the Nazis could have penetrated that without you. . . . Roger Martin . . . Amos Hilliard . . . It was *you!*" Metcalfe could feel his heart thudding.

Chip's ruddy face was shiny with perspiration. His watery gray eyes seemed dead. "You give me more credit than I deserve, pal. I just point the SD in the right direction, give 'em names and locations when I learn stuff. They have people who do the . . . housecleaning."

"The housecleaning . . ." Metcalfe echoed. A gruesome mental image of Scoop Martin, garroted, flashed into his head. Of Amos Hilliard. Of Derek Compton-Jones and Johnny Betts, in Paris. . . . Now a surge of anger overtook him. He looked at the barrel of the gun that was aimed directly at him. It was like a fierce staring black eye. He raised his glance to Chip's eyes, which looked like another set of boreholes. "Put down the gun, Chip," he said.

"Look, sometimes patriots have to make ugly choices," Nolan said. The gun didn't waver. "The world isn't a pretty place. You've got to choose sides."

"Choose . . . *sides?*" Metcalfe exploded. "And you're on . . . what side? The side of the *fascists?* The *Nazis? Adolf Hitler?*"

"I'm on the side of realism, fella. I'm on the side of a stronger America. Not the soft socialism of the welfare state, which is what Roosevelt and his pro-Soviet New Dealers have been trying to turn America into. See, Metcalfe, if you weren't so blinded to what's going on around you, maybe you could face the brutal facts. There are thousands of Communists on the payroll in Washington, and Roosevelt knows about it. What does he say? He says, 'Some of my best friends are Communists.' Who's his closest adviser?"

"Harry Hopkins. Put down the gun, Chip."

"Correct. Harry Hopkins. A known Soviet agent of influence. Actually *lives* in the White House. Most of Roosevelt's Brain Trust are card-carrying members of the Communist Party. Trucklers to their 'Uncle Joe.' 'Uncle Joe is a good man to know,' the comrades say. What's the first thing Roosevelt did when he came into office? Recognized the Soviet Union—legitimized the thugs who stole Russia, the Bolshies who made it clear they want to spread Communism around the whole goddamned world. Roosevelt and his Red-loving cronies want to hand the world over to the Soviet slave empire. Establish one-world government, run out of Moscow. You don't get it, do you, Metcalfe?"

"I get the fact that you're a goddamned *fascist*," Metcalfe said quietly.

"That's just a word," Chip snapped back. "The National Socialists, the Nazis, the fascists—call 'em what you will, I don't care—you better pray they're the wave of the future. Whether you agree or disagree with Hitler, you'd have to be a fool not to see how he took a rotten, decayed country, overrun by Jews and Communists, and cleaned it up, built it into a goddamned *powerhouse*, the strongest, most powerful nation in Europe."

"A tyranny is what it is."

"No, pal. A 'tyranny' is what the Slavic hordes are perpetrating in Russia, with their genocide against the white race. Tell me something, Metcalfe: did your rich Social Register parents raise you to be a pinko, or did you get converted at Yale?"

Metcalfe smiled. "So that's what you think—that I'm a Communist."

"No, you're not a Commie, Metcalfe. You know what you are?

You're what Lenin called a 'useful idiot.' That's what he called all the mindless pro-Soviet apologists and lickspittles in Western democracies who always seem to defend the Communist Internationale no matter how brutal it is. Now all you useful idiots are trying to push us into a war against a nation that poses no threat to us. So millions of American boys can die overseas to make Europe safe for Uncle Joe."

"The 'nation that poses no threat to us'—you're talking about Nazi *Germany?* The Third Reich? Whose tanks have already rolled into France and Poland, Norway and Denmark and Holland—"

"*Lebensraum.* Call it breathing room. I guess you haven't noticed how your Uncle Joe's been grabbing up real estate right and left while we've been staring down Hitler, huh? He's already invaded Finland and Lithuania, Latvia and Estonia, big chunks of Romania, Poland. . . . And the war's scarcely started. Roosevelt and his Bolshevik masters aren't happy with the way Hitler defeated Communism in Germany. Nazi Germany is the only brake on Bolshevism we've got. No wonder Roosevelt wants to get us into war. This is a titanic global conflict, buddy, and America's being pushed over to the wrong side of it. The White House and the striped-pants boys in the State Department, they're all whoring for Uncle Joe, and then Roosevelt had his asshole buddy Alfred Corcoran sending agents all around the world to fight Hitler, the only real friend we have. Agents like you, Metcalfe, are actually doing something. You're in the field, conducting operations, and that makes you a real menace. Because if men like you aren't stopped, your friends in Moscow will soon be going through Europe like shit through a goose."

Metcalfe just nodded. "I'm getting the picture now. That's why you wanted to know about Kundrov. You weren't sure whether Soviet intelligence was on to you. You were afraid he might have blown your cover."

Nolan shrugged. "There was only one way to be sure. I had to meet you myself and look into those puppy-dog eyes."

"Which means we must be alone," Metcalfe went on, half thinking aloud. "You'd never show yourself to the rank and file. Not you. You just might be the Reich's most highly placed asset in the United States intelligence services. There'd be too many possibilities for exposure."

"You're right that I'd never allow myself to be seen that way. No, if I had any backup, it would have to be someone I had complete confidence in. Someone I'd worked with personally. Discretion is all-important, naturally. But you know us G-men. We're great believers in the buddy system. Not like your gasbag Corcoran, with his fucking *compartmentation*. Christ, what a phony he was. A goddamned phony, and a menace."

"Was?" Metcalfe said weakly.

"Ah, the past tense. Right. I'm afraid my friends paid him a visit a few hours ago. I'm afraid he's no longer with us. I hear the old man pissed his pants. Pity about his housekeeper, Frau Schibli, but she was just in the way."

"You *goddamned bastard!*" Metcalfe roared.

Nolan released one hand from the weapon and made a slight signal.

Metcalfe heard a movement from behind, like the whispery sound of a striking snake, and suddenly something drew tight around Metcalfe's neck. *He couldn't breathe!* Some sort of wire sliced into his throat.

"Thanks, Herr Kleist," Nolan said. He made another gesture with his hand, and the wire suddenly loosened.

Metcalfe coughed. The pain where the wire had cut into his throat was intense, like a band of fire.

"My German friends have a few more questions for you," Nolan said. "We're just going to have to go through them. Now, one more time: what were you doing in Berlin?"

"Drop dead, you miserable bastard!" Metcalfe's voice was gravelly; the wire had already bruised his larynx.

"After you, kid," Nolan said, giving him another grotesque wink. "After you. Listen, you can forget all the game playing. The noble defiance? Duly noted. But you're performing to an audience that isn't here. You ever see a calf that's got itself caught in a fence, and finds itself slowly strangling? Guess not, not where you come from. But it's a horrible sight. There's something primal about it—it's like you're drowning ever so slowly, and you're panicking, and it's just the worst thing. A horrible way to die."

At a hand signal from Nolan, the wire around his neck grew incrementally tenser. Metcalfe felt his face grow red, as if blood were being pumped into his head but couldn't leave. It seemed that tiny cluster bombs of agony were being detonated inside his skull.

I just point the SD in the right direction . . . They have people who do the . . . housecleaning.

It was the assassin from Paris, from Moscow! The one who'd killed Roger Martin, Amos Hilliard, the men in the Paris wireless station. . . .

Nolan's voice sounded far away as he spoke in a voice of inexorable calm. "Just let it all go, Stephen," he said, almost tenderly. "Everything you ever did, and everything you never got to do. All the women you screwed, and all the women you never got to screw—you've just got to let it all go."

Another hand signal: abruptly the wire loosened and the agony began to drain away. "You begin to see what I'm talking about? Understand, I hate to do this. I truly do. But like I say, you've gotta choose sides, and you chose the wrong one. Now, you gonna level with me? No?" A sorrowful look. "Herr Kleist, kindly resume."

"Wait!" Metcalfe blurted out.

"I'm sorry, Metcalfe. I take no pleasure in this. But there's the greater good to be considered."

"You're absolutely right," Metcalfe gasped. "I *have* been used. I've been a *tool.*"

Chip stared back suspiciously. "Forgive me if I take this deathbed conversion with a grain of salt."

"Truth is, it's been on my mind for a while now," Metcalfe

said. Speaking was painful, but he forced himself to go on.
"Guess you can't lie to yourself forever. I just didn't know what
Corky was getting me into. He sent me over to Russia to enlist
certain influential government officials in a plan to attack Germany. But you knew that already, didn't you?"

Nolan peered closely at Metcalfe's face and nodded fractionally.
"Go on."

"That's what I'm here working on. I—Jesus, Chip, what the
hell did I know? I was just a kid fresh out of college with stars
in my eyes, I was going to save the world, and this wise old
mentor takes me under his wing. Jesus! I *have* been blind."

Now Chip seemed to hesitate. He didn't lower his weapon, but
Metcalfe could see the tension in the FBI man's trigger finger
slacken just a bit. The bait was irresistible to Chip; he couldn't
pass up the lure. "Tell me about the plan," Chip said.

"God, it's brilliant. I mean, really amazing," Metcalfe said con-
fidingly. He glanced to one side, then the other, as if making sure
he wasn't overheard. *Action's always twice as fast as reaction,* Metcalfe thought. *The sudden, unexpected movement. That's the only
way.* Yet where was the assassin behind him? The angle of the
grip around his throat suggested that the killer was approximately
Metcalfe's height, and the fact that he couldn't feel the warmth
of the man's breath suggested that he was standing at least two
feet away—and, given the mechanics of the garrote, probably no
more than two feet away. Metcalfe went on: "This guy Kundrov
that I met with earlier today? Obviously you know he's GRU,
right?"

Chip nodded.

He's not aiming now, Metcalfe thought. *He's listening raptly,
paying attention to what I'm saying; he can't focus well on two
things.*

"Well, here's the clever part." He leaned in toward Chip, a
natural motion of a man confiding a secret, felt a warning tug
around his throat. Suddenly, with lightning speed, he shot out
his right hand and grabbed the barrel of the gun close to the

trigger guard, abruptly shoving it upward. At the same instant, he jackhammered his left elbow backward, in the anticipated direction of his strangler's solar plexus. A sudden expulsion of breath from behind him confirmed the accuracy of his powerful blow. Now he spun his body away from the line of fire before lunging forward, diagonally, at Chip. The Colt exploded deafeningly, echoing in the vast space, the bullet pinging against the corrugated-steel ceiling, just as Metcalfe threw his weight against Chip's body and slammed the FBI man to the floor.

Crumpled on the floor, a few feet away, was a handsome, aristocratic-looking man with finely wrought features.

"You *bastard!*" Chip roared as the two men wrestled for control of the gun. With one final thrust of his hand, Metcalfe managed to wrest the Colt from Chip's hand, but it went flying into the air, then clattered to the concrete floor fifty feet away. Chip turned to see where the weapon had gone, and at that moment Metcalfe slammed his knee into Chip's groin. "Goddamned *Nazi!*" Metcalfe shouted, then kneed Chip again once more for emphasis.

Chip screamed in pain and doubled over.

Metcalfe turned toward the second man—Nolan's "Herr Kleist"—who had bounded to his feet and was now racing like a jackal toward the Colt. Metcalfe had to get it first. He withdrew his own gun from the small of his back and bounded after the assassin, his eyes alert for the telltale glint of metal. *Where was it?* The gun was nowhere to be seen. And where was the German? Both had seemingly vanished.

Metcalfe looked around him. There were too many hiding places, too many pieces of heavy machinery that could conceal an armed assassin. And the gun in his hand gave him no advantage.

He had to get out of there. *Now.*

Metcalfe raced down the nearest aisle and out into another area of the lot. He ran, his legs pistoning, for what seemed half the length of a football field before darting into another enclosed soundstage. He had to make a plan—had to turn himself from prey to predator.

The consequences of failure were too great. The rendezvous point would be turned into an ambush, ensuring not just his own death but Lana's as well.

He slid to the floor, beside a papier-mâché Alpine peak, breathing heavily. Probably the two were fanning out, each covering half of the lot. But had either one of them seen him enter?

A faint noise, then a louder one, provided his answer. He heard footsteps and immediately recognized Chip's lumbering walk.

He had to get out of there, stealthily. In the gloom, he made out a wooden door, a hundred feet away. Quickly, quietly, he made his way there and grabbed the knob.

Which came right off.

The door was a fake! It was nothing more than a painted board, the door frame and door an appliqué of thin wood a quarter of an inch thick glued on top of a piece of lumber four by eight feet.

Metcalfe shoved it, but it was too sturdy, probably reinforced from behind.

Then he heard Chip's footsteps grow nearer, saw Chip running down the aisle toward him, his Colt in his hand once again. Fifty feet, thirty feet . . .

Metcalfe was trapped.

To his left was a large metal trash bin four feet tall and six feet long. It was dented and rusted, but its several layers of sheet metal would serve as a shield against the Colt's bullets. Just as Chip came to a halt and assumed a two-handed firing stance, Metcalfe dived behind the trash bin. There was silence: Chip was probably repositioning himself to try to aim around the steel obstruction.

Metcalfe took advantage of the lull to get his Smith & Wesson chambered and ready to fire.

Suddenly there came a volley of gunfire, and Metcalfe felt an icicle-like incision in his right shoulder. A bullet had lodged just below his collarbone. He gasped; the pain was incredible. How could this have happened? As warm blood oozed into his clothing, he realized with horror: This was no metal trash container. It was stretched muslim on a frame of wood! The bullet had easily pierced a few sheets of cloth before entering his body.

He rolled over on the concrete floor, hoping that at least the change in position would protect him from another round. Another shot, and then one more, penetrated the prop but missed. Metcalfe scrambled to his knees and scuttled along the floor, the prop now serving as a curtain at least to obscure him from Chip's aim.

Another lull. Was Chip repositioning, racing closer? Why wasn't he just firing again? After all, he couldn't have been more than ten or fifteen feet away.

Then Metcalfe heard a metallic clanging on the floor, and he recognized the sound of an ammunition cartridge being ejected. Chip was reloading! Metcalfe leaped to his feet and raced down the adjoining aisle, not daring to look back. In a moment he was easily thirty or forty feet away; he knew he could count on the inaccuracy of Chip's handgun at more than twenty feet. He began weaving erratically from side to side as he ran, almost lurching like a drunk, but there was a logic: he knew that an unpredictable moving target was extremely difficult to hit, especially as the distance between them grew. He glanced back now, saw that Chip had once again assumed his firing stance and was shifting his weapon back and forth, trying to hone in on his target.

Chip recognized what he was doing and lowered his gun, then raced toward Metcalfe. A moment too late Metcalfe saw a ten-foot-high scale model of a castle—Mad King Ludwig's famous Schloss Neuschwanstein. He was too close; he couldn't stop himself in time from colliding with it. The plywood shuddered, chunks of plaster came raining down, and one of its spires flew off. With a long creaking sound, the castle tipped forward, smashing onto the floor directly in Chip's path.

The plywood wreck knocked Chip off balance, buying Metcalfe a few more precious seconds. He spun around toward Chip and squeezed off a carefully aimed shot. A metallic cough was followed by a guttural cry. He had hit Chip!

He squeezed the trigger once more, but nothing.

The gun was empty.

He reached into his pocket to grab a handful of bullets, but they were gone. They must have fallen out at some point. *He had no more ammunition!*

He had no choice, now: he had to keep running. Metcalfe searched for a way out and saw one, a few aisles down. A steel door: he thought it was genuine, though he couldn't be sure.

A long row of wooden crates separated this aisle from the next. The crates were too tall to jump over, but in front of them was a wooden worktable that was low enough to use as an intermediate step from which to vault over them. He leaped on top of the table—and it collapsed. Shit! It was a balsawood breakaway table, another prop, probably left over from some slapstick comedy.

His knees slammed painfully onto the concrete floor. Pain was now flooding his body, from his knees up to his collarbone. He was breathing hard, finding it difficult to catch his breath. He could feel that his shirt was soaked with blood: a good deal of blood had been lost.

A shout: Chip's voice. "I heard that," he said, breathing hard as well. "Out of ammo. Tough luck, kid. You should always be prepared. One of those lessons you learn a little too late, huh?"

Metcalfe didn't reply.

"You're going to die today, Metcalfe. You might as well face it. But look on the bright side. It'll be the most valuable thing you ever do. The planet is gonna be a hell of a lot safer without you on it."

As Metcalfe got to his feet, his eye was caught by one of the crates a few inches from his head.

It was filled with weapons.

There were antique machine guns, some ridiculously outdated. Some MG-34s, some MP-43 assault rifles, MP-38 machine pistols. Antique stick hand grenades, some smaller egg-shaped ones. They were World-War-One-vintage dummy weapons that had been used in the Brandenburg Studios' many war films.

Quietly Metcalfe reached into the crate and removed a Luger 9mm Parabellum semiautomatic weapon, a P-38. Also circa the Great War. But it was entirely plausible. It wouldn't fire—but it looked authentic. Glancing to his left, he saw Chip's legs flailing as he tried to free himself from the plywood debris. He slipped the Luger into his coat pocket, then raced farther down the aisle until he came to the replica of the Manhattan apartment, complete with ivory grand piano and a large chandelier. The chandelier hung low over the apartment, apparently intended to be within the camera frame, but it dangled from an ugly plain rope that was tied to what looked like a tall iron ship's mast, another section of iron rod jutting forward at a perpendicular. It appeared to be a microphone boom that had been retrofitted. Metcalfe pulled at the iron mast and knocked it over toward where Chip was just getting to his feet. It missed him narrowly but blocked his path.

Metcalfe shoved at the barrier of wooden crates, and a few of them gave way. He managed to crash through to the next aisle, then ran toward the steel door.

It was *real*, he saw with relief.

He pulled it open, saw that it did not lead to the outdoors. There was a dark stairwell that wound around down, presumably to a basement, or up. Up where? A roof?

The roof seemed a safer alternative than the basement, where he might find himself trapped. He sprinted up the stairs, trying his best to ignore the pain in his shoulder, which was steadily increasing, and the dull ache in his kneecaps. Soon he reached another steel door, flung it open, and saw that it gave onto the roof of the building. A flat tar-and-gravel roof. The moonlight provided ample illumination, allowing him to run across the expanse of the roof. When he neared the edge, he realized that the drop to the ground had to be a hundred feet: enough to kill him or at least injure him so badly that he would not be able to move. One of the dummy brick buildings was close, however; it was no more than six feet away. Smoke poured from its four chimneys. If he took a running leap he should be able to make it. He had jumped across wider chasms between Paris rooftops.

A clamor of footsteps told him that Chip had followed him up. A few seconds later, Chip burst through the doorway.

"Go ahead and jump, asshole!" he shouted. "One way or another you're dead. I don't really care how it happens." He advanced across the gravel slowly, deliberately, his gun drawn.

Metcalfe backed up a few feet, took off running, then jumped into the air, pulling his feet up under him in preparation to break his fall.

Then everything seemed to happen all at once. He was propelled through the air and landed square onto the bluestone roof of the brick building, just as Chip shouted, "Die, you bastard!" A moment later, Chip fired off a shot; Metcalfe could see the deliberate, calm aim of the FBI man and knew that the bullet was going to hit him.

But even as Chip was shouting at him, Metcalfe could feel his feet crashing through the bluestone roof as if it were made of marzipan. As he plummeted down, he felt the bullet whiz by so close he could feel the disturbance in the air.

In the next instant, Metcalfe hit something hard. The floor of the building? No, it was the ground, the earth soft, recently plowed. He groaned, wondered whether he'd broken a leg. He tested himself, felt both of his legs. He had not. He was in pain— Christ, yet *more* pain!—but his limbs were intact.

He'd known the brick structure was fake, but he hadn't known how flimsy it was. The roof must have been some sort of fabric, painted to look like bluestone; he had torn through it, the fabric slowing his descent just enough to keep his landing from crippling him.

Now Metcalfe looked around in wonderment. The "building" was nothing more than a large box constructed of beams and joists of two-by-four lumber, an armature over which was stretched canvas that, outside, was painted to look exactly like brick. As his eyes swept the interior, he was jolted to see several men standing by one of the ground-level windows. Then he realized that they were mannequins—lifelike human dummies attired in men's clothing, posed near the cut-out windows to simulate factory workers. Arrayed around the ground were four rectangular metal boxes, each connected by a short length of pipe to tall two-hundred-liter oil drums. Emerging from each contraption was a long, wide hose that ran all the way up to the four false chimneys.

He knew what these were instantly. They were the mechanical smoke generators that pumped out the smoke billowing from the chimneys.

On the battlefield they were used, usually on tanks, to generate a smoke screen over a wide area for tactical deception, to screen troops, to foil reconnaissance and surveillance. The British used crude versions of them, called smudge pots, to hide the Vauxhall Motors plant at Luton from daytime enemy bombers. The Germans used these more sophisticated devices by the thousands to conceal the oil refineries they'd seized at Ploiesti, Romania.

The machines ran on diesel fuel that flowed from the attached oil drums. Here they furthered another type of deception: they created the illusion of a working factory.

He heard footsteps, *two* sets now! Obviously Nolan's German partner, the SD assassin, had heard the noise and rushed over.

Swiveling his head around, Metcalfe saw that there was just one entrance; it would not be safe to exit there, since his pursuer or pursuers were surely entering that way. He ran behind a storage cabinet, out of sight, just as Chip's voice boomed out: "You're a cornered rat, Metcalfe. No way out of here. Throw down your weapon, hands in the air, and we can talk!"

Talk funeral arrangements, maybe, Metcalfe thought. One of the smoke generators was within reach, connected by hoses to both a fuel drum and the chimney directly above.

He shot out his hand, yanked off the smoke exhaust hose. At once a great cloud of white smoke began billowing into the enclosed space, creating a low, white cloud.

But Chip had already reached the other side of the cabinet. Metcalfe could see him through a crack in the cabinet; the FBI man was limping. Chip had been shot in the leg. But his concentration seemed unaffected. He was looking from side to side, obviously considering which direction to turn.

Metcalfe did not want to give him the benefit of the choice.

He drew out his dummy Luger revolver and suddenly leaped out, aiming the weapon at Chip's face. Chip flinched, raised his gun as well.

The fog was filling the structure, already having risen to the level of the men's knees.

"I told you, Stephen, you're gonna die today," Chip said.

"After *you*, asshole," Metcalfe replied. "Looks like a standoff to me."

Chip's eyes locked on Metcalfe's, but there was a flicker of uncertainty on his face. The fake gun had worked. It did not have to be fired to be effective.

Metcalfe continued with bravado, as if the gun were loaded with 9mm cartridges, "So what's your move, Chip? Who's gonna win?"

"Depends on who has the bigger balls," Chip snapped. He attempted a smile.

Metcalfe saw in his peripheral vision the German assassin slipping in through the entrance from outside. "Or who least minds dying," Metcalfe said. "I'm just a small fish, right? One of many field operatives trying to fight the battle. Whereas you're a major cog in the machinery. One of the Nazis' favorite turncoats. If you're killed, it's a big loss for the fascist world—isn't that right?"

———

The violinist stepped silently through the thick white haze. He could see nothing. Worst of all, he could smell nothing. The acrid smoke burned his delicate nasal membranes, blunting his olfactory sense, his finest weapon.

Without it, he felt lost. He felt a curious disorientation verging on panic. He wandered cautiously through the fog, his hands outstretched, his left hand clutching the violin string.

He thought he heard something.

Rattlesnake-fast, he struck. Grabbing the other end of the violin string to form a loop, he lashed out, drew it tight around his victim's neck—

And then he realized that he was garroting something hard, something wooden.

A *mannequin.*

In disgust, he loosened the string and forged ahead through the cloud.

Without his olfactory weapon, the violinist knew, he was disabled. But that would not stop him, he vowed, from completing his assignment.

The smoke had reached their shoulders already. It was an eerie sensation, as if they were standing immersed in a cloud, just their heads sticking up. The smoke, denser and more opaque than any naturally occurring fog, stung Metcalfe's eyes. Where was the second man, the one Nolan had called Herr Kleist? *Must be alert—must not let the other one sneak up on me while I'm engaged in this standoff with Chip.*

"Actually, I don't plan to be killed. You, on the other hand . . ." Chip hesitated, lowered his gaze to the weapon in Metcalfe's hand. "I didn't give you a Luger," he said.

Metcalfe shrugged. "You're not my only source of armaments."

"A German gun, huh?"

"Strange thing," Metcalfe said glibly. "The Jerrys only seem to have Jerry guns. Can you beat that?"

"It's an *antique!*"

"You take what you're offered. Wartime privation, and all that."

"That's. Jesus, that's . . . that's a goddamned *fake!* The god-damn borehole's *plugged*—!"

Metcalfe did not wait for Chip to react. He lunged, slamming himself against Chip with all his weight, knocking him backward onto the dirt, the two of them enveloped by the oily smoke. Metcalfe's eyes burned as he wrestled with Chip for the gun.

His body was wracked with pain, which diminished his strength markedly. But Chip seemed equally weakened. Still, he reared up with enormous strength, roaring in anger, unwilling to relinquish his grip on the weapon, even as Metcalfe gradually forced it backward so that it was pointing back toward Chip himself.

"Hey, Yale boy—it'll be skull and bones at last!" Chip Nolan panted, a sneer on his lips, his right hand and arm trembling with muscular exertion as Metcalfe forced the other man's hand back toward himself. It was some grim variant of arm wrestling. "*Your* skull and bones." The gun, firmly in the FBI agent's grip, pointed first toward Metcalfe, then back at Chip, back and forth like a child's toy. With a sudden furious surge of strength, Chip shoved the gun toward Metcalfe as he began to squeeze the trigger. His hand spasmed; the gun shook violently. Yet Chip had overestimated his own strength, and he could not withstand Metcalfe's counterforce. At the very instant that Chip's finger squeezed the trigger, the FBI man's wrist gave way, snapping backward, the gun pointing up at Chip's eyes, which widened in terror as the realization dawned of what was about to happen.

The explosion filled Metcalfe's ears as he saw the horrifying sight of the back of Chip's head coming off. Blood spattered his face. He collapsed, sinking back to the ground, utterly spent.

Acrid white fog surrounded him entirely; he was blind, immobilized by the pain of his wound, gasping for breath.

He heard a scuffing noise.

A whispering, slithering sound, like a snake in the sand.

Some vestigial instinct made him reach a hand behind him. He felt something touch his neck, his wrist, something cold and metallic, and suddenly draw tight around his neck, constricting it with immense force. He was being strangled—and with a ferocity ten times greater than before! He lurched upward, whipping his body to one side and then the other, summoning reserves of strength he didn't know he still possessed. He roared, but all that came out was a gurgle.

A few fingers of his right hand were trapped against his neck by the wire, or whatever it was, rendering his right hand useless. He thrust out his left hand, balled into a fist, swinging around until he connected with his attacker.

They have people who do the . . . housecleaning.

This was the man who did the housecleaning.

The assassin from the *Sicherheitsdienst* was going to finish his assignment. The vicious killer who had garroted the men in Paris and Amos Hilliard and his good friend Roger Martin . . .

And who intended to garrote Metcalfe.

Images of the dead men flashed across his eyes as the metal wire sliced into his neck, only the fingers of his right hand keeping the garrote from severing his carotid artery, slicing through the delicate tissue of his neck. He couldn't see, his stinging eyes blurred by the dense smoke, everything around him a blur. He was surrounded by opaque white smoke; he couldn't see more than a few inches in front of him! He arched his back, furiously rolling over, kicking at his would-be murderer, punching, connecting with the other man's body. But this time the strangler was standing too close for his blows to have any force. The wire drew ever tighter against his neck, cutting off the circulation until Metcalfe felt light-headed, pinpoints of light flashing in the opaque white haze. *He couldn't breathe!*

No, he *couldn't* give in to the killer; he couldn't let the man from the *Sicherheitsdienst* vanquish him. There was Lana, always Lana. She would be arriving momentarily, in a car driven by Kundrov, and a few minutes after that a British Lysander plane would land and he and Lana would climb in and be flown to England and then back home, home to safety. Lana would be saved; she would be free, and all the work they had done, the documents she had given von Schüssler, would be legitimized, believed by high-level Nazi officials.

Lana would be safe, and the Nazi war machine, embroiled in a conflict it could not hope to win, would be defeated. It had to happen; it *would* happen! Everything hinged on Lana arriving and the two of them getting on that Lysander and being spirited away to safety. The fate of two people hung on it; the fate of *millions* hung on it.

He could not be killed now!

With his only free hand he grabbed hold of one of his attacker's hands at the back of his neck, a hand that was pulling the garrote so unbelievably tight against Metcalfe's throat. As Metcalfe arched his back again, struggling with all of his body, he seized several fingers of the killer's hands, separating two of the fingers, peeling them apart from the iron grip, pulling, *pulling* against them. Now the killer was drawing the wire even more tightly against his neck, tighter than Metcalfe thought possible, and he was on the verge of losing consciousness. His trapped, gashed right hand was useless in the struggle—though it was at the same time saving him, for without his fingers there, the wire would have already sliced through his neck.

Metcalfe's whole body was trembling, shuddering with exertion. He would not let go of his grip on the killer's fingers; finally, he was able to grab hold of the fingers fully, pulling them backward until he felt, *heard,* a snap. He had broken the fingers! The killer screamed in pain and fury, and the choke hold went slack. Metcalfe took in a gulp of air. His feet swung around, hitting something, a hard object he couldn't see but realized was one of the two-hundred-liter fuel drums.

Yes! The *fuel!* The *oil . . . slippery* oil!

If only he could knock over the drum, let its viscous, greasy contents pour out.

He scissored both of his feet forward, letting go of the assassin's broken fingers with his only free hand, lunging to one side even as the garrote pulled tighter . . . and then he shoved hard against the barrel. It tipped over, the hose tearing free of the opening, and the liquid began to gush, to spray out freely.

But it was not engine oil, it was *gasoline!* It was not greasy; it would *not* work.

Suddenly the wire at his throat came loose.

The assassin screamed as the gasoline sprayed into his eyes, temporarily blinding him; drenched, the German jumped back, out of the way. Metcalfe broke free, lurched forward. He stumbled into a hard object, shrouded in the opaque fog. One of the smoke generators: he could see the blue flame at its base still burning the gasoline that remained. Metcalfe shoved the machine toward the German. It crashed into him and fell noisily to the floor by his feet.

And then there was a flash of light.

An orange flash that, a split second later, exploded into an immense, blazing fireball. Metcalfe heard the bellow of a wounded animal, and he saw the sphere of flames moving toward him.

The pain was incalculable, extraordinary, even exquisite. The violinist knew he was being burned alive. He screamed with every fiber of his being, as if screaming would diminish the agony, though in fact the agony was unbearable.

It was not as unbearable, however, as the knowledge that he was not going to complete his assignment—that the American would not be killed.

He screamed until his vocal cords gave out, as the flames engulfed his body. He knew he was going to die; he was unable to snuff out the flames by rolling in the dirt. The fire was too great, too consuming, and he could no longer move, in any case.

But then he was pleased to notice that his sense of smell had returned. His nostrils were filled with a distinctive overpowering odor, which he identified at once. It was, he realized, the smell of burning flesh.

His own burning flesh.

Through the penumbra of the fireball, Metcalfe saw the man's limbs flailing. The scream was shrill, weirdly high, a horrible keening, an animal noise. In another couple of seconds, the fireball had stopped moving; it roared, shooting flames high into the air, licking against the wooden frame of the decoy structure, which immediately caught fire as well. Metcalfe turned back around and ran, just as the entire building burst into flames.

He did not stop running until he had reached the pavement, and then he sank to the ground. The plywood-and-canvas structure was now a massive, roaring fire. He could feel the heat, even a hundred feet away.

The killer was dead.

Both killers were dead. But where was *Lana?* Where was *Kundrov?* He looked at his watch. The plane was scheduled to touch down momentarily, and he hadn't even set up the flares. If the pilot saw no flares, he would assume the rendezvous had been scrapped and he would not land.

As Metcalfe headed toward the field, which was now illuminated by the orange light of the burning structure, he heard the screech of brakes. He turned and saw Kundrov behind the wheel of a black automobile. The door was flung open, and Kundrov jumped out.

"*Bozhe moi!*" the Russian shouted. "*Pozhar*—the fire!" He ran closer. "You—you've been shot! What happened?"

"Where is she?" Metcalfe said

Kundrov, grim-faced, shook his head.

Metcalfe grabbed him by the shoulders. "Where *is* she?" he repeated. Kundrov's eyes were red-rimmed. "You were supposed to pick her up at the *schloss*—what happened? What have you *done* with her?"

Kundrov shook his head again. "She wasn't there."

"What do you mean she wasn't there?"

"Von Schüssler was there. She was gone."

"*Gone?* What the hell do you mean, *gone?* The NKVD came early, is *that* what happened? God *damn* you, did they come for her *early?* How could this happen?"

"No!" Kundrov shouted. "She told von Schüssler that there was an emergency in Moscow, that she had to return at once. She asked to be taken at once to the railroad station."

"But that was the *ruse,* she understood that!"

Kundrov spoke in a feeble monotone as if he'd been hypnotized. He shook his head slowly. "Von Schüssler was distraught, but he said she insisted on being taken to the station immediately. He agreed to have his chauffeur take her to the Ostbahnhof. The chauffeur found that the Daimler was missing—I can see where it went—and took her in another vehicle."

"Did they kidnap her?"

"I seriously doubt it. She went voluntarily."

"But why?" Metcalfe cried. "Why did she *do* this?"

"Let me tell you something. I have amassed probably two thousand dossier pages on this woman. My observations of her have been more extensive than any other surveillance ever conducted on a Soviet citizen. I have watched her closely, intimately, for years. Yet I cannot say that I understand the woman."

Metcalfe looked up at the moonlit sky. A faint high-pitched whine in the distance, which he'd been vaguely aware of for the last minute or so, had become the distinctive buzz-saw drone of a Lysander. It appeared just over the horizon.

"The flares!" Metcalfe shouted.

"For what?" Kundrov called back. "Without her, what's the point?"

"Jesus Christ!" The two men stood there frozen, staring up into the sky as the Lysander made a slow loop above the field. In a moment it was gone.

Metcalfe glanced at his watch again. "In less than half an hour, the train stops at the Ostbahnhof. If we drive at top speed, we can just make it there."

They arrived at the Gothic cathedral-like railroad station, its grimy facade unlit, sodium-yellow light coming faintly through the tall windows. The station was deserted; their footsteps echoed as they ran, stopping only to look up at the timetable sign to locate the platform number.

The platform was empty. The train waited there; sleeping passengers could be seen through its darkened windows. A final alarm tone was sounding as they raced down the platform.

A small group of men in dark suits were clustered at the far end of the platform, the only people boarding the train. Metcalfe ran as fast as he had ever run, running through the pain, seeing only Lana's face ahead of him. But the men had gotten on the train by the time he got there, and he could see no woman among them. *Was she truly here? Was she already on the train?*

Where was she? He wanted to scream out her name; he was screaming inside. His heart raced, fear flooding his body.

Where was she?

Kundrov caught up, panting. "Those men were NKVD. I recognize the type too well. She must be on the train. They're escorts, the followers."

Metcalfe nodded. He stared into the train compartment that the men had just entered, walking by slowly, looking into each one, desperate, terrified.

Lana!

He screamed silently.

Then he screamed aloud: "Lana! Lana!"

With a pneumatic hiss of the brakes, the train came to life and started moving. He ran alongside the train, looking into each window, screaming her name. "Please, Lana! Dear God!"

Then he saw her.

She was seated in a row with the dark-suited men on either side of her; she looked up. Their eyes met.

"Lana!" he screamed. His voice filled the station, reverberating hollowly.

She was wearing a head scarf, the only makeup the rouge on her lips. She turned away.

"Lana!" he screamed again.

Once more she looked up, and again their eyes met, and now Metcalfe saw something in her beautiful eyes that chilled him to the core. It was a piercing look that said, *I know what I'm doing. I've made my decision. Stand back.*

This is my life, her expression told him. *This death shall be, too. I will not be deterred.*

He shouted again, this time a question: "Lana?"

He saw the resignation and determination in her face. She gave a tiny, fractional shake of the head and then turned away.

"*No!*" he shouted with fathomless agony.

Now she looked straight ahead with a grim, steely resolve. In her luminous face were terror and defiance and, curiously, the deep serenity of someone who has at last made up her mind.

CHAPTER THIRTY-EIGHT

Moscow, the Lubyanka

The small, pale-haired man with the ghostly pallor turned around and walked out of the execution chamber. For all the executions he had witnessed on behalf of his boss, Chief Investigator Rubashov, he still found them horrifying. Then again, everything the NKVD did was repulsive to him, which was why he felt fortunate to have been given the opportunity a year or so ago to work secretly for the Germans. He would do anything to defeat the Soviet terror machine. About the Nazis he knew little; all he needed to know, all he cared about, was that Hitler was determined to vanquish the hateful Soviet state. If the intelligence he secretly provided to Berlin could hasten the day of Stalin's downfall, he counted himself a lucky man indeed.

The pallid aide-de-camp mentally clocked the precise time of death. The *Abwehr* would want to know all of the details. They would also want all transcripts of the interrogations of the woman. She was an extravagantly beautiful woman, one of the greatest ballerinas in all of Russia—and yet she, too, was an agent for Berlin! The torture she had undergone had been brutal, but eventually she had confessed to having stolen top-secret military documents from her father, a general, and passed them to her lover, a German diplomat.

To the pale-haired man, the ballerina was a heroine. She had been a secret enemy of the Kremlin and a spy for Berlin, just as he was. But she had withstood many hours of torment beyond imagining before she had confessed. He wondered if he possessed the fortitude, the courage, that this woman had shown before she finally broke down and told all, as everyone eventually did.

The tarpaulin that had been spread down on the floor of the

execution chamber was sprayed with the beautiful woman's blood, an image that remained in his mind and would remain there forever. Soon the body would be taken away, and then the cleaning woman would come to mop up. All the details of Svetlana Baranova's execution would be buried by the NKVD, her death intended to be anonymous.

But he would see to it that this brave woman did not die in vain.

Tonight when he returned home and wrote up his report to send to the *Abwehr,* he would reveal to them everything he knew about the woman's valiant service on behalf of the Nazis.

Berlin needed to know the truth. Not only was it his job to report everything about it, but he also felt it was the least he could do to honor the ballerina's bravery.

Berlin

Admiral Canaris had to admit that he relished what he was about to say. He addressed his remarks directly to Reinhard Heydrich, who had been raising questions all along about the authenticity of his source in Moscow.

"Our assets in the Lubyanka have just confirmed our numerous secondhand reports: that the source who has been providing us with so many valuable documents on Stalin's Operation WOLFSFALLE has just been executed."

"So the pipeline has been cut off!" cried Field Marshal Wilhelm Keitel. "This is a disaster!"

Canaris watched Heydrich's reptilian eyes. Heydrich was an evil man, but he was also brilliant. Like Canaris, he understood what this meant. But Heydrich would say nothing. His campaign to undermine Canaris and the *Abwehr* had just been defeated.

"It is regrettable," said Canaris calmly. "It is a most unfortunate development. It is indeed tragic that this woman gave her life for our cause." He did not have to spell out what everyone now realized: the fact that their source had been executed proved her authenticity.

There was a long moment of silence as Canaris's statement sank in. Then Hitler got to his feet.

"A young woman paid the supreme price that we should learn the truth of Stalin's treachery. Let us honor her bravery. The invasion of Russia, which we are now calling Operation Barbarossa, must be put into motion. It will now commence, and there will be no turning back. Does anyone around this table disagree?"

Some shook their heads, but no one spoke.

"Believe me," the Führer continued, "we only have to kick in the door, and the whole rotten structure will come crashing down."

"Hear, hear!" said Keitel. His cry was joined by several others.

A wide grin lit up the Führer's face. "Our campaign against Russia will be like child's play in a sandbox."

CHAPTER THIRTY-NINE

Yalta, the Soviet Crimea, February 1945

The Nazi defeat was imminent. Officially, Berlin had not surrendered, but everyone knew it was merely a matter of time, perhaps a month or two. President Roosevelt's plane landed at an airfield in the Crimea at a few minutes after noon. Among the many aides aboard the flight was a young man named Stephen Metcalfe, an assistant to the President.

With Alfred Corcoran's death, the Register had been disbanded. That had been just as well, for the moment that Metcalfe learned that Lana Baranova had been executed by the NKVD he knew he had to resign. He knew he had accomplished something great, but the cost had been too high to bear. He had placed the only woman he had ever loved in harm's way, and harm had taken the advantage.

Metcalfe had returned to Washington a dispirited, guilt-wracked man. For a few months he had lived at the Hay-Adams Hotel and drunk heavily, never going out, never seeing anyone. His life was over.

But at last his many friends had intervened, telling him he had to find a job, had to keep working. The family business had been going along just fine without him, and his brother, Howard, made it clear that he didn't want Stephen's help. Metcalfe would never want for money, but he needed a purpose.

One day Metcalfe received a message at his hotel room from a man who had been the most important member of Corky's Register: President Franklin Delano Roosevelt. FDR wanted Metcalfe to come by the White House for a brief chat.

By the next day, Roosevelt had hired Metcalfe as a junior White House assistant and Metcalfe had a purpose again.

The presidential motorcade drove the eighty miles from the airfield at Saki to the Livadia Palace in the mountains, which had once been the summer residence of the czar. During the entire five-hour drive, the road was lined with Soviet soldiers, each of whom saluted with the distinctive Soviet snap as the cars passed.

The destruction that had been wrought upon the Soviet land by the Nazis, the gutted buildings, the wreckage, was appalling. By the time they arrived at the palace, it was already evening. The Germans had stripped the Livadia Palace of everything they could take, from plumbing fixtures to doorknobs, but the Russians had restored the buildings just in time for this conference of the Big Three—Stalin, Churchill, and Roosevelt—who hoped to iron out most of their differences here and come up with a plan for the postwar world.

It wasn't until the third evening that Metcalfe finally had the opportunity to stroll through the grounds. He was despondent over the way things were going here. The President was seriously ill, and his attention wandered. His public remarks were rambling. He would not be alive for much longer, though very few people knew that. His chief adviser, Harry Hopkins, was seriously ill as well. Roosevelt had only two goals here: to convince Stalin to join the final battle of the war, against Japan, and to create an international organization, which he called the United Nations. Everything else paled next to those goals, as a result of which the President was giving in too readily to Stalin's demands. Roosevelt was giving Churchill the cold shoulder, refusing to listen to the British leader's arguments. Roosevelt persisted in referring to Stalin as "Uncle Joe," which indicated his naïveté about Stalin's true evil. Metcalfe tried to make his arguments, but he was too junior; his role here was as little more than note taker at all the plenary sessions. No one would listen to him; his frustration grew by the day.

At least when I was a spy, he thought, *I accomplished something. Here I'm nothing more than a bureaucrat.*

A silhouetted figure was hobbling through the shadows toward him. His old instincts kicked in, and he froze, the adrenaline

pumping. But he relaxed when he saw it was a one-legged man
or, rather, a man with a wooden leg, not a cause for alarm.

"Metcalfe!" the one-legged man called out as he drew near.

Metcalfe stared in shock as he took in the blazing red hair, the
proud, almost arrogant mouth. "Lieutenant *Kundrov?*"

"*Colonel* Kundrov now."

"My God!" Metcalfe shook Kundrov's hand. "*You're* here, too?
What happened—?"

"Stalingrad happened. The Battle of Stalingrad. I was a lucky
man—I only lost a leg. Most of my comrades lost their lives. But
we prevailed. Invading the Soviet Union was Hitler's greatest miscalculation."

"It's the reason he lost the war," Metcalfe said with a nod.

"You were right." There was, it seemed, a twinkle in Kundrov's
eye.

"I'm sure I don't know what you're talking about."

"Indeed. These things must not be spoken about. The secret
history of the war must never be told."

Metcalfe ignored Kundrov's remark. "I hear that Rudolf von
Schüssler was executed as a traitor on Hitler's orders, after the
Battle of Stalingrad."

"Most unfortunate."

"But what I've always found puzzling is why the Red Army
was so unprepared. Stalin must have been warned that Hitler
planned to attack."

Kundrov's expression grew solemn. "Many tried to warn Stalin. Churchill warned him. Even I myself dispatched several
warnings to the Kremlin, to Stalin himself, though I doubt he
ever received them. But the warnings went unheeded. It was as
if Stalin could not believe Hitler would betray him."

"Or that Hitler would do something so staggeringly foolish."

"We will never know, but it is a terrible shame." He paused.
"I understand you are now working in the White House."

"A man has to work."

"Do you have the President's ear?"

"Only at a distance. I'm a young man, and the President listens only to his most seasoned advisers, which is as it should be."

"But unfortunate. You understand Russia better than his old men."

"You're too kind."

"I'm correct. You have seen Moscow in ways that none of them ever have."

"Perhaps. I know that I hate your government but love the Russian people."

Kundrov did not reply, but Metcalfe believed he knew what the Russian was thinking. Neither man would ever mention Kundrov's attempt to defect. That, too, was a secret best left buried.

"Quite the coincidence that both of us happen to be out for a stroll tonight," Metcalfe said with a poker face.

"Your president is dying," Kundrov said. "Hopkins is dying, too. Perhaps that is why they are giving away the store, as you Americans say."

"How do you mean?" asked Metcalfe, alarmed.

"You are letting Stalin have what he wants in Berlin. You are handing Poland over to us. The Kremlin will take control of the whole of Eastern Europe as a result of your carelessness here; you may take my word for it. And your president is not united with Churchill, which makes Churchill most disgruntled. That only emboldens Stalin."

"How do you know about Churchill's private conversations with Roosevelt?"

"Why do you think I am here? Our intelligence agents are working through the night here to transcribe Roosevelt's private conversations and translate them into Russian to give Stalin at breakfast."

"You're bugging the President's private suite?"

"Surely you're not that naive, Metcalfe. You know how we work. Every word your president utters is transmitted to a listening station nearby. I know this, because I command that listening station."

Metcalfe smiled. "The irony is that I'm powerless to do anything about what you tell me. Even if I did warn Roosevelt, I wouldn't be believed."

"Just as my warnings to Stalin went ignored. We are small cogs in a large machine, both of us. Perhaps one day we both will have the power to affect the course of our two governments. Until then, we must do what we can. And we must always remember the good that we've done."

"And the bad."

Kundrov gave Metcalfe a sad smile but said nothing. He drew from his jacket pocket a folded sheet of coarse paper. "Just before Miss Baranova was executed by the NKVD, she was allowed to write one letter." He handed it to Metcalfe. It was covered with Lana's fine script, though much of the ink was blotched.

Kundrov, seeing Metcalfe's raised eyebrows, said quietly, "Her tears made the ink run."

Metcalfe read it by the pale moonlight, his hands shaking, his own tears running down his cheek. When he finished, he looked up. "My God," he whispered. "The bravery of that woman."

"She knew that the plan we came up with was only a halfmeasure. It was not likely to fool the Germans. She was convinced that only her execution would convince Hitler's men that she was a genuine spy."

"She could have lived!" Metcalfe cried. "She could have come with me to America. . . ." He couldn't continue. He couldn't speak the words.

Kundrov shook his head. "She knew her home was Russia, and that she wanted to be buried there. She loved you deeply, but she knew that only by making the ultimate sacrifice could she save your plan. She did it not just for Russia, and for freedom, but for you."

Metcalfe felt his legs weaken. He felt as if he was going to collapse. He felt as if all the strength had left his body.

"We must return to the Grand Ballroom," Kundrov said.

As they entered, each man was handed a glass of the finest

Armenian cognac. Another endless round of toasts was about to begin.

Kundrov raised his glass to Metcalfe's and, drawing close, said quietly, "Her sacrifice was greater than we ever expected."

Metcalfe nodded.

"And her gift to you—the gift of love—was greater than you will ever realize."

"Not true," Metcalfe said.

But Kundrov kept speaking. "Maybe someday you will understand. But until then, let us both drink to the most extraordinary woman either of us will ever know."

Metcalfe clinked his glass against Kundrov's. "To Lana," he said. And for a long moment, the two men were silent, pensive, before they drank.

"To Lana, my one, my only love," Metcalfe said again, this time to himself. "To Lana."

Moscow, August 1991

Ambassador Stephen Metcalfe began telling his story to Stepan Menilov, the tale of a young American businessman who fell in love with a beautiful Russian ballerina half a century ago.

Menilov listened with a look of puzzlement and annoyance that soon gave way to rapt attention. His eyes did not move from Metcalfe's.

Before Metcalfe had finished, the Conductor stormed: "This is some kind of trick! Some tactic devised by your American psy-ops specialists! Well, it will not work!"

With trembling hands, Metcalfe pulled the pistol from his breast pocket.

Menilov stared at it, thunderstruck. *"Bozhe moi!"* he whispered.

Metcalfe had felt a twinge of sadness whenever he looked at the ornately tooled dueling pistol. He would never forget the day fifty years earlier when, in the depth of his drunken misery at the Hay-Adams Hotel in Washington after he'd learned of Lana's execution, he had received the heavy package, couriered over from the Soviet embassy, which had been sent from Moscow via the diplomatic pouch. Inside the case, packed well in excelsior, was an antique pistol with ornately carved walnut stock and a barrel engraved with flames. He recognized it at once as one of the pair of dueling pistols Lana had shown him. They had belonged to her father, he remembered. An unsigned note–from Kundrov, he was certain–told him that she had bequeathed it to him in a letter she had been allowed to write at the Lubyanka, her last. He was moved by this precious final gift, knew that it meant her father was dead, and wondered why she had given him only one of the set. It had always filled him with the deepest sorrow.

"Take it," ordered Metcalfe.

Instead, Menilov opened a drawer in his desk and took out an identical dueling pistol whose walnut handle was carved with acanthus leaves and whose octagonal steel barrel was engraved with flames.

"The missing half of the pair," said the Russian.

"Your mother told me that they once belonged to Pushkin," said Metcalfe.

A flush had come over Menilov's face. He spoke slowly, haltingly. "I never knew who you were," he said. "Mother called you Stiva—only Stiva. But she named me after you." He sounded as if he were in a trance. "My *babushka* told me that Mother wasn't surprised when the Chekists came to take her away, you know. She went with them serenely. She said she knew that her Stiva loved her. And that whatever sacrifice had to be made was one she made proudly."

"You must have been no more than six," Metcalfe finally brought himself to say. In Stalin's Russia, a Russian child whose father was an American would have been a second-class citizen or worse. He would always be suspect. Lana must have known that in order to protect her child, she could never tell Metcalfe about him.

"Yes. I have very few memories of her, of course. But there were pictures, and her grandmother—whom I called my *babushka*—always told me stories about her, to keep Mother's memory alive. I know she was a very brave woman."

Metcalfe nodded. "Brave like no one else I've ever known. And I know that she passed that bravery on to you. The history of our two countries is filled with so many missteps, so many terrible errors. You have the opportunity to set things right, to take the right step, make the right move. And I know you will do it."

Ambassador Stephen Metcalfe's limousine pulled up at the Sheryemetyevo Airport outside Moscow. There were no photographers to meet him here, no television cameras, no journalists. That was the way he wanted it. He had flown into Moscow quietly, and he would leave quietly. Let others grant interviews, claim credit.

One of the most earthshaking moments in the twentieth century—a century filled with earthshaking moments—was over. The coup attempt had collapsed: without the support of the man known as the Conductor, the plotters could not go on. Statues of the old tyrants had been pulled down; the streets were filled with rejoicing.

History had been made; no one needed to know who had made it. The world had no idea of his role in changing history half a century ago. It would never know about the role he had just played now, either. The only ones who would know were the son he had never known and Metcalfe's old friend, a red-haired GRU lieutenant named Kundrov who had become a white-haired three-star general.

The marine Metcalfe had been assigned by the U.S. embassy helped him with his bags. The crew-cut young man seemed starstruck in Metcalfe's presence, thrilled to have met someone of such eminence.

Metcalfe was cordial enough, but his mind was elsewhere.

A special gift, Lana had said. *The gift of your love.*

And for the first time in his eight decades, Stephen Metcalfe understood that certain gifts are indeed beyond price.